S R Masters grew up around Birmingham in the UK. After having his brain scrambled by a philosophy degree, he moved to Oxfordshire where he lives with his wife and children.

His short fiction and novels have been published internationally. Labelled as "a writer to watch" by *Publishers Weekly*, his other books include *The Killer You Know*, *The Trial* and *How To Kill With Kindness*.

www.sr-masters.com

instagram.com/SRMastersAuthor
facebook.com/srmastersauthor
youtube.com/@srmastersauthor

ALSO BY S. R. MASTERS

The Killer You Know

The Trial

How to Kill with Kindness

THE DROP

S. R. MASTERS

One More Chapter
a division of HarperCollins*Publishers*
1 London Bridge Street
London SE1 9GF
www.harpercollins.co.uk
HarperCollins*Publishers*
Macken House, 39/40 Mayor Street Upper,
Dublin 1, D01 C9W8, Ireland

This paperback edition 2025

1

First published in Great Britain in ebook format
by HarperCollins*Publishers* 2025

Copyright © S. R. Masters 2025
S. R. Masters asserts the moral right to
be identified as the author of this work

A catalogue record of this book is available from the British Library

ISBN: 978-0-00-867193-8

This novel is entirely a work of fiction. The names, characters and incidents portrayed in it are the work of the author's imagination. Any resemblance to actual persons, living or dead, events or localities is entirely coincidental.

Printed and bound in the UK using 100% Renewable Electricity
by CPI Group (UK) Ltd

All rights reserved. No part of this publication may be reproduced, stored in a retrieval system, or transmitted, in any form or by any means, electronic, mechanical, photocopying, recording or otherwise, without the prior permission of the publishers.
Without limiting the exclusive rights of any author, contributor or the publisher of this publication, any unauthorised use of this publication to train generative artificial intelligence (AI) technologies is expressly prohibited. HarperCollins also exercise their rights under Article 4(3) of the Digital Single Market Directive 2019/790 and expressly reserve this publication from the text and data mining exception.

For Dibby and Toppy, the best brothers a guy could have

PART ONE
THE NO TOMORROWS CLUB

CADY

Thursday 20th June, 7.30pm
Celsius: 19°, Fahrenheit: 66.2°

Cady Ellison was only a few hours away from the most exciting adventure of her life. The weeks of planning and dreaming and anticipation were finally behind her, the airport was just a mile away – and now she had to deal with this. An … *intervention*. A low-key one, yes, but what other word was there for it?

She hid in her parents' kitchen, slicing up a supermarket sponge cake, the wall clock ticking, the fridge purring. They were all silently waiting for her in the lounge. Waiting for her to explain. To reassure. Cady lowered the knife and cut another slice. And another. Barely paying attention. They meant well, but why now, when her head was already close to bursting?

She'd fled the scene in the hope that by the time she got

back with this loving, daughterly gift, picked up especially on the journey down from Manchester, the conversation might have moved on. That they'd taken the hint, and she wouldn't have to expend vital energy on answering their questions and placating—

She dropped the knife and sucked in breath through pursed lips, a sharp pain commandeering her attention. She held up her left index finger. Blood oozed from a small wound, which she took to the sink and held under the tap. Proof, if proof were needed, that she didn't have the bandwidth for anything but work right now.

Cady returned to the lounge wearing a plaster, and she put down three plates on the coffee table. 'There we go.' She placed her hands on her hips, and waited for them to dive in. To block up their mouths with her generosity.

No one moved. Instead, they stared at her. Dad said, 'Well?'

'I think she was hoping we'd forgotten,' Mum said.

'Can we maybe talk about it when I get home?' Cady said with a smile that beamed with assurance. When none of them replied, Cady took a deep breath. 'Okay, maybe one way to think about what I do is … it's just like a roller coaster. It might seem scary from the outside, but you're more likely to die in the car on the way to an amusement park than *on* the roller coaster. Do you know what I mean?'

Mum and Dad looked at one another across the empty sofa seat between them. Then they turned to Tom, Cady's boyfriend, sitting over on Dad's ancient recliner. Tom forked the fingers of his right hand into the blond thatch on his head, puffed his pinkening cheeks, and became instantly fascinated by the knitted 'Follow Your Dreams' wall art above her parents.

'I'm sure you're right,' Dad said, gesturing for her to sit

down in the empty sofa chair across from them. 'It's just a funny … lifestyle, isn't it? Lots of strangers watching you.'

'Dad,' she said, laughing gently, 'it's not a lifestyle. It's a job.'

'Sorry, yes. Job…' Again, he looked to Tom. 'I don't think we quite understand how it all works. How you keep yourself … safe?'

Cady sighed. She rubbed her stinging finger with her thumb. Had this all been impromptu, or had they planned it in advance? It felt planned. Was that why Tom had offered to drive her all the way down to Birmingham Airport? Was that why he'd suggested they drop in here for tea before she flew?

Then again, her parents weren't really the intervention types, were they? Ockham's Razor suggested Tom had simply failed to remove his big, overly fretful American heart from his sleeve when she'd gone hunting for mobile reception earlier, and her parents felt some British obligation to act on his worries for fear of being viewed as sociopaths.

It felt strange though, suddenly having so much of their attention.

'But … did someone attack you, Cady?'

'No, Mum.' Cady made a *Really?* face at Tom.

'It wasn't an attack exactly,' Tom conceded, retaining his interest in that wall art.

'I'm not sure what Tom has said, but there was just this little incident with someone, and I dealt with it months ago. So it's fine.'

'It sounded frightening,' Mum said.

'It's fine.'

'Tom.' Mum turned to him with the tiniest smirk. 'Is it fine?'

He held up his hands and sighed. 'I'm really not an expert. I bow to Cady on this.'

Cady drew another long breath. She had so much still to do and think about, exciting things, fun things. She wanted to get on that plane in a positive state of mind, damn it, not dwelling on this old news.

'Well, all due respect, but Tom is a worry wort, Mum,' she said. 'All jobs have risks. You work in offices. And you know what offices have?' For a moment she couldn't think of how to finish her point. Looking around the room, she noticed a candle on a side table, and said, 'Fires.'

Nodding slowly, Dad asked, 'So how do you deal with a person like that, then? Out of curiosity.'

'I posted a video. A serious one that told this ... *person* not to do it again or there would be consequences.'

'Well, we saw that, darling,' Mum said, 'that's what had us worried.'

'Okay, well great,' Cady said, 'so since then, it's been fine.'

'Did you tell the police?' Dad asked.

She shook her head. 'There wasn't really a crime, was there? It was a one-off, bad luck type of thing. I wasn't attacked. Honestly, it's all fine. Tom just ... likes to worry.'

She gave him a loving look that he returned with a thin smile. She was going to kill him when they got back in the car.

'Well, I don't know, Cady,' Dad said. 'Videos about you travelling is one thing. But where's this camping-in-funny-places come from?'

'It's an experiment, Dad. You have to keep things interesting.'

Cady let gravity assist her into the sofa chair. She took her phone from her pocket and swiped it to reveal the time. Seven-thirty. Still over an hour before check-in, so there'd be no quick escape. Her head was starting to hurt around her temple, a classic sign she was stressed. She shut her eyes and waited for the pain to pass. When she opened them again, she pressed the icon for her YouTube studio app. It wouldn't load. She refreshed it. Refreshed it again. But despite having two bars of signal, she couldn't get online.

'What's the problem?' Tom said.

'I still can't get any internet. Can you?'

Tom sighed and took out his phone, swiped his screen a few times and shook his head. She didn't bother asking her parents. The reception on their phones had been so poor since they'd downsized to the flat that she usually called their landline. Recently though, even that had been impossible because Dad had fallen out with their broadband provider and appeared to be in no rush to replace them.

'I'm really sorry, but I need to find signal. I need to know if my latest video's uploaded.' She looked up at Mum and Dad.

Dad held up the palms of both hands. 'Of course, darling. But you don't think there's anything for us to worry about, then?'

She nodded. 'No, Dad. I'm fine. I'm just ... not that scared of the world, you know?' She stopped herself from adding, *unlike you three*. 'Most people are good. A few bad apples shouldn't spoil it for everyone.'

Mum straightened. 'A few?'

Cady rolled her eyes. 'One. One odd person.'

She was trying to stay diplomatic, but they were making it hard. The reality was she'd finally, after all these years of solitary creative projects, made a success of something, and now suddenly they wanted input. She couldn't look at them. Instead, she stared at the screen print of the Twin Towers above the fire. Dad had worked there during the 80s before moving back to the UK. He still loved everything American – including Tom. He'd have taken his concerns seriously.

'I don't think *anyone* is suggesting you stop, Cady Bug,' Dad said. That was low, bringing out the nickname. 'But do you not feel that this … YouTube thing has all happened to you a bit fast? I mean, the numbers Tom mentioned are … wow. Perhaps you need a little stop-and-think, you know, about how you do things. Assess the risks. I know you don't like to be still, darling, but sometimes … slow and steady wins the race, no?'

She had no idea what he was talking about now. Her head hurt. So did her finger. And she really, really didn't want to deal with this. She wanted sun. And sand. And a way out of here.

'I can't slow down. That's not how the algorithm works. I need to keep making videos, speaking of which…'

It was all becoming a bit oppressive. She wanted to say as much, but she knew what Tom would make of that. He'd be thinking, yes, of course safety *is* oppressive. But it's good oppression, like the rules in the hospital where he worked.

When she stood up, towering above her parents, they seemed so small, their faces now indented with deep caverns of worry. How old they were all of a sudden. How quickly the world was changing around them. Tom meant well, but she wished he hadn't dragged them into this.

'I really appreciate what you're saying,' she said. 'So thank you. But I am safe. I'm sound. And if anything changes, I'll—'

'Take a breather,' Dad said, nodding like this might tie a bow on it all. 'Be still.'

'Exactly,' Mum said.

She brightened her smile, so glad she'd not told Tom *everything* that happened that night in Sherwood Forest. Like the sounds of that man's breathing just centimetres away from her on the other side of the tent fabric. Those strange things he'd said.

Cady returned Dad's nod, happy for any sort of conclusion. But she wasn't going to slow down. Nothing was going to stop her now she'd found her way.

She'd be still when she was dead.

CADY

Thursday 20th June, 7.49pm
Celsius: 19°, Fahrenheit: 66.2°

She sat on the windowsill in the spare bedroom, the way her Grandad Sal used to when it was too cold to smoke in the garden, one arm extended outside seeking phone reception, the other hooked around the top of the window recess to stop herself falling three stories. Much like the rest of the flat, the room was free from the sort of lived-in clutter that had been ever-present in the semi where she'd grown up. The only personal touch was a framed collage of photographs above the bed, childhood snaps of Cady and her late brother, Robbie, and the family-iconic images of Mum on stage in her am-dram days, and Dad singing into a mic with his rock band in the early 70s. In one, Cady and Robbie wore green Oxfam t-shirts. God, they'd been such a pair of goodie-goodies.

Cady could hear the distant murmuring of the others down the hall. But she didn't want to dwell on what had just happened. The embarrassing, irreversible reality of it, which demanded to be dealt with. Yes, that strange man at the campsite had been bad, as evidenced by the fact she'd even told Tom about it – well, some of it – knowing how likely it was he'd go into panic mode. And fine, he was allowed to worry a little bit. That was their whole dynamic, Cady pushing him out of his comfort zone and Tom protecting her from her own exuberance, and it had always worked. But why had she started to get a sense from him lately that he'd be happy for her to give up, even if he never said so directly?

Or maybe that was unfair. Maybe she just didn't want to acknowledge how unsettling the whole thing had been, and what that might mean.

You in there, Cady?

She forced the man's voice from her mind and brought in her phone. The screen now thankfully displayed her channel's home page. At the top was the logo, her silhouette in front of a tall roller coaster. 'Coasting with Cady' had gained another twenty or so followers since she'd last checked a few hours ago. But that fact barely registered. Because the top of her list of recently posted videos should have shown her recent visit to Thorpe Park. Instead, it was still last week's visit to Legoland.

Instinctively, she tried to open up her complete list of videos to check what was happening, but the connection wasn't good enough. She refreshed the page and held her arm out the window. She brought it back. Nothing. She tried again. Finally, when the page loaded, the issue revealed itself. Her video had stalled while processing.

'Oh, damn.'

She'd have to reupload the whole video now. Of course it

would happen tonight, when she was stuck without internet and due on a seven-hour flight to the Middle East. Of course it would happen the one time when she had nothing pre-loaded and ready to go live well in advance.

Leaving it until she landed wasn't an option. Like most creators on the platform, Cady had no idea how the YouTube algorithm *really* worked. Why her videos were watched hundreds of thousands of times and other channels were ignored. But ever since it had first deemed her worthy, she'd kept everything she could exactly the same for fear of slighting that fickle god. So she simply had to release a new video at 9pm, as she did every Thursday.

There was only one option. Only one way to get her video out on time before her flight. The idea brought a small smile to her face. She lowered herself from the windowsill and walked back to the lounge. She'd have to go to the airport early.

Mum and Dad waved them off from the doorstep looking haunted and small. She'd again insisted they not worry, and suspected that, once the car turned the corner, they wouldn't. Out of sight, out of mind, as it had always been with them outside of Christmas and birthdays.

Tom drove to Birmingham Airport in silence, his shirt sleeves rolled back to reveal two taut forearms. His fingers, white-knuckled, squeezed the steering wheel. The roads grew fatter and busier, and they were less than a mile away when finally Cady looked up from her phone and said, 'Do you want to talk about … anything?'

He shrugged. 'What's to say?'

'Why did you bring *them* into it?'

'They saw your video and asked if I was worried. What was I supposed to say, that I wasn't? What are they going think of me if I just say: Oh, yeah, I think it's great she's camping illegally with random men stalking her?'

'Man. One man. And you could have reassured them.'

'How?'

'I mean, God, we've talked about all this.'

'Have we? When? If I get even five precious minutes of your time, you listen to me go around in circles until I'm dizzy, then just say, don't worry, it's fine, it's fine. And okay, I've had to accept all the creepy blokes in the comments and coming up to you in person. But this was different. It wasn't fine.'

'Well… I just think… Nothing happened.' She looked out her window, catching sight of another car far behind them, its headlights on despite the late summer light.

Tom shook his head, and took a moment to gather his thoughts. When he spoke again, his voice was soft. 'Yeah, well I'm worried, and they are, too. What if he turns up again?'

Her blood was up, and she couldn't help herself. 'Did you even give them the other side? Did you tell them how much money I'm making now?'

'They know you earn good money. That's not the point.'

'I just … why does everyone suddenly have an opinion about my life? It's a bit … suffocating.'

He exhaled slowly through pursed lips. 'I mean … this is the thing, Cade. Me worrying about you being stalked by strange men—'

'Come on, once. It happened—'

'—seems to get turned back on me to make out I'm being … controlling. Is that really how you feel? Controlled.'

'I don't know why you feel that way. But sometimes I think

safe old Cady with a desk job and her vague dreams locked up safely in her head is the version of me you want to be with.'

'That's… You think that's fair? Really? I'm happy you've found this. I'm happy it makes you shit tons of money.'

'Then what?' She laughed in an attempt to hide her irritation. 'What is it you all want?'

He took another moment before responding. 'I think a sense you can still perceive danger would go a long way. I mean, you wouldn't even report it to the police. Get something on record in case it escalates.'

'But Tom … we really have been through this.' Cady folded her arms. 'Sometimes I feel the only issue here is that you don't listen to me.'

His jaw tightened. 'Fine. Fine, maybe that's true. This week apart has probably come at a good time, then.'

That didn't sound good. 'Yeah?'

'It can give us both some time to think.'

They reached the road approaching the airport, and she watched in the mirror as the car that had been behind them moved into the outside lane and overtook them, heading for the long-stay car park. They stayed left, and followed the signs to the drop-off area, where stern yellow jackets paced back and forth menacingly, moving on cars outstaying their welcome.

'What things do we need to think about?' she said softly when he'd pulled over. 'There aren't *things*, Tom. Just one little disagreement.'

He wouldn't face her. 'Well… I wouldn't say it's little.'

'What do you actually want Tom, if it's not to give up?'

'I don't know,' he said and shrugged. 'Just your time. Maybe not being instantly dismissed. That would be a start. I'm going to head off. I need to cool down a bit.'

'But it's going to hang over us now.'

'You're the one that wanted to get to the airport early to use the Wi-Fi.' He opened his door, still refusing to look at her.

'Tom.' He finally turned. 'We'll go away when I get back. Me and you.'

He laughed at this. 'Yeah?'

'I'm serious. A week. Two weeks. We can talk properly and… I know it's always so busy, and I'm always promising that we'll spend time together, but…' She looked at her phone, at the time. She raised her head again and smiled. 'When I get back. And I'll think about what you've said while I'm away. I will.'

'Uh huh.'

Tom stepped out of the car and retrieved her bag from the boot. She stepped out and met him on the pavement where he hugged her politely. She really didn't want to leave him like this. He went to leave and stopped. 'Will you message me when you land? Let me know you're okay.'

That was good to hear. He couldn't be that angry if he still wanted a text message. 'Of course I will. What sort of person do you think I am?'

But he knew exactly the sort of person she could be when distracted. Still, she sensed this was the closest she was going to get to an affectionate goodbye from him, so she'd have to take it. Still, both of them hesitated.

'Tom,' she said, her voice sounding unusually small.

He smiled, held up a hand, and walked away.

CADY

Thursday 20th June, 10.40pm
Celsius: 17°, Fahrenheit: 62.6°

Cady looked up at the departures board. She had some time before take-off, but it was already flashing 'Go to Gate' and she was still land-side – a gamble, but she didn't want to get to departures and find there was bad signal. At least here she had functional hotspot.

On her laptop screen, the HD processing was stuck at 96% and hadn't moved for a few minutes. She chewed her thumbnail and glanced around, hoping she might see Tom. That he might have come back and they could make up. But Tom would be home in Manchester now. This doomy feeling was coming to the Middle East with her.

Cady shook her head and snorted quietly. As if she'd once

believed that being paid to do something she loved would be the end of her problems.

She had met Tom six years ago on a casual night out with friends. She ended up taking him home with her and he never really left. At that point Cady had been drifting along working in PR for a theatre company, bouncing from creative project to creative project in her free time, the way she'd done throughout her adult life, in search of a calling. She'd found Tom a refreshing, grown-up change to the artsy, thin-skinned boys she'd been with before. He was a doctor, a sensible person in the actual, real world. Not that he lacked passion by any means. He just wasn't flash with it. He burned quietly to make things better. For her. For his patients at the hospital. Even in his darkest, lowest moments. All because as a kid he'd watched medics perform miracles on his sister when she had cancer, and now felt duty-bound to pay something back.

Sometimes her own bohemian ambitions felt incredibly selfish next to his. But he never made her feel that way. His view had always been that there was no point saving people's lives if the world didn't have music, and art, and films.

For two years life had attained a run-of-the-mill bliss. Tom's work demanded a lot of his time, but her relative freedom meant they'd always make the most of his days off. They travelled at lot, explored the city in which they were both strangers, but they were equally content just lying in bed watching TV or shagging. They rubbed along well, as Tom's mum had put it, their differences in temperament complimentary, their arguments for the most part able to attain a lightness that kept them impersonal.

Then the pandemic had hit, and the world shut down. No more travel, no more trips to the cinema, no more gigs. Cady lost her favourite comedy night. Her open mic. Her writing club. Stuck at home on furlough, she tried writing a play, but the anxiety out in the world leached into her daily thinking, rendering her creatively inert. Tom working right in the firing line every day didn't help either, and she lived in fear of the inevitable day he came home from the hospital with that still-mysterious illness, carrying around sacks of guilt that she wasn't able to do anything more useful – a jester in a plague.

Given his sacrifice, she decided to throw herself into making Tom's life easier, her metamorphosis into 1950s housewife her bit for the cause. But in a flat the size of theirs, there were only so many rooms to clean, and only so many pre-prepared meals she could jam into the freezer. It was all too easy to spend a little bit more time in bed each day, and allow the time between taking her pyjamas off and putting them on again to gradually shrink.

Trying to summon a sense of hope and stimulate her drive, Cady became addicted to YouTube videos. It started with comfort-watching shows and interviews featuring favourite actors, musicians and comedians, before the algorithm, like some devious drug peddler, began offering her little tempting glimpses of other related YouTube subcultures. Soon she found herself up at two in the morning watching strangers playing retro computer games, or absorbed by an hour-long video essay about Klaus Kinski, or drifting off after lunch to a woman with zebra-pattern nail varnish chopping up kinetic sand.

At some point she clicked on a video in which a couple went around the world reviewing amusement parks, and from that moment the algorithm knew it had found her poison. Perhaps it was because they reminded her of childhood, when she and Robbie had terrorised Drayton Manor and Alton Towers. Or perhaps she simply missed being able to leave the house. But day and night, every free bit of time she had she'd fill watching men and women from all over the world filming themselves either talking about or visiting amusement parks.

Like many during the pandemic years, Cady was radicalised by the internet. But not for her wild conspiracies, or the politics of the far right, the far left, or the far-too-certain-of-themselves. Instead, Cady became a YouTube zealot, coming to believe after years of scepticism, that the platform was meritocratic, a way for creative types from all walks of life to find an audience, and even earn a living, doing things they loved, without being subject to the whims of big entertainment companies and the homogenising mallet of profitability.

Her first video had been in an empty, post-lockdown Blackpool Pleasure Beach, a mask affixed to her face. It was light-hearted, daft even, Cady cataloguing the rides she went on, the newly implemented hygiene procedures, pointing out the things that had changed since her youth. She made it with no expectations. It was just another creative whim in a life of them.

But it didn't mean she wasn't disappointed when 'Post-apocalyptic Blackpool Pleasure Beach Adventure' had attracted only nine viewers after a week. And she felt an unpleasant little jab in her belly each time she saw the desolate bar graph reflecting her channel's views in the last forty-eight hours. It was objective proof of her worthlessness. Her lack of talent. She was close to deleting the whole thing when a notification interrupted dinner one evening, alerting her to a comment someone had left on her video.

This is funny.

Not exactly effusive, but she experienced a little frisson

nonetheless. No one had called her funny since she'd dabbled in improv years back. Interestingly, the video had also obtained sixty views over the last hour. And thirty in the hour preceding that. Was something happening?

Over the next few days it became clear something definitely was. Views and comments mounted. Users demanded more videos. By the end of the following week, she'd reached one hundred subscribers. By the end of the month, she was close to the one thousand subscribers needed to monetize her channel. Within two months, from a single silly video, she sailed past the required number of hours and started earning money.

By the end of all the lockdowns, her poorly paid day job was actually in the way of her maximising her earnings potential, as Tom put it when he finally started to get his head around what was happening. And without fully realising she'd been carrying it around, decades of guilt about her life's direction, and a deeply internalised sense of failure, sloughed away in a matter of weeks.

Sitting in the airport now, the processing at 97%, she felt a tug of longing for that time when Tom had been an enthusiastic cheerleader of her YouTube career. Some nights they had sat together watching her subscriber numbers going up in real time, drinking shots every time it reached a multiple of ten. He'd always been upset by the comments where she was sexualised or demeaned, but she was able to delete most of them before he saw them. But in the last two years, when her Disneyland and Harry Potter videos began to do views in the millions, the comments came in quicker than she could delete them. That was when Tom's naturally cautious nature had began to sour him on the whole thing. The drinking games stopped. They began talking about her job less and less, except on occasions he'd been particularly unsettled by a comment he'd read. Once, he came with her to Chessington, and had grown quieter and quieter the more people recognised Cady and said hello.

'Everyone online has to put up with stuff like this,' she would always say, 'please don't worry. It's just edgy kids and bots.'

She mostly believed this, too, but even if there were genuine psychos watching her, they didn't really scare her. Not as much as living timidly did. She'd been through too much, lost too much, to not embrace every day she had.

Sherwood Forest had really been the embodiment of all Tom's worst-case-scenario nightmares, though. Cady had spent the day filming at the Nottingham Goose Fair, and had decided to 'stealth camp' for the night in Sherwood Forest. Stealth camping videos – an outdoors sub-genre where campers set up their tents in highly unusual locations without being detected – were doing good numbers on YouTube, and she was experimenting with adding the element to some of her own output – much to Tom's confusion. But risk was like a blood sacrifice to the algorithm.

It was October, and pitch-black when she found a secluded spot on the forest floor in a ring of trees a few miles from the car park. She was making her tea on a camp stove to camera, and when she finished she looked up to see a figure standing at the edge of the light circle created by the flames. She screamed, and the figure raised a hand. Dark as it was, she saw enough for a police description, should it be needed. Tall and slim, with a sloped stance. Jeans. A bright yellow beanie. A beard.

'Don't mind me,' he called in some indecipherable accent that at times might have been Yorkshire, Welsh or Geordie. 'You out here alone?'

She told him her boyfriend was getting things from the car, and after a moment he wandered off. Ten minutes later, he came back and stood in the same spot.

'Where's your boyfriend?' he said.

'On his way,' she said, trying to hide her growing alarm.

'Why are you lying?'

'I'm not.'

'You are, *Cady*. I'm a fan. Big one. You always come out by yourself.'

'Sadly, you've stepped behind the curtain,' she said, quick as a flash. 'I never do anything without someone being within screaming distance. Be mad not to.'

He'd stood saying nothing for a while before vanishing back into the forest without another word. She'd been so close to packing up. But if she did, she'd have to admit to herself that she'd messed up. Which would only strengthen Tom's then growing concerns about her new stealth camps. Besides, she wasn't going to let some random, ever-so-slightly sinister fan cost her a video.

So she stayed. Drank wine and got her head down in the tent. At around two in the morning, she awoke to that crunching sound just outside her tent. She lay in the dark, eyes open, heart thudding. It was hard to hear anything over the rustle of the tent fabric in the wind. Then, practically in her ear from the other side of the canvas, the voice came:

'Cady. You in there, *Caaadyyy*. You're full of it, Cady. You're a little bitch.'

She said nothing, pretended to be asleep like a child hiding from monsters beneath the covers. Whoever was there chuckled softly. With great care, she reached out to her rucksack, opened one of the pockets, and took out her Swiss army knife.

Time dragged on, and perhaps an hour later, likely more, she finally found the courage to get up and go outside. She surveyed the area with her torch, packed everything up, and walked to where she'd parked the car. A battered yellow fiat was parked right behind hers, and a man was sitting inside. Her man, perhaps? She watched him from the trees for what felt like hours, and eventually he drove off.

For the next few months, she kept seeing yellow fiats and bearded men in beanies everywhere – not least in the backgrounds of her own video footage, blurred figures in the crowds, faces in the shadows. This much she didn't tell Tom. She'd done everything she could to convince him it was a one-off, which is what she believed herself. Mostly. The rest was paranoia and post-traumatic stress. She'd get over it, in time.

Up on the departures board, it still said Go to Gate. Processing was now at 99%. She sighed, weighed down by her thoughts. She scanned the airport for Tom one last hopeful time. He wasn't there.

But someone *was* watching her. A tall, slim man, leaning against the glass window to the right of the entrance, close enough to her that she could make out the smirk on his face. He started coming towards her. She tried to appear busy.

'Cady?'

She raised her head slowly. He stood a metre away with no luggage. He wore jeans. And a yellow beanie.

'Oh, my days,' he said, putting a hand to his forehead. 'It is you, isn't it? From YouTube. Oh, Cady, I'm Nick. Massive, massive stan.'

Stan, such a fun portmanteau. Stalker. Fan. Processing hit 100%. She closed her laptop and stood up. 'Hi Nick, really nice to meet you. I'm so sorry. I have to catch a flight.'

'Yeah, of course. It's a Thursday. You always have a video on a Thursday.'

Was this the same voice she'd heard that night? A little gravelly, a strange, hard-to-place accent. It was hard to tell. And not every slender man in a yellow hat was a stalker.

Up on the screen, it said her flight was now *Boarding*. 'Thursday like clockwork. Nick, did you say?'

'Yeah.'

'Great, Nick. I'll give you a shout out on the next video.' She slightly raised the hand carrying her computer and started to walk away.

'Where you off to?' he asked.

She tried hard to be kind to her fans, and felt bad fleeing him this way. Negative comments spread quickly. Annoyed with herself for letting all that had happened tonight get to her, she threw him a bone. 'I'm off to the Middle East.'

'To a park?'

She gave him a mysterious waggle of her eyebrows before picking up her pace in the direction of the security gate.

Cady was indeed heading to a park, one that hadn't even opened yet. But that didn't even scratch the surface of what lay ahead for the weekend. Danson, a dear old member of her university friendship group, was an amusement park project manager. He'd invited her to fly out as part of an exclusive group of celebrities and influencers to be the first to ride on the royalty-financed theme park's flagship roller coaster, which was set to break all the records.

Her plane tickets, a week in a hotel, and her travel were all paid for, and Danson said she could film the whole experience. She'd never had this sort of exclusive access before, and it was going to be a real coup for the channel. And while Danson hadn't told her who else was going when she'd asked, he'd sent a cryptic text that, on further analysis, had contained the titles to at least three Taylor Swift songs. It was going to be mind-blowing.

She took out her selfie stick and phone to record some b-roll footage – subtly though, because she knew other people could find it obnoxious. When she took a last glance back, her stan had gone.

She didn't have to queue long for security, and felt calmer about everything once the braided lady at the metal-detecting arch met her with a smile. Nick wasn't coming this way without a ticket.

'I've got a metal plate in my head,' Cady said, tapping herself like the woman might be unaware of what a head was. 'Do you need to know?'

The lady shook her head. 'What's it made of?'

'Titanium. It usually isn't an issue but they say to mention it.'

'Probably won't be, but let's see.'

Cady walked through without a problem and thanked the lady with a little nod. She'd had the plate since she was thirteen, the legacy of the car accident that had killed Grandad Sal and Robbie. Other than the occasional headache, being a bit bad with times and dates, and a freak-out while caving when she was eighteen, it was easy to forget she was part metal. She did often dream of the crash, but given memories of the accident itself were very patchy, she had no idea how true to life they were.

With first-class tickets, she walked onto the plane without an issue, although the departure board now glowed *Final Call* in red. In her seat, she took out her phone to film some build-up material for the next video, and messaged Danson that her flight was leaving on time. Only after she'd turned off her phone did she consider sending Tom a message. Just something to let him know she was thinking of him.

But was that letting him off too easily? No matter her sadness, she was still annoyed at how he'd handled tonight. He could wait until she landed. Like he'd said, they could both do with some time to think.

The plane lurched forwards and headed for the runway, briefly passing a long window in what looked like a viewing area. A tall figure stood watching their departure, hands behind his back. She couldn't make out the details of his face, but she could see he wore a beanie.

CADY

Friday 21st June, 4.52pm
Celsius: 17°, Fahrenheit: 62.6°

It was a long way down. Her room – an apartment really – was on the tenth floor of an American chain hotel by the beach. No sea view from her window, though. Forty metres below, on a street of hotels, traffic swarmed. Cady watched through the screen of her camera, filming to pass the time while she waited for the driver to call. Sometime between five and half-five, Danson had said. It was almost five now.

She turned the camera on herself. 'Waiting for my lift. Dead time, do you know what I mean?' She crinkled her face up and enunciated the phrase again: 'Dead time. Those little nothing pockets between … stuff. How much does it all add up to in someone's life? Years?' She paused, distracted by the cut on her left finger gripping the top of her screen. Returning to her face, she noticed how rough she looked in this light. 'Ugh, sorry about the bags today.' She poked the skin under her eyes. 'Long flight. Maybe I can get some sort of dodgy treatment while I'm here. A bleaching. An eye-bag bleach. Is that a thing?'

She started chuckling and turned off the camera, aware she was talking rubbish, the excitement sending her silly. She shut her eyes and yawned. She'd not slept well on the plane, and when she reached the hotel she'd dozed off with her phone beside her. The power had drained and her alarm hadn't gone off. She'd lost half the day. She had missed calls from Danson, but thankfully he'd messaged over instructions.

The main event with all the razzmatazz, he said, would be tomorrow evening. Tonight, she was getting a special, private tour and dinner. It was a low-key thing, casual dress and strictly no filming. The last part was a shame, but not unexpected – from what she'd gleaned online the entire project was locked down and there had been very few photos leaked. They wanted those first park images to be special. Taylor Swift special. But getting a little preparation time 'off the books' as Danson had put it, was no bad thing.

Once she'd got her head together earlier, she managed to get some footage of the hotel. After that she'd passed away the afternoon nibbling on food from the hotel café and catching up with channel administration on her laptop. Commenting, liking, occasionally deleting. For the same reasons she kept a tight release schedule, she never wanted to leave her viewers unanswered for too long, particularly the regulars. Jodie, Miguel, PuffyCheeksASMR. They were the foundation of her success. Then she'd showered, put on light make up, and changed into jean shorts and a loose T-shirt – casual, conservative and cool. While this was considered one of the more modern emirates, Danson had advised erring on the side of caution.

Her phone still in her hand, she opened her messages, aware she hadn't yet heard back from Tom since texting him that morning. She narrowed her eyes. She suddenly understood.

'No. No no no no.'

Delivery failed, it said, did she want to resend?

Yes. Of course she did, yes. Tom didn't use WhatsApp, something to do with their data policy, so she'd had to use old-school SMS. Perhaps the phone hadn't been connected to the local network at the time. Or perhaps there was a permission issue; had she turned off roaming? Oh, why did he have to be so difficult? But it wasn't his fault, was it? He'd asked her for one thing and she'd completely failed. He was going to be heartbroken.

She was typing a new message to explain when the phone rang. It was her driver, waiting down at reception. Okay, that was fine, she could send Tom a message on the way. Conscious of those bags under her eyes, she grabbed the wooden pocket make-up kit Tom had bought her as a birthday gift, and walked out. Cady strolled through the hotel and down to the lobby, still wearing the light cardigan she'd put on to shield her from the air-conditioning.

A slender man in a suit and tie held up a sign with her name on it. She waved. His face, brown skin plump and flawless, was open and friendly, the smile he offered genuine.

'I'm Jag, Cady,' he said with a trace of an accent, Indian perhaps. 'Do you want to follow me?'

Just beyond the reach of the air-conditioning, the lurking desert heat met her like a shove. Despite it being early afternoon, the outside temperature on the dashboard of Jag's white Mercedes saloon read 36 degrees Celsius.

He drove out of the city bustle, onto a ribbon of motorway laid between expanses of sand and mountains. The roads were busy, enough to make her wary every time Jag overtook a vehicle, yet once the city was behind them a creeping sense of isolation began to take hold.

'Do you work at the park?' Jag asked. 'At Dreamland?'

From the back seat she saw he was looking at her in the rear-view mirror. 'No. I'm a guest.'

'Ah.' He nodded, although she could tell he was still curious. She had to be careful what she said, though, Danson had asked her to be discreet about anything concerning the park and her visit. Sensing Danson was perhaps bending the rules a little to accommodate her tonight, she chose her words carefully.

'I'm meeting the project manager. Do you know much about the park?'

He nodded eagerly. 'Probably *too* much.' He paused thoughtfully and added, 'I'm passionate about amusement parks. And roller coasters.'

'Me too. Have you been here before, then?'

'No. But I'm very excited by this job.' Again, he seemed to hesitate before continuing. 'When I was a boy, we lived not far from Nicco Park in Kolkata. Have you heard of it?'

Cady nodded and would have loved to mention her channel. But she played it cool. 'It has a big wooden coaster, doesn't it? Called Cyclone, is that right?'

'Yes,' he said, his smile enormous.

'I've never been, but is it good?'

'It's a very good park. But I've also never visited. Some of my family worked building it, though. But Nicco Park is nothing like Dreamland. It will be the best park in the world when it is finished.'

Cady had visited the links to Dreamland's official page, with all its hyperbole and futuristic computer-generated renderings, but details outside this were scarce. The wider coaster community had drifted into wild speculation, fuelled by distant drone photographs of building equipment and unclear images of what may or may not be parts of a roller coaster in a sandy location.

'I'm not actually sure what I'm walking into,' she said. 'Do you know how far along the work is?'

'No one knows anything.' He laughed. 'We know the royal family want to compete with Dubai and Saudi, so they've been very secretive. I was warned about filming or taking pictures before coming tonight. They said it's illegal.'

'Really. Wow.'

'Yes,' he said, shaking his head. 'I know there are supposed to be eight different lands, you know, with different themes. Filmland, Spaceland.'

'I heard that.'

'And of course, Hysteria will be in Musicland. That's what I'm most excited about seeing.'

She was enjoying Jag's enthusiasm about the park, so she played dumb and asked, 'So, is that the big roller coaster? Hysteria.'

Jag blew air into his cheeks. 'Big is not the word. Tallest, biggest drop, steepest drop, fastest, longest, most inversions. Corkscrews. Loops. Bunny hops. A zero-G stall. It's going to destroy the one in Saudi Arabia, if it really happens.'

'How tall are we talking, exactly?'

'The tallest point is about two hundred metres, with a very

steep drop. Are you English?' Cady nodded. 'Someone told me it's taller than the depth of the English Channel.'

'Really?' Cady said, a little surprised by the comparison. But yes, she supposed it probably was. That would also make it five times as high as the drop from her hotel room earlier. She was suddenly having trouble picturing the thing.

'Yes, but … as I say. *If* it happens. Because you never know here in the Gulf. These vanity projects … well, have you heard about The Line? Or the Palm Islands?'

She nodded. 'From what I've heard, I think the roller coaster has been built, though.'

'Really?'

'Well, I hope so. I've been told I'm going to get to go on it.' Jag's mouth formed an O. Had she said too much? 'Although, got to say I'm a bit worried now. Maybe I misunderstood.'

'You must go on it, Cady. For me.'

She laughed. Secretly, she couldn't wait. Half joking, she said, 'Do you want me to ask if they'll let you have a go, too?'

His thick eyebrows drew together and his eyes grew fearful. 'Please don't.'

Cady knew about the problematic working conditions out here – not to mention the human rights abuses – and inwardly cringed at having been so glib. She didn't want to get Jag in trouble.

'No,' she said. 'Don't worry, I won't. I was just joking.'

A moment passed before Jag said, 'Perhaps, if I am selected to pick you up again, I could hear all about it.'

'Of course. Can I ask for Jag when we call you?'

He smiled and nodded. 'I'd really love to hear how it is.'

Jag followed a slip road off the motorway down to a security barrier, where a neat-bearded security man sat staring out at the horizon from inside a booth. Jag rolled down his window, told the guard that he was dropping off Cady Ellison, and the barrier opened.

They drove onto the black tarmac of a motorway recently laid. Sand powdered the surface of the four lanes, and Jag's tyres rolled along the imprints from other sanctioned vehicles. Ten minutes passed, twenty, all around them only dusty, anaemic-yellow land, indistinguishable but for rocky outcrops and patches of colourless scrub. A few times Cady turned to look behind them, which only heightened her growing sense of isolation. What was she looking for? A car, perhaps. A little yellow Fiat?

She was grateful for Jag's company. His pleasant, distracting chatter. Every so often, similar-looking cars to theirs drove by in the other direction – would there be other guests tonight? Or were these workers clearing out for the night?

'My word,' Jag said a little while later, hunching to admire the sight ahead of them.

Cady leaned forward and her abdomen tightened. Rising from the land at the horizon like a skeletal sail was the triangular top of an enormous roller coaster. A steep-angled climb crested before what looked like an almost vertical drop.

'Oh dear,' she said, laughing nervously.

'It's real.' Jag slapped his steering wheel and laughed, too.

They drove closer, and she found herself unable to look away. Rectangular mountains rose into view underneath, the ride dwarfing even their flat peaks. It was soon apparent that the park had been built on a plain encircled by the mountains, to provide shade, Jag suggested. Cranes and parts of other tall rides soon became visible, multi-coloured tubes and tracks, and something that looked like a giant's crown suspended high above the ground, all shimmering in the heat.

At last, they reached another checkpoint. Beyond this they

followed the paved road into the park through a wide opening in the mountains. Nothing appeared finished but for the multitude of white workers' tents – although she'd not seen a single soul yet. It was a Friday, though.

Great levelled areas, cordoned off by wire fences decorated with strips of red-and-white flagging tape, were home to static excavators, and trucks, and giant parts of unfinished attractions, which emerged from the sand like the half-buried remnants of a lost civilisation.

Every so often they would pass below a section of Hysteria's gold and blue track or beside one of the elephantine support beams, the coaster looming over and encroaching upon all the other rides within its enormous footprint.

'This is just incredible,' Jag said, barely able to keep his eyes on the road ahead of him. 'Although it's not going to be ready for next summer, is it?'

They finally reached a car park, which was mostly empty but for a few construction vehicles and what looked like… She gave a disbelieving snort. It was an old yellow Fiat. She couldn't see the number plate, but it obviously didn't belong to her—

Stalker.

—fan from Sherwood Forest. Or to … what had his name been, Nick? What, did he travel in the world's fastest ferry, after seeing her off at the airport? Despite the improbability of the idea, the sight disturbed her. What were the chances?

She shoved her paranoia aside because she needed to start working. Taking mental notes on how she was going to film this place tomorrow. Jag cut across the car park and pulled up at the foot of the wide concrete stairs leading up to the entrance. She tipped him with her phone, and Jag thanked her.

He climbed out and opened her door. Once more the evening heat surprised her.

'Hope to see you again,' she said.

'Have a wonderful time, Cady.'

He walked back to the car and drove away, and that feeling of isolation she'd felt before intensified.

Jag was gone. He'd left her alone. But of course he hadn't, because she could hear laughter coming from the direction of the entrance. She climbed the eight steps and reached a paved, circular concourse, on the other side of which stood thirty or so ticket booths. Above these stretched an enormous arch, decorated with onion-shaped turrets and domes, at its centre golden letters spelling out the park's name. Higher still ran a section of Hysteria's track. And looming over everything in the distance was the enormous lift hill, as imposing as any of the surrounding mountains.

'Cady,' someone shouted.

Four people stood around a table erected below the arch. She approached, and the figures beside Danson, their eyes concealed by sunglasses, were at first only a blurred cause for puzzlement. But then there was an initial flicker of recognition, and once close enough to see the champagne flutes and the unopened bottles in buckets of ice, Cady's disbelief became trepidation. Looking back at her were all of them. Her university gang.

Femi. Naseem. Winston.

Along with Danson, it was every single member of The No Tomorrows Club.

How very lovely. How very awkward.

CADY

Friday 21st June, 6.10pm
Celsius: 38°, Fahrenheit: 100.4°

If she had her dates right, it had been four years since she'd seen them in person. At a reunion in Oxford that ended with a very *memorable* encounter in a hotel room. That was just a month before the pandemic really took hold, and if any of them still felt residual embarrassment about what had happened, it didn't show on their smiling, barely-aged faces. God, they were a good-looking bunch. Thank flip she'd managed to put on a little concealer in Jag's car to hide those rubbish sacks under her eyes.

'What the *actual*?' Cady said, holding out her upturned hands either side of her.

They laughed and uttered elated whoops. It *had* briefly crossed her mind on the plane that Danson might have invited them, too. After all, each one of them was far more successful and influential than her. But seeing them out here in the middle of nowhere was no less shocking.

Danson, who had been the only one not in the Oxford hotel room that night, walked around the table to hug her. There was no denying that he appeared to have aged a little. Despite the heat, he wore a navy-blue blazer over a shirt, which hung from his lanky frame like it was too big for him. She squeezed only air at first before eventually meeting the resistance of his body. She looked up at a long, grey face, and tired eyes propped up on high, prominent cheekbones.

'Welcome to Dreamland, old friend,' he said.

She peered around him. 'Did you guys know?'

'No, they didn't,' Danson said. 'I kept it all … a surprise.'

'And *what* a surprise,' Femi said, walking around the table now and clapping him on the shoulder. Beside Danson, he looked like a professional wrestler, his white T-shirt straining against his chest, his biceps throttled by the armholes. 'Hello, love.' He grabbed Cady in one enormous arm and pulled her to his chest. Her cheek pressed against his gold chain and she heard his powerful heartbeat.

When he let go, she stepped back, noticing grey hairs under the rim of a branded baseball cap at his temples, either a recent development, or one he covered up when he was on television. He still somehow looked younger than when she'd last seen him, though, likely because, for his most famous role, he wore a beard.

She greeted Naz next, long gone now the goth princess she'd been in their youth. This rounder-faced descendant wore a floaty cream maxi-dress patterned with primary-coloured slashes, the final form of a transformation that had started after she sold her first novel.

'You,' she said, taking Cady's face into her hands. 'You.'

'You,' Cady said back, breathing in her exotic perfume and enjoying the sudden rush of affection she felt.

Winston sidled over next, hands in the pockets of his chino shorts, a sideways smile on a face part-concealed by sunglasses. 'Hi, Cady,' he said in his syrupy, Anglo-Californian drawl.

'Hey, Maestro,' she said.

The sleeves of his white shirt were rolled up over arms heavily tattooed with abstract, plant-like patterns, and his top buttons were open to reveal an already sun-reddened chest.

Danson poured champagne, and the gang made small talk about their journeys like they hadn't all once shared formative years, and holidays, and beds together. Danson, still on the job it seemed, poured none for himself and sipped instead from a plastic water bottle.

'So can you tell us what we're doing here now?' Femi said to Danson, perhaps trying to wrest back his old leadership role. 'Was all this a little ruse to get us together?'

'I wouldn't say a ruse,' he replied, his right hand rising to rest at the back of his head while his index finger tapped out quick triplets. Cady had forgotten this little tic of his, and felt oddly comforted by its appearance. His expression remained serious, which was pretty normal with Danson, but had Cady seen a ghost of a smile there briefly? 'We'll get to all that, but can I just say thank you for all coming to this. It's made my dreams come true.'

'Thank *you*,' Naseem said. 'Sounds like this is the place to be.' She held up her drink, and they all clinked glasses.

Danson was seemingly on top of all their recent career developments, and quickly had them all deep in catch-up chat: Femi and his star-studded gossip from behind the scenes of a movie he'd been filming, Winston revealing all the hidden stress and costs that went with an invite to play on *Jools Holland* with his band, and Naz downplaying the high-profile award for which her latest novel had been shortlisted.

'And of course,' Danson said, seeming to have noticed Cady had drifted to the periphery of the conversation, 'now Cady is more famous than any of you. When I polled the kids in my office, she was the only one they'd heard of.'

'No, they hadn't,' Cady said, assuming he was yanking her chain. 'I'm comfortably small time.'

Femi swatted her arm lightly with the back of his hand. 'I'm a subscriber.'

'Get out,' she said.

'Seriously. I have a secret account. I watch your videos before bed some nights.'

'Easy, tiger,' Winston said.

'They're very comforting,' he clarified with a laugh. 'They remind me of old times.'

'Yeah,' Winston said, dragging the word out. 'She does have a way with the camera.'

'Very … authentic,' Naz said, her expression hard to read behind her round, oversized shades.

'Stop it, you lot,' Cady said, waving a hand, genuinely surprised they had any idea what she was up to. For the longest time she'd viewed them all as occupying a different, rarefied world to her, the world of the successful creative. It was hard to imagine them doing something as mundane as watching what were glorified home videos. 'I'm not sure I'm really important enough to be here.'

'What's being a YouTuber like?' Naz said, no interest in her attempts at self-deprecation. 'Do you get recognised?'

She had to laugh at that. As tempting as it was to unburden

herself, she didn't want to darken the vibe. 'Honestly, it's mostly admin. It's not – Sorry, it's just strange you've watched.'

'It's so great you finally found your niche,' Naz said, and after a pause gave a contented sigh.

If it were anyone else saying this to her, she might perceive it as barbed. But Naz was a lot of things, prone to gaffs certainly, but she was never cruel. And if she said she was happy for Cady, she really was – even if the implication of her remark was that she had viewed her, until now, as a bit of a failure. Or maybe that was Cady projecting.

Danson started fretting about losing the light – they *really* had to make the most of the view on Hysteria – and the sun had vanished behind the mountains, plunging them into a still, stifling shade, so he ushered them in the direction of a sand-swept pathway further into the park. This suited Cady, who had only sipped at her champagne, and didn't fancy getting drunk and dehydrated her first night out here. She already felt a little tug of thirst.

'Is there water where we're going?' she asked, noticing Danson was bringing his bottle with him.

He nodded, made his way to the front of their little caravan and turned to face them while walking backwards. 'If anyone needs a drink, let me know. I'm sure you're aware, but the desert is trying to kill you even as we speak.'

'I could do with more booze?' Winston said, and Femi laughed.

'All in good time. But seriously, we did sadly have one worker who went out to explore the mountains without water and got disorientated or lost or both, and tragically we found him too late. The temperature even now is up near the forties and stays that way overnight. It's not like the Sahara where it cools down. So anyone needs anything, just shout.'

'Gotcha,' Femi said.

Danson shook his head and smiled now, drinking them all in with his sunken eyes, quenching a different thirst. 'I still can't get over how well you all look. I'm so, so, so glad you came.'

'Right back at you, D-man,' Femi said, and Cady was grateful. Better an actor deliver that lie than her. If anyone wanted walking proof that the desert was out to kill you, Danson was your man.

CADY

Friday 21st June, 6.33pm
Celsius: 37°, Fahrenheit: 98.6°

They walked into Musicland, passing the shells of future shops and attractions clustered beyond the entrance sign. Three ten-metre structures, like closed umbrellas, rides maybe, or a decorative feature, towered in the haze of an otherwise empty plot. Unplumbed mist sprinklers, heads hooded in plastic bags like gang victims, lined the first section of their route to Hysteria.

'I know how this all looks at the moment,' Danson said, turning to address them as they moved, 'but it'll all be different tomorrow night.'

Cady found that hard to believe, although who was she to doubt the resources of the royal family?

He continued, 'Tonight you are getting a sneak preview. You'll technically be the first ever riders.'

'Uh, is that good?' Naz asked with a nervous laugh, staring up and ahead at Hysteria's approaching lift hill.

'It's been safety-tested, obviously. But you'll be the first *guests* to get the full Hysteria experience. To *ride* her.'

'Sounds fun.' Naz gave a smile that was part grimace.

'You've never liked heights, have you?' Danson said. 'I won't be offended if you want to stay with me on the ground.'

'No, no.' She raised an outward palm in defiance. 'All for one and one for all.'

'So it goes right up there,' Winston said, head raised, squinting. Danson nodded enthusiastically. 'It's … big.'

Cady looked up too, the structure appeared to sway in the wind slightly. A tremor of excitement passed through her. 'This is so cool. Danson, thank you. I know people who'd have paid through the nose to be the first to ride this.'

"Yeah,' Femi said, 'thanks, mate. Got to say, proud of you man. This is all… impressive stuff.'

'Well, when a mad, wealthy prince writes down his impossible idea on a scrap of paper, and his handlers give you the task of making it a reality… I think when you pull it off you should be allowed a bit of licence to celebrate how you see fit, don't you? To treat your oldest friends in the world to an unforgettable night.'

It was nice to hear Danson felt this way about them all still, despite how they'd drifted over the last few years. They'd been so close at university – had lived together for two of their three undergraduate years – but while they still kept in touch online as best they could, since graduating their reunions had become further and further apart. Cady knew Danson had sometimes felt a bit neglected or out of it once the others had found success. Up until her own breakthrough, she'd related. How great was it that they'd both found their way in the end, and with it, some peace?

As if sensing he'd gone too mushy too soon, Danson said, 'You guys know I like to be honest though, so let me be straight. I do have a bit of an ulterior motive as well.' He gave a little sideways smirk.

'Here we go,' Femi said.

'Ruse alert,' Winston said.

'Well … no … but… Dreamland hasn't entirely been as dreamy as it could have been lately. There have been a few … hiccups.'

'Really?' Cady said. 'Like what?'

'I'd have thought a place like this couldn't fail,' Femi added. 'What did I read it cost, four billion?'

'Thereabouts,' Danson replied. 'But… I'm told the prince has been getting cold feet. Keep this to yourself, but we've actually stopped work on whole sections of the park, and the plan is they're going to open Hysteria first as a sort of … market test next month.'

'Oh no,' Cady said.

Femi raised an eyebrow. 'A bit late in the day for that, isn't it?'

'You'd make an excellent project manager, Fem. But it's not as bad as it sounds. The winds out here are fickle, and hopefully a good bit of early word of mouth might help right the ship. Hence why…'

'You've called the big guns,' Femi said, and Winston snorted.

'Exactly,' Danson said. 'And why I wanted to give you a ride ahead of the others. I'm not really supposed to, but screw it. I imagined Cady might quite enjoy the honour, and it will give you all a chance to maybe prepare something.'

They reached the end of the paved path, Danson shepherding them along a graded route marked out by oversized fence blocks the shape of pulled teeth, more stick-of-rock-coloured tape tied between each, trembling in the wind. Large mounds of sand rose from the desert floor, seemingly at random, and Danson joked that the workers made them when they had nothing else to do. They followed a twisted section of Hysteria's track, which stood ten metres or so from the ground, purple here, like the skin of an exotic snake. Cady couldn't keep the awed grin from her face.

'I'm not really one for false modesty,' Naz said, 'but I'm not exactly sure how strong the crossover is between the literary world and theme-park enthusiasts.'

'What did *The Times* call you?' Danson asked.

'A generational talent?' Winston offered. 'Voice of a generation? Something like that.'

Naz rolled her eyes. 'I don't think it was quite *that*. Still, I'm not sure anyone listens to writers these days, if they ever did. Especially not on the topic of theme parks.'

'Well, it's about all of you together,' Danson said. 'In concert. The earlier the better, too. A cultural blitzkrieg. But you know … only if you enjoy it, of course. I don't want to put words in your mouth. No pressure.' He gave a big showman's smile.

At the foot of the lift hill, Cady started getting ideas for filming the next day. Doing a piece to camera right below the drop would be incredible, because from here you could also see how the track in the distance climbed up onto the mountains before another spectacular drop. The scale of Hysteria was genuinely terrifying – it looked big enough to see from space. Her eventual video was going to blow her behind-the-scenes-of-Diagon-Alley to smithereens.

She peeled away the front of her top from her chest and wafted it to cool her down. 'I think I might take you up on that drink,' she said.

Danson held out his bottle to her. 'Here you go.'

She thanked him and swallowed a warm mouthful before offering it to the others. They declined, their attention fixed on the roller coaster.

Finally, they reached the entrance to another paved concourse, above which hung a sign emblazoned with the ride's name in a yellow, scrawled font. They all stopped and the desert silence closed in on them. Cady looked around. She hadn't seen anyone else since arriving. If she closed her eyes, she'd have no idea she was even in an amusement park.

Danson guided them towards the start of a winding queue line, before walking up the exit line, telling them he needed to get things ready and that he'd meet them on the other side. The path zig-zagged back and forth, passing signage designed to build anticipation.

Tallest. Fastest. Longest. No turning back from here. Point of no return. Last chance.

They entered a dim building, illuminated in yellows, violets and reds, with air-conditioning so strong Cady instinctively reached down to the cardigan around her waist. The queue line continued, winding past artwork, videos and information boards about the ride's inspiration, a multi-million-selling rock album from the 1980s. Halfway around, melodic heavy metal music started to boom through the speakers.

When they finally reached the front of the queue line, they had passed through a tunnel and into a cavernous final building where Danson stood waiting for them. 'What did you think?'

'Question.' Winston held up his hand like he was on a school trip. 'Are these guys still big?'

'Have the Gen Zs in your office heard of them?' Cady asked.

Danson smiled, his hand at the back of his head again, tap, tap, tapping. 'They certainly have now.'

'I bet.' Cady turned to look up at a giant mural of the album cover on the wall behind them, a warped human-animal face the focal point. She remembered it from the cassette copy that had circumnavigated its way around Dad's cluttered Mondeo during her childhood, along with the greatest hits of Queen and Dire Straits.

'The prince is a big rocker,' Danson said, 'and he insisted this be a monument to the greatest album ever made. So. Here we are.'

'Rock on,' Winston said and made two devil horns with his hands.

Danson looked at his watch, and gestured for them to follow. He led them through a set of gates to the first and second car of the roller coaster train. The coaster's sculpted front was sleek and feline, a snarling lion, ears pinned back by the wind. The fibreglass body, more of that gold and deep blue, gleamed, factory fresh. A clear plastic screen angled into each two-seated car, a bird screen, and understanding what this implied, Cady asked, 'How fast does this go?'

'Top speed is about one hundred and fifty-five miles an hour. It hits that speed twice.' Danson looked out of the ride exit, at the glimmer of pinkish twilight in the sky. 'I'll need all your loose items, if that's okay. The way this thing shifts, if anything comes free it'll be a war zone.'

He brought over a tray, and the group obliged, dropping in sunglasses, watches and phones. Femi threw in his chain and hat. Cady patted her pockets with increasing alarm, unable to find her lovely make-up kit. Had it fallen out in the car maybe, when she'd put on her concealer? That was going to be another mark against her when she confessed to—

Tom. Oh crap, she still hadn't messaged him – what a flipping idiot. How could she be such a dozy cow? There was reception and 5G here, too. Oh, Tom was going feel so abandoned. She considered asking for her phone back to quickly message him, but Danson was already walking away with the tray. She noticed his arms appeared to be trembling a little under the weight. Cady let it go, they'd be back in a flash. Five minutes wouldn't make or break their relationship.

'If you want to get in car one, you'll get the best experience,' Danson said from over by the operating booth. They all looked at one another before moving slowly towards the front of the train.

'Do you guys have a preference?' Cady said to the others.

'The second car gets the best air time,' Danson called back to them.

'Air time?' Naz looked to Cady.

'The feeling you're floating out of your seat.'

'Oh,' she said. 'Car one it is, then.'

Naz took the right-hand seat, Winston the left. Cady went in next, sitting behind Naz in car two. Femi took the seat to her left.

'The ride is quite rare,' Danson said from over at the booth. 'It's a real Frankenstein's monster. It's got elements of the fastest launch roller coasters in the world, mixed with more traditional elements, like the two hundred metre lift hill – that was another specification from the prince. He wanted to recapture the magic of *The Big One* in Blackpool when it first opened.'

'I've been on that one,' Naz said. 'How much bigger than that one is this?'

'Four times, more or less,' Danson said. Naz turned to look through the seat gap at Cady in horror.

Winston reached across and patted Naz's shoulder. 'But it's all been tested, yeah?' he said.

'You'll be fine guys, don't worry,' Danson said, enjoying himself now. 'You've got at least two minutes on the way up to contemplate your life choices. Then there's a bit of a scary pause for dramatic effect before it absolutely hurls you down that slope using a booster. Do you think your heart can take all that, Fem?'

Cady turned to Femi, as did Naz, her face appearing through the gap between the tall seat backs. As a teenager, Femi had collapsed during a game of football, a hitherto undetected heart anomaly the cause. He'd lived with a heart device ever since, and at university he'd always been nervous about exerting himself. They'd joked darkly about it back in the day, although something about Danson using it now felt ill-judged. Femi didn't seem bothered though, and yelled 'Bring it' at the operating booth. Cady guessed he and Danson had perhaps already discussed it. They'd always had something of a special bond, which at times bordered on paternal. She'd noticed it earlier, when Femi told Danson he'd been proud of him.

Danson's voice suddenly boomed from the speakers above. 'Everyone set?'

'Actually, I think I want to go home,' Naz said and stood up. Winston reached up and guided her back into the seat, all of them laughing, appreciative of the break in tension.

There was a sudden hiss, and Cady jumped. A clamshell-shaped lap restraint descended on a bar over her shoulders and stopped just above her thighs. She pulled it the rest of the way down and gripped the handle on the clamshell's front, her forearms resting in two grooves on top. Just to check, she pushed up with her knees, but the locking mechanism pushed back, immovable. She leaned against the seat back and pushed up again. But the restraint wasn't going anywhere.

Danson reappeared from inside a booth, reaching over to manually check each restraint, tugging and shoving. He checked Cady last, leaning across Femi's lap and grunting. Check complete, he closed his eyes, took a deep breath. And another.

His eyes didn't open.

'You okay?' she asked.

Danson nodded, took another breath, and his eyes opened again. He smiled. Femi helped him back up to the platform. 'Sorry, head rush. Told you, this place is trying to kill you.' With a weary smile he returned to the booth. Cady turned to Femi, who grinned back excitedly.

The lighting lowered, and a voice began wailing along with heavy guitars and pounding drums. A deeper voice counted back from ten and the roller coaster jerked forward. Passing the booth, Cady saw Danson through the window. He brought something up to his mouth, and chased it down with a swig from his bottle. Then he turned his back to them, and leaned forward, hands out to prop up the weight of his upper body.

Before she could give it any more consideration, the roller coaster left the station and turned sharply right. Ahead of them was the lift hill, stretching up impossibly to the darkening sky. At that moment, it wasn't possible to concentrate on anything else.

CADY

Friday 21st June, 6.53pm
Celsius: 37°, Fahrenheit: 98.6°

clakclakclakclakclakclakclak

The coaster climbed. Cady, tilted up thirty-five degrees, surveyed the surrounding mountains and desert. She wished she'd been allowed to film today. To get her genuine, first-time reaction to all this. Not that she couldn't act, and she did occasionally do second takes if her camera failed or it didn't feel right the first time. But authenticity was important, both to her and her audience. And this view, and the whole park really, even unfinished, was blowing her mind.

A quarter of the way up, a little round sign informed them they'd reached fifty metres. Already quotidian perspective had gone. On either side, the tops of tents and dwarfed construction equipment marked the mostly empty land stretching out to the sheer mountain walls. The routes of unbuilt roads and footprints of attractions still only dreams appeared now as a piece.

clakclakclak

To the left and right of the car, beyond a half-metre gap, an emergency staircase ran alongside the track, its outer handrail demarcating the edge of the safe world.

Catching her staring across him, Femi said, 'I wouldn't fancy coming down on those much.'

'No,' Cady said, even though in reality she'd love it. Perhaps Danson might let her climb up to film over the next few days. It wouldn't hurt to ask.

Femi leaned towards her. 'It's so good to see you.'

'I know, what an amazing surprise.'

He nodded with a tight smile for just a bit too long. He looked like he might be gearing up to say something. Maybe about Oxford. She really didn't want to go there, it wasn't necessary. She tried to hijack the conversation. 'Such an amazing view.'

'Uh huh. I don't know if you even remember,' Femi said. 'You probably don't. But sorry about what happened … you know. At Danson's birthday thing. In Oxford. I know it's been ages.'

So they were doing this, then. She didn't have a choice. She flapped her hand. No big deal. Which was true when it came right down to it. It wasn't like *she*, or they, had anything to be embarrassed or apologetic about. They were all adults. Still…

It had been a surprise party for Danson, the location chosen as it suited Southerners, Northerners and Midlanders. The city's similarities to Cambridge allowed them to slip back into their old roles: Femi roguishly egging on the birthday boy to do shots with him and flirting with all the staff, Danson quietly bowled over by their attention, Winston impulsively taking on an enormous food challenge on the menu, Naz rebelling against the bad meals and awful service by charming them a discount, and Cady powering the conversation with enthusiastic questions and prompts until they were all drunk enough to interact unaided.

And after dinner, they'd gone to a bar and drunk even more, other men and women present unable to stop themselves glancing over covetously – again just as it had been at university. Their glamour and energy and optimism radiated from them, enhanced by their togetherness. God, they'd been so full of it that night.

Danson, always sensible, had left to get a coach back to Birmingham, but because the rest of them had all been having so much fun, they went back to Femi's room at the hotel for a few more drinks. The chat got pretty intense. Relationship and sex-life stuff; an old-fashioned Chamberlain College deep-and-meaningful-and-reckless. That stuff, it seemed, was in their group DNA, too.

So it hadn't been too wild for Femi to suggest, no matter how jokingly, they play spin the bottle. Like they were kids again. And why the hell not? Naz had just ended a big relationship. Winston was, by choice, eternally single. And Femi had just split from his first wife.

Only Cady hadn't been up for it. So she'd excused herself, gone to get another bottle of wine from the bar, and while waiting to be served she decided she was done for the night. She and Tom had been together two years by then, and she had no interest in risking what was turning into the most serious relationship of her life for a little nostalgia snog. But when she returned to drop the wine off, Naseem was standing between the other two with her knickers around her ankles, Femi on his knees with his face to her crotch, Winston kissing her from behind with his hands under her top. They hadn't even noticed Cady enter, and when she placed the wine on the dressing table with a view to a quick exit, all three turned to look at her. Then Naz had smiled, shrugged, and gestured for her to come and join them.

But even though the night had reminded her of how much she loved them, and that moments like this had often threatened to break out at university but never had, so in some respects this was unfinished business, she really was trying to move on with her life. So she smiled, shook her head, and left. And the next morning, she'd gone home before seeing any of them again, picking up a petrol-station Twix for Tom, because they were his favourite.

clakclakclakclakclak

'We were all really, really, drunk,' Femi said. 'Sorry if you were— If it was upsetting or weird.'

'Honestly. It wasn't.'

clakclakclakclakclak

'Hey,' she said, again derailing. 'Did you think Danson seemed okay?'

'Yeah. Can't believe he got us all out here. What a guy.'

'Do you think he looked a bit … pale?'

He shrugged. 'Maybe. But I imagine it's hard work on your body living out in this climate.' He reached up and pressed his fingers to his damp forehead.

'Yeah, but you'd also expect him to have a tan.'

clakclakclakclakclak

'You guys okay?' Femi shouted.

'Did I mention I fucking hate heights?' Naseem said.

'You'll be fine. Just don't look down.'

One hundred metres. Europe's tallest. One hundred and

fifty. Aeroplane high, the ground a map now. The breeze was cooler here, but not by much; it cut across from the tops of the nearest mountains, above which they were now ascending. Beyond these were more mountains, the c-shape range reaching far into the desert and concealing the horizon all around them but for the opening where they had entered the park. That was the direction the lift hill faced, and from her seat Cady saw the motorway tapering towards the magenta sky.

clakclakclakclakclak

Still they climbed. So much track to go. Of course, she'd been on *The Big One* in Blackpool, too. Plenty of times. She had three different Blackpool videos on her channel. Her parents had taken her when it first opened, when it had been the tallest coaster in the world. It had seemed galactically big to her then, visible from every part of the town. And it wasn't exactly small, even as a grown-up.

It had been sixty-five metres. *Only sixty-five metres*. More or less what they still had left to climb.

clakclakclak

Cady raised her face to stare at the wispy clouds above.

World's tallest now.

170 metres.

190.

The apex approached. The track stopping improbably, impossibly, at the vanishing point just metres ahead. Beyond that…

Who knew? They'd seen the coaster from the ground, but what if…? What if there was nothing there? What if it had all been some horrible trick, and the roller coaster wasn't finished yet and was about to plunge into an abyss? But of course it would all be fine. It always was, wasn't it? Safer than the drive here, ha ha. Still, amazing Hysteria had caused in her, a seasoned rider, the briefest moment of doubt – good job, Danson. Her dissipating fear cleared the path for a burst of excitement, just as the coaster reached the top.

The train began to straighten. They passed two large lights, there to alert aircraft, followed by a pole with a tip like fusilli – a lightning rod.

But no drop. Not yet. Instead, the train moved down a short, gently sloped straight, allowing riders to enjoy the appearance of the unobstructed panorama: the park, the entrance, the desert, the mountains, and that single road in and out. It was a bit different, but Cady appreciated the suspense.

Femi made a last terrified face and let go of the handle on his lap restraint, putting his arms above his head. Impressed, Cady did the same, the grin on her face impossible to stop.

A sign below a weathervane read, 'We're going to fly!'

clakclakclak

The lion's face at the front of the car passed the point of no return. Winston and Naz's seat backs then began to lower as their car entered the start of a steeper decline. Femi glanced at Cady apologetically, and grabbed his handle. She laughed and braced herself for the fall.

clakclakcla—

The car halted. Time, too.

Without the sound of the chain, it felt almost silent. But the weathervane *eeeeked*. The wind caressed their car.

Ten seconds passed. Twenty. The suspense delicious. Femi shifted in his seat, vinyl squeaking, clothes rustling. A look in any direction offered no reprieve, only confirmation of how far they were about to plunge.

'No,' Naseem said. 'No, no, no. Don't like this one bit.'

Thirty seconds. Forty. Femi turned to Cady, saw she was

still smiling, and let her mood inform his. The slight furrow in his brow retreated.

'Jesus,' Winston yelled. 'This is nuts.'

'They're going to make millions,' Femi said, and raised his arms once more.

Another thirty seconds passed. Naz yelled, 'What if it's broken?'

Winston's face appeared in the seat gap of their slightly lower car, eyes seeking answers from Cady from the other side of the bird screen.

'It's all part of it,' Cady said.

With some effort, Cady looked back through her own seat gap, at the four empty cars stretching back on the straight. The lift hill was no longer visible. The rails vanished into thin air. Turning back, she could see the ornamental front of the car had already descended the gently sloped start of the drop. At that point the tracks fell so steeply you could only see sand and sky beyond.

Ninety seconds.

'This really can't be good for your heart,' Cady said to Femi.

Femi gave a sideways grin. 'Don't you worry about me,' he said, sounding slightly short of breath. 'I'm golden.' He lowered his arms to the handle again, his right hand briefly touching his jaw on the way down.

Two minutes.

No time at all on the ground, but up here, too much. Surely, too much. Parks needed to funnel riders through as quickly as possible, there was no way the design would allow for such a pointless hold-up. Especially as it was kind of diminishing the tension. Unless Danson was maybe heightening the experience for them. Playing a trick.

Femi leaned towards her again. 'At what point do we worry?'

'I'm worried,' Naz called back.

'It's fine,' Cady said. 'I'm sure it's fine.'

Yet why was a different species of tension now slithering through her? She felt poised and alert, like she had been that night in her tent. She pressed her feet against the car floor and leaned back to counter their slightly forward tilt.

Winston's face appeared in the gap again. 'I've gotta say, it feels like something's happened.'

Femi hummed a note of concern. 'I mean, if this ride was happening in the day, it's a long time to have people without hats and sunglasses exposed to the sun, isn't it?'

'I really don't want to hear this,' Naz said.

'It'll be fine,' Cady said, trying to keep herself and them calm. 'If it is an issue, which it probably isn't, Danson will be able to fix it.'

'He said there was a wait,' Winston said to Naz, trying to be helpful.

'Not this long, though,' Naz snapped back. 'Not this long.'

'Naz,' Femi said, 'if Cady says there's nothing to worry about, then we should probably listen to her. We're not in actual danger, are we?'

He gave Cady a hopeful glance, and she tried to project assurance. 'No, not at all. It'll be fine.'

Except Danson hadn't looked well, had he? He hadn't looked well at all. What if he'd collapsed? What if they'd broken down and he was lying on the ground down there, unconscious?

Cady swallowed. She filled her lungs and shut her eyes. That hadn't happened. Danson was fine. He had to be fine.

She looked around the park again, noticing some workers

had made a smiley face using mounds of sands far, far, down to her right. She noticed a few scattered palm trees around the park, and how spindly the other sections of Hysteria's track looked from up here. How spindly their own section of track suddenly felt.

And still, the train didn't move.

CADY

Friday 21st June, 7.05pm
Celsius: 36°, Fahrenheit: 96.8°

The four friends sat silent in the gloaming. For ten minutes or so they'd taken turns shouting to alert Danson, their panic growing steadily more audible. But if he hadn't noticed them stuck up here by now, he'd definitely be wondering why the train hadn't returned to the station.

'The lights aren't on,' Winston said, voice raised to be heard, barely moving his head, keeping his gaze straight in front. All of them were speaking this way now, not daring to move too much, like Hysteria might fall down if they did.

'What lights?' Naz said, alarmed.

'The ones running on the sides of the tracks,' Winston said. 'There's probably an electrical problem.'

'Electrics,' Femi said, seemingly to himself. He ran a finger along one side of his jawline. 'A power cut.'

Naz jabbed her head at a caged white bulb by the weathervane. 'That one's on, though.'

'It's probably on a backup,' Femi said. 'Maybe that's it. A power cut. That's an easy enough fix, isn't it, Cady?'

'Yeah,' she said, trying to stay positive. 'I mean, yeah. Sure.' She looked back to see if she might be able to glimpse the station building through the tracks but they were too far from it now.

'Why hasn't he come yet?' Naz said, her voice ragged from their yelling. 'Or … or … shouted up to us, at least.'

Cady glanced to her right, the distant features of the landscape already being consumed by darkness. 'I'm not sure if we could see or hear him from here.'

'Bloody super,' Naz said. 'So no one can hear us, either.'

'Can anyone get out?' Femi asked, trying carefully to slide under the clamshell lap restraint pinning him in his seat. Eventually he shook his head when the bottom of the clamshell dug into his lower ribs.

'I'm not going anywhere,' Naz said. 'What, and jump that gap to the staircase if I escape? Uh uh.'

Femi gripped the chair's plastic sides and tried to push himself up with the intention of getting high enough to pull his legs through the waist-sized gap beneath the clamshell. But to do so required him holding his body in a banana shape while climbing up the chair back with backwards-facing hands. He was strong, stronger than the rest of them, but clearly his gym regime hadn't involved this extreme form of reverse dip. After a few failed attempts, he banged his head against his chair back in frustration.

Cady looked down at her clamshell restraint. She certainly wouldn't be able to lift herself up and out. It was under or bust. The flat bottom of the clamshell hovered a little above her thighs, the back just a few inches from her belly. There wasn't a big gap, but it looked a fraction bigger than Femi's. And she was much smaller than him. But even if she could navigate the angles and squeeze her rib cage through, her head might not fit – and that wasn't the only problem. The slight upward tilt of the seat bottom countered the effect of the shallow gradient they were on, but still any forward movement into the car's leg recess was a battle with gravity, one she would have to face with core strength and leg power alone. She would also have to clear the small, slender fin at the end of the seat that was designed to separate her legs – all the while hoping the ride didn't start again, and that she wouldn't get herself into a position from which she couldn't extricate herself.

She steadied herself and tried it anyway. Just to know if it was possible. But scooting her backside under the clamshell contorted her body so that her chin became wedged uncomfortably against her chest. The fin jabbed her coccyx, and suddenly the idea she might get trapped like this overwhelmed her. Her anxiety was all-consuming. Like when her friends had taken her caving for her eighteenth, and she'd panicked about her head cracking so much she'd frozen and had to be rescued by the guides. Now her legs started to shake, and a whiny voice in her head insisted she back up.

Overcome with claustrophobia and the sudden conviction persistence would split and snap her, she pushed against the car floor with her feet and resumed her sitting position. She was surprised by how heavily she was breathing, and unpleasant adrenaline coursed through her. Her head ached around her right temple, and she reached up to touch it.

'It's impossible,' she said. 'The ride's designed to hold you in place.'

Winston, abandoning his own half-hearted attempt, concurred.

As ashamed as Cady felt at her own overreaction, Naz couldn't even summon the courage to try. She was now concentrating on her breathing, puffing in and out like she was in labour. Staring straight ahead. That's why she saw it first.

'Is that a car?' she said.

'Where?' Femi said.

'On the road in,' Winston said, pointing where Naz wouldn't; her hands hadn't left the restraint handle since they'd got on the ride.

Two pinpricks of light glided towards the horizon. Who would be leaving the park at this time? All hands were presumably on deck if there had been a power cut or an emergency.

'It's probably the security changing over,' Cady said, mostly to reassure herself.

'What if it's Danson?' Naz said. 'What if … what if he's had to get someone to help, and he's left us here?'

'He wouldn't do that,' Femi said. 'Not without telling us.'

'What if he doesn't want to waste time doing that? What if … what if he's driven off to get help and something happens? His car breaks down or … or he crashes. And we're up here. Oh my God, it's the weekend. It's the bloody weekend. We might be stuck here for—'

Winston said something to her, trying to stop her talking herself into a panic attack. All Cady heard was a low murmur. Through the bird screen she saw Winston take Naz's hand. Then, his voice audible now, he said, 'Worst case, so what?

Tomorrow's party night. This place will be full of people setting up all day.'

'Yeah?' Naz said.

'Hey, maybe they even start tonight.'

'A place like this doesn't sit empty very long,' Femi added. 'Just keep it ... we're all good, guys. We're all good.'

Cady found herself nodding, reassured by this train of thought. 'Hey, Taylor Swift might even come to our rescue.' Naz managed to force a laugh.

'You think it's really going be that big a deal, then?' she said.

'Why would Danson lie?'

'Did he actually say Taylor Swift was coming?' Femi said. 'Or did he imply it, like the way he did to me about Ryan Coogler?'

'He strongly implied it,' Cady said after a beat.

After a moment, Winston said, 'Well ... any of them rescuing us would be just fine by me. And it'd be some marketing stunt.'

All of them fell silent. Cady glanced over the side again, the height dizzying her briefly. It really *would* be a great marketing stunt. Four well-known, if not *famous*, people stuck at the top of a roller coaster in the desert. That sort of thing might generate a lot of press. The sort of press Danson had been desperate for.

Like they'd all been thinking the same thing, Naz said, 'But Danson wouldn't do this deliberately, would he? Not like this.'

'Nah,' Winston said. 'Danson? Nah. He's our boy.'

'What if ... what if he thought we wouldn't find out?' Naz said. 'Or, talked himself into thinking it was fine because we'd get publicity for ourselves, too?'

Winston squeezed her hand again and shook it gently. 'He's down there now sorting it all out.'

'Or what if he's cross with us? About something we did?'

'He's not cross with us,' Femi said. 'Everyone just—'

'What if it's because he heard about what happened in Oxford?' Naz said.

'Why…' Winston turned to her. 'Why would he know about that?'

'Because Femi told him.'

Winston turned to look through the seat gap. 'You didn't,' he said. 'Did you?'

Femi shook his head. 'I just got a bit drunk with him in town and it kind of came out. I didn't… I didn't want it to be this big secret between us. I thought he'd appreciate it.'

'Ah, Fem.'

'You told me he looked upset,' Naz said.

'No, I said he was probably annoyed he'd missed it—'

'You didn't say that—'

'—but he certainly didn't want to imprison us. Come on.'

'You sure of that?' Naz said. 'What if this is a punishment?'

'Uh, can I just remind everyone I wasn't involved,' Cady said. 'So … if hypothetically that is why he's angry, why would I be here?'

Femi paused. In a calmer tone, he said, 'I didn't exactly name names exactly. I just sort of said we all ended up… you know. So maybe—'

Cady shook her head, annoyed but not entirely surprised by his braggadocio. 'Femi.'

'It was years after it happened. And I was wasted. I'm really sorry. It wasn't like a massive thing. I made a throwaway remark and … he went a bit quiet.'

'When exactly was this?' Cady said.

'I don't know,' Femi said. 'About a year ago.'

Cady shook her head and stared out at the horizon. What if something had gotten back to Tom? It could have really caused Cady problems. She could only imagine how distraught she'd have been had the roles been reversed. Especially after Tom had been so cool about her friendship with them all, particularly with the boys. One previous boyfriend had really struggled with that element, and his jealousy had been a large part of why they broke up. God, how she missed Tom suddenly. Was he checking his phone still, or had he given up on her completely? It would be about 4pm back in the UK. From his perspective, he'd waited a whole day to hear from her. And now she was stuck, unable to do anything about it for God knew how long.

'None of this feels right,' Naz said.

'Isn't it more likely that he's collapsed or something?' Cady said, and when Femi glared at her, she added, 'while we're entertaining morbid possibilities. As much as I'm sure he'd have felt a bit left out by … the whole massive gang bang thing, didn't you all see how frail he looked? He nearly passed out checking my harness. What if the stress of all this…' She looked at Femi. 'What if he's fallen and hit his head or something?'

'He didn't look great,' Winston said.

After another silence, Naz said, 'I liked it better when Taylor Swift was coming to rescue us.'

'She definitely is,' Cady said. 'Taylor wouldn't leave us.'

She had the urge to cross her legs but the restraint wouldn't allow for it, so she shifted her weight from one side to the other for the umpteenth time. Oh, what she'd give to get one knee on the near side of the clamshell. Wedge her whole body in place and ease the pressure on her back.

In the distance, she could make out the shadowy shape of the arch at the entrance. It blocked any view of the yellow car she'd seen there. Had it perhaps been the one leaving just now? Despite the heat, a shiver travelled the length of her spine at the sudden notion that all this might have something to do with her stalker. That he had perhaps arranged all this somehow. Found out her plans. Followed her here. Done something to Danson.

Perhaps he had put some sort of tracking device on her. Was that how he'd been following her?

No, that was stupid. She was losing her composure. It was too early for that. The idea of her stalker being here was even more ridiculous than the idea Danson, gentle, contemplative Danson, had imprisoned them up here because he was jealous of an imaginary foursome.

Danson, Then

I have survived Fresher's Week. Just! Everyone here is nice enough, and I've been hanging out with some people from my little concrete 'blockhouse' – though I've not clicked with anyone yet. Chamberlain is more Soviet than I remember from my interview, very different from the grand old buildings of the other Cambridge colleges. Lots of brutal oblongs and cubes set out on regularly tended lawns, each with a Hepworth-esque sculpture at the centre. Other than the art, it looks a bit like school, so I should feel at home.

But I don't. Not yet, anyway. Like I said, everyone is friendly. But I get a sense when I'm talking to people I'm only being half looked at, that they're keeping an eye out for a better opportunity. Everyone here is so smart and focused.

Properly. Talking about the economy and the Venezuela situation and how they are going to do this and that when they graduate. I haven't got the first clue what I'm going to do next week, let alone in three years.

I shouldn't be here. Last week Dr Pinter caught me daydreaming in his lecture and called on me. My answer was so far off, the whole theatre groaned. I think maybe I'm not actually that clever, and that I'm just very good at following instructions. It got me through exams, and through the interview process here, but now I'm being found out. Maths at Cambridge is all about being quick. You can't just be right. You've got to be right last week. I've started skipping lectures. Maybe I'll catch up over Christmas at my own pace, but also what's the point? I'll cram before exams, like I did at school, and hope for the best.

Everyone seems to have settled into their friendship groups now first term's coming to an end, and while I've somehow ended up at the periphery of more than one, I still end most nights reading in my room like a sad sack. I don't think I'm the only one still adapting, though. There's this girl I've seen around, who also seems on the outskirts of things. She's pretty and punky. Sticks gems to her face. She was alone in the lunch hall the other day and made eye contact. I nearly went to sit with her but bottled it at the last minute.

I've been re-reading a lot of comfort books, some of the stuff about magic Nan bought me as a kid. I started working on some card tricks, entertaining the ludicrous fantasy that I might be able to use them to impress people in the college bar.

Got sick of feeling sorry for myself, so I threw myself into things this last week, and now I feel I'm ending term on a bit of a high. Last Thursday, I went to an open cast and crew audition for *Little Shop of Horrors*. It's only for the college dramatic society, but there were a lot of the student glitterati there. You know, the sort that stand out in a geek-farm like this, well-groomed, attractive, nice clothes. Juggernaut auras. The crazy fools plan to do the whole thing next term, which is surely impossible.

I'd gone there wanting to get involved in the technical side. There's a lot of crossover between magic and stagecraft, and I was curious as to how they'd do it with the big alien plant puppet and everything. But we all had to do a bit of acting and singing and dancing, and I hadn't sort of realised until we were all standing in a circle taking turns to sing lines of 'Happy Birthday'.

I was always okay at drama, and sung in a punk band at school, so I resisted the urge to run, and gave it my best shot. And in the end, most auditioners were pretty terrible, and it was all so much fun no one minded I was bad. That was largely down to the director, this confident Adonis-of-a-bloke called Femi, who I'd seen around and always assumed was a second or third year. He put everyone at ease and got us all in on the joke. It was impressive, actually.

After, a bunch of people were heading to the bar, and Femi asked me if I was coming. While we were there, some dick called Sampson made a crack about my singing. I almost lost it, wanting to go for him in a way I'd not done since being at school back when Matty Tamplin said I smelled of piss. Femi, sitting on the other side of the table we were at, heard it, though. He leaned forward, raised his voice, and said, 'No. That's not happening.' Everyone went quiet and gave Sampson evils, and the guy eventually slunk away.

There were about four or five of us at the end of the night, including Femi and a few of the cool kids, who, of course, had been the best singers and everything else. They were actually really nice. The attractive girl with the face gems was there, too. Her name was Eloise, and because she worked behind the bar she did a lock-in. I don't know what it was, but the atmosphere was just … it clicked. A load of creative types, lots of energy and ideas, bouncing off each other. Unlike others I've met here, there's a vibe the future is a blank canvas, and that five-year-plans are for suckers. Hilariously, Femi told us his family, all medics, had no idea that he'd secretly switched courses to study history and was currently trying to put them off coming to visit in case they found out.

I have to say, I felt pretty shy most of the night, so at times found myself spectating. But after a pint or two I couldn't help myself. I felt all my creative juices flowing again. So I did the torn corner card trick for them. And they only bloody liked it. Best night I've had since coming here!

I've got so much to catch up on here. Things have been manic!

So the first thing I find on arriving at Chamberlain was a note in my pigeonhole telling me I actually got a part in the show! Okay, it's not massive, but I get to play a street urchin. AND, I'm sort of like the Stage Manager, too. Yeah, it's dogs-body work really, mainly running around after Femi, who's the one making the big calls. But I don't mind. That guy is a serious talent. He's doing the voice of the singing plant, and it's crazy how good he is.

The guy leading the band, this laid-back whippet of a dude called Winston who seems to be able to play every single instrument amazingly, well, his mum apparently knows someone who can lend us the scenery and stuff from the actual touring production. How mad is that? Slightly worried we have to perform the thing in six weeks, but there's a lot of energy and enthusiasm happening, so I'm sure it'll work out.

Interestingly, Eloise has become the show's costumer – I think Femi charmed her into it. We were in the lunch queue together the other day and had a polite little chat. She's got this really warm, womanly voice, and I noticed a slight accent. Turns out, she's from Wolverhampton. So I told her I was from the West Midlands too, and she joked we were probably related. I laughed, and so wasn't quite sure I heard what she said next correctly. So I just smiled at her, and that was the end of the conversation.

I'm probably deluding myself, but what I think she said was, 'shame'.

Quick catch-up: there's been some Eloise developments. Tonight, after rehearsal, I was with Naz and Cady, two of the actors from the show, and they caught me staring at Eloise working behind the bar. It was like having an angel and a devil on my shoulders.

Cady, who is like the personification of a child's drawing of the sun, asked me if I liked her, and when I said 'sort of', Naz, who has this no-nonsense chic goth thing going on (that I think is a bit of an act) asked if I'd spoken to her. I told them about the Midlands chat, not mentioning the 'shame' part, and Naz rolled her eyes. I told them I thought she was a bit out of my league, and Cady looked appalled. 'You're absolutely not,' she said, and told me there were no leagues in love.

Naz got up then, and, worried, I asked where she was going. She ignored me and my desperate head-shaking, and was soon at the bar talking to Eloise, looking over at me and pointing. I was mortified. When Naz came back, she didn't say a thing. Not even when I asked.

At the end of the night, Eloise stopped me and asked if she could have a word. She locked us in and started collecting glasses and wiping tables. She had on these plaid trousers and a crop top, while her blonde hair, streaked with pink, was tied back in a high, tight ponytail. She looked amazing. Eventually, she told me that 'my friend' had said to her that I was looking for work.

I didn't have a clue what to say. Cambridge doesn't let you have a job term-time because you're supposed to focus completely on studying. So what was this about?

Quickly, I pieced it together. I'd told Naz about my mum taking that cowboy builder to small claims court over the new kitchen. And about all the hints she's been dropping about needing help with her bills. I'd also wondered out loud why Eloise was allowed to work behind the bar given the university policy. Clearly Naz had killed two birds with one stone. I didn't know whether to be annoyed with her or if I now owed her a drink.

Eventually I told Eloise I sort of, kind of, maybe was looking for work. And Eloise told me about how, if you were poor enough, the college would give you a job to do in exchange for a discount on your fees.

So I asked how they decided if you were poor enough, and Eloise sort of gave me a once-over followed by a wicked little sideways smile. Then she vanished with her glasses, and that was the end of the conversation.

Of course, dear reader, I probably don't need to tell you that I'm now in love.

CADY

Friday 21st June, 7.35pm
Celsius: 37°, Fahrenheit: 98.6°

With each passing minute their collective belief that things were in hand weakened. Half-an-hour later and it was almost fully dark, the park now a grim patchwork of blacks and greys, only the dimmest band of burnt orange at the horizon. The stars, and the slender moon behind them, offered little illumination, while the emergency bulb gradually created a light bubble around them, further limiting the range of their view beyond it.

Their movements now emboldened by the diminishing view of how high up they were, Femi suggested that they all try and throw their weight forward at the same time. Perhaps it might send the train over the edge. Cady didn't argue, despite her scepticism.

It didn't work, and Cady's stomach ached from where it had repeatedly struck the clamshell. Her legs ached too, as did her core and her back, all from having to fight the slight decline to stay comfortable. Gravity kept pulling her forwards, away from the seat back and into the restraint, putting extra pressure on her thighs. She had to keep swapping where she held her weight, sometimes extending her legs to push against the front wall of the car, sometimes pushing against the back of the clamshell with both palms, squeezing with her core. She didn't complain though. Whatever she and Femi were experiencing would be much worse for the other two given their tilted position beyond the straight. Naz had already complained about her legs and the tummy pain from having to let her weight rest on the clamshell. Cady could cope – for now.

After a quick inventory, all they had between them was a sachet of sugar in Femi's pocket, and a bag of coke in Winston's.

'Let's not mix those up,' Cady said.

Only Femi laughed, and even that was strained. Through the gap, Cady could see Winston rubbing the opening of his baggie between his thumb and forefinger.

'So, we've got no water,' he said. 'No sun cream. No extra clothing. No hats.'

No one replied. Winston's fingers picked up pace.

'And what time does the sun come up?'

'We won't be here then,' Femi said, irritated that Winston had spoken these things aloud.

It was no surprise when Naseem started shrieking again. 'Help us. Help us. We're stuck. Please.'

Eventually Winston, perhaps out of guilt, took over yelling when Naz started losing her voice. Cady was happy to go next.

She needed a distraction from the slight pressure in her bladder, and from the acidic taste of fear in the back of her already dry mouth. A distraction from all this *dead time*.

But when Winston's cries started breaking up, Femi intervened. 'We need to have a better strategy than this. We're all going to blow our voices.'

'I agree,' Cady said. 'What do you think? Should we take it in turns? Every half-an-hour?'

'Yeah, sounds good. But I think we all do it together. It'll be louder. And we should sustain it for exactly a minute. It makes it like a pattern, rather than just random theme park noise. I'm sure I've read somewhere that's what to do.'

'The SAS Guide to Roller Coaster Malfunctions,' Cady said.

'That's the one.'

'Solid read.'

Femi's little laugh was warmer this time, perhaps appreciating Cady's attempts to keep their spirits up. To keep things normal. And calm.

It wasn't working on Naz, though. 'Can you speak up? We can't hear you when you talk quietly.'

'It wasn't anything important,' Femi replied. 'Just that we should be yelling together in a pattern, on the hour. Or half hour.'

'How will we know the time?'

'It doesn't have to be exact. I'm sure we can all agree on when it feels like the time has gone.'

'Well, it feels like an hour now.'

'No way,' Winston said. 'Jesus.'

Femi rolled his eyes and took a deep breath. 'You know,' he said, a funny smile appearing on his face. 'If the worst does happen, and no one comes for us, you just have to outlive me and you'll be fine.'

Cady couldn't work out if it was a joke she wasn't getting. 'What do you mean?'

He pointed to his chest. 'I've had an upgrade. A state-of-the-art ICD. It's a pacemaker and a defibrillator all in one.' Something in his manner changed, and instead of addressing them he began to address his lap. 'I don't know if you remember years back my dad died.'

'Yes,' Cady said. 'Of course.'

'He lived on his own. And he was old. But the way he died… It was his heart. And he'd been in his otherwise spotless flat three days before anyone found him. That gave me a lot of anxiety. You know? Especially given our relationship. If only someone had been around… If I'd been around.'

'Of course,' Cady said.

His hand rose up to touch his jaw again. The left side. The right. 'Because yeah, I've got my device in my chest. But I got thinking, what if I'm away somewhere and it's not working? Or it can't fix the problem and I'm … like lying there dying and no one knows. In some hotel or out hiking. I had a few nightmares and turned down a few jobs because of it. Pissed my agent off no end.' He paused. 'Sorry, what's my point? My point is I did some research, and I got on a trial for an ICD with a 5G alert system built in. So there you go. If my heart stops, this little thing connects to 5G and sends an SOS with GPS coordinates. Someone in a call centre somewhere will send an ambulance or two to this very spot. Problem solved.'

Naz turned to peer at them through the gap. Deadpan, she said. 'Can we just kill you now, then? Save the waiting around.'

They all laughed, but it quickly evaporated. Because they weren't going to kill Femi, and an hour really was a long time, wasn't it? A big, round amount that even irrepressible Cady couldn't ignore. If you were waiting for a date to turn up at a restaurant, when would you give up? Half-an-hour at the most. Maybe forty if it was a busy night and traffic was bad. Never an hour.

'Guys,' she said. 'Do you—'

Femi put a hand across her chest. 'Do you hear that?' With some effort, his feet on tiptoes, he leaned out of the car to look back the way they'd come.

'What?' Naz said.

They all listened. Then Cady *did* hear it. A hollow, metallic thud, travelling up the stairwell every few seconds. Cady twisted her neck to look back.

'Someone's coming up,' Femi said.

'Don't joke,' Naz said.

'I'm not.'

'Thank Christ,' Winston said, throwing up his arms like he was casting off every suppressed emotion.

'Is it Danson?' Naz said.

'I assume so,' Femi said. He cupped a hand around his mouth. 'Danson, you bastard. What took you so long?'

Their visitor didn't shout back.

'Danson,' Cady called.

Still, he didn't reply.

But it had to be Danson. Didn't it? Or maybe one of the workers.

By the now harsh illumination of the emergency light, Cady made out the first details of the person approaching them when they emerged from the shadows where the stairs became a flat walkway. The person who still wouldn't respond.

Her heartbeat quickened and the acidic taste in her mouth returned. Their apparent saviour wore a hat of some sort.

CADY

Friday 21st June, 7.59pm
Celsius: 36°, Fahrenheit: 96.8°

'Danson,' Winston yelled. 'Is that you?'

clonk. clonk. clonk.

Whoever this was, they weren't in a rush.

Cady wouldn't panic though. This wasn't her stalker. It couldn't be. She was having a stress reaction, her mind was playing tricks.

And yes, the closer the figure drew, the less that yellow hat looked like a beanie. In fact, more and more it looked like a hard hat. Which made more sense, especially if this was a rescue worker. And the sinister, snail's-pace approach? Well, that was just because it was a 200-metre climb – no wonder they didn't have the puff to call back.

Still, Cady couldn't quite think her muscles loose. Her

twisted neck ached looking back through the gap, but she daren't look away.

'Danson,' Femi said, the figure close enough that they could hear laboured breathing now. 'It's Danson.'

It was without doubt their old friend, revealed in full by the emergency light, still dressed in the clothes he'd been wearing when they left the station. He looked exhausted, but wore the slightest smile on his face.

'Hey … guys,' Danson said, trying to catch his breath.

'Bloody hell, Danson,' Naz said. 'Bloody hell.'

With great effort, Danson kept going until he was level with them on the walkway. Then he allowed himself to collapse into a sitting position, still clutching the railing with his right hand. His shirt clung to his body and sweat beaded his forehead.

'Where the hell have you been?' Naz said. 'We've been losing our minds.'

Danson held up a hand, wanting a moment to recover.

'I think what Naz means,' Femi said, 'is that we're bloody glad to see you. Are things … under control?'

'Yeah. It's … all … under control.' Danson gave a weary laugh and shook his head. 'Did you … like the view?'

'It was good for the first hour,' Cady said. Danson shook his head and grinned apologetically.

'Mate,' Femi said, 'are you able to get us down?'

'Sorry, just … it's so much more difficult than … I expected. I'm in bad, bad, bad shape.' He held up a hand while he took a series of deep breaths. 'You guys must have been so worried up here. Did you think … I'd abandoned you?'

'No way,' Winston said, 'we had faith. You're a fixer. Always have been.'

'I am.' He took another few breaths and softly repeated himself in a whisper. *I am.*

He descended into what looked like a reverie. Cady tried snapping him out of it by asking, 'So how's that going? The fixing?'

'Do you know the story of the woman ... in the vinegar bottle?' he said.

'What's that got to do with anything, Danson?' Naz said. 'Can we get down, please?'

'I'd be surprised ... if you hadn't heard of it, Naz.'

Cady shifted in her seat. Her knees pushed against the immovable lap bar. Her relief at seeing Danson flickered. Why was he asking them about the view, and about women in vinegar bottles? Why wasn't he reassuring them with every ounce of his being?

He didn't reply to Naz, and by way of response Femi darkened his voice. 'Look, what's the plan, mate? We're getting a bit stressed here, in case you couldn't tell.'

Danson cocked his head like a bird and stared at Femi. 'The plan? Okay, you want to know the plan. The plan. The *plan*. Well, the *plan* is ... that you need to get out, don't you? But you can't because the restraints on Hysteria have been built by the brightest, best paid ride engineers in the world, whose sole job was to keep you in those seats. You've probably realised that. So, to get out, you need a key to free the restraint.'

'Which,' Femi said, 'you presumably have.'

Danson held up a hand again, asking for patience. 'Can you see a little slot on the front wall of the car, just beneath the screen? Credit-card sized. Pop the key in there, and boom, all that hydraulic pressure keeping you safe in place vanishes.'

'So, where's the key, Danson?' Naz couldn't hide her irritation.

'You must have been so worried. Stuck up here. No one due to be on site for another week.'

'Dan, can you just—' Winston started to say before Femi cut him off.

'A week? There's a party here tomorr—'

'Is there?'

Now Cady's relief was extinguished. She sensed something similar occurring with the others, too, because no one said anything for a moment.

Through a barely open mouth, Femi said, 'You told us there was a big party. That's why we're here.'

'Did I?' He shook his head. 'I said there was a big event. And there will be. I never lie.'

'Oh, Jesus,' Winston said, having reached his conclusion already. 'Dans—'

Danson's head flicked to him. 'Please.' In a thin tenor, he sang, '*Have a little ... patience.*'

'What's happening, mate?' Femi said. 'We've been up here over an hour now.'

'A bit longer, actually,' he said and brought his watch up to his face. 'It's eight o'clock.'

They all stared at him but he met no one's gaze. He crossed his legs, let go of the rail, and when he spoke again he dropped his voice and spoke without any hint of the mateyness he'd employed until now.

'Guys, I've made sure no one is going to be on site for at least a week. Security think temps are covering tonight. They're not. No one but the two security guards you saw on the way in know you're here. They've gone home and think you're loss adjusters. And the drivers I hired to bring you here were from four different companies. None of them will be asking why they didn't get the return journey.'

Cady grabbed the handle on the lap bar like it was the ride

plummeting not her stomach. Why was he telling them these things? Why?

As if she didn't know.

'I'm not well, guys…' Danson stood up and grasped the handrail once more. A hot breeze tousled the hair poking out from beneath his helmet. The weathervane shifted noisily. 'I had all these plans. So many plans. I'd do this big, well-paying job, then get back to all my creative things later with some money in the bank. Alas, so many plans, forever skeletons. I've got a year at best, they tell me.'

He allowed this to settle, and eventually it was Femi who found his voice. 'I'm sorry. That's awful. Are they… Is there any treatment?'

'Irrelevant now. But, I'm telling you because … because it did help me focus on what was important. Especially when I found out that the prince, fickle man that he is, was no longer very passionate about his pet theme park, and instead wants to refocus his resources on building a space … a space … a space hotel.' He started laughing. 'But waste not, want not. I came to understand that all of it was connected. You. Dreamland. Hysteria. My illness.'

'Get us down, Dan,' Naz said, dropping a diminutive like it might help change his mind. 'Get us down and we can talk. Now, please.'

'Naz, I don't think you're quite understanding the situation—'

'Enough,' Femi yelled. 'Let's talk about this on the ground, yeah?'

Danson shook his head slowly. 'No. Femi, no. What I realised was that—'

'What do you mean, no?'

'—despite not having achieved the same things you did, I

could say one thing about my life. And that's that it was honest. I did what I did with the best intentions, with love, and I did it honestly, in a way I could look myself in the mirror each day. Which is to say that I have lived a life in service of the truth. That's what I've always valued. That was such an important revelation to me. Can you all say the same, do you think?'

Femi tried forcing up his bar, and Cady could see he was losing it. She put a hand on his shoulder. Her gut was screaming at her that their survival depended now on handling Danson, not attacking him.

'Are you getting us down or not?' Winston said. 'Can we cut to the chase?'

'Guys, listen. If you interrupt again, I'm going to walk back down and never come back.' His hand went to the back of his helmet and his fingers began a hollow tap tap tap, tap tap tap. 'When the sun rises, you'll be cooked. You'll perhaps last the day. You won't last two. Any search party looking for you will arrive too late. Your skin will start burning tomorrow morning. You'll be dehydrated by lunch time and experiencing hallucinations by early afternoon. You'll stop sweating, and your dehydration will be severe. By then it will be truly awful for you. In the clothes you're wearing, no shade… The good news is you're up here, where it's about two degrees cooler than the ground. Bad news is, it'll still be well over forty degrees, unless you luck out on some unexpected cloud cover. That'll just drag things out for you, though, as you'd then have to survive the first night with very bad sun stroke and likely organ failure.'

A startled noise escaped Naz. Cady became aware of her skin tingling from the small amount of sun exposure she'd had today.

'So, all of you … listen, please? I'm giving you a chance.

Listen. Or ... prepare yourself never to see your families and loved ones again.'

Femi started to say something, but fell silent when Cady squeezed his arm.

'Thank you. Okay, so ... so ... so you have all been on a quest, haven't you? All of you incredibly... focused.' He repeated the last two words to himself. *Incredibly focused.* 'Ever since university, at least, but maybe from before then. My theory? Well, I think what united us all was our parents not loving us or giving us enough attention. Something ... anyway, we all externalised our need for affirmation. When we couldn't get it at home, we wanted it from an audience. To our generation, it was the people on television, in films, people who wrote books we copied when our home life didn't provide it. The problem is, it's made you all so focused on yourselves, I don't think you've ever stopped to think about the effect you're having on the people around you. On the world. The damage you've left in your wake as you trawl through the ocean of ... no, a better metaphor is this. Your lives have been like roller coasters. You've been hurtling around, unable to stop. But now look, I've stopped you. I'm stopping you to let you breathe. And think. Think about the truth.'

His mouth smiled and his gaze had become dreamy. His fingers tapped away.

'And if you get to the truth, I think ... everything is going to be okay.'

'Am I allowed to speak?' Femi asked through gritted teeth.

'Yes.'

'What *truth* are you talking about?'

Danson let go of the handrail. He leaned forwards, his head over the gap between the walkway and the car. 'What do you think?'

Femi stared Danson down, his hands repeatedly squeezing the restraint handle. 'I don't know?'

'It's probably hard when you're an actor, isn't it, Fem? So many lies. All the time.' He moved back to the handrail again and grabbed it. He started walking away. One step. Then another. 'Well. What I'd *really* like to know. Really, really, really. Is the truth about Eloise Draclin?'

No one said anything, but immediately the atmosphere in the cars changed.

They all knew who he was talking about.

He took another step away from them. 'Have a think about it,' he said, and started to leave. Ignoring the sudden hullabaloo of their distress, he called back, 'Talk about it between yourselves. Have a good, honest think. Then we'll *really* talk.'

And with that, he made his way back to the staircase, and shortly after, the *clonking* resumed.

Danson, Then

Last night the truck arrived with all the *Little Shop* stuff and it was dumped in the main hall. There's too much of it. I could tell as soon as the back door rolled up. Femi and Winston didn't seem to get it, but I stayed there going through it all long after we'd unpacked, fretting and getting ill from the mothbally stink of it all. Later, Eloise popped her head in, and I told her it wasn't going to fit on the hall stage. That we had nowhere else to store it. That we were four weeks away from the performance and had no time to reorganise.

She could tell I was in a bit of a state, so she ordered me to take a break and follow her. I did, and we walked to the porter's lodge, a turreted concrete keep adjacent to the hall.

She called the porter by his first name and asked for 'the keys'. He handed them over without a word.

We walked around the back of the lodge and through a door where we accessed a staircase to the roof. She offered me a cigarette and I took one, even though I didn't smoke. She hopped up to sit in the gap of two turrets and looked out at the Cambridge skyline. Calm and familiar as you like, no issue with the ten-metre drop inches behind her. After a moment she shuffled to lie flat with her legs up against the opposite turret.

I asked her how come she was allowed up here, because I'd thought only the teaching staff had access.

No joke, she said, 'I'm very charming. Haven't you noticed?'

She exhaled and the smoke drifted up around my face. I breathed it in and couldn't help but think about it having just been inside her. She told me she liked it up here because it was peaceful, and that it was too crowded in college. Apparently, she could hear the couple above her having sex at night.

When I said nothing, she asked if I was still thinking about a job in the bar.

I wasn't. I never had been. I imagine she knew that. I explained that I had too much work on but would keep it in mind. She nodded slowly. Then she asked if I had sent Naz over to talk to her that day in the bar. I denied it, and told her that I really had been interested in the job.

'Interested in me, more like,' she said, and let smoke drift from her open mouth.

My face burned, and I had no words.

Then things went a bit strange. She started telling me how much she hated that we were all on top of each other at Chamberlain but none of us ever touched. She told me how important she thought touch was, said that we crave it. 'Endemically'.

I said I agreed with her, and suddenly found swallowing very difficult.

Then, no joke, she said, 'If I asked you to rub my tummy, would you?'

I laughed. Then I nodded. She pulled up her top, and I got down on my knees and stroked her in little circles with my flattened hand. This went on for a while. We didn't talk. Eventually she jumped down and asked if coming up here had helped me relax.

I nodded but remained crouched to hide my very obvious erection.

Later, outside my blockhouse, she hugged me, and commented on how nice it was for two people to be intimate without being sexual. Quick as a flash, she cast a glance down at my trousers. Then she turned and flounced off.

———

Something awful happened tonight. I'm sorry about the bad writing. My hands are still shaking. I offered to drive Femi, Naseem, Cady and Winston from the show out to a pub in Girton village for a change of scenery after rehearsal. I had my car up because I'd needed it to move all the extra *Little Shop* stuff after Femi decided to go with my suggestion to do it in a more minimalist style. I'd been hoping one of them might bring up the deposit money I was owed for securing the storage locker, but my ancient Firebird is a glorified biscuit tin, and the rain pelting the roof made conversation impossible.

They didn't bring it up at the pub though, and while they got squiffy, I got into a sober funk. On the way back I was still up in my own head. The roads were slippy, and on a country lane I hit a sharp bend that had come from nowhere. I wasn't going fast, but the car just went. It spun 180 degrees across both lanes, ending up on a patch of grass facing the way we'd come from. A blink later, an enormous lorry rushed by in the lane beside us, its driver oblivious to how close we'd all come to a collision.

I spent the night apologising to them all and slunk off to my room to cry. An accident like that at Cambridge would have made the papers. Bloody hell, I nearly wiped out Chamberlain's brightest stars. I would have been infamous. My whole life defined in that one moment. They all looked so haunted afterwards, their giant auras somewhere back on that road.

I can't sleep now. And sorry. This isn't helping either. That lorry... A heartbeat away. A breath.

I'm in a better state of mind today. It's been a week since the accident. What I didn't write before, because I thought they were just trying to stop me crying, was that the others believed I saved their life. Their view was there was nothing I could have done about the skid, that I'd been unlucky, and that, in fact, my driving skills were responsible for the car ending up safely on the other side, rather than in the middle of the road where we would have most certainly been smashed to bits.

I have to say, I had no idea that was what I'd done. I'd just sort of... reacted. It didn't feel like I had much control. But I do remember I fought the wheel. So perhaps, in my guilt at being in a mood with them, I'd misremembered the situation.

I've no doubt of their sincerity. They've been making half-serious jokes about them owing me their life whenever I see them. In fact, morbidly they all seem really inspired by it. Like our brush with death should inspire us all to succeed even more because life is so short. They've taken to calling us The No Tomorrows Club.

Also, yesterday, Femi, Naseem, Cady and Winston called at my room together, and took me to the bar to ask if I wanted to live with them next year in Churchill House, one of the second-year blockhouses at the far end of the college. They had one spot left. I'd been convinced one of the other *Little Shop* people, Nick, or Araminta, or Camille, would be in there with them. But no. Maybe because of the accident, maybe not – perhaps there is some other alchemy at work here – but I'm part of their club. Crazy.

The final show went really well, a big improvement on night two! At the after party, Femi toasted me for organising all the drinks and behind-the-scenes stuff, as well as throwing in a cryptic little in-joke about me being a lifesaver – which I don't think referred to my idea for us to go minimalist. I got kisses and hugs, which was lovely. I'd still quite like my few hundred quid back though, although maybe it's a price worth paying to be part of the in-crowd.

I mentioned this in passing to Eloise when she turned up at my room at 3am, asking for a tummy rub, yet again. While lying on my bed, in the dark, she asked if I could afford to write off that much money. She already knew I couldn't. We'd had plenty of chats about our single mums and our lack of cash growing up. But my overdraft could cope. In a sleepy voice, she told me she didn't believe my cool act, and that I'd looked ready to kill someone the night she'd found me in a panic about the *Little Shop* props. That wasn't my memory of it, but I didn't challenge her.

Maybe because she was drunk, and possibly high, but she repeatedly insisted I needed to be blunt with them. 'It's the only language people like them understand,' she said.

'People like them?' I asked.

But she had fallen asleep beside me. I lay there with her so close, yet feeling very alone, trapped in this little box on my shoulders. It's a sad thought to think it's always like this really. None of us ever any closer than this.

I'll miss Eloise over Easter. Even if I am a bit confused about what it is we're doing.

———

I'm on the floor of my room surrounded by printed off revision notes and books. That's all there is to summer term. I'll write again when I have the time.

———

Everyone passed their exams. No one is getting thrown out, despite how stressed everyone got. And last night, I had sex with Eloise Draclin. Twice! I can still smell her on me now. I'm in dreamland.

She wasn't working tonight, so she drank with The No Tomorrows. The others seemed too exhausted to include her, though, and I could tell she was getting bored of them by the end of the night. She asked to go back to my room in a whisper, and so we did. We lay on the bed, and I stroked her, and she asked me if I was gay. I confirmed I wasn't, and she said she didn't believe me, because I never made a move on her.

I got sort of puffed up with confidence then, and in my head I sounded like James Bond, when I told her I'd make a move if she wanted me to.

'I bet you won't,' she said.

She lay on her back, and I was on my side with my hand on her stomach. I pushed my lips to hers, and she opened her mouth. I felt her smile. She was cigarettes, wine, and vanilla, and honestly the sex was like we actually merged, became just this one content being. Towards the end she was on my lap, and we were pressed together face-to-face, and she was still for so long I wondered if she'd stopped, was maybe even crying. But then she came, and after, she did cry. But she reassured me it wasn't because it was terrible. Then it went a bit weird again.

We were lying beneath the covers for ages when she started up with all her 'people like them and people like us' stuff. 'Why would you want to live with those people when they don't really respect you?'

I said she needed to get to know them better, that they were good guys. There was some sort of class war thing going on with her, which I didn't want to get into. Sure, some people have money, some don't. But wasn't that the great thing about a place like Cambridge? That 'people like us' got to go if they were bright enough. Didn't that show that class might sometimes be a story people tell themselves to justify their failures?

She kept at it, though. And we lay in a spoon at odds, her seemingly goading me into slagging them off. I wouldn't do it, though. I wondered if maybe she was just jealous of my closeness to them. At one point, she rolled over so we were face-to-face.

'You're sweet,' she said. 'But they aren't what you think.'

I moved away from her hand and stroked her hair to reassure her. Told her that I appreciated her honesty, but suggested we change the subject.

She pushed her face towards me, and said quietly, 'Danson, listen. If anything happens to me, anything bad, I need you to know that one of them did it.'

Now I had no idea what she meant.

She put her finger on my lips and grabbed my dick with her other hand. 'I want someone to know. If anything happens, it's one of them.'

Those were her exact words.

I asked her to clarify who she meant, and she closed her eyes like she was losing the will to live. Then she spoke their names. Cady. Naseem. Winston. And Femi.

CADY

Friday 21st June, 8.07pm
Celsius: 36°, Fahrenheit: 96.8°

The vibrations of stairs grew quieter until the only sound was the thud of Cady's heart in her ears. She shifted her weight to the left again, her lower back sore and her backside numb.

'He's joking, isn't he?' Naz said. 'Please tell me you're all in on it.'

Winston sighed. 'I don't think so.'

'What does he *want*?' Her cry died in the air around them.

'The truth about Eloise,' Cady said. 'Whatever that is. I remember she worked in the bar. And did costumes for *Little Shop*. Danson and her were friends, I think.'

'He fancied her,' Naz said. 'I remember that. He took what happened to her hard. Harder than we did.'

'Did he?' Cady said, trying to cast her mind back twenty years.

'But it was puppy love,' Naz said.

'Maybe it wasn't,' Femi said.

They all fell silent.

'He's ... gone, hasn't he?' Winston said. 'Didn't you see it in his eyes? He got a death sentence and cracked.'

'If he's *lost it*, then we're absolutely stuffed,' Naz said. She took a deep breath to compose herself. 'I really don't like that story, Win.'

Winston said nothing in reply, perhaps having run short on the compassion required to keep placating Naseem.

But Naz had a point as far as Cady was concerned. Stories were important, and Cady suspected they'd stand a better chance of escaping if they kept telling themselves a positive one. 'Speaking of stories,' she said. 'What did he mean about that woman in a bottle?'

'Exactly,' Winston said. 'He's lost it.'

'The woman in the vinegar bottle,' Naz said, still talking quickly but with more composure than she'd had since they'd left the ground. 'It's a fairy tale. I can't remember exactly how it goes. An old woman gets punished for living in a vinegar bottle ... or something. I don't know what he was talking about.'

'I wish he hadn't found out about Oxford now,' Winston said.

'Yeah,' Naz said with a pointed snort.

'Look,' Femi said, 'I've apologised. Can we just drop that, please?'

'I'm really not sure our supposed orgy is the issue here,' Cady said. 'Can we talk about Eloise? What do you remember about her from that first year at Chamberlain?'

'Not much,' Winston said.

'No,' Naz agreed.

Cady couldn't think of anything, either. From what she remembered, Eloise had always been on the periphery of their group. She'd been likable enough, but had kept people at arm's length. Cady had certainly never been close enough to Eloise to know any secrets about her. And how exactly was Eloise connected to all that other stuff he'd said about them? About her. The idea that Cady had hurt people on her rise to the top didn't ring true – not least because she'd only just found the most transient and insubstantial success. But she wasn't arrogant enough to assume she wasn't guilty of something back in the day, and perhaps she'd just not noticed the damage she'd done, the way you simply didn't when you were a kid.

'This is a nightmare,' Winston said. 'I can't bloody die on a roller coaster.'

'If it makes you feel any better,' Femi said, 'imagine all the records your band will sell.'

'Funny,' Winston said.

'Does he think we're somehow responsible, maybe?' Cady said. 'For what happened to her. Is that possible?'

'Who knows?' Winston said, and Femi stared off into space.

Cady sensed the others were being a little bit evasive. It was annoying. 'Put it this way,' she said, 'if Danson comes back and we don't have anything to say about Eloise, I think he's going to be annoyed. So, let's try to have something, okay? Try and think of anything, any detail, about what happened before her accident that might have upset Danson. Especially if he had a thing for her. Or … don't even think of it like that. Let's just think of anything we can about her first. Let's … brainstorm.'

Too much time passed, and Cady shook her head. 'So, no one, none of you, can think of anything of note about Eloise, a girl we all lived beside for a year?'

'I'm trying to think, Cady,' Femi said.

'And me,' Naz said.

Cady was getting too frustrated with the others to even concentrate on her own recollections. Why was she having to push them so hard?

A sharp pain in her temple made her wince. It was likely the stress, because she'd not had pains this strong since her exams at university.

And that was when it struck her. A realisation, a memory. She'd had a strange interaction with Eloise right after first year exams. Because of what had happened afterwards, she'd never been able to explain it.

It probably meant nothing in the scheme of things, but she decided to mention it anyway. It would at least get the ball rolling.

Make it feel like they were *doing something*.

PART TWO
THE DROP

CADY

Then

After Danson's car came off the road, the five of them drove back to college and went to the bar to take stock and calm down. It was Eloise on shift, and she'd been about to close, but when she learned what happened she let them take a table and locked the bar door. Danson, lost in black clouds of shock, sat staring at the carpet, tapping the back of his head absently.

'It really wasn't your fault,' Cady kept telling him when he tried to apologise. Unlike the other three, she actually drove, and she knew how cars could just go from under you when the weather was bad. Could he have slowed down a bit going into the bend? She didn't think so, and he certainly hadn't been speeding.

The others toed Cady's line until Danson went to bed, at

which point Femi said, 'The idiot nearly bloody killed us. Jesus.' He put his face into his hands and bent over his knees.

'I can't stop thinking about that lorry,' Naz said, shaking her head, pushing her long, dark hair from her face with both hands.

After letting the remarks stew, Winston said, 'I don't know, guys. That was some nasty rain.'

'If anything,' Cady said, 'Danson's driving saved us. He steered that car off the road.'

'He was never in control,' Femi said, kicking the table leg, his tone sharp and dismissive. 'We were lucky, Cady. That car of his shouldn't even be on the road. Don't defend him.'

He'd never spoken to Cady that way before. Her eyes unexpectedly filled with tears, so she looked to one side. At Eloise, standing on the other side of the bar, just inside the fire door, smoking, politely looking elsewhere.

A few nights later, Femi invited everyone but Danson to the bar having arranged with Eloise for their own after-hours lock-in again. Femi apologised to them all, to Cady in particular, explaining he'd been upset, and that he masks his sadness with anger, and that he knew that it had been an accident really. He hadn't meant to blow up at her.

'It's fine,' Cady said, grateful he'd said something, acting like it hadn't been making her miserable since it happened. 'We were all in a bad place.'

'I was out of order,' Femi said. 'I don't expect forgiveness, and I don't want to make excuses. But I wanted to sort of explain…' He shook his head like he was deeply disappointed with himself. 'When I was fifteen I collapsed playing football in the park. I actually died for a bit. Thankfully, Mum and Dad are doctors, and they were … well, here I still am. Hi.'

'Hi,' Winston said. 'Glad you made it.'

'Thanks, Maestro.'

'Was that your heart thing?' Naz asked.

He nodded. 'So, yeah, the other night… It brought back…' He looked up at the ceiling. 'I think my personality … my drive comes from … sticking it to death. Seizing the day, you know? Felt a bit like that accident was death having a word. Putting me back in my place.'

'No way,' Winston said.

'I don't know. It just hit me how cruel it all is. The idea of us all being obliterated in such a bloody dumb way was…' A hand came up to cover one eye and his mouth turned down. His shoulders began to shake.

The others went to him, knelt with him, held him.

'Unfair,' he said, wiping his eyes with the back of his sleeve. 'It would have been unfair. But, that's the universe, isn't it? It doesn't care.' He took some time to compose himself. Then he sat up straight and shook his head. 'Or maybe it does, and it was trying to tell me to go back to medicine. To do something useful.' After another moment's thought, though, he added, 'Honestly, I think art – a good song, a painting, a poem – that can save lives in its own way. Maybe more than medicine can, in a way. Does that sound mad?'

He looked like he might go again. 'No,' Cady said, at first only to soothe him. 'I understand. I understand completely. I… I completely…'

Her voice caught and a tear ran down her cheek. Their attention shifted to her at once, and when she finally got hold of herself, she apologised, embarrassed that she must be coming across as a right attention-seeker. But she hadn't been able to help it. She knew exactly what Femi meant.

Since the accident, she'd not slept well at all. She'd been having ... not dreams exactly, or even nightmares really. Because these scenes in her head had actually happened. Replays was what they were, triggered memories from her childhood that she'd done her best to try to hide in the attic of her mind.

Looking around at their faces, so supportive, so forgiving, like they would back her no matter what she might tell them, she told them about her own life story. About what had made her what she was. About Robbie. And Grandad Sal. And how she'd nearly died in a car before.

It had been an unnoteworthy Tuesday in the summer holidays. Cady was thirteen, and the gossip and dramas of the playground were in hibernation until September. Mum and Dad were at the caravan in the Brecons for a weekend, and Grandad Sal had charge of Robbie and her. It was his first time alone with them, the cigarettes finally having caught up with Nan the year before. He was in his seventies, a Spanish man with a nicotine goatee, and whose English was only marginally better than when he'd arrived in the country fifty years ago, rendering him taciturn from lack of confidence. Robbie, whose mispronunciation of Katy as a child had led to Cady's lifelong nickname, had recently turned sixteen and sat his last GCSE.

Age difference usually decreed Robbie should have been in the passenger seat that day. But for reasons she'd never been able to remember, she was in the front of the car and Robbie was in the back. A bright green Toyota Starlet, built in a more carefree era, it had never stood a chance. Grandad was driving them to the shops in Marlstone, and he pulled out from a muddy country lane onto a dual carriageway. But for some reason, Grandad crossed over to the fast lane just as two cars, one in each lane, sped around the corner. Grandad had made an odd guttural sound. Cady turned to see a white saloon filling the back and rear window, and Robbie's disbelieving expression. The brown curls of his fringe were being blown back by the wind from Grandad's open window. He gave her a sad little smile, one she'd think back on for the rest of her life, an expression that said, *What's Grandad gone and done now?*

Then she woke up on her back in the road, voices all around her. The world flashed red and blue, and she could smell bonfire night and petrol station forecourts. Pain in the right side of her head swamped her like idling paparazzi suddenly spotting a celebrity. When she awoke again she was being carried on a stretcher. She turned her head to see firefighters putting out the blackened Starlet. But where were Robbie and Grandad?

Her adolescence began with comas and funerals. A lonely summer of catching up on missed schoolwork. More operations. Headaches. A wig. Ugly-short hair. 'I am sad, and I am angry,' she read to the congregants at her brother's funeral. Sad, because Robbie had been her idol, and his phantom poked her memory in every room of the house they'd lived in their whole lives. Angry, because his brilliant exam scores, stuffed in a drawer out of sight as soon as they'd been collected, his body still lying unburied, had been attained for nothing.

All that work, those late nights and early mornings, all that stop-playing-computer-games-and-focus stress. Pointless.

Mum and Dad watched television now. In the day. In the evenings. She'd come down and find one or both of them asleep on the sofa with the twenty-four-hour news still on. Mum stopped working. They forgot things. Sometimes they never remembered them in the first place. This made her sad and angry, too. So did her old friends moving on. They were still nice to her, but, terrified they might have to talk to her about Robbie, they drifted away.

So she made new friends. With the scruffy, dreamy kids into skating and punk. She went to parties, took drugs, joined a band. She heard a fast song with screechy vocals talking about living like there was no tomorrow. It burrowed into her soul, became her mantra.

At first this expressed itself as rebellion, shedding her instinct to always 'do the right thing'. She stopped trying. Why should she? What was the point following rules and listening to the advice and cautions of miserable adults? Live every day like you might get thrown through a car window. Just in case. She shoplifted. Stabbed her thighs with a compass in dull lessons. Broke a few hearts just because she could.

But sometimes she felt like her intermittent headaches, her nightmares of being trapped somewhere dark and smoky, were messages from Robbie, watching over her, disapproving. Her serious, wise-owl brother, who had always been kind. Even when they'd squabbled, it had never been serious. She couldn't remember them ever falling out longer than an hour or so. He'd been a good kid. They both had been. She still was good, really. Deep down. And in the end, she started to feel her clichéd little rebellion was dishonouring Robbie in some way.

So, in the end, she knocked the worst stuff on the head –

not that anyone really noticed, especially Mum and Dad. But unlike Robbie at sixteen, Cady found herself with no firm plan for her future. Robbie would have taken those A grades of his and studied science, and eventually medicine. Lived in a house with an attic room overlooking the sea with a red-headed wife. He'd had it all mapped out. But Cady wanted to be so many things. A singer. An actor. A writer. A director. A painter. Separately and all at once. Her interests shifted with each new cultural discovery she made at sixth form – and her exploration was fuelled by that instinct to make the most of life, and a promise to herself that she must not regret her life the way all the adults around her seemed to. She must *do something* in the world.

It wasn't clear when or how or why that *something* became synonymous with a creative pursuit. But it was those things which brought her praise, which nourished Cady. That she could do quite a few of those creative things adeptly made her stand out, attracting the attention of teachers and peers, convincing her more and more that not only *must* she *do something*, she *could do something*.

But Robbie would have argued that she needed to understand the world first before *doing something* in it. How else would you know whether you were doing the right *something*? And he would likely have agreed with her sociology teacher, that people, whether in the arts or otherwise, would take her more seriously with qualifications under her belt.

So, as much as she wanted to pack it all in for Hollywood or RADA or the flipping circus, she knuckled down and did the boring work. Her grades had never really suffered, but being accepted into Cambridge to study Social and Political Sciences still shocked her. The interview had felt like a disaster, her answers to the questions she'd been posed nothing but nervous drivel. She went to Robbie's grave in the village where they lived first, to tell him before anyone else. And later, when she told her parents, they hadn't looked up from the television.

'I thought you'd already gotten in there,' Mum said.

When she finished talking, the others nodded silently. She knew instantly she'd made the right decision: they truly understood, didn't they? Femi held her hand. Naz got up, her leather skirt creaking, and kissed Cady's forehead with tears in her own eyes. Winston lowered his head as if in tribute.

She pointed to where the metal plate was in her head, and said, 'So, if I'm ever a bit spaced out sometimes, or you know, if I forget your birthday, now you know why.'

Ever since she'd met them, and they'd effortlessly drifted into each other's orbit, she'd sensed a special bond between them all. Right now, that bond was being sealed for life. These people, strangers last summer, already felt like family. The life she'd had before meeting them now felt like simply existence, colourless and empty.

'So funny how similar we are,' Femi said. 'Feels a bit like we've been drawn together by the fates. That the accident is part of it.'

'Maybe,' she said, still trying to stop herself bursting into tears. 'Or perhaps every creative person has ... something to burn. Or a hole to fill.'

'My hole's fine, thanks,' Winston said.

Femi smiled. 'Easy, Maestro.'

Naz ignored him, and said wistfully, 'Everyone's got their story, don't they?'

'What's yours, then?' Winston said.

There was a long silence. It wasn't uncomfortable, though. They all sensed something important happening.

Eventually, Naz said, 'Well, it's not like you two. Not really. But in a way I died this summer. I stopped wearing the hijab.'

'Wow,' Winston said.

'How long had you...' Femi said.

'Since I was about twelve. And my family are pretty conservative.'

'God, Naz,' Cady said. 'How did they take it?'

Not well, she'd told them. Her dad and brother had been particularly bothered, and in their minds she'd suddenly been corrupted, or gone crazy. Up until then, she'd been a good Muslim girl, so it had to be that someone must have done this to her. But really, she said, she'd been atheist for years and just kept quiet about it.

'What corrupted me was television. And the cinema. And the bookshop.'

'Hear, hear,' Femi said, holding up his beer bottle.

'I always read a lot,' she said. 'Watched a lot of films. Starred in a ton of plays at school. And when you expose yourself to so many fucking stories, you get picky about the ones you like.' She raised her glass of wine to match Femi. 'Anyway, here's to seizing the day, and living like there's no tomorrow. To time ticking.'

Everyone put up their drink except Winston. 'I still don't think that lorry was as close as you think,' he said. 'But ... I like the sentiment.' Now he held up his beer can.

Naz narrowed her eyes at him. 'So do you have a story, Winston?'

He smiled mischievously, but then his gaze vanished momentarily into middle distance, and the smile lost its sheen. It was for a second, maybe two, but in that instant

Cady knew for certain he had been about to tell them something.

'Nah,' he said. 'I'm dull as shit. Came from a musical family. They loved me very much. Now I play music. I'll go on to play music. Still, I'm all for seizing days. And let me say, the days I've seized with you this term have been awesome. And I'm sorry about all the fucked-up stuff you've had to deal with.'

'Love you guys,' Femi said. 'You're the people I dreamed of meeting here.'

'Soppy bastard,' Naz said.

'To the No Tomorrows Club,' Cady said, raising her glass. They all looked at her.

'No Tomorrows Club,' Naz said. 'Love it.'

All of them drank.

'That's what this accident has to mean,' Cady said. 'It made us have this talk. Reminded us time's short. So, we have to make sure we do something in the world, guys. We'll … all help each other. A rising tide raising all boats. We'll take over the world.'

'Woah, nelly,' Winston said, and everyone but Cady laughed.

'Hear me out,' she said. 'We all came to Cambridge. We didn't go to art school. Or start auditioning or… We came here. Because we were clever enough, and because it was safe. A good little entry on our CV. Well … bugger that.'

Femi whooped and raised his arms. Naz laughed, her head dropped and her hair fell over her face.

'I'm serious.' She stared steadily at each one of them until the atmosphere in the room shifted, darkened a shade. The intensity of their attention caused a mad power to swell in Cady. 'There'll be lots of people that will try and talk us out of it. Tell us to get serious and grow up. Unhappy people, mostly. They, and the world, will throw obstacles down to stop us. But damn them all. I declare, here, today, and for all time, that we, The No Tomorrows Club, are going make the very most of this short life we've been given.'

Some time later, Eloise brought them out a last round of drinks and they talked about how bad they felt for Danson. How he was such a great guy, and how his general helpfulness and low maintenance would make the perfect fit for their shared blockhouse next year. They had to decide soon, otherwise they'd be put in one of the four-beds miles from town, and how much would it mean to him now given how low he'd been after the accident?

With a final toast to their completed house, they headed their separate ways. Cady was just getting into bed, her digital clock displaying 02:14 in a devil-red glare, when Femi turned up at her door.

'I just wanted to say I really appreciate you sharing what you did tonight,' he said, a bit too loud.

She felt a little daft standing there in her pyjamas, so kept the open door between them. 'You too,' she whispered, not wanting her neighbours gossiping.

Nodding, Femi glanced left and right, checking the corridor outside her room before lowering his voice. 'I liked your speech, too. Very rousing.'

'Well, you kn—'

He leaned in and kissed her through the gap. Seizing the moment.

She was still quite drunk, and he *was* extremely attractive.

But, after letting the kiss possess her momentarily, she pulled away.

'No?' he said.

'Bad idea,' she said, and smiled in a way that suggested his advance hadn't been completely unappreciated.

But only a week earlier, Cady had seen him getting off with Naz in the dressing room, and he was always flirting and having intimate one-on-ones with the female members of the cast. He'd even been flirty with Eloise, he couldn't seem to help himself. And Cady didn't want to fall out with anyone. Not with two years left at Chamberlain. And not after tonight of all nights. If Femi was a womaniser, she didn't want it wrecking things. Particularly because Femi, of all of them in the group, had the most stardust in his blood. He was someone you wanted to hitch your wagon to, as Dad might say. He was going to go far, and she didn't want to be just some notch on his university bedpost.

'You sure?' he said, one eyebrow raised. But he'd already taken a step back from her door.

'Trust me,' she said. 'It's for the best.'

Eventually, Cady started sleeping again, the accident gradually being replaced by other concerns. Exams being the main one. During the summer term, everyone in the group grew edgy and solitary as they drew close. The play had been a great success – *The Cambridge Student* had even singled out Cady's turn as Audrey in their five-star review. That had been nice, because she had always felt Naz was the better singer, and had worried Femi made the wrong choice just because she could do a good impression of Ellen Greene in the film. But there was real concern from the college, especially in Femi and Naz's case, that their extra-curricular pursuits might have distracted them from work. Directors of Studies became involved. Pastoral workers, too. But in the end, everyone in The No Tomorrows Club got the grades they needed to stay on next year.

A few days before they would all depart for the summer holidays, those connected to *Little Shop* threw a small party on the roof of the porter's lodge. Someone brought a speaker. Joints circulated. Danson went back and forth collecting extra beers from his fridge. Cady sat on the cool floor, her back pressed to the wall. At some point, her old song came on. *Live like there's no tomorroooow*. One of the others must have found it. She listened, smiling, staring up at Eloise who lay in a nook between turrets, cigarette smoke floating around her.

'I know,' Eloise said, catching her staring. 'You said before. I should give up.'

'Did I?' She vaguely recalled telling Danson to put out a cigarette once, but not Eloise.

'I think you'd had a bit to drink. You said your nan died of lung cancer. But you were right. I should.' With that she took in a big lungful of smoke, leaned perilously over the edge of the building, and breathed out.

'Sorry, that was rude of me. I sometimes … say stupid things when I drink.'

Femi and Naz had gone off somewhere, and she hadn't seen Winston since the start of the night. The only one of them from The No Tomorrows Club still there was Danson, who was in the opposite corner trying to limbo under a sideways flagpole with the trumpet player and Damo, the guy who played Seymour.

'It's fine,' Eloise said. 'How are you doing, by the way? Last time I really saw you all you were still freaking out about that car accident. You sleeping any better?'

Cady was taken aback. She hadn't told Eloise about her bad dreams. She must have overheard them all in the bar. Cady wasn't sure how she felt about that. What else had she heard?

'It's fine now,' she said. 'I'll sleep when I'm dead.'

Eloise snorted. She gestured for Cady to come closer, and when she did Eloise took hold of her hand. Eloise lowered her voice. 'I see you, you know. The little battery keeping all these people going. When we all leave here, it'll be you organising the reunions. You keeping everyone in touch. Groups always have a *you* in them. And they're always unsung.'

'You think?' Cady didn't know what else to say to that. 'Thank you.' The girl was a funny one. She liked Eloise, but there was something flinty about her, something you could occasionally glimpse if you held eye contact long enough. It scared Cady.

'I've been meaning to talk to you,' Eloise said. 'I have something to ask.'

'You want more smoking advice, don't you?'

Eloise laughed. The gems on her cheeks sparkled, but her eyes... There was no other word for it. Flinty. 'Can I come to your room tonight, when things finish here?'

Cady glanced down at her hand, which Eloise still held. For lack of reason to say no, she agreed, and Eloise let go. With that, Eloise stood up, arms held out for balance, and jumped down beside Cady. 'Wee time,' she said, and left.

That night she fell asleep in her room awaiting Eloise's arrival. She'd probably been high and completely forgotten. Maybe she didn't know where Cady lived and hadn't realised until they'd separated.

At some time after 2am, she was awoken by knocking. Still a little bit angry with the dream version of her nan, who she'd been telling off for smoking in front of her, she crossed the room still dressed in her jeans and her top.

Recalling now her conversation with Eloise, she was surprised to pull open the door and see Naz, biting her black-varnished nails and staring at the floor, her skin paler, her eyes fearful.

'Naz?'

She looked up. 'It's Eloise,' she said. 'I think she's died.'

CADY

Friday 21st June, 8.24pm
Celsius: 36°, Fahrenheit: 96.8°

Eloise had been found by the night porter at the base of the lodge on the front drive. A halo of blood pooling around her head. Cady had only heard about that later, from the students who had shown up before the ambulances arrived. By the time she and Naz got down, staff had formed a loose circle around the scene to stop anyone getting near.

The porter initially claimed Eloise must have stolen the keys, but in the investigations that followed it was suspected he'd come to some arrangement with her, about the nature of which people were left to speculate. He lost his job.

In Cady's own interview with college staff, she recounted how they often went up to the roof with her, and how she would always sit precariously close to the edge. In her little turret seat. Smoking. Others said the same. And while she kept to herself, she hadn't seemed suicidal, although the relevance and meaning of that was up for debate. Yet she'd had no previous interactions with mental health services either, and so, whether or not it was true, what happened to Eloise Draclin was eventually deemed a terrible accident. A fall caused by too much drink and bad luck.

Now, Cady stared at the desert far below them, imagining Eloise's final moments, and shuddered. 'I told the college that she'd asked to meet me that night,' she said to the others. 'But I didn't know what it was about. I mentioned she'd asked about the accident and seemed worried about me. I told you guys about it, too. But no one seemed that interested, so I just let it go. I think maybe that was because I assumed you all might know something more about why she fell that I didn't.'

'What do you mean?' Femi said, perhaps a little bit too quickly.

'I just meant, maybe people thought she jumped. Deliberately. Rather than fell. I didn't really know how well any of you knew her outside *Little Shop*. So, if there were personal things involved, I didn't want to pry.'

'Ah.' He nodded, making no effort to hide his diminished interest. He said nothing else, and neither did the other three. Not a single remark from any of them about her revelation. About whether or not it might be relevant to getting off this bloody roller coaster.

Perhaps they were all too lost in their own thoughts, frantically shuffling through old memories long since filed away. But that wasn't how it felt. To Cady, it really felt like they knew more about Eloise than they were letting on, and simply weren't saying. And if she was honest, it had felt that way from the moment Danson spoke her name.

A wind passed over the roller coaster, and the lift hill swayed ever so slightly. Cady's stomach lurched like they'd driven over a humpback bridge too fast. She stretched her legs and pressed her feet against the front wall of the car. God, she didn't want to be here. Didn't want to be thinking about Eloise Draclin and Chamberlain College. Why had she ever wanted to leave home in the first place? That was the question now. So she could film videos of herself and get applauded by random people online. When she had a loving partner and a comfortable flat right there. It all felt suddenly very silly.

'So,' Cady said, determined to make some headway, '*did* any of you know anything more about Eloise? Do you guys know why she wanted to speak to me?'

'I don't know,' Winston said eventually.

'What don't you know?' Cady asked.

'I just don't know. About any of it. Anyone else any ideas?'

After a pause, Femi said, 'No. None here.'

'Guys,' Naz said, and Cady leaned forward in anticipation. Hopefully she would get things moving. 'I don't mean to be crude,' she said, 'but does anyone else regret drinking that champagne?'

Cady sighed and arched her back to lean against the headrest.

'You need to go?' Winston said.

'It's not desperate yet. But I think I'm ready to try and get under the restraint. Win, if you put your hand under the small of my back.'

Cady turned to Femi, who ignored her and focused his attention on the gap in the seat back, at what Naz was doing.

What was happening here? Why didn't they want to talk about Eloise?

From the other side of the bird screen came the sound of

shuffling and muttering. 'You push up against my … there … push… No, that hurts. Yeah, like that.'

'Naz, it really is impossible,' Cady said, overwhelmed again by that claustrophobia and dread she'd felt trying it herself earlier. 'Be careful.'

'I'm okay. I think I can do it.'

Perhaps she could? There wasn't much in it, but she was smaller than Cady. And their seats were already a little way over the drop, which might give them an assist from gravity.

'Just don't hurt—'

Too late. Naz screamed. She began swearing in staccato bursts. The position of the high chair back prevented Cady seeing what was going on, although Winston was now visible in the gap leaning over to help Naz.

'What's happened?' Femi asked.

'She's got stuck sliding down,' Winston said, voice raised to be heard above Naz's stream of profanity.

More panicked shuffling followed, and a disturbing series of agonised mewls, preceded a sudden movement that prompted Winston to say, 'Gotcha.'

'You okay, Naz?' Femi said, sitting forwards as far at the clamshell would allow.

'Naz?' Winston asked. 'Naz, you okay?'

She was sobbing. 'I think I've twisted something in my back. It really fucking hurts, guys. I need to stretch it out.' Cady heard and felt her ramming the restraint with her knees again. She screamed. 'Oh, shit, I need to stand up and stretch it out.'

Her aggression ebbed. Her sobs resumed.

'What happened, Maestro?' Femi said.

'I don't know, she got quite far down but it was the bottom bit—'

Naz cut him off. 'It's like a cramp or I've slipped a disc or… I can't sit up straight. I can't sit up and—'

'Take a breath, Naz,' Femi said. 'Nice and deep.'

'Fuck off, Femi. I'm not in labour.' She cried out again. 'I can't be here anymore.'

'Just try and stay calm—' Winston tried softly.

'Please don't tell me to be calm. Please.'

It took a good few minutes for her to settle, but Naz eventually managed to find a position leaning to one side which minimised the pain in her back. But it meant there was now pressure on her lower back, which was gradually ratcheting up. They all began to call out for Danson again. A long time passed. Twenty minutes. Maybe half-an-hour. Dead time. Eventually, their voices tired and their cries grew more sporadic.

Cady was getting ready to try and ease them back onto the topic of Eloise when the stairs began to shudder again, and a while later Danson reappeared on the walkway.

'Naz is hurt, Danson,' Femi said when he approached. 'She's twisted her back. Can you let her out, please? Enough is enough. She's in agony.'

Danson said nothing and continued walking until he was level with them. He sat down, in one hand a bottle of water, under the other arm what looked like a wooden chest. He set them both down at his side.

'Dan, Naz is hurt,' Cady tried.

He nodded. 'So, Eloise Draclin. Anyone any thoughts?'

'Danson,' Naz said. 'It really hurts.'

He reached over and picked up the bottle of water. 'I bought this up because I thought you might have something for me. It's been an hour now, what have you been talking about? Do you even remember her? Did it all mean so little to you that—'

'We remember Eloise,' Cady said. 'We remember her.'

'What do you remember?'

Cady told him what she'd told the others. It was a paltry offering, and she felt a stab of annoyance that the others hadn't contributed a thing to help.

Danson turned his attention to Femi. 'And did you lot have anything to add to that?'

'Well, Naz hurt herself,' Cady said when nobody spoke. 'We've been calling for you.'

'Fine. It's more time you need, is it?' Danson laughed. 'I've got all night, so fine. I'll give you an hour. Or maybe two.'

'No,' Naz yelled.

Danson allowed her protest to vanish into the darkness. Then he stood up. He opened the water bottle. 'Such a shame. You know my watch says it's thirty-six degrees up here right now. And it won't get much cooler. You'll already be dehydrating.'

Cady hadn't wanted to say it out loud, but the pressure she'd felt in her bladder earlier had already abated. Was that an early sign of dehydration?

Danson stuck out his tongue and poured the water over it. It dribbled down his chin, down his neck, soaking his shirt, some of it cascading down on the walkway.

'Man,' Winston said, 'what the…'

He slowly held the bottle in front of him and let go. It fell through the gap between the stairs and the track, striking some support beam on the way down with a hollow *bonk*.

'I'll give you a little clue, then,' Danson said. 'Before she died, Eloise told me that something bad was going to happen to her. And if it did, I was to suspect you lot.'

'That's bull,' Winston said. 'She was a…'

'What was she, Maestro? Finish the thought.'

'She was a liar.'

'How do you know that, Winston?'

'I just do.'

Danson nodded for a while, Cady sensed for effect rather than because he was truly contemplating anything. 'Well … put yourself in my shoes. She says she might die, and then she does. What am I to think? For all these years, what I thought was that you guys weren't really capable of hurting anyone. I defended you in my mind and kept quiet about what she'd told me. Even when the police interviewed me. And I must have been right, no? Because look at all the good work you do now. Femi, all your social media posts about climate change and representation in the arts. Can't be an actor without being an activist these days, can you? And Naz, all that amazing mentoring work you do for underrepresented authors. So, so noble. And Winston, you went big on raising money after that earthquake, didn't you? And I loved that very earnest video you did about food banks, Cady. Not your highest rated video, but very worthy.

'You're all so stunning and brave. But, here's the thing. Being good, and being stunning and brave, means telling the truth. And here is my truth: I know for certain you know what Eloise was talking about when she said that to me. And I'd also bet the house someone here knows what Eloise wanted to talk to Cady about.'

'None of us hurt Eloise, Danson,' Femi said. 'I know these people. You do, too. Or you did.'

'That's a shame.' He bent over and picked up the wooden chest on the step. 'All I want is the truth. I think I'm going to go.'

He walked away, and Femi started shouting after him to come back, drowning out Naz's muted little pleas to be let free. Femi started pushing on his bars again. Growling with his already weary vocal cords. To Cady, he sounded like he was losing it. That he was starting to finally believe that they might be in trouble. And that tomorrow, the sun would rise, and they would be unable to do a thing to stop it scorching them.

Cady's own heart picked up pace. Winston was yelling after Danson now, and someone needed to step in to keep it all together. Keep everyone focused on their escape, the best route to which right now was keeping on Danson's good side, surely?

'Everyone be quiet,' Cady said. 'Stop shouting at him. It's not going to help.'

'He needs to know that this has gone too far,' Femi said. 'Fine, he's got some grudge. But he's not going to leave us here to die, is he?'

Cady took a deep breath. 'I think he might. If he really thinks one of us pushed Eloise off the lodge. Or drove her to it. That's what's happening here, Fem. Like Naz said, if he was in love with her.'

'No. I don't believe it,' Femi said. 'He would never believe that of us. Not after everything we've been through together. Years and years of good friendship. He's just had a bad reaction to the park being in trouble, that's all, and … and…'

Naz whined again. Winston turned to look through the gap. 'Guys, can we all stop messing around now, okay? I know for a fact that someone here knows something about Eloise Draclin that they're keeping quiet about. This has been coming, so why don't we—'

'It's all bollocks, Win,' Femi said.

'It isn't, though,' he said. 'Is it?'

'It sounds like *you* know something, too,' Cady put to Winston, frightened about where this was all leading.

'Well ... I'm not going there alone.'

He obviously wasn't talking about Cady, because she'd already shared her memory of Eloise. Which meant it had to be one of the others. 'Naz, Fem?'

They both remained silent. Again, the atmosphere felt leaden with the unsaid. Cady's gaze drifted to her walkway, and she remembered that odd wooden chest Danson had been carrying. She felt a squirm of disquiet. What had its purpose been in all this?

Naseem let out another exhausted and agonised groan. It made Cady wince in sympathy.

'God damn,' Winston said. 'I knew I should have stayed home. God. Damn. Okay, this has got to stop. This is what I know. But you guys promise me something. When I'm finished, we stick together, okay?

'Well, that sounds ominous,' Femi said.

'Or at least until we get down. Promise me, Fem.'

'I promise,' Naz said. 'Femi, promise too.'

He shook his head.

'I promise,' Cady said.

And finally, with a sigh, Femi said, 'Fine. Let's get this over with.'

Winston, Then

He sat in the college bar. *At* the bar. It made him feel close to Dad, or at least the idea of Dad. They called it the 'college bar', but it wasn't really a bar, it was more like a pub. The sticky carpet, the squat red stools like toxic mushrooms, old photographs of college sports teams on the exposed brick walls. What even was the difference between a bar and a pub? One was American, one British, maybe. Pub. Public house. Perhaps if it felt like home, it was a pub.

Dad had loved all things British – had even married an English, as he used to say. Bunting of tiny Union Jacks framed the family piano on which Ms Fenton would give Winston lessons. Resting on top had been a stack of vinyl records, The Beatles' *Abbey Road* facing outward eternally. Dad would often sit to play *Pretty Ballerina*, a trippy 60s song, singing in a fake English accent that was silly, but accurate enough to retain the song's haunting effect.

Winston murmured it now, winding his empty shot glass into the bar with both hands.

'Winston.'

Such a strange melody. Such a strange chord progression. And was that the Lydian mode it used? How Dad had loved it. Like he'd loved the little 'English Pub' in San Francisco.

'Winston.'

He used to talk to strangers, Mom said. It was how he got to know what the common man was thinking.

'Maestro.'

He looked up to see a face across the bar. Pretty, in a pinched sort of way. Pretty in pinched. Hadn't that been a film with Molly Ringw—

'I've got to lock up soon,' the girl behind the bar said. She knew his name and the silly name Femi had started calling him. And he knew her name. He absolutely knew her name. They saw each other all the time. Was it Louise? No, not that. Close, but— *Eloise*. That was it. Eloise, he was certain.

'Sorry,' Winston said, and chickened out of saying her name. He swivelled on his stool. His tall stool. Not like one of the stumpy stools around the tables in the little wall nooks. The mushroom stools. Wait, was that why they were called toad stools? Because they looked like little seats for amphibians. Must be.

The bar was empty. The *pub* was empty. Everyone had gone to drink in their rooms, or, as was more likely here at Cambridge, gone to get an early night before morning lectures.

'I nearly didn't see you there,' she said, and gestured at his cinnamon-coloured hoodie. 'You blend in with the bar.'

'Ah,' he said. Noting her blonde and pink hair. So brilliant it hurt his eyes, perhaps. 'No, I'm here. I think, anyway.'

'Where's your usual lot gone? Femi and them?'

He shrugged. 'I don't know.' And that was fine by him this evening. He loved those guys, but it had gotten so intense lately. The conversations they had. The sleep they missed. The drink they put away. It had been worse since Danson had spun the car going up to Girton. They'd all gone mad after that. Damn, at the first dress rehearsal last week, he'd gotten so wasted just to keep up with them that he'd been ill for days. The girls had been taking mescaline Danson had got them from somewhere. He'd be glad when the shows were done next week. Things would be more normal then, as much fun as it all very much was.

He placed his palms on the bar, ready to get up and leave. But it wasn't what Dad would have done. He'd have stuck around a bit. Maybe made a new friend. He had his mom's personality in the main: pragmatic, laid-back, a sense that the world did what it wanted with you and for the most part you just had to watch. Like being the passenger in an out-of-control car, whatever will be, will be, as the old song went. Only very, very rarely could you cause things. But sometimes it felt fun to just try every once in a while. Make life happen a bit, where it was safe. And right now he was feeling at home enough to be a bit Dadly.

'Hey, where's your accent from?' he said. 'This is probably going to be completely wrong, but it sounds a bit like Daphne from Frasier.'

She scrunched her face in apparent disgust. 'She's from Manchester, isn't she?' Appraising him, she seemed to soften. 'I'm from Wolverhampton. Only seventy miles off. You done with that glass?'

He nodded and she took it.

'And what about yours? Sometimes you sound American, like a surfer dude. And then you sound like you're from Kent. Somewhere southern.'

A little laugh escaped him. 'That's actually impressive. I grew up in California.'

'Oh, cool? Where?'

He had to be careful here, didn't want to fly too close to that West Coast sun. Any detail was too much detail, he'd long ago decided. 'By the ocean. Then I moved to Rodwell when I was a kid.'

'By the ocean.' She gave him a funny look, flat and faintly amused. It was still kind of cute, though. 'Nice. And Rodwell's in Kent?'

'Yeah.'

'I think I knew that. There's a posh school near there, isn't there?'

His eyebrows rose and he cast his gaze down at the bar. 'Yeah.'

She didn't build on the thought. And mentally he shrugged, let her judge, if she wanted. If she wanted to be chippy, as Mom liked to say, that was on her. She didn't know anything about him. She didn't know their life. And about how far he'd fallen behind after Dad died. How much energy they'd had to spend on starting again. Him and Mom had needed all the help they could get, then.

'So have you always studied music? Like, properly? You're so good. I mean, you did that one rehearsal on the piano, and then I saw you with a guitar the next day teaching Cady one of the songs.'

He raised his head, and she was leaning on the bar on her folded arms, staring at him. The little plastic gems twinkled prettily in the bar lights. 'It's sort of the done thing in my family. My grandad was quite a well-known … a conductor.'

'A *conductor*?'

He narrowed his eyes. Why'd she asked that? Like she knew he was lying. That she'd known he'd been on the cusp of saying pianist before realising that was too specific. Too searchable on the internet. He was bad at this. Bad at being Dadly. That was a good thing, really. He should take pride in being as little like him as possible.

'Just locally, he was known. But it's sort of … what I grew up with.'

'You read music?'

'Yeah. I mean, you sort of have to on the music course.'

'But you weren't reading any music during rehearsals.'

'I mean…' He shrugged. How to explain that even though he'd studied the *Little Shop* score over the Christmas break, and memorised many of the flourishes, the songs were just simple doo-wop tunes really and he could play passable versions of them from the top of his head. 'Yeah.'

She shook her head, her eyes wide. 'I think that's amazing.'

'Do you like music?' With her piercings and heavy eye make-up, she looked like she did.

'Me? Yeah, I love it. Rock and indie. Metal. That sort of thing.'

'Do you know any progressive rock stuff. Like early Genesis, or Yes?'

She shook her head. 'I liked that thing you were singing just now. Under your breath. What was that? Sounded spooky.'

It took him a moment to recall. Then he blushed, had he been singing aloud? But she didn't appear to be mocking him. She was staring at him still, and there was something in her gaze beyond the surface curiosity. There was a hunger there, he was certain. For him. He was overcome by a sudden rush of excitement, the whisky in his blood suddenly drowning his inhibitions. Pinched, sminched, the girl was more than cute. She was hot. And damn, he needed to keep them both safe, keep Mom safe, sure, sure. But surely he could enjoy life, too? Have a bit of twinkly fun once in a while.

'It's this song from the 60s. No one really knows it. I've a copy of it on CD.' He swallowed. 'In my room. Do you want to hear it?'

'Now?' she said.

'Well, whenever.'

'I can come when I've locked up.' She suddenly averted her eyes, perhaps embarrassed by her own keenness.

Winston liked that. Not wanting her to change her mind, he stood up. 'Well, no worries if you change your mind. But I'll be up late anyway. I'm on the second floor of the blockhouse by the fountain. Room—'

She nodded and gave a tiny little smile. 'I know where your room is.'

She stepped inside trailing a scent of tropical fruit. Had she been back to her own room, put on some perfume? Just as he'd quickly brushed his teeth and tidied up. She confidently sat in the flea-bitten armchair by the window, and he put on the song. She listened, her head slightly cocked. He found it incredibly attractive that she didn't talk over it. Winston couldn't have music on without listening to it.

'It's brilliant,' she said after. 'Again.'

They listened to it three more times, and each time Winston

sat back down a little bit closer to her. He was in touching distance now, and very much hoped she might take the next step. The pressure was mounting within him that he ought to make a move. Because she might *just* be here for the music. Which in a way would be a relief, as well as a disappointment.

'You know what it reminds me of?' she said. 'There's a song by a band called Memories called 'Things I Know That You Don't'. Have you heard of it?'

'I'm not as great with modern music as I should be.'

She stood up and held out her hand. 'Come with me. I'll play it you.'

They crossed the quad outside, over to the blockhouse near the front of college. They walked along the periphery of the central quad, in the shadows of the outside wall. Over by one of the statues, Danson, Femi, and Cady were sitting in a little circle drinking.

'Don't let them see us,' Eloise whispered, and Winston felt a little electricity in his chest.

Eloise's room was on the top of the blockhouse on its own. They climbed four flights of noisy stairs, and Eloise opened the door and turned to face him.

'There is a box, Winston,' she said, holding up one finger. 'And everything right now is in the box. And it can stay in the box. Like nothing ever happened. Just keep that in mind.'

He leaned down to kiss her, and she pulled away with a laugh. 'That's... Come inside.'

He followed her, and she closed the door behind them. Her room was lit by fairy lights hung around a mirror on her desk. The walls were decorated with posters of bands and musicians, most of the faces meaning nothing to him. But he did recognise Frida Kahlo, staring at him moodily from a postcard. Eloise walked over to the desk and pulled out the chair, offering it to him. He didn't know what was happening, but he obliged, and only when he sat down did he begin to understand what all the bits of paper were spread out on the desk in front of him.

Sweat broke over his body. He couldn't breathe.

He stared. At print-outs and photocopies. Accusing headlines.

POLICE SEARCH GARDEN OF HOME IN STANTON IN MURDER CASE

BODY FOUND IN SOFTWARE DEVELOPER'S GARDEN

PROSTITUTE KILLER DIES AFTER STABBING

The world spun. He grabbed the desk's edge to steady himself. How had she found out? There wasn't any way, was there? He'd done everything in his power to protect them. To protect Mom. This really wasn't possible.

'I always found it funny how sometimes you wouldn't answer to your name, Winston.' Her voice was close. He looked up to see her sitting on the sill of a large sash window. Her little eyes burned with delight. 'Like in the bar just now.'

He had failed. That's what this meant. The mission he'd been on since finding Mom's note at the back of her bedside drawer after Dad died, when he was still only a child really. A note written in her neat, beautiful cursive, yet exploding with love and regret for something that hadn't even happened yet. *I'm so sorry*, she'd written. *Sorry. Sorry. Sorry.* But he'd done everything to keep that note from ever being placed inside the empty envelope he'd found beside it. Or so he'd thought. But now it was over. The world was going to know. And Mom would break all over again.

'I'm not a bad person, Winston,' Eloise said. 'I'm just realistic. Do you know about Realpolitik, Winston? Politics stripped of emotion and idealism.'

A sudden numbness overcame him. And with it, acceptance, similar to what a gazelle must feel when the jaws of a lion close around its neck. Hadn't he always known this was coming? Hadn't he always suspected that one day it would all catch up with them? The way a lion pursued a... Was that what lions ate? Gazelles? Or was it antelope?

'Remember what I said, though,' Eloise said now.

'What?' His voice sounded minuscule. Tinnitus in a concert hall.

'Everything is still in the box. And it can stay there, if you want it to. That much is up to you.'

CADY

Friday 21st June, 9.14pm
Celsius: 35°, Fahrenheit: 95°

'Eloise had found out my father killed three women,' Winston said, his voice deep and measured. 'Sex workers. Two before he married my mom, one after. I don't know how she found it out, she never said, but that she knew seemed impossible to me. We'd changed our names. We told *no one*. We wouldn't let him define us.'

'Oh my God, Winston,' Cady said.

'You know, I was in a great place at Chamberlain. I'd managed to put him in a box in my head. I just remembered the good stuff about him. Because to me, he *was* a good dad. That's the crazy thing. They even thought he arranged his own murder in prison so we'd get his insurance. But when she …

seeing all these newspaper clippings from when it happened laid out on her desk.'

'That's awful,' Cady said. 'How old were you? When it happened.'

'Ten when they found the bodies in the garden. That's how he got caught. The first two he buried in the garden of a house he lived in with his first partner. They demolished the house to build an entire suburb. The whole secret was close to being buried under concrete, but then they dug up a body by accident. They traced the property back to Dad and came looking in our garden.'

After a long silence, Naz said, 'I don't know what to say. I'm so sorry.'

'I got moved to my mom's friend's house, so I didn't really understand any of it. Mom said that they were doing emergency work on our house. She struggled a lot. Mentally. At some point I remember her lying on my bed with me and saying that the police had found out Dad had done some evil things. He wasn't evil, but he had done evil things. And that he had to go to prison. I remember her stroking my hair, and I just stared out at the swimming pool through the window, watching the way the sun flickered on it, thinking it was strange how people might still want to go swimming in the world after what had happened to us. Like every pool should be drained as a mark of respect.'

'Christ, man,' Femi said.

'I think had we stayed in California Mom might have… She used to practise suicide notes, which I found.'

'No,' Naz said.

'Yeah. But, next thing I knew, Dad was dead and we were moving to England. And I wasn't called James Junior anymore.'

Cady closed her eyes, remembering what a solid, gentle presence Winston had been back then. It broke her heart that they'd never known all this about him. Never been able to help or comfort him. Especially given how her own family tragedy had been such a part of her outward identity. A pang of shame made her squeeze her eyelids together even tighter.

'Winston,' she said. 'I wish we'd known. We could have…'

'You couldn't have done anything. I needed it to stay a secret. It was a point of pride. If it got out, I was worried Mom would… Well, you know. It was the only thing I really cared about. And yet, somehow, Eloise found out. My only guess was that maybe I said something. Like when I'd been really drunk that night of the dress rehearsal. Either that or… Well, your guess is as good as mine.'

'So, what did she want?' Cady said. 'Money?'

'Yeah, pretty much. I panicked. I showed my hand too early, said she couldn't tell anyone, because of Mom. And then it was like, what's that worth to you? I should have handled it better.'

'It wasn't your fault,' Cady said. 'You must know that.'

'Whatever, she said I was a have, she was a have not. Said she knew all my clothes were high end. That I had to have had years of lessons to play like I did. That it wasn't personal. She had it all figured out, it was like each month I had to meet her in town and hand over cash. She told me to take it out in small amounts. And also to buy other things with cash that I'd normally put on a card. So it wouldn't ever look suspicious and there would be an audit trail. She bloody called it an audit trail.'

It struck Cady in that moment that Winston suddenly had a very strong motive for murder. The idea was unwanted, treacherous even. Especially, in this, a moment of real vulnerability for him.

And yet, there it was. Where there had been simple confusion at Eloise's name, now there was a story. An uncovered secret. Blackmail. Was this the reason they were all stuck here, then? Had Danson found something out?

He was the son of a killer, too. What did that mean?

She stopped herself. Horrified. Appalled at her own mind. No, no, no, she refused to consider that.

'I wish you'd told us,' Cady said. 'We could have helped you.'

'I'm so sorry,' Femi said again, his tone flat, his head moving slowly from side to side.

'There were times when I was drunk or we'd done pills, I came so close to telling you. That's how much you guys meant to me. I bloody loved you all so much, especially after that night when you all told each other about your lives back at home. I thought it was amazing we'd all come together. But I couldn't tell you the other stuff. About Dad. I just couldn't. So I kept it all in.'

It had been some time since Naz had made a sound, but she moaned now while trying to shift in her seat. Winston asked if she was okay.

'My lower back's gone numb. It doesn't hurt but I'm not sure that's good.'

'Winston, why did you make us promise to stick together before?' Cady said. 'Did you think we'd … what, think less of you for who your dad was? We love you. We'd never—'

'I haven't finished, Cady,' he said. 'There's more. Just let me… You know, when my band started doing well, it was nice. But it really wasn't supposed to happen. It was a hobby. I was meant to end up an anonymous member of some low-rent orchestra. Or a wedding pianist. Or a music teacher like Mom. But it blew up in a heartbeat. And I started to worry. It's always been in my head that, if Eloise found out about Dad, someone else might, too. That it was inevitable someone would, one day. Some journalist, or an overly keen fan. And it would be everywhere, wouldn't it? They'd want to talk to me. Talk to Mom. They'd track her down, hound her, bring it all back up.

'I'll be honest, guys, I've not been, you know, my best the last few years because of it. I've cancelled shows, and I've skipped rehearsals. The songs I've written are … bad. They're just *bad*. Because I can't write about what's really on my mind. About how this truth… I feel like it's coming for me. Coming to ruin everything. I've been seeing a therapist, and I didn't even tell them about Dad. I just skirted around it, but it became obvious it was the issue. That I probably needed to either tell the other guys, or just leave the band. So I told them I'd do one more album, and one more tour. Then the band should go on without me.'

'Mate,' Femi said. 'You are the band. You sing half the songs. You write most of them. The best ones.'

'Fem,' Winston said, his voice, having risen in pitch, now sounding like he was close to tears. 'Just… I did a terrible thing. Okay. I love you all. So much. But the amount of money she asked for initially … it was ridiculous. Do you remember in *Austin Powers*, when he asks for one million dollars, and everyone laughs? Well, it was sort of like that, in that it was a poor person's fantasy of what someone well off might have to hand. I told her I couldn't afford it. I explained what I got given from Mom, and what portion of that went on rent and living expenses. I spent weeks terrified. I genuinely thought I might try and steal the money from the college canteen.

Because like, really, we weren't well off. We had assets. A house. A first-class education. But Mom was a music teacher. She spent her inheritance on chasing her dream, mostly. We weren't—'

'What did you do?' Fem said.

'I told her that I would have to steal the money. Because I couldn't get it. So she asked if I had anything to trade. I had no idea what she meant, but then she said, I'll trade you a secret. A good secret, like yours.'

'Secrets,' Cady said.

'Yes. Did I know any secrets about anyone else?'

Pieces began to fall together in Cady's mind. What Winston had said about how he knew one of them knew something about Eloise. The strange atmosphere in the car since he'd said it. Femi's body language beside her. That she'd been the only one asking any questions.

'And what did you say?' Femi asked, suddenly upright in his chair, jaw clenched.

'Well, someone here knows what I said already. And—'

'You told her a secret of ours?' Naz said.

'—maybe they ought to tell their side of it. And God... I'm so sorry.'

Cady waited. Waited for one of the other two to speak.

It was Naz that broke the silence. 'Winston, I can't—'

'Sorry,' Femi said, cutting her off. 'I think I should probably say something first, if that's okay?' He didn't leave time for an answer. 'Maestro, I really appreciate you telling us all this, okay. I know it can't have been easy. I think I'm starting to get a picture of things here, so I should probably say something. But I just want to reiterate what he said before, about us sticking together. It's clear Winston was in an unenviable position, and in situations like that, people can make horrible choices, largely because there aren't any good ones. Yeah?'

'Yeah,' Cady said, more as a question than in agreement – where on earth was he going with this?

'I've also got a feeling now Danson knows more than he's letting on to us about Eloise. I suspect it's all coming out, one way or another. So – in the spirit of the Maestro's bravery – I want to volunteer some information, too. About Eloise.'

'O-*kay*,' Naz said.

'And please … let's just all … try and be fair.'

Femi, Then

"Please, whatever they offer you, don't feed the plants.

"Don't feed the plaaaaaants."

The final note of the first dress rehearsal dragged on, the actors on stage raised their arms and faces to the Gods of musical theatre, their voices cascading and intersecting in soaring, climactic harmony. Then with a nod of his head, Winston silenced the hall.

Femi, standing at the back of the room, brought up the microphone he'd been holding to deliver the lines of the plant, and said, 'Guys, that was, *astounding*.'

The assembled performers and the small, hand-picked audience erupted into cheers. Femi grinned, taking in their happy, proud faces. They had absolutely no idea how terrible it was.

'Party in the Mason Library,' he said, and stepped out into the quiet of the hallway and went hunting for the nearest toilet.

What a stupid idea it had all been. You couldn't do a minimalist version of something like *Little Shop*. Why had he listened to Danson, of all people? This wasn't Shakespeare, it was bloody Broadway.

He found a disabled toilet and locked himself inside. He propped himself up on the sink and stared at his face. At his jaw. Left side. Right side. It looked normal. That was good, because it meant he wasn't about to have a cardiac arrest. It was bad, because it meant his difficulty breathing and the crushing anxiety he felt were a response to the dress rehearsal.

Just to be sure, he checked his jaw again. Left. Right. Underneath.

Your mouth's doing something funny.

He'd hoped doing something as ambitious as *Little Shop*, especially at college level would make his name across the university theatre scene. Fast track him. That wasn't going to happen with this show. Okay, so it wasn't *really* terrible. But it wasn't *astounding*, was it? If he was lucky, it might be pleasantly forgotten.

Christ, if only the posters hadn't gone around already. If only he hadn't emailed the reviewers at *Varsity* and *The Cambridge Student*. He touched his jaw again. Took a deep breath.

Your mouth's doing something funny.

It wasn't, though. He was fine. Just overreacting. This wasn't anything like that day when he'd been fifteen, his football team two-nil up. The afternoon he died. Scouts were watching him, but he'd not been stressed by that. He'd scored both goals. But why had he come over all exhausted? Why was he so anxious all of a sudden?

Your mouth's doing something funny, Fem. Fem, you okay?

The world had gone white. Dad, Mum, his two older brothers, all medics, rushed on the field and saved his life. He woke up in hospital later with a raging thirst, and his dad talking gravely about Femi needing an operation.

Days later, he was still at the hospital, now with a scar in the middle of his chest. He'd thanked the doctors, and his parents. But his father had said he didn't want his thanks. That this was what they did in their family. This was their purpose.

'One day, Obafemi,' he said, 'you will be a doctor, and you will save someone else's life. You will save lots of lives. And you won't do it for thanks.'

Standing before the mirror now, the toilet light flickered as he appraised his reflection. 'An electrical problem,' he said to no one. That was the difference between a cardiac arrest and a heart attack, the surgeon had told him. Electricity.

'Can I play football again?' he'd asked him, and his family, standing nearby, laughed a bit too hard.

'In time, yes. You shouldn't overexert yourself at first, but yes. You can live a normal life. Run a marathon. Drive a racing car. Ride on a roller coaster.'

But he didn't want to play again. It had been his secret dream to play professionally. But it wasn't worth the risk, was it? He knew not to trust doctors. Their 'certainty' all came from probabilities when it came down to it. But just because something was improbable, it wasn't impossible. Life could be short, and he didn't want it to be now. He kept thinking about that whiteness that had closed in on him, had eaten him alive, that day. That nothingness from which we came and were all doomed to go to again. No thank you. He had things to experience. Places to go. Girls to meet. Man, he'd nearly died a virgin.

In the month he spent off school recovering, he watched films in the dark of his room. Three or four each day, wondering how you even became an actor, or a director, or a dolly grip. These were real jobs, as real as any job in medicine, so there must be some career path? The idea of ever having to go back into a hospital again, even as a doctor, filled him with stomach-clenching anxiety. So a new dream began to form, filling the vacuum left by football. His mind needed it, too, to distract from what had happened. And what might happen again.

Sometimes at night, his mind no longer occupied, Femi would dream of his own ghost standing over him at the foot of the bed, still dressed in a football kit, and he would wake up convinced that he *had* died that day on the football pitch, and everything since had been some hallucination in the stretched final seconds of his consciousness.

Or worse, perhaps he was the unwitting victim of some deception, like in *The Truman Show* or *Total Recall*. Or the subject of an experiment, his dad in the white coat maybe, or perhaps he was in *The Matrix*. Because after he died, everything felt just a little bit ... wonky. A little bit ... unreal.

He gave himself a last look in the mirror. Ever since Danson had nearly killed them all early that term – and he would never be convinced that wasn't what happened – the world had felt wonkier than usual. But in this moment now, his mouth and his jaw weren't doing anything funny. Not on the right. Not on the left. That was good.

So, it was the play bringing out those beads of sweat on his forehead. It had to be the play.

Unless it was something else entirely. Something he kept

pushing to the back of his mind because he really didn't want to deal with it.

Everyone was getting wasted at the party, but Femi wasn't in the mood. He nursed drinks all night but only pretended to sip.

'What's the matter?' Cady said to him, slurring. He sat between her and Naz on a leather sofa by the window while the party circulated around them. 'You look sad. No need to be sad, is there? We're a flippin' hit.' Her head flopped on to his shoulder.

'I'm not sad. No.' He reached over and gave her a hug. Naz narrowed her eyes. It was just for a second, but it definitely happened. 'I'm golden, Cady. I was just thinking about … how we all achieved this. It's not really fair my name's on it as director. We've all put this together. You two, Winston, the other cast.'

'Danson,' Cady said.

'Yes, Danson. Who could forget *Danson*.'

'Yeah, but you were our fearless leader, oh fearless leader. You drove this car.'

'Yes, fearless leader,' Naz said with a trace of sarcasm, 'this is all on you.'

No, there was no getting out of this. He couldn't charm himself into winning this time.

He looked up and his blood pressure suddenly rose.

She was here. Standing in the corner talking to Danson.

A chill rippled across his shoulders.

Perhaps the play was fine. Perhaps the reason he felt so anxious was because of *her*. Because of Eloise Draclin. She of the tiny body, mousy little face, and the blackest of hearts. Just the sight of her caused his pulse to quicken unpleasantly. He'd been trying to forget about her and the conversation they'd had in the days after the car accident. About the money she'd demanded in exchange for not telling his parents about his little lie.

Bloody hell, how idiotic he'd been to have been so brazen about it. He'd assumed the more people he told the less likely there would be an accidental slip up should Dad pay one of the surprise visits he used to give Femi's siblings. But no, she'd been so keen to know about it, hadn't she? And like a dope he'd thought she was flirting.

Gosh, it must be so hard having such expectations on you. How do you even deal with that pressure? You really think he'd disown you if you weren't in medicine?

And of course, the killer question, *'And you plan to keep this up your entire life?'*

To which he'd laughed, nodding. 'Probably.'

So now she was going to blackmail him for the rest of his life. And there wasn't anything he could do about it, was there? Other than murdering her like in some Agatha Christie thing. And obviously he wasn't going to do that.

He'd had enough and left the library, sensing Eloise's eyes on him the whole time. On the way to his room, Winston stumbled into him coming the other way, so drunk now he didn't even recognise Femi.

He was woken at three in the morning by a soft tapping on his door. His body stiffened. It was going to be Eloise. She was going to ask for more money. Only he couldn't afford any more. He was already lying to his parents about needing extra for private tutoring. His dad was already getting suspicious, asking him medical and course-related questions he couldn't answer, necessitating Femi spending more time researching the medicine tripos than working on his history degree. He may as well have just studied bloody medicine the amount he now knew.

But it wasn't Eloise at the door. It was Naz. Her eyes were hooded, sort of sexy. At the end of last term, and at the very start of this one, they'd done the deed. Casually, just two young lovers, as Naz put it. Friends with benefits was how he put it, but Naz turned up her nose. He'd been sort of expecting things to pick up at some point. Had she come back for more now? She put a palm on his chest.

'Did I wake you up?'

'Do you care?'

She grinned. He grinned.

'I'm afraid dearest Winston is in a bit of a bad way.'

'How bad is the damage?'

'He's supine behind the sofa in the Mason Library. Talking utter fucking gibberish. I think he needs to go to bed.'

Femi nodded and followed her down. Cady was sitting on the leather sofa holding a pink alcopop bottle. 'He's here.' She pointed into the gap behind the sofa and the curtains, and gave a laboured blink.

Winston lay with his eyes closed and a little smile on his face. Femi worked out a few times a week in the college gym so didn't have any trouble getting him to his feet. But he bore a good share of his weight on the slog back to his blockhouse and was sweaty and tired by the time they reached Winston's room.

He eased Winston down on to his bed and took off his

trainers, but that was the extent of the undressing he was prepared to do. He switched off his bedside light and covered him with the duvet.

Femi opened the door, and a chink of hallway light fell on Winston's soft-smiling face. 'Sweet dreams, Winston.'

The smile curdled into something resembling anger. 'That's not my name.'

Femi snorted and shook his head. 'Okay, come on, Maestro.'

'I'm James. I'm not ashamed to be James.' His words were a sludge through his barely open mouth.

Femi took a few seconds to play back what he'd heard. 'Okay, *James*.'

He stepped into the hallway and began to close the door. Winston rolled onto his back.

'I'm not ashamed,' he said again. 'James Robert Weatherall. And I'm not ashamed.'

For no reason he could discern, the name made him uneasy.

He hadn't thought about Winston's unusual remarks for a few days, but he was struggling to find anything useful about Gladstone and his reforms on the computer in the main college library. It was such a strangely specific name. And what had been all that stuff about being ashamed? Song lyrics, maybe, coupled with the name of a favourite musician.

He typed 'James Weatherall' into Google and browsed through some of the hits. Most of them were British, and none of them meant much to Femi. He typed in 'James Weatherall California', and he began to half-interestedly read about a serial killer who had murdered three prostitutes and buried them in the garden of his family home. Femi shook his head. What was with all the serial killers in California? Too many bad drugs in the 60s.

He'd skimmed past the photograph at first. A picture of James Weatherall with members of his local church. It was easy to miss amongst the other photographs in the article. Weatherall had one arm around the waist of a pale brunette, the hand of his other arm on the shoulder of a smiling, wholesome boy with a mop of brown hair. According to the text directly under the photo, these were Weatherall's wife and child, Mandy and Junior. The photo was ten years old. The boy looked about eight or nine.

'Huh,' Femi said to himself.

He printed the image and cut out the little boy. Over the next week, telling them it was a photo he'd found in a random catalogue, not giving away his discovery, he showed the photo to Naz, and Cady, and Danson. To get a second opinion. They all said the same thing that he'd thought.

He checked the mirror. Left. Right. Left again. His jaw was fine. He walked into town and met Eloise in The Eagle. They sat opposite one another in a booth by the window. She wore a beanie and an oversized hoodie with the words No Doubt on the front.

'Everything okay?' she said.

He looked up at her. This tiny thorn causing him so much pain. He took out a wedge of cash from the pocket of his coat and looked down at it. He'd brought the full amount. Because he still didn't know if he could really do this to someone. Ruin someone's life just to make his own easier. No, not someone, a friend. A No Tomorrows Club member, whom he cared about, and admired, but could probably afford the money without causing himself any problems given his connections. And the way he dressed. And really, when you got down to it, they'd only known each other a few months. It was hardly like... Hardly like...

His chest pounded, and something else his dad had said to him at the hospital returned to him. 'You have a weak heart.'

Eloise had asked him once if his family really would disown him. If he wasn't just overreacting. And he'd told her about his older sister, Abi. Who had chosen to move to London to become an actor instead of studying medicine. He'd gone to visit her with one of his brothers, and she had been living with three other people in a flat littered with empty take away boxes and dirty plates. Black mould adorned the walls and mouse droppings mingled with breadcrumbs on the sticky kitchen counters. Abi looked thin and miserable.

'Is this worth it?' his brother asked her. And Femi had wanted her so badly to say 'Yes.' Because in his mind she had been away from them all every birthday and Christmas because she was living a better life.

But she shook her head. 'Not really.'

'Then why don't you come home?'

'You don't think I've tried? It's not happening. I said no to him, and that's it now. That's the one crime you can't commit. He's like a mob boss.'

It was true that Dad ran the family like an organisation. But instead of drugs and money, Dad dealt in the currencies of principle and the greater good. Saving and improving lives through medical science was an altar on which you had to sacrifice yourself. But Abi hadn't wanted that, and neither had

Femi. It wasn't Dad that had helped him deal with all those deep, existential anxieties his death had thrown up. *Harold and Maude* had done that. *Wild Strawberries. Beaches*. He'd been too busy working or up some mountain with his hiking group. Okay, fine, medicine saved lives in a literal sense. But films had saved his. And music and television and books and theatre. These things had saved Naz, too. And Cady.

Yet he didn't end up living in squalor, either. Abi's mistake had been to be too honest. To realise that their family's wealth was the trick to getting a leg up in the creative arts. What Dad didn't know, wouldn't hurt him, Femi truly believed that. Just like he truly believed the world would benefit as a result of this deceit.

Now, he reached into his pocket again and put the printed photograph of James Weatherall's son on the table. Then he counted out half the amount he owed and put the rest back in his coat. He took a deep breath and stared at the picture. He'd be able to afford it. He'd be able to afford it.

Then he handed the money and the picture to Eloise.

'What's this?' she said.

'You said a fifty per cent discount.'

'Yeah, it has to be something useful, though.'

He pointed to the picture. 'Who does this look like?'

'I don't know.' She looked annoyed. Then she picked it up and after a moment said, 'It looks like Winston, the guy doing the music in the show.'

Femi nodded. 'That's because it is.'

CADY

Friday 21st June, 9.45pm
Celsius: 35°, Fahrenheit: 95°

When Femi finished his story, they all sat stunned, processing all it entailed. Cady still hadn't got to grips with Winston's revelation. Now she was supposed to get her head around this... betrayal. She let gravity take her body, and with her weight taken at the middle by the clamshell, she folded her arms and pressed her face into the crook of her elbow.

She felt so naïve. What a child she'd been, wandering around Chamberlain all that time completely oblivious, happy in her own world thinking how magical and perfect their friendship group was. What amazing, wonderful people they all were.

Winston needed to speak first. But he remained quiet, massaging the baggie between his fingers once more. Could she blame him? After everything Winston had been through, for it to have been Femi that told Eloise…

He'd told them all to stick together. What chance was there of that now?

The wind around them picked up again, like it couldn't bear the silence. It offered about as much relief from the heat as standing in front of an open oven door. Cady sat back up.

'Winston,' she said. 'Are you okay?'

'Maestro,' Femi said, as softly as he could without his voice being inaudible through the bird shield. 'I'm sorry.'

'Don't call me that, please.' His tone was cold. 'I never liked it.'

'Winston. Genuinely, I am so sorry. I know on some level you must understand. About the position I was in. And I was such a selfish person back then. We all were, weren't we? I didn't really have any conception of what all that must have been like for you. I knew the secret had value, I can't pretend I didn't, but I didn't have the capacity to appreciate the anxiety it must have caused you. I was so focused on me, and all my … shit, that I just thought you'd pay her like I did. That you had the resources. Obviously, if I'd known what I do now, about your life… I'm utterly, mortified, my friend. And I don't know what else I can say.'

'Just shut up, maybe,' Winston said.

'Yeah, of course. Of course.' Femi brought up his hand to his mouth and ran his shaky fingers around his jaw.

Naz made a nasal groaning sound. Was it physical discomfort, or because of what had been revealed? Either way, it was as much as Winston could take. He blurted, 'Screw this.'

'No, Winston,' Naz said, sounding more animated than she had been in some time. 'Come on.'

There was the sound of a sharp snort.

Femi sat up straight. 'Is he doing what I think he's doing?'

'Do you think he's just snorted a fuck load of coke?' Naz asked.

'It'll keep me focused.'

Cady knew how crushed and how angry Winston must be feeling. How confused. She felt all those things herself. But how was being coked out his mind going to help them escape?

'Do you not think we need to keep our heads clear?' she said.

'This will help,' Winston said, sounding wired now. 'And yeah, it's all coming together now. This is our punishment, isn't it? The piper's come to get paid.'

'I don't know what you mean?' Cady said.

'You've never felt it on your back before, Cady? That thing reaching out for you, demanding payment. It came for me at Chamberlain, dressed like Eloise. And now it's Danson. But really it's something else. Some old God or something. Because you don't get real success like we've had without the downside, do you? Ask Robert Johnson. Or the 27 Club. What goes up, must come…' He started giggling, high and unhinged. It made Cady's skin crawl, but not as much as what he said next. 'We're not getting out of here.'

'Mate,' Femi said, at the same time Naz cried out, 'Don't.'

'Shut up, man,' he said to Femi. 'You … you fucking traitor.'

Cady tried to intervene. 'Can we just take a sec—'

'Look, be fair,' Femi said, low and firm. 'You've already implied that you traded a secret with Eloise. Stones and glass houses and all that.'

'You think our situations are comparable?'

'They're not that far apart.'

'So wait,' Cady said, hoping to get in a word before

Winston retorted, 'let me try and understand this. Eloise knew about Femi's secret, and she used that to get Winston's secret. And Winston, you gave away someone else's secret to her, and that person is in this car. And it's not Femi. And I know it's not me.'

'Eloise played each of us off one another, didn't she?' Winston said. 'She embedded herself amongst us like … like a cuckoo.'

Another silence followed before Cady said, 'Naz, did Eloise…'

'I always thought it was an accident,' Naz said. 'That I'd just been horribly unlucky. But Winston, are you fucking saying what I think you are? From all the way up there on your high horse? You massive fucking prick.'

'I think it's pretty obvious that's what happened now,' Femi said. 'We really don't need to drag up the details and put Naz—'

'And you,' she said. 'You knew about Eloise all along, didn't you? And you never said a thing to me after I told you.'

'Naz, I can explain my thinking.'

'I don't want your thinking, you fucking wanker.'

'Wait,' Winston said, 'so Femi knew Eloise had your secret. And he never mentioned it was his fault in the first place. Perfect. Nice one, Fem.'

'It wasn't his fault,' Naz said, her tone venomous. 'You did it to me. But fuck you both for all of it. What I went through… Fuck. And even now, you're trying to smooth your way out of it, aren't you, Femi? Jumping in with your little confession first, acting all noble.' She dropped her voice into a mocking baritone. 'Oh, be fair, be fair, my dad made demands of me, wah, wah, fucking, wah. Oh, we don't have to drag up the details and upset poor Naz, especially if it makes me look bad.'

'Guys,' Cady said. 'Come on. What is happening here?'

'Oh, don't worry, Cady,' she said. 'I'm going to tell you everything. It would be good for you to know what you're dealing with here.'

Cady saw her fist appear in the gap between the seats. It looked like she was about to strike Winston. But it remained in place until it began to shake and Naz started to sob. It didn't last long. And once she regained her composure, she began to speak.

Naseem, Then

This just wasn't part of her story. That's how Cady had put it, and now she nodded to herself as if hammering the idea back into place. Naseem might want kids one day, in the distant future. But not now, not before she'd done a single fucking thing of note with her life.

She looked around the waiting room of the clinic. So many plants, and paintings, so many soft furnishings. Like the whole place was in denial about its purpose. But no, not in denial. Fuck that. This wasn't a bad thing she was doing, she'd already decided that. Morally no different to a period, as Cady put it. This would free her, as it had freed so many women who, years ago, would have been doomed to a life they didn't want or for which they weren't ready. That was a good thing, no matter what other people thought. Like her parents. And grandparents. And Tasha, her best mate at home.

Just because it was hard didn't mean it was wrong. She had to keep reminding herself: she was the plucky protagonist in this book or movie, and what had happened was one of the obstacles she would have to overcome. And this place ... well, in some ways, it was sort of horny, if you thought about it in the right way. It was where people came to get the pill, and Johnnies, and lube. All the young lovers. Getting down to some fucking for fun.

What she'd decided, after years of questioning her faith, was that when you got down to the quantum mechanics of it all, reality was just stories all the way down. And you could basically pick and choose the ones that worked for you.

The electric doors to the clinic whooshed opened. She turned her face away, hiding it beneath her hair. Eventually, hearing nothing else, she looked up and saw the clinic was still empty. No one sitting with her. No one at the reception desk. She felt so exposed, sitting here. Couldn't they have put her in a back room? Out of sight. Then again, even if someone came in, they wouldn't necessarily know why she was here. She might be applying for a job. Or waiting to get some of those sexy prophylactics.

Now *those* would have been a good idea back at the start of term. But Naseem hadn't wanted to spoil the fun, had she? She been trying to play it cool, like she did this sort of thing all the time. So she'd said she was on the pill, even though she wasn't, because when she'd tried it once she'd spent the month crying and feeling fat.

Her crossed legs, hugged by tights and poking out from a

red leather skirt, bobbed up and down. See, that was the thing. Everyone said the pill was fine, and yet it hadn't been, had it? So, what if it was like that with *this*?

What if she was going to regret it forever?

What if all those things she'd seen on that stupid website, which she knew were bollocks, weren't actually bollocks at all? Made the story a bit harder to believe, didn't it?

She stood up. But she didn't move.

'Everything okay?'

Naseem looked up and smiled at the lady behind the desk. 'Just stretching my legs,' she said.

'It won't be long.'

She sat down again. She was fucking doing this. It was like Femi said, ultimately the decision was both of theirs. And even if a small part of her had doubts, she was mostly convinced. And Femi was completely against it. She'd seen it on his face when she'd told him the morning she'd found out, not long after the dress rehearsal. His horror was almost funny. So the maths was like, 90/10 in favour. 85 maybe.

And that was the other thing to keep in mind. She'd drunk and smoked so much since conception that the baby was probably damaged. And what about that mescaline ice cream Danson had given her and Cady? Who knew what she might be giving birth to? What sort of life she and *it* might end up having?

She felt her eyes welling up and didn't know why. She imagined her mum holding her. The way she'd done after Naseem woke up from having grommets put in as a six-year-old. That pain had been so unbearable. She wished she could talk to Mum now. But that could never happen, obviously.

She stood up and strode out through the doors.

For a while she stood at the top of the clinic steps, in full view of the road. But no cars passed by. No pedestrians. No mothers pushing buggies. The door kept whooshing open and closed behind her. Sensing her presence but not sure what she wanted.

She should forget about Mum. Mum was part of the problem. She never spoke up for herself. Hadn't the whole time Naseem had been alive. She never defended Naseem when she fought with her dad and Has. She knew Mum agreed with her, that she had doubts too, but she wouldn't do anything to upset the family. Really, the whole idea of family was part of the problem, too. Nice idea in theory, but it was a misogynistic trap in reality. Religion, family, babies, all weapons of control. Fuck every one of them.

Better to choose who you keep close. Like The No Tomorrows Club. They were sort of her family now. Her Chamberlain family, anyway. Their group chemistry was off the charts.

Eventually a voice spoke from close behind her. 'We're ready for you now. Do you need a minute?'

A bus went by, on the side a poster for the latest Mariah Carey album. How she'd loved that woman once, when she'd been younger, before she'd discovered metal and Emo and punk. Not now, though. She was a different girl now. A different woman.

Something Cady said came to her then, from that night Naz had told them all about her summer. She'd felt so close to them then that her family suddenly seemed like aliens by comparison. What Cady had said was they all had to promise to each other that they would try to make the most of the short lives they were given. And Naseem had promised, hadn't she?

'No,' Naseem said. 'I'm fine.'

She turned around and went inside.

Other than a very mild cramp, Naseem felt nothing walking back into the waiting area. But the anaesthetic had made her feel groggy, and she was exhausted. All she wanted to do now was climb into bed. She wished it could be her bed at home. But it would have to be her bed at Chamberlain. The bed that started the whole mess.

With a deep breath, she shook her hair so it drew around her face like curtains and left the building. She was reaching down into her bag for cigarettes straight away and wasn't looking where she was going. She walked into someone heading up the stairs and dropped the pack on the floor. Cigarettes tumbled down towards the pavement.

'I'm sorry,' she said, scalding heat rising in her chest and face.

'Sorry,' the woman she'd bumped into said at the same time.

Both of them knelt down to retrieve the cigarettes. 'You don't have to…' Naseem started, but when she looked up she saw a familiar face, and the rising heat burned even stronger.

How could her luck be so bad? It was Eloise Draclin, from Chamberlain. She was dressed in an oversized coat and a beanie. A disguise. But she knew that sharp little face anywhere.

'Oh,' Eloise said, eyes enormous and full of the same embarrassment as hers.

Both of them got up and stared at one another for few seconds before Eloise began her ascent, and Naseem continued down. At the bottom, she turned. Eloise was looking back at her from the top.

'Are you okay?' Eloise said.

Naseem nodded. 'Yeah. Are you?'

'Hope so.' She turned for the door and Naseem watched her enter the clinic. Too exhausted to work out what it meant, she walked to the taxi rank and went back to Chamberlain.

It wasn't really an option to avoid Eloise. Two days later she had to meet her for a costume fitting for *Little Shop*. They met in the auditorium, Eloise on stage surrounded by different garments she'd assembled using the small budget given to them by the Chamberlain Dramatic Society. They communicated in small smiles and short sentences, until Eloise, her gaze firmly on her feet, said, 'If you ever want to go for coffee, you know, to talk.'

'Oh.' The last thing Naseem wanted was to ever think about what happened again. It was all she could do to turn her own brain off sometimes.

'It's none of my business, but, you know. They said to have someone there with you. And I didn't. And you didn't.' Eloise shrugged. 'I'm making a lot of assumptions, I know. You might have been there for anything.'

Surprising herself, Naseem said, 'You can make them. Only one thing happens there on a Wednesday morning, doesn't it. Have you been okay?'

'I'm okay.' She shrugged. 'Sort of. You?'

'Yeah. Good.' She started to feel herself go.

They met in town for coffee, finding a nook at the back of The Eagle. For some reason, the house playlist kept playing 'Tragedy' by the Bee Gees, which was funny until it wasn't.

Eloise was forthright, and Naseem appreciated it. Her fear going into town earlier had been the awkwardness of them both easing into the conversation. Beating around the bush.

'So, the dad didn't go with you, either?' Eloise said.

'Dear me, do we have to use the D word?'

'How about sperm donor?'

Naseem laughed. 'No, he didn't. He offered but I didn't want it to be a thing.'

'Was it Femi?'

Eloise really wasn't messing around.

'I probably shouldn't. What about you?'

'Me? Dan.'

'Sorry. Danson was...?'

'The sperm donor. Yeah.'

Naz couldn't keep the surprise from lifting her eyebrows and causing her mouth to tilt in an odd smile. Not that there was anything wrong with Danson, per se. It was just ... she couldn't really imagine him fucking. 'Oh. That's... I didn't know.'

'What's to know? We had a couple of shags. It's not like we're getting married. I'm like you, I didn't want anyone else there. Not that I was spoilt for choice, you know? Can't exactly invite my mum and dad.' Eloise smiled, acting like she was reporting a visit to the dentist. But there was something else glimmering in her eyes.

'God, yeah, tell me about it,' Naz said. 'My family... Yeah, that wouldn't be good.'

'Pretty traditional?'

'About some things. Not about others. My mum's okay, but

my dad and my brother… My brother particularly. Well, let's just say his faith's gone funny since September 11th.'

She told Eloise about ditching her hijab, and how her brother hadn't spoken to her for days.

'Oh, wow.'

'Yeah, so you can probably imagine how well all this would have gone down.'

'What do your parents do?' Eloise asked, that little glimmer in her eyes burning more brightly now on her mousy face.

'My dad started a restaurant chain. He's been doing it since his twenties.'

'He does okay, then?'

'Yeah, he does fine.'

'Went to a nice school, then, did you?' She took a drink from her herbal tea and stared off to her left at nothing in particular. 'It's funny, I always knew about Oxbridge being like it is. But it still surprises me that even the normal-seeming people went to private school.'

'I mean… I started in a state school,' Naseem said, finding it odd she should suddenly have to defend her education. It wasn't like she'd had much choice in it. She suddenly felt as exposed as she had while sitting in the clinic. And that look in Eloise's eyes, as if something in her head was hastily trying to burrow out. Maybe this had been a mistake. 'But yeah, I went private from secondary.'

After a chasmic silence, Eloise spoke into whichever abyss she was still staring into: 'My mum was an assistant librarian at a *very* illustrious private school. You know, the sort that makes prime ministers. She wasn't chippy, though, my mum. She was grateful to get to work in such a posh place. And she would tell me all these stories about how the other half lived. It was insightful. Mum stuck around there years hoping to get a staff discount for me to go. Got me a scholarship exam which I fucking aced. But still, 70% of a lot of money is still a lot of money. I think she'd convinced herself that, if she worked hard enough and long enough, they might do her a deal or something. But no. Mum was an optimist until the day she died. But she wasn't even on their radar.' Eloise shook her head. 'She never had a pay rise in twenty years.'

'That's awful. I was lucky, my school really valued the library. I loved it. The librarian turned me onto the Brontes and Jane Austen. I—'

'Do you ever wonder why people are drawn to each other?'

There would be no salvaging this now. Eloise was unsettling and Naseem wanted to leave. How was she going to do it without offending her, though? Go to the loo and pretend she'd had a phone call. That was the only way to do it. 'I don't actually. Eloise, I just—'

'I've got a theory,' Eloise said, 'and it's hard to prove, but I'm getting there. So, my theory is, we all have different chemistry with each other, don't we? Humans. We accept that. I know you agree, because I heard you and your mates all talking about being drawn to each other in the bar when you'd had that accident. And I agree that chemistry is linked to circumstance. But here is my thing: I think people with secrets, they tend to be similar types of people. And they tend to congregate. I don't know why this happens, but perhaps it's because keeping a secret poisons your personality in some way. And when you meet someone who is poisoned like you, you gravitate towards that ... familiarity. Like how girls and boys drift towards their own at primary school. Or how people with similar backgrounds can just tell. People with the same *cultural capital*.'

'Or how me and you are having this conversation,' Naseem

said, in the hope of de-escalating what felt like a prelude to an attack.

Eloise grinned. How had Naseem ever thought Eloise's face mouse-like? The way those canines dominated that smile was all wolf. And Naseem felt in her bones that she was quarry.

'Naseem,' Eloise said. 'Do you know any secrets?'

CADY

Friday 21st June, 10.10pm
Celsius: 35°, Fahrenheit: 95°

Cady drew a deep breath of air laced with the fake vinyl scent of the coaster seats. Realising she'd been gripping the restraint handle, she let go. She was scared to ask Naz what happened next. But she needed to. Because now it was all too obvious why the other three were here. They were all Eloise's victims, and therefore, they all had a motive to harm her.

The question was, why the heck was she sitting here with them? And did it have anything to do with what Eloise had wanted to talk to Cady about that night before she fell? Given what the other three had just revealed, didn't it follow that Naz had betrayed some secret of Cady's to Eloise, and that perhaps Eloise had been planning to blackmail Cady next? It had a dark and inescapable logic to it.

Yet it couldn't be right, primarily because Cady didn't have any secrets. Nothing that Eloise could have used to get money from her, anyway. Other than that brief period of rebellion during her teen years, Cady consciously prided herself on always trying to do the right thing. At heart, she was still the same goody-goody, Oxfam-t-shirt-wearing kid from that photograph at Mum and Dad's. And Eloise wouldn't have gotten very far telling people Cady once stole a lip balm from Lush.

Perhaps, then, she was here because of a misunderstanding. Had Eloise named Cady specifically, or had she simply said something generic like 'your friends' when she'd told Danson they meant to harm her? Danson might have simply assumed she meant Cady.

Feeling braver suddenly, Cady asked, 'So did you?' She gathered just enough saliva in her mouth to swallow. 'Did you know any secrets?'

'Of course I did. I…' Naz paused, overwhelmed by a spasm of pain in her back. 'I knew about Femi lying to his parents. But I'd never have betrayed him. And it wouldn't have been much of a secret. He fucking told anyone who'd listen.'

Femi said, 'I was just trying to—'

'Shut up,' Winston said.

Femi glowered, but it soon softened into something more like a sulk.

'So,' Cady said, 'what, you just paid her?'

'I agonised over it. Didn't fucking sleep. Eventually, I told Femi, because it was sort of his secret, too. I knew I wasn't supposed to tell anyone, but I needed someone. I thought he might have an idea. Or at least offer to help pay. But of course, he was already paying her, wasn't he? So that was never going to happen.'

'I'm sorry I didn't tell you,' Femi said.

'Stop saying sorry,' Winston said. 'It's pathetic.'

'And Femi lobbied pretty hard for me to pay her off,' Naz said. 'That I wouldn't want it on my conscience to betray someone. Ha.'

'Can I just say something,' Femi said.

'No,' Winston said.

Femi ignored him. 'I was speaking from experience. You didn't want it on your conscience. And by then, don't forget, I knew she was blackmailing me, and Winston, and you now. I understood how dangerous she was. I wanted to stop her from hurting anyone else.'

'Who are you even talking to?' Naz said, her voice clipped at the end of the sentence and she gave a dry cough. 'You could have told me, Femi, and we could have teamed up against her. Trapped her or something. But obviously you were too worried about your parents finding out any one of the terrible things you'd been up to. Or maybe you were scared if I dug too deep, I'd find out what you'd done to Winston.'

'I don't think that's entirely fair,' he said. 'I can't deny probably some of all that was in my head. At the very back. But also, think about it, you didn't know about Winston, but you knew Eloise traded secrets. If I'd told you about my situation, you might think I'd told Eloise to turn up at the clinic that day. To save myself. You were always suspicious about her bumping into you there.'

'And you fucking told me I was being paranoid.' Again, her voice cracked. 'I asked Eloise once, after she blackmailed me, if she'd even really been pregnant with Danson's kid, because I just never really bought that they'd fucked, and she just gave me this really ugly, smug smile. Like she knew all the world's secrets and I never would. I know why now, but at the time, I thought you were probably right, Femi, because only you, me and the clinic knew the exact appointment time. And you so clearly wanted nothing to do with the baby, so I doubt you'd have been telling anyone else—'

'Hey, come on, Naz. You know all that bloody broke me.'

'I know nothing anymore. Wait, did you ever suspect that Winston might have been the one to tell Eloise? That you'd indirectly caused all of it?'

'No,' he said, outraged by the idea. 'I genuinely believed you'd been unlucky running into her, Naz. I told you, I assumed Winston had paid her, and that had been that. That's why I was so confident telling you to do the same. I knew she'd keep her word.'

'What the fuck does it even matter now?' she said and coughed. 'I feel so … violated. Everything I've shared with you over the years. Both of you. Fuck.'

'Naz—' Winston stopped himself.

'How did you even find out, Winston?' she asked. 'Did Femi fuck that up as well?'

'No, it wasn't him,' Winston said. He snorted, but added nothing else.

'Was it Cady?' Naz said.

Up until then Cady had become so absorbed in their conversation that her own thoughts had been in a gobsmacked stasis. At the sound of her own name, she came back to herself. 'Me?'

'Yes. No offence, darling, but you do like a fucking chat when you're out of it. And you were the only other person who knew about me being pregnant.'

'I didn't.'

'You did. I told you on the night of the dress rehearsal.'

'What? Naz, I don't think so.'

'I hadn't even told Femi yet. We got really, really drunk and you'd had way more of that magic ice cream Danson's druggie mate gave him than me. We went deep. You asked me why I was drinking so much, and so I told you I was trying to kill it. I felt horrible about saying it the next day, and it always made me a bit nervous that you never brought it up again. That maybe I'd offended you or something.'

Cady burned with shame. 'Oh, my God, Naz. Really? I'm so sorry.' Of course, Cady remembered the night. It had birthed one of the worst hangovers of her life. Despite that, and waking up with a deep regret of unknown origin, she had always held on to the sweet memory of her and Naz waking up spooning on Cady's bed like two sisters.

'It wasn't Cady,' Winston said. 'I was asleep behind the sofa that night.'

'Wait,' Naz said. 'You were wasted. Femi had to carry you upstairs.'

'Well, yeah. But I woke up and heard you talking. Then I passed out again and the next day it was about the only thing I could remember. I was never going to tell anyone, though. But then … fuck, I'm sorry, Naz. I didn't have a credit card or anything like that. All my money in my bank account was sort of budgeted for. She wanted like £500 quid a month.'

'Same,' Femi said, staring out at the shadows of the mountains. Perhaps even beyond those.

'She didn't ask me for that much,' Naz said. 'Maybe because she already had your money. She told me she wanted it for her student loan, so maybe she had a set figure in mind. She was really cautious. Made the amounts small and had me sign this contract she'd made up saying she was giving me writing lessons.'

Winston huffed. 'Same. For music lessons.'

'What about you?' Cady said to Femi, sensing the seeds of a truce being sown and eager for them to sprout.

He grunted absently. 'Guitar lessons.'

'Oh my God,' Naz said, 'if only we'd said something. Worked together.'

'We couldn't, though, could we?' Winston said. 'She'd have brought us down.'

'Surely…' Naz trailed off and repositioned herself. 'I did have a credit card. And I knew my parents would pay it off at the end of the year without asking questions. Even if they did, I'd say I spent it on clothes, and they'd have just given me a lecture on being more responsible. But yeah, I couldn't have risked letting my parents know about what happened. Not with the little narrative my brother was trying to spin about me with Dad. I used to be so scared of Has. Still am, to be honest.'

Cady had suspected before, but now had no doubt, Naz's break-out second book, *Corruption*, about a young Muslim woman murdered by her fanatical brother, had clearly been more than a little bit autobiographical. Had they read it? If so, that can't have been an easy time for her.

Winston took another snort and said, 'Naz, I never would have said a thing. But I couldn't let her ruin everything. Honestly, I'd have probably killed someone had she asked me to.'

'Well,' Cady said, 'that's comforting.'

No one laughed, and Cady wished she'd stayed quiet.

'Just … fuck you, Winston,' Naz said. 'And give me that.' Cady saw Naseem's hand reach across the gap between their seats.

'Hey, what the hell,' Winston said.

Cady watched the baggy fly over the edge of the coaster and disappear into the night.

'If I have to go through this sober, you do too.'

'It's probably for the best, Win,' Femi said. 'Coke is going to dehydrate you, which isn't—'

'Shut up, Femi. You had your chance to be a doctor.'

'Winston, I don't know what else to say but sorry.'

'Yeah, we're all bloody sorry, aren't we? But now what? Are we going to tell Danson we all despised the girl he loved because she was blackmailing us? Because sorry isn't going to work if he thinks we did something to her, is it?'

'Are we supposed to be finding out if one of us pushed her off?' Naz said. 'Because given the levels of utter deviousness we've discovered tonight, I'm not sure one of you didn't.'

'Glass houses,' Femi said.

'Femi, as relieved as I was when she fell, and when no one came asking any questions about all the money she'd taken from me, in the aftermath, I didn't actually kill her.'

Femi and Winston both denied it too.

Cady said nothing. She wasn't part of this conversation. Because Eloise hadn't tried blackmailing her. Yet what had she wanted to talk about that night?

'Cady,' Naz said. 'Did you push Eloise?'

'Guess it must be me,' she said. The other three actually laughed. Not in a pleasant way, though. More in the mad fashion of soldiers about to go over the top.

'I don't think Danson wants a confession,' Cady said. 'My reading was that he just wanted to know what Eloise's comment meant. And now we have something to tell him. We can let him know what a monster she was. We need to be careful how we do it, though. Be sensitive. But hopefully he'll already have his suspicions, and this will confirm them.'

'But now we have clear motives?' Winston said a little bit too quickly. 'How is that going to help if he does think one of us did it? And he loved her.'

'To which I say, does anyone else have a better idea?' Cady said.

Of course, no one did. And so they uneasily agreed that they would approach him as if he were a growling Dobermann. That they would make clear that they completely understood why he might have thought something had happened to Eloise, but that actually *they* were the victims. The likelihood was she simply fell, as everyone had always believed.

It would have to do, even if Cady wasn't entirely sure she believed it anymore. The heat, and the panic rising like floodwater, was affecting her judgement, though. Yet the things they'd done to one another showed how little she'd ever really known them. They would have given her away to Eloise in a heartbeat had she had anything worth knowing. So why wouldn't they have taken the chance to shove her off the lodge had it presented itself? And it *would* have presented itself, the way Eloise used to sit up there. Like that drop didn't exist.

Means. Opportunity. Motive. All of it was there. And capability, that's what she now couldn't rule out. Winston was genetically related to a killer. Hadn't she read about genetic inheritance in such cases? An unfair thought, maybe, but even put to one side, he'd betrayed Naz. And Femi, how easily he'd sold Winston out, and lied about it all. Not to mention how callous he'd apparently been about his baby with Naz. Cady didn't entirely trust *her*, either. All these years she'd never once mentioned what Eloise had done to her – even when it was safe to do so after her fall. None of them had until now. Was that because they knew it might make them suspects? Or did they have something else to hide?

They called for Danson. He didn't come. They called again. And again.

Likely an hour passed, they couldn't be sure. It felt like two. None of them wanted to consider that he might have left them for good now. So they didn't talk about it. For much of the time they sat in silence, brooding, unpicking the past and stitching it back together. It wasn't much better than the angry arguments from before, and more than once Cady tried to bind them together with small talk and hope, only to be harshly rebuffed.

Finally, they heard the sound of the steps. No one spoke. Cady shifted her body. Her clothes stuck to her skin. Her skin stuck to the vinyl seat. She couldn't free herself from one discomfort without instigating another. Her knees, and side, and back, and neck all ached.

It was exactly 11pm when Danson sat down on the walkway again and placed the wooden chest beside him.

'It's been four hours now,' he said, smiling in wonder.

Eloise, Then

She lay in the dark listening to Danny snore. Each little honk serenaded her closer to sobriety, but that didn't halt the falling sensation she experienced every time she closed her eyes. Like the bed wasn't there and she was plummeting through the floors of the blockhouse. So she stared into the blackness, his cum gradually oozing from inside her.

What had come over her tonight? Some of it was the booze. But if it was *only* that she'd have seduced him long before tonight. And it *had* been a seduction. A juicy one, too. She'd absolutely pounced on him.

Yeah, she'd needed some relief after the stress of exams – nowhere near a fail, but nothing too flash that might draw attention to herself – that had been part of it. But also she'd felt pity, Danny going on about his magic in the bar earlier, while those supposed *friends* humoured him. Facts were facts: his tricks were bad. And the bourgeois was too strong in *them* to spout anything but empty encouragement. Tonight, though, they'd been exquisitely phony, and Danny had started to notice.

It was Eloise's fault. They didn't know how to act around her now. They were too absorbed in trying to pretend they were all mates, having seemingly grown even closer after betraying one another. Too busy avoiding eye-contact with Eloise. They had no mental energy left for their politeness.

Then Cady had arrived, and that had been the final straw. She was the most fluff-brained, bright-side-of-life privileged bitch she'd ever met. The ray of sunshine that turned your moles cancerous.

So she'd whisked Danny away. *Danny* not *Danson*, as they all called him, because apparently Winston or Femi had thought he looked like the actor from *Cheers*. And later, when he'd started rubbing her belly, she'd got so wet fantasising about jumping his bones, imagining his shocked little face as all his dreams came true, that she'd only gone and done it.

Rafael's voice had been in her head then. Telling her she was doing reeeeally well. That she was truly freeing herself from the chains of oppression. And that had helped, too.

The surprise had been that she'd enjoyed the actual sex as much as he did. Given he'd let her take complete control, perhaps it shouldn't have been a surprise. But she'd forgotten that she liked the way he looked until his clothes came off. And hadn't he been so present. Not like Raf, who always seemed like he was thinking about something more important.

Why she'd cried she had no idea. Maybe it was because she felt like she'd cheated on Raf. Some tyrannical biological thing going on. But it wasn't like she had real feelings for Danny. Not like she did for Raf. For fuck's sake, why was she even comparing them? No, she'd slept with Danny because he *really* lapped up all those little compliments those wanker friends gave him. Didn't see them for what they were. So maybe in amongst all the other stuff, she'd wanted to show him what a real compliment was. What real attention and a real connection was. Slap him into reality. Slap him with a good fuck.

In the dark, she grinned. She'd certainly done that.

On the ceiling, amorphous shapes danced – the blood vessels in her eyes playing tricks. She blinked. It reminded her of the pink elephants in *Dumbo*. That had been one of two video cassettes that had been in her house as a child. *Dumbo* and *Robin Hood*. Her Disney dads. She always used to specify she had the Disney versions at school, because some of the other kids on her estate had knock-off *Disneys* bought down at Chelmsley market. She'd watched those two cartoons endlessly in the hours she used to wait for Mum to come home after school. Dawn, her fourteen-year-old cousin, was meant to stay with her, but she always got bored and left.

She'd joked to Raf that her Marxism was born from watching Robin Hood steal from the rich and give to the poor. Of course, Raf being Raf had said that if it *truly* was, she needed to reassess her motivations, to ensure they were *truly* rational. Everything had to be done *truly*, according to Raf. Truly and rationally. Which was why she loved him, and knew he loved her. He pushed back, made her ask herself questions, didn't just accept things at face value and whinge about it all when it went wrong, after it was too late to do anything about it. If you loved someone, push them.

But she had only been joking about Robin Hood. She had other reasons both rational and irrational. She didn't need a cartoon to explain how the world worked. She'd seen the lecherous men from that well-off school, managers *and* parents, promise Mum the world before disappearing. Particularly in those years before the lines on Mum's face became too deep to bury in make-up. Back when she didn't need to mention out loud that she'd once done a stint modelling.

One of her teachers had told her about Marx. Had even lent her the communist manifesto. And at fifteen she'd started hanging out with the local Socialist Worker Party chapter with her friend Letisha, principally because there were older boys there. Men really. But Letisha hadn't been able to handle the debates, while Eloise loved them. She was good at them.

Eventually, Eloise decided the Socialist Worker Party were all just grinding out personal issues under the guise of politics. She needed action, and so she joined Worker's Fight, a group of ex-SWPs that preferred *doing something*. That's where she met Raf, a long-haired, beautiful Italian in his early twenties. She'd been seventeen but told him she was a year older. They fell in love over illegal sit-ins and occupations, and when she wasn't at sixth form, she was hanging out with him at a filthy squat in Birmingham city centre, bed sheets for window glass and woodlice for pets, arguing about the Spanish Civil War and nuclear disarmament, and what happened to the middle class when the revolution came.

What they talked about most, though, was how soft other socialists were. How they were never really willing to *truly* overthrow everything that oppressed them. They picked and chose. To really be free, you couldn't be bound by social expectations and antiquated morality. That was why they never called themselves a couple. And why they were both free to sleep with whomever they wanted. Eloise didn't really take advantage of that, but she suspected when she got gonorrhoea that Raf did. But she never doubted he loved her.

It was Raf who first suggested she take revenge on one of those men from Mum's school. Eloise's stories had really got under his skin. He'd done it before, he said, lots of times. The secrets of the rich, he said, were like gold dust. So they'd looked this one man from the school up, found he was still some big deal in finance. Still married too. They wrote him an email containing a cash figure and a drop-off location. In exchange, they wouldn't tell his wife about the watch he'd left at Mum's before ditching her like a used condom. The watch engraved with a wedding anniversary on the back, which Mum had told him later that she couldn't find, and that she'd told Eloise she was going to sell, but that had long sat inside a sad little jewellery box under Mum's bed with other memorabilia, like the tyre company card, on the back of which Eloise's late dad had written his new phone number in Spain, a number that had never worked.

Raf had collected the money himself after watching the guy drop off and scarper. Then he'd invited Eloise over to watch him set the bag on fire in a metal bin. Just because they could. Of course, the gesture only worked if the money was still inside the sport's bag, and afterwards she wished she'd asked him to show it to her first. Not because she didn't believe him, but because the gesture would have been even more powerful had she actually seen the queen's face alight. That was all.

It had also been Raf that was honest enough to tell her what bullshit it was that a supposed true revolutionary had applied to and been accepted by Cambridge. The elite of the elite. And that changing the system from within was a lie every sell-out told themselves. When he found out, he said he didn't want to associate with her. But then she told him her plan. And reminded him that rich people's secrets were like gold dust.

Yes, he loved her. And she couldn't wait to go and visit him in Italy this summer with the money she'd made. Tell him how she'd listened and learned from him. How she'd got a job at the bar, and listened carefully to all the rich kids' drunk conversations. How she'd ensconced herself in a group of daft wannabe luvvies. How she'd even managed to catch the porter drinking from a hip flask of whisky one night and been able to make him dance whenever she willed it. It had been a few months now since Raf had written to her, though, but he'd been moving around a lot, so it really wasn't a surprise. It wasn't like they were betrothed.

Perhaps that was yet another reason she'd slept with Danny tonight. That distance from him had made it easier to break those particular oppressive chains. The ones that made free people want to chain themselves to the people they fuck. Sentimental nonsense.

Danny had stopped snoring. He placed a hand tentatively on her chest, just underneath her boobs.

'Eloise... I love you.'

Oh dear. That wasn't good. Or had she secretly expected it? Either way, she should probably respond soon. Time was passing, and she couldn't say nothing. So she took the hand on her chest and moved it onto her breast. To distract him. But also it felt good.

'Thanks, Danny.'

His hand came off her. 'I mean... I just mean, like, as a friend. Like, how I love all of you guys from *Little Shop*. We've all ... got such a good chemistry.'

It was weird. Even though she really didn't want him falling in love with her, she was annoyed he was trying to take it back. That he was putting her in the same category as *them*. She wasn't from *Little Shop*, and she wanted him to know. Outside of Cambridge, people like *them* would as soon wish people like Danny and her dead as they would look at them. She'd certainly felt like they might like to kill her tonight, in those few moments they'd failed to avoid her gaze, and all their hatred of her had burned in their eyes.

She started questioning Danny about them. Not wanting to outright say it, but pushing him towards the truth. That they didn't *really* like him. Not like *she* did. And that they were, frankly, dangerous. Rich people were everything wrong with the world. The real problem behind all problems. She wanted him to understand, to awaken him from his slumber. But to do that, she would need to tell him all of it. Tell them what cowardly little backstabbers they were when their own interests were at stake.

And she couldn't do that, could she? So instead, she told him a version of the truth. That they all had it in for her. And that, if anything happened to her, it would be one of them that did it.

It was mysterious, and it raised the stakes, and best of all, it was true. Sometimes she really did lie awake at night thinking about whether she'd taken on too much. That she'd gotten greedy and power hungry, like that idiot Orwell always said people like her did. And that one of them might come into her room and slit her throat.

And in the end, because he was confused by what she'd said, and because she really wanted to, she fucked him again. It was better than lying in the dark. Falling.

Friday 21st June, 11.00pm
Celsius: 34°, Fahrenheit: 93.2°

'So, what did you all find out?' he said. He sounded exhausted, his breathing even heavier than the last time he'd completed the climb. He still wore his blazer, and plump beads of sweat decorated his forehead, oddly reminding Cady of the face gems Eloise used to wear. 'And please. Be honest now. I really don't have it in me to do this climb again.'

'Are you sure you're okay?' Cady said. 'You don't sound great. I mean, if anything happened to you now, we're—'

'I'll be fine. I've thought it through.' He patted the chest beside him. What that meant was anyone's guess. 'Now. Talk. Or forever hold your peace.'

Having been the one to corral them all into agreement, Cady began, 'Danson, we—'

But Femi cut her off. 'Firstly, we wanted to say that we completely understand your position.'

Cady scowled, her eyes wide with annoyance. Femi was not the right person to speak for them. Not after what they'd all just learned about him. And certainly not after how wound up he'd gotten earlier. The implication had been that *she'd* talk. She was in the best position to, having neither been harmed by Eloise, or been on the end of a direct betrayal. She was calmer, able to keep her head. But Femi didn't turn to see her face, to see her anger, and he began to lay out everything they'd talked about in all its heartbreaking detail.

Cady threw back her head and closed her eyes. She wavered between feeling sad for them all, and being mortified that her version of these people, particularly Winston and Femi, whom she'd always had on such a pedestal, had been so spectacularly wrong. Winston chimed in occasionally. Naz once or twice. But she mainly contributed moans and groans of discomfort, perhaps to play on Danson's heart strings, perhaps because her agony was getting worse.

'And if we were you, we would completely think the same thing,' Femi finished, concluding where they'd begun, like all good arts students were taught to do when structuring an argument. 'But Dan, honest to God, we didn't have anything to do with her fall.'

Danson's hand rose and started tapping the back of his skull, hard enough that Cady could hear each finger strike. He appeared to mull over what they'd said, and finally replied, 'Don't think I don't appreciate your honesty. But... we're missing something.' He winced, like his head hurt.

Femi gritted his teeth, and before he could say anything, Cady got there first. 'What are we missing, Danson?'

He looked up at her, unimpressed by her tone. 'Well, *Cady*… Why are *you* here?'

'Why am— I'm here because…' Well, that was the question, wasn't it? The one she'd been avoiding. Panic began to creep up from its lair in her belly. Because of how he'd asked the question, and because she wanted to keep Femi from jumping in again.

'I don't know,' Cady said. 'Did she really say my name? Or did she just—'

'She said your name, Cady.'

Any hope she'd had that this might be some mistake burst from her like refuse from the bottom of an overstuffed bin bag.

'Well,' Naz said, struggling to raise her voice. 'Maybe Eloise fell before she got around to getting any dirt on Cady.'

'Yeah, that's a good story, Naz. I can see why they give you prizes. But it isn't what happened, is it?'

'You only know what she told you, though,' Cady said.

Danson's head dropped and he began shaking it. Hunched over in the brilliant light, he looked like a slate etching. After a while he got to his feet. 'We got so close.' He collected his chest. 'Can I ask, how did it make you feel, learning how full of it you all were? How close you were all pretending to be, when all along you were stabbing each other in the back.'

'After what you've put us through,' Femi said, 'it's about par for the evening.'

Danson laughed and started walking.

'Are you coming back?' Cady said.

'Nah. I'm done.'

'I don't know what this has to do with me,' Cady said, struggling to keep her composure, to keep the Dobermann happy. 'I've told you everything I know.'

He stopped. Smiled. 'I know. But Naseem hasn't.'

'What did Eloise tell you?' Naz said to Danson. 'Because … because…'

Danson was walking away, but slowly. Cady knew this had to be something to do with her. 'Naz, whatever it is, say it, okay? I'll forgive you. We'll stick together.'

Naz said nothing. And now Danson was speeding up.

'Naseem.' Femi's voice was thin and angry.

'Please,' Cady said.

A frustrated cry rattled in Naz's throat, before eventually she cried, 'Fine. Danson, come back.'

Slowly, Danson turned and came back. He sat down once more and shook his head. 'Please don't make me get up again.'

'You obviously know,' Naz said. 'So I told Eloise something about Cady. Okay? That's what she wanted to talk to you about that night. Because I couldn't… I couldn't just put the money on a credit card. That was a lie. My dad went through my bills every month. He called me to go through it when it came through the door. He was a proper fucking arsehole about it, frankly. So I made a choice. And… and… I told her… something.' Another shift. Another moan. 'Listen, Danson, I've said this much. I really don't want to talk about what it is I said because I don't think it's fair. It's really not fair to Cady.'

Cady's body felt like it was petrifying, every muscle and joint. What had Naz said? What was it she thought she knew about her?

'Was it fair when you told Eloise?' Danson said.

'Danson,' Naz said, 'Cady and me were wasted, and she was tripping on that fucking mescaline you gave us, okay? So I thought it was all bollocks, anyway. But if it wasn't, there's a chance Cady was dealing with a repressed memory or something, and that's not really fair to bring it up now, if she—'

'And still you told Eloise?' he said.

'A repressed memory?' Cady said. 'What are you talking about? What did I say to you?'

'So, if you knew all this?' Naz said to Danson. 'What's this all about? Why—' This time, her attempt to get more comfortable made her yell. When she spoke again, her voice was much higher, weaker, desperate. 'Why are we here if you knew all this? Let us go, you fucking prick.'

Danson sighed the sigh of a God having to explain himself to mortals. 'What I said was that I wanted to know what happened to Eloise. And that I wanted the truth, given what she told me. But we're not quite there yet.'

'How do you know that?' Naz yelled.

'She told me everything, Naz. I know *everything*.'

'You knew this stuff all along?' Femi said, twisting the handle on the front of the restraint.

'Of course I did.'

'You've known all this time and only now you've decided one of us might have pushed her?' Femi shook his head.

Danson laughed. 'Pushed her? No. No, no, no. I'm sorry if that's what you all thought. Is that why you thought you were here? Because you thought I wanted to solve a mystery?'

They didn't reply to this. Cady squeezed her own lap bar handle, dreading what might come out of his mouth next. She wanted to be home. She wanted to buy Tom a Twix at the airport. She wanted to wake up in bed with Tom and tell him … tell him they'd go on holiday the next day. Or that afternoon, if he could get his work to agree.

'No,' Danson said. 'I did want the truth. I wanted *you* to all know the truth about *each other*, which would never have sounded as good coming from my lips. I wanted you all to understand who you really are. But, God, no, I never once thought you pushed her off. I mean, I know you didn't push her off. In fact, I was there when she fell.'

Cady tried to swallow. Tried to breathe. She couldn't. Thoughts and images churned. Had he witnessed her suicide, then? Did he think maybe they were responsible for that in some way? If he'd seen such an awful thing, and had her damning words about them all in his head, perhaps...

But Danson's shining eyes looked suddenly unmoored in that horrible white light. And Cady knew he hadn't finished yet.

'Danson,' Femi said, 'what do you mean you saw her fall? You were there?'

'Yeah.' He blinked, and a tear fell. 'I pushed her.'

Danson, Then

I'll have to tear this out when I'm done, another entry for my growing lost journal – but I need to get my thoughts together. Like Naz, my brain works better on paper. I'll replace this with something else when I'm done, just in case anyone asks any questions. But I don't think they will. Eloise was never very proud of us, so I don't think I'll be high on anyone's list of suspects.

There was a party on the roof tonight for *Little Shop* people. Eloise must have arranged it with Femi. Everyone was there. I don't know how it didn't get shut down. I kept waiting to get Eloise alone, but I knew I'd be in for a long wait. I watched her in her turret nook. Watched her deliberately avoid my gaze, as she has ever since we slept together.

She never stopped talking to people. To people she didn't even like. Conveniently gregarious. It got well past midnight, so I left without telling her. Maybe she would wind things down once she thought I'd gone. I hid inside the petals of the flower sculpture opposite the porter's lodge. Seymour Krelborn. Consumed by a hungry plant. I remember wondering if, perhaps, had I had a bit more confidence, I might have played that role alongside the others. In a world where I'd pursued the music and not the magic.

Within ten minutes the last few stragglers emerged from the back of the lodge. Eloise wasn't with them. I climbed the stairs, expecting to find her at the top, struggling with the door like she always did. But no, she was still sitting between her turrets, staring out at the city.

I called out to her softly, so she didn't jump.

'I thought you'd gone,' she said.

I know you did, I didn't say. I stepped inside and walked halfway across the roof. She turned to face me, swinging her legs so they hung into the roof terrace. We made some small talk. I offered to grab her a beer from the box holding open the door. But of course, she wanted to go to bed.

She still wouldn't meet my gaze, either. In the days after we made love, I felt so full. Like the top of a freshly spun hourglass. Grain by grain, I emptied. The hope needed to explain away her blanking of me gradually grew wilder. And now this brush-off. I can't describe how quickly that old raging injustice welled up in me. I hadn't felt anything like it since I was a kid, back when Dad was still knocking around.

She knew we needed to talk. I told her again I loved her. She couldn't ignore that forever. Even if she didn't feel the same way, we could at least establish that and move on. Be real friends again.

I won't lie, I'd been going out of my mind. Femi said I'd lost weight. Naz asked if I was sleeping. Cady wanted to know why I looked so troubled all the time. The sort of questions people who really care about you ask. But I kept quiet. Because I wanted to talk to her first.

So I asked her if we could be honest for a bit. And she gave it some thought, and looking right into my eyes, she said something like, 'Okay, but are you ready for that?'

Her tone appalled me. It wasn't the time to be playful, if that's what she was being. I deserved her seriousness. Of course I was ready. I said we should talk about us, and what had happened, and how we were feeling.

She started stargazing, swinging her legs and shaking her head. Creating this hellish, embarrassing atmosphere between us, like we were two kids in the playground.

'The truth?' she said.

Suddenly I wanted to say "no." But I didn't.

So she told me she had a boyfriend. An older man who lived in Italy. He'd told her to be free while they were apart, but now she had been, she realised how much she didn't enjoy that particular freedom. She said she was sorry if she'd led me on, but that she'd had a really good time, and that I was her favourite person at university. She said we were kindred spirits. But she didn't love me that way.

How I fell then. Ungracefully. Unmanfully. I tried saving face on cowardly instinct, again insisting I hadn't meant love *that way*. That I loved her the way I loved the other *Little Shop* people, and had simply chosen the wrong moment to say it. That the sex had meant nothing, and I'd just wanted to make sure.

Strangely, she took exception to this. She groaned before unleashing a torrent of invective about how this was the perfect example of why I couldn't handle the truth. That I was utterly blind to how terrible the others were.

I'll admit, I was drunk and liable to confusion and anger. But I was so sick of her opinions about them, how wrong she was. I demanded to know why she had it in for them. Why she couldn't see that, even though they were rich, fine, they were nice. And most importantly, they cared about me.

That made her laugh. I hate to use the word against a woman, but it was a spiteful witch's cackle that made me feel like a piece of shit on the bottom of her boot. And off she went then, ranting about how they looked through me, and that she'd heard how they talk about me behind my back, and that they only kept me around in case I was useful to them after university. That's how the private school lot treat friendships, she said, as networking opportunities.

I told her how ridiculous she sounded, and she practically hissed, 'If you weren't at Cambridge, they wouldn't piss on you if you were on fire.'

I wasn't stupid, I knew some people at Cambridge were the way she was describing. But not many. And certainly not anyone from The No Tomorrows Club. I understood then that she was a zealot. Utterly deluded and hateful. Brainwashed, even.

It got so much worse then, because when I suggested I had a better grip on the truth than her, she paused. No, not paused, she froze. Like a robot with a mechanical glitch. Then back to life she came. And she asked how much truth I could take, and since we were in for a penny, in for a pound, I didn't back down. And so she said: 'Your. Magic. Tricks. Are. Shit.'

I laughed. What else could I do with all the stuff inside me, heating up like atoms, bouncing around, looking to escape? She went on, though, about how the others placated me, encouraged my delusion. She said anyone with a pair of eyes can work out how my tricks are done. It's just not what I was good at.

'The thing is,' she carried on, 'they don't consider you worth correcting.'

I had tears in my eyes then, and I started pacing around, turreted wall to turreted wall, turning sadness into kinetic energy. It's always worked for me, but I couldn't do it fast enough. I asked why she was saying all this, was it to make me hate her to soften the blow of rejection? I got another patronising laugh, and she called me a muppet for not realising this was her way of respecting me.

I didn't buy that one bit. Now I had the idea she was feeling sorry for me, backing off a bit. That just made me angrier. Neither of us spoke for a while. My thoughts were a blizzard.

I wanted to ask her what they'd been saying about me behind my back. But I decided I actually didn't believe her. That she was doing anything she could to turn me against them for her own messed up reasons. I wanted to catch her out, so I asked her why she'd told me the No Tomorrows would want to bother harming her if we were such specks of dust to them?

Just because we couldn't be together, she told me, didn't mean we weren't kindred spirits. And that because of that, and because she could tell I didn't believe she really respected me, she was going to tell me the complete, unvarnished truth.

She started with this Rafael, and about their twisted Marxism. She said she'd come to university prowling for opportunities to challenge the social order. That's how she put it. She listened. And waited. And pounced. Turning Femi on Winston, Winston on Naseem, and Naseem on Cady. She told me their secrets, and about how she was going to use them to redistribute wealth. Pay off her student loan. Her mum's debts. Buy a house with Rafael in Italy.

I paced faster and faster, terrified about what would happen if I stopped. She was a maniac. A complete monster.

I don't know what she had expected, but she could tell I was distraught. She tried again to point out how bad they'd been to one another. How instrumental their friendships were when push came to shove. But she was mad. She'd put them in a terrible position. Given them agonising choices using such personal secrets. Bloody hell, what she told me about poor Winston. And lovely Cady. And what Naz and Femi must have gone through, such agony.

I understood now why everyone had seemed so strange and distracted this term. I thought it had been the exams. They were all going through these private hells. And why? Because Eloise had decided they were too privileged? Part of some fuzzy concept called class that she believes is concrete.

None of them were mega-rich, certainly not by Cambridge standards. Especially Cady, whose inclusion baffled me. I said as much to Eloise, again sensing another flaw in her supposed logical reasoning. Why had she targeted her?

She hadn't, though. Not yet. She was meeting her tonight. Sweet Cady, who had always been so kind to me. Who, just the week before, had realised that none of the others had paid back the money they owed me for *Little Shop*. She made sure Winston and Femi knew, causing them to apologise to me, take me out for dinner, and pay me back in full.

'Cady's the worst of all,' Eloise said, and when I asked why, her exact words were, 'Because I'm Robin Hood. And if you need it explained to you, perhaps you're stupider than I thought.'

My poor friends. I was barraged by memories of their friendship. Femi defending me against Sampson after the first audition. Naz cheekily breaking the ice with Eloise for me. Winston jumping immediately to reassure me after I spun the car from the road. And all of them inviting me to join Churchill House, when they could have had their pick. Bloody hell, how was that going to play out, with all of them under Eloise's thumb? And me knowing.

I stopped pacing a few steps from her. I didn't look up. I demanded to know how long she planned to blackmail them for.

I could hear the shrug in her reply. 'Until the revolution.'

It was so stupid and flippant. The hurt constricted my heart. I told her again that I loved her. Out loud it sounded like a question.

'I respect you, *Danson*,' she said. 'I don't love you.'

It was too much. I didn't charge at her. I think she thought I was going to hug her. She shuffled back to evade me, which helped. I didn't push her. I grabbed her two dangling legs and quickly brought them up to shoulder height. She called my name, and I smelled the rubber on the soles of her Converse. I shoved upwards, before she could grip the front of the turrets either side of her. Over went her head, her shoulders, and after that, the rest of her, very quickly.

I ran to the exit. I don't think I even heard her land.

Afterwards, when I closed my eyes to sleep, I didn't think about her at all.

Instead, I kept thinking about that old fairy tale Mum had loved so much. About the old woman who lived in a vinegar bottle.

CADY

Saturday 21st June, 11.22pm
Celsius: 34°, Fahrenheit: 93.2°

His story done, Danson sat back and sighed. 'I've wanted to tell you all this for so long.' He rested his head on the walkway's meshed fence. 'I knew all your secrets, and *still* I loved you. And what I wanted was to *earn* that knowledge from you, for you to want to confide in me in those years after she fell. I kept creating opportunities, opening my heart to you. But you all … all … all stayed quiet. And sometimes I wanted to just tell you what I knew, for parity. But also I found myself *enjoying* that you didn't know I knew. It was a power, of sorts. When you hurt me, knowing what you'd done to each other lessened the pain and reminded me that you weren't perfect.'

Cady had no idea if Danson was telling the truth, but that he had lost his mind was no longer in question. Any plan to placate or reason with him was out the window. All they could do was not make things worse.

After a while, he said, 'You understand, I pushed her for you. To free you from her. Because I loved you.'

'Mate, you...' Winston said, but coked up or not, he stopped himself finishing the thought.

'If you love us so much, why are we here?' Femi asked through barely open lips.

'I've already told you. I want the truth.'

Femi raised his voice. 'You already know everything.'

'No. I don't.' He looked at Naz, and then at Cady.

Cady didn't like that one bit. Especially given Eloise had supposedly singled *Cady* out as being the worst of them. That's what Danson had said. The worst. Which had to be a mistake, like this supposed secret Naseem knew. The worst thing she'd ever done in her whole life was ... well, was probably the way she treated Tom, wasn't it? The way she shot down any of his concerns, insisting to him that there was no danger at all, even when she knew damn well that there had been danger. But Danson didn't care about that.

The irony of it all wasn't lost on her. God, had she not tuned Tom out so completely, she wouldn't be up here. She'd have listened to her gut when it started trying to tell her Danson didn't look well. That it was a little bit strange him bringing them all together this way. And that the park looked not unfinished but abandoned. All because she didn't want anything to slow her down. To get in the way of her hard-won success. Not even love. Not even her own safety.

'What did Naz tell Eloise about me, Danson?' Cady said. 'Whatever it was, I can guarantee it was rubbish. I've never done anything to anyone.'

'We loved you, too,' Naz said, trying to assert control in

spite of her failing voice. 'We never did anything to deserve this.'

'Do you think you are good people, then?' Danson said.

'Good?' Femi shook his head. 'We're normal, flawed human beings, Dan. Like you, like everyone.'

Danson considered this. His hand rose, and his fingers began their triple meter on the base of his skull. 'Let me ask you all a question. Is Eloise alive or dead?'

No one said a thing. Cady had a feeling someone, somewhere, had told her that she had died. It might even have been Danson. But why wasn't she more certain? Now it seemed vital that they know, Cady cursed herself for never having been more curious over the years.

Of course, she knew Eloise Draclin had survived her dreadful fall, at least in a sense. But her injuries had been severe – 'bones like marbles in a sock' a fellow student had tastelessly commented afterwards. Her brain injuries left her in what the doctors called a minimally conscious state, which had a technical definition involving brain scans, but boiled down to the rare occasions Eloise would show signs of recognising her own name, or be able to wiggle her index finger to answer a basic question. She wasn't really conscious the majority of the time, and she wasn't locked in. Fleetingly, though, some part of her would return.

For the time they were at university, the college council organised a fundraiser and visits to the care home where she ended up. Eloise's mum encouraged those visits at the start, when there was some hope about her consciousness edging away from minimal. Cady went twice with The No Tomorrows Club during their second year. In the third year she went once, with Danson.

Looking back on that now, what had the others all been

thinking in that room while Eloise lay there? At the time, Cady assumed they didn't come in the third year because it was too much for them. But Winston, Femi and Naz must have been so relieved about what happened, and also terrified about her returning. Had they really sung songs from *Little Shop* to her on that first visit, to stimulate her brain activity – how ridiculous. The whole time the others would have been silently praying for her to stay still. While Danson… Oh, it didn't bear thinking about.

Her head ached at the temple, and she drew up a hand to rub the skin there. Everything she'd been through at university and beyond needed re-evaluation. All the years they'd lived together in each others' pockets. Celebrating wins, commiserating losses.

In the second year, when Femi's dad had shown up unexpectedly, and they'd all had to go to dinner with him and pretend to be medics. Winston, who'd done absolutely no acting in his life, had put on an incredible show.

Or in the run-up to finals in the third year, when there had been an outbreak of head lice in their shared house, and their initial disgust had turned into much needed comradery and an oddly life-affirming trip to the pharmacy, which culminated in them all sitting in the bathroom together, gently combing eggs out of each other's hair. God, she'd sat in Danson's lap then, hadn't she? Found his fingers on her scalp unexpectedly blissful, had become ever-so-slightly aroused. That had been the year Femi had made a calendar of all their exams and plotted out all the times they'd be free to hang out and de-stress. It had hung in the kitchen, and Cady secretly suspected he'd done it partly to help her, because the year before she'd muddled up the dates of her exams and nearly missed one.

Or in that second year of living together in London, when

they'd gone up to Edinburgh to put on a show Naz had written, and turned the misery of their smelly accommodation and single lukewarm review into a triumph by laughing every second of every day they were there. So many beautiful memories, all tinted darkly now by this new lens through which Danson had forced them to look.

'None of you know, do you?' Danson said. 'Once it was obvious she wasn't coming back, she may as well have been dead to you.'

Femi snorted a laugh. 'You think we're bad people for not visiting her? After what she did to us.'

'No, you all knew I had feelings for her. Or at least you did once.' He let them consume this for a moment. 'And I'm just surprised not one of you kept tabs on her. Just in case. At least in the years after university. Maybe not Cady, and maybe not you, Femi, because your family were bound to find out about your little lie eventually.' Femi only glared, giving away nothing. 'But no, why would any of you keep tabs on her? You're all so used to things working out in your favour, that it wouldn't have crossed your minds that she might come back. Because under all your sad faces, you were delighted, weren't you? All your secrets locked in her head. Did any of you think about finishing her off? Maybe sneaking in and putting a pillow over her face? I bet you did.'

'Did you?' Femi said.

Danson stared back at Femi, his face impassive.

'I would have stood by what I'd done,' he said. 'For the longest time, I would have.' He reached over and picked up the wooden chest he'd brought with him. 'But I really *was* shit at magic. And as the years went by at Chamberlain, I did start to have doubts about what I'd done. And about all of you. I watched the way you carried your secrets so easily. Adept little liars, getting on with your successful little lives like you'd learned nothing. And, every day, I woke up seeing the shock and betrayal on her face just before she went over.

'I remember those days, too,' Cady said. 'Whatever went on in secret, we still all loved each other. None of that was fake.' Did she really believe that any more, though? God knew what strange guilt, or obligation, or regret might have bound the others. And why wouldn't Naz tell her the secret she'd given Eloise? Like she wanted to convince herself, though, she continued, 'Those second and third years were good years, Danson.'

'Maybe,' he said. 'But what about afterwards?'

Cady couldn't keep hold of his gaze, it was too intense. She looked down at her lap and shook her head. 'I was always there for you.'

'In retrospect,' he said, 'I suspect maybe Eloise did love me after all. Perhaps she had just been scared of her feelings for me. Found them too … oppressive. I talked to her boyfriend, Rafael, years later. He didn't even remember her. Funny. You, on the other hand. *You*. I tried killing her for you, and you didn't even understand you had a guardian angel in your midst.'

'Sounds to me like you tried killing her because she spurned you, mate,' Femi said, and shook his head. 'Very incel-y.'

Cady cringed, not sure what Femi hoped to gain by goading him. He might not have studied medicine, but he damn sure knew what the Hippocratic oath was.

'Believe that, if you want.' Danson sighed and pulled himself to his feet using the mesh. 'It's getting much later than I intended, guys. I have somewhere to be and lots still to do.'

Femi sat up bolt upright. 'Where?'

'What do you mean?' Naz said, distressed.

Danson shushed them. 'Calm down. Calm down. I'm not going to just leave you here.' He bent over and picked up the chest he'd brought with him.

'What is that?' Winston said, unable to keep the dread from his voice.

'This?' He glanced down at his hands. The chest was ten centimetres across and made from a thick, unvarnished wood. 'This is a mystery box. I used to build them in that basement of Churchill House, for my shows, do you remember? They were never any good, but I think this one is.'

'So, there's something inside?' Cady said.

'Ah, you remember?'

'What's in it?' Femi said.

'Your way out. Do you remember I told you about the key slot for the restraints? It's a bit of plastic that looks like an oversized credit card.'

Cady and Femi both looked at that dark slot in the front wall of the car and understood Danson's game. Femi reached forwards, his hand still far from the opening. 'I can't even reach it.'

'You'd have to do it with your feet, I imagine. But it *is* doable. I put a lot of thought into all this. Years, really. And once the release key is inside that slot, up go the restraints. Easy.'

'So how do we get it?' Femi said.

'Well, to open the box, I need you all to dig deep into yourselves. I'm not saying it's going to be easy, but I think between you, you can do it. You see, over the years I've been testing you. I gave each of you a test of your character and of your supposed love for me.'

'You're fucking joking,' Naz said.

'You all failed it, which is why you're here. But I'm hoping by the time you manage to escape, you'll have learned something important. Something that can benefit you and the world after I'm long gone.'

'This is crazy,' Femi said. 'You must know that.'

'I do. I do. But love is fucking crazy, isn't it? Did Shakespeare say that, Naz? Also, you lot were all so obsessed with legacy, weren't you? It rubbed off on me, definitely. But my legacy won't be Dreamland anymore, will it? But it might be saving your souls.' He smiled in a way that had genuine warmth, which only made what he said more upsetting. 'I'm your guardian angel, okay? And this is your chance to finally *slow down* and understand who you really are. And the damage you do.'

'You're not leaving us here, you bastard,' Femi said. He was working himself up again, and that really wasn't going to help.

'How do we get into the box?' Cady asked quickly.

He brought up the box to the level of his face. 'You'll see there are four combination locks on the front. Each has six numbers. They correspond to a month and a year. Each lock belongs to one of you, and the specific time I tested you in the years after university. From left to right it's in alphabetical order. So Cady, the first lock belongs to you. Winston, yours is the last. Easy, isn't it?'

'I don't understand,' Cady said. 'What do you mean, you tested us? Tested us how?'

'Cady, are you stalling for time? I told you. I tested your love. Now, part of me suspects you don't even remember. That's sort of what the game is. Your one chance of redemption is that you do. That at least I wasn't completely invisible to you, and that there is hope. That you're not what Eloise Draclin always insisted to me you were. If you can remember the test, and when it was, you can open all four locks and be free. If not, you'll die here knowing the truth.'

'Fine,' Femi said. 'Give us the box and go.'

Danson stared at Femi a moment. 'I know you're thinking maybe you'll smash open the box. Or perhaps you'll just try all the combinations through the night in the hope you can crack them by morning. But unfortunately, I've built the box in quite a clever way. So do those things at your peril. You must enter the correct date the first time of asking, otherwise everything inside will be destroyed.'

'Destroyed how?' Cady said.

'Like I said, it's a very clever box. And you don't want to find that out. Treat it like you'd treat a baby. Or a bomb.'

'Wait,' Naz said. 'You're entrusting our lives to remembering some random encounter with you.'

'Random,' he said. 'Interesting word. Put it this way, if you were the people you think you are, you *would* remember.'

'We're fucked,' Winston cried out, laughing bitterly.

'No, don't be like that,' Danson said. 'I've watched each one of you go on to live the dreams we all used to talk about. I was the only one who…'

Danson cut himself off and slowly turned towards the front of the coaster. Cady, who had been working herself up to ask him one last time what Naz had told Eloise before he went, turned her head in that direction and immediately saw what had silenced him.

Two pinpricks of light shone through the black sheet draped over the desert, at about where the road had tapered towards the horizon. They all stared in silence, and very slowly the lights grew brighter and bigger. A car was heading *towards* Dreamland.

Danson's composure fell away in an instant. He hurriedly put down the box on the walkway. 'All of you stay quiet.' He started to walk away and briefly turned back. 'I'm deadly serious. If you start making a noise, there will be consequences. I have a gun down there, and trust me, I'll use it.'

CADY

Friday 21st June, 11.32pm
Celsius: 33°, Fahrenheit: 91.4°

He'd stood down his staff, including security at both gates. Cady understood now why that was: he hadn't wanted anyone noticing that he'd left the park without the four people who had gone in earlier. Which meant perhaps someone, or preferably a group of someones, had chanced their luck driving down to get a look at the secret new amusement park. Or maybe it was one of the staff, coming back to retrieve an item they'd left behind. Or maybe, in a perfect world – please, please let it be that world – their earlier cries had been heard on the desert wind, and the police were here to investigate.

Danson's reaction had said it all. This wasn't part of the plan. And that meant it might be their one chance to escape.

Whatever grievances they now held against each other, they had to put them aside to make the most of this.

'So, when do we start yelling?' Winston said, Danson comfortably out of earshot.

'You're not worried about him shooting someone, if we do?' Naz spoke so softly that Cady struggled to hear her.

'He's going to cook us alive, Naz,' Winston said. 'We're sitting ducks here. At least whoever is down there has a fair chance, if we warn them. There might be a whole group. They could overpower him before he gets a shot off.'

They watched the car getting closer. It showed no signs of slowing down or turning around.

'I agree,' Femi said. 'He's not exactly at fighting weight, either. And I think he was bluffing about the gun. He's a terrible actor. In fact, do you guys even believe any of what he said just now? That he pushed Eloise off the porter's lodge. And he kept it all a secret. That they were having some sort of relationship that none of us knew about and saw neither hide nor hair of. I don't know. Part of me wonders if it's all a power trip. Mind games to give us a good scare. A bit of showmanship. Is he really going to leave us here to die horribly? Is he really a killer? Danson? Really?'

'I believe him,' Winston said, in a hoarse monotone. 'But I still think we need to take our chance.'

Cady turned to Femi. 'Why wouldn't you believe him? I think we need to consider what we do very carefully. I'm not saying we don't call for help, but he is dangerous, Femi. Even if he is bluffing about some of it, already what he's done to us, to imprison us this way, it's insane. Can't you feel that? Who knows what he's capable of.'

'Obviously all of it is insane. He had some chip on his shoulder that he's got all mixed up with Eloise's death and the fact he's going to die, and he's taking it out on us. But look, he's leaving us this magic box of his, isn't he? So clearly he intends to eventually let us out. If we yell, he probably won't do anything but run off. His plan's been ruined. As usual with him, he's overestimated his ability.'

'And you're happy risking all this with someone else's life?' Cady said. 'Without any discussion.'

'I can't believe after everything,' Naz said, 'you're still going to be this cocksure.'

'I'm just stating my opinion,' Femi said.

'You don't get to have an opinion,' Naz yelled. In a calmer voice, she continued, 'If we start yelling after he's explicitly said we shouldn't, he might take the *mystery* box away. Or he might not even come back up again. Or, what if this visitor and him fight and hurt each other? And they are both stuck down there?'

'That's a good point,' Winston said, perhaps just to side against Femi now.

Femi slammed his fist on his plastic arm rest. 'God, damn it. I'm not going to let you all sit here like meek little lambs when the universe has opened the slaughterhouse door.'

'Don't yell,' Winston said. 'They have a point. If, like you say, he plans to let us go eventually, why not let it play out?'

'Because what if he leaves us and his little box doesn't work? Is that out of the question, given he's lost the plot? Given how those boxes he made never bloody worked.' Femi shook his head. 'Come on, guys. There's no debate here really.'

'Femi, please,' Cady said, irritated that he was even trying to assert his dominance again, let alone choosing this exact moment. 'We're just thinking this through.'

A stillness permeated the bubble created by the light.

Eventually, one of Winston's arms appeared above his seat. 'Okay, well I still vote we say something.'

'Just to be clear,' Femi said. 'This isn't a vote. When that car gets within reach, I'm yelling my head off. I've let you all down in the past, but not now.'

'And you'll take the blame, if it goes wrong?' Naz said.

'I'm not scared of owning my mistakes. By the way, how's your back feeling, Naz? You got another day or two in you?'

'It's numb, Femi.' She paused. 'And I'm scared. But not so much we do something stupid.'

They all watched the car approach, and it entered into the area that must have been the large car park at the front. It very slowly circled, and appeared at one point to be turning around, prompting Femi to mutter *no, no, no* like an incantation. It was hard to tell at this height and distance, in the dark, through the glare of the emergency light, but the car appeared to take one of the dirt roads into the park itself. It briefly vanished, disappearing behind the city of tents and empty buildings. When it became visible again, it was right at the foot of the coaster. Before its lights switched off, and the park returned to darkness, Cady was able to make out the shape and colour of the vehicle. From this height, it reminded her of the micro-machine toy cars Robbie had collected, the ones her mum and dad used to always tread on and playfully threaten to throw away. It was maybe a saloon. A white saloon.

Cady felt a sudden sinking sensation and reached down instinctively to her pocket. Her empty pocket.

'Shall we, then?' Winston said, peering through the gap at Femi, sealing their uneasy alliance.

'Think so,' Femi replied.

Jag

Growing up, Jag's elders had always taught him to be fearful of snakes. But he had always been curious, often wandering the fields of his grandfather's farm seeking an encounter. After dropping off the lady at Dreamland, Hysteria had slithered through his mind. Its colours, its size, the way it commanded the skyline like a great serpent god. Stunned but regretful, he'd pulled over twice on the access road to look back at the gigantic coaster. How lovely it would have been to take a photograph, but he had been given explicit instructions not to, so his phone remained in his pocket.

But perhaps he should have said *yes* when she had offered to ask if he could ride it. But he'd made the error as a younger man of mistaking politeness for kindness. He'd once been so thirsty on a job, he'd mentioned it to a wealthy client. They'd then insisted he stop and refill his water bottle. Later, he discovered the man told Jag's bosses, and his bosses fired him.

Dreamland far behind him, Jag pulled over for petrol on the way back to base. He opened the rear door and checked the back seat, something he usually did as soon as a client left but had been too awestruck earlier. Hidden partially by the seat-belt socket, he found a circular wooden object that must have belonged to the lady he'd dropped off. He picked it up and examined it in the harsh light of the forecourt. The wood was engraved with numbers and letters, a C and an E. Cady. It opened like a shell, revealing two mirrors.

He had to yank the reins on his heart, which very much interpreted this as a sign, perhaps from the Goddess Saraswati, that something important awaited him back at Hysteria. But Jag wasn't a fool, and he didn't want to confuse his own desires with those of a deity.

Still, he sat in the car for a while. He drank a coffee and rested, watching the slow drip of a tap sticking out of the building's side. It was a quiet night, and unless he got a big enough job through, he might just go home. But there was still a chance the lady from Dreamland might request him for the return journey. So he messaged Tariq asking if anyone had called. No one had.

It wasn't as if she'd invite him to ride now if he went back. He'd missed his chance. Still, it would be nice to see the coaster again. Up against the night sky. He used to go looking for kraits at night. That was when they liked to hunt.

Perhaps he might drive back to Dreamland then, take Cady her mirror. It would be an expense he'd have to bear himself, if he didn't get the job to pick her up.

It had just gone ten o'clock. It would take him an hour to

get back there. Or perhaps it wouldn't this time. If they let him through, there were no restrictions on that road, he could...

Ah, but that was the thing. The security would stop him and likely take the mirror from him to give the lady on her departure. Why would *he* need to drive all that way down? And he needed to consider that it had been four hours or so since he drove away from the park. She might have left already.

Still, at least the mirror would be with people who knew her. Maybe security would let him park at the entrance and wait there in case he still got a call to collect her. They'd also know if she'd left or not.

Yes, he'd go there. He took out his phone and switched off the GPS. He was sure Tariq wouldn't kick up that much of a fuss if he saw him driving back, but better safe than sorry.

He came off the slip road and found the booth empty. The barrier was down, but there was room to go around it if he wanted. After a good ten minutes of drumming his steering wheel and staring out at the headlight-illuminated tarmac, he depressed the accelerator. Even with his full beams on he could see only road and the desert's edges. It was like driving into oil. Above the stars burned but ahead there was only blackness.

Earlier he'd been excited to make this drive. Now he was nervous. But he wasn't doing anything wrong, really. He was being helpful.

An eternity later, the booth at the end of the access road emerged from the darkness. Jag drove into the car park by memory and skirted the front edge. Somewhere deep within he saw light. It shone like a halo above some shadowy obstacle. He found an unmarked road and went hunting the source, all the while suspecting his every movement, as well as his number plate, was being picked up on security cameras. Still, no one stopped him, and when he found what he was looking for he pulled over and realised he was at the foot of Hysteria. Like it was calling him.

Tentatively, heart racing, he stepped out of the car clutching the mirror. Above him loomed the lift hill. His stomach flipped trying to comprehend its size and imagining the plummet from that drop.

'Hello,' a voice called. Jag headed towards it, in the direction of the ride entrance and that ring of light coming from behind the ride's main building. Walking towards him was a very tall, very pale man in a blazer. He had an almost rectangular head anchored by a strong jaw. He looked official.

'Can I help you?'

Jag and the man approached one another. At first, Jag was reminded of a scarecrow, but when he drew close he sensed something in the man's walk that felt hostile. Snake-like. Hunting him in the dark. But that was a childish thought. Besides, he wasn't afraid of snakes – they were more afraid of you.

'I'm very sorry,' he said. 'I'm looking for a woman, Cady. She left something in my car. I dropped her here tonight. Earlier tonight.'

The tall man came to a stop before him and smiled. It wasn't a very nice smile. His forehead was dappled with sweat beads and, when he spoke, he struggled for breath. 'I see. Yes, Cady is one of our VIPs tonight. If you hand it to me, I'll make sure she gets it.'

Jag hesitated. He didn't trust this man. And hadn't he been

hoping to see her in person again? 'I'm very sorry, I would like to confirm it is hers first, as it may belong to another of my passengers.'

The tall man held out a hand. It was shaking. 'May I see it?'

Reluctantly, he gave him the mirror. After inspecting it, he nodded. 'It has her initials on and her birthday. I'd say it's hers.'

Jag nodded. 'Would it be at all possible to give it to her in person?'

'Can I ask your name?' Venomous words, designed to get Jag to back off. To go home.

Jag shook his head. He'd already come here without permission. Was perhaps even trespassing now. This man could make a lot of trouble for him. He certainly did not want to lose his job or end up getting arrested. He had too much to lose. His family back in India relied on him. 'It's fine. I can leave it with you, if it's not possible to do it myself.'

He thanked the tall man and walked back to the car, pleased to be putting some distance between them, but also disappointed he hadn't seen Cady again. At least he hadn't gotten in trouble, though. At least—

A sound caught his attention. Voices calling from far, far above him. He looked up. The voices were faint, drifting in and out of audibility on the breeze. But no, they weren't calling. That sounded like yelling. Anxious and urgent. Jag looked up and cocked his head to one side. He turned and walked towards Hysteria.

Help. He could hear that word, couldn't he? And screaming now. But not the joyful screams that would occasionally drift over from Nicco Park when he'd been a child. And why wasn't it running? Why couldn't he hear any clacking sounds of the lift hill, or see the train whizzing around the track, sections of which were all around him?

'Did you really come all this way to return a mirror?'

The voice was right behind him. He jumped and spun around. The tall man stood between him and the door of the Mercedes.

'Of course.'

'Which company are you from? Elite? Desert Cars?'

'Desert VIP.'

'Do they know you're here?'

Jag smiled. 'I did this on my own time, so there is no issue. The lady, Cady, seemed nice so I wanted to return her belongings.' The man stared and said nothing. Above, the shouting continued. 'She … was very kind. She even said she would ask if I could ride it. But of course, I told her not to. Even though I love roller coasters very much.'

'You do?'

'Yes, I've been very excited about Dreamland opening. I've followed what I can online.'

'So did you take any pictures?'

He held up both of his hands. 'No, not at all. We were instructed not to.'

'Can I see your phone?'

Jag didn't know what to say. The cries above him sounded even more agitated than before. 'I can show you my phone.' It didn't feel right. But he walked over to the car and unlocked it with the fob.

The tall man followed and opened the door for him and said, 'I bet you're wondering what all that racket up there is.'

Jag leaned in, holding his breath while he reached into the side compartment. He kept expecting the door to slam him in the side. When his fingers grasped the phone, he jerked himself out.

'Did Cady tell you why she was coming here?' the tall man asked.

'No.'

'We're doing some last-minute tests tonight. I'm measuring the sound of the coaster from different points in the park. The screaming and shouting.'

'Oh,' Jag said, and smiled with sudden relief. That made perfect sense, of course. 'They are up there now?'

'At the very top. We need to know if the sound carries and if so, how loudly.'

'Ah yes.' He told him about the screams from Nicco Park. The tall man nodded politely before gesturing for the phone. Jag typed in his code, opened his photo app and confidently handed it over. 'Please look. I didn't take a single picture. I know this is a top-secret project.'

The man was nodding. 'I'm impressed. What was your name again?'

'It's Jag, sir.'

'Well Jag, you like roller coasters, do you?'

'Very much.'

'Do you want to ride Hysteria, then?'

His calves and thighs complained with every step now, and he was grateful that the dark concealed how high up they really were. He wasn't scared of heights usually, but out here he felt exposed. He pressed his body to the handrail on the left, and he gripped it tightly. It had been a long time since he'd needed an inhaler, but he'd have loved one right now. No breath seemed sufficiently deep. The yelling far up ahead was more sporadic, but he was close enough to hear what they were saying and he started to wonder if he'd made a terrible error. The cries of *help* and *we're stuck* and *he's dangerous* sounded very genuine.

'They're old friends of mine just messing around,' the tall man said when Jag paused and looked back. Jag didn't entirely believe him. Something was off in the way he carried himself. The guy had still got his phone, claiming it might fly out when he rode the coaster down. That was likely true, but still, it made him feel vulnerable and paranoid.

But if he went back now, he might cause offence. Jeopardise his job and cost him the opportunity of a lifetime. They were probably messing around, like he said.

Yet the higher he climbed, the stranger the whole idea of having to walk up here instead of riding it from the start became. On the ground he'd been too excited to question why the car couldn't just come back down and go back up with him inside. He'd just accepted the man's words that it was to be the last drop of the night.

'I think I've changed my mind,' Jag said, turning to face the tall man.

'Don't be silly,' he said. 'We're nearly there.'

Jag paused, braced to stand his ground, and instead remembered how regretful he'd been earlier. He turned again and kept climbing. They reached a flat section of walkway at the very top of the ride, and the train came into view in the light of a brilliant white emergency light. The people inside, four of them, clearly saw him now.

'Oh my God,' a man said, 'Mate, he's trapped us here. He's trying to kill us.'

'Please help us,' a woman screamed. 'Stop him.'

Jag froze and stared at the people looking back. Two men. Two women. All of their eyes were wide and pleading. But what could he do? He was five foot eight. He abhorred violence and had only ever been in fights started by others.

'Jag.' That was the woman. Cady. 'We don't have time. Believe us, he really is dangerous. Help us, please.'

Still clutching the rail, he twisted again to look back. 'What is happening here? Are they still messing—'

The tall man was closing the distance between them with a handgun in his outstretched hand. On instinct Jag raised his arms. Jag was made to walk until he reached the front car.

'I'm sorry, Jag, my friend. Wrong place, wrong, wrong. wrong time. He brought back your mirror, Cady.'

'Jag,' the white man sitting in the very front seat said, 'he is planning to kill us. He wants us to burn in the sun unless we—'

'None of that is true,' the tall man said, sounding genuinely hurt.

'He'll kill us all,' the strong-looking man in the second car said. 'You, too. So, unless you want that, stop him.'

'What did I specifically say to you all?' the tall man said. 'Don't listen to them, Jag. They're being dramatic. They also aren't taking me very seriously, which is a problem. I suggest you do, Jag. Now, this gun is loaded, so please do as I ask. Can you stand on the edge there by the second car. You'll have to let go of the handrail. Let go of it and walk to the edge facing the car please. Keep your hands up.'

'You're imprisoning him up here, too?' the girl sitting beside the white man asked.

'Do it now, Jag.'

Jag reluctantly let go of the rail. His whole upper body shook. He shuffled across the stairs, keeping his focus on his inexpensive dress shoes and the corrugated surface underneath. The man closed the distance between them, and for a head-swimming moment Jag believed he might be able to knock the gun from his grip and push him over. Maybe into the gap between the rails and stairs. Was he meant to? Was that why he'd been sent back here? But this would kill the man, and he didn't—

Hands pressed against his back. He cried out.

'Steady,' the tall man said. 'I'm just searching you.'

But Jag travelled light. The man retrieved the fob for the car and continued past him along the walkway so he was closer to the front of the train. He was still aiming the gun with both his hands on the handle. He didn't look practised at this. Perhaps he had no intention to shoot. Could Jag run now? Escape and get help? His way was clear.

'Jag, please look at the car, not at me. Thank you. Does your car have any sort of tracking device. I'm going to check anyway, but this will help me.'

'No, it doesn't,' he said, trying not to look down, pushing with his legs to keep them extra straight and steady. If the man wanted him to cross the metre-wide gap to the car he wasn't sure he could. Feeling that more information might help his situation, he added, 'We all ask for it, but they won't pay.'

'And is the phone you gave me your work one or home?'

'It's both.'

'Do you have children?'

He turned his head to the man, who had moved to the left side. 'Children? No, I don't have children.'

'Face the car, please.'

'Jag,' Cady said. 'Run, now.'

'What about a wife?' Jag shook his head. 'Or a girlfriend?'

'Jag. Run, for God's sake.'

'Not a... There is a girl I grew up with called Mishti. She is not my girlfriend, but...'

He was still picturing her, smiling at him from above a row of wheat in his grandfather's fields, hair tied back and smile so mischievous, when the snake struck the back of his head.

CADY

Saturday 22nd June, 12.13am
Celsius: 33°, Fahrenheit: 91.4°

It all happened so quickly. The gun fired and everyone cried out. Jag's head jerked backwards and he collapsed onto the walkway. Those in the car, including Cady, began shouting at Danson, who stood staring at Jag like he hadn't meant to fire the gun, which he still held out in front of him.

Jag wasn't dead, though. He lay on his side, body moving in such a way that it looked as if he intended to get up. Danson stepped away from the handrail and approached him.

Bang. Bang.

Cady shut her eyes and hunched her shoulders, the gunfire painfully loud. Jag had been struck again, but he still wasn't dead. He initially rolled towards the handrail, but regrettably rolled the other way, no longer cognisant of where he was.

The lovely man who'd driven her here, who had been so excited about one day getting the chance to plummet from this 200-metre-high structure, fell through the gap between the walkway and the train.

Someone yelled 'No', and Cady realised after that it was her. Naz was asking what was happening. She couldn't twist around to see.

'You killed him,' Femi yelled. 'You … you…'

Cady looked back at Danson and realised that somehow Femi now had a grip on his arm. She'd missed whatever had happened, but given the way he still held the gun in his right hand, his left must have been flung outwards by the gun's recoil.

'Let go, Femi,' Danson said, teetering on the brink of the gap himself.

Femi wasn't having any of it. He yanked Danson, who had to jump across the gap or risk following Jag.

'No,' Cady shouted.

Danson crashed against the car, and Femi threw his enormous right arm around his neck and pulled him to his chest. Danson wound up bent over the car edge backwards, feet on the rail, hands clutching the car sides. The gun fell from Danson's hand and clattered to the floor by Cady's feet.

'You're going nowhere,' Femi said, an enormous, crazed grin stretching his face. He punched Danson twice in his ribs. Danson grunted, but he didn't cry out.

Cady picked up the gun with her feet and passed it carefully up to her hands. Its weight gave her hope. It was over now, surely.

She pointed it at Danson shakily but steadied her aim with her non-trigger hand.

Ashes to ashes, dust to dust, finger to finger, thumb to thumb.

She'd learned that at the shooting range by Tom's old place in Wycombe. They'd gone there on a date. Yes, she could use the gun, if needed – but from this distance it was risky, especially with Femi in the way.

'Well done,' Danson said. 'You have me. Now what?'

'You just killed a man,' Femi said.

'No, you killed him.' Danson's voice strained against the arm at his throat. 'I told you not to make a sound. You didn't listen. I was seconds from sending him away. But I couldn't once he heard you, could I?' Femi yanked him and the side of the car pressed further into Danson's back. He growled.

'He was a bloody kid, Danson,' Cady said, no longer able to restrain herself. Her hands began to shake at the memory of his youthful, open face, as his stories of childhood roller coaster dreams filled her mind. He'd never get to ride Hysteria. He'd never get to do anything now. And all because he'd been kind enough to return her mirror. Why hadn't she checked when she got out, for God's sake? Why was she so bloody self-involved?

'I didn't want to shoot him, Cady. I wanted you to be quiet. But I made my mind up long ago that what happens here *must* happen now, no matter what. And once he heard you... Well, better he die that way than being trapped here in the sun alongside you.' Femi punched him twice in the head. Danson absorbed the blows almost silently, and after a moment spoke with eerie composure. 'So, what is your plan, Femi? Beat me to death? Shoot me? Throw me off?'

Femi started shaking his head from side to side, ensnared by his own thoughts but unable to speak.

'Perhaps I should make it clear,' Danson said, 'nothing in

this park ever happened without me. I oversaw and organised every team, every staff member, every diary. There is no one coming here to save you. Your only hope is in that box on the other side of the gap. So kill me. You'll never get out.'

'You didn't expect that guy, though,' Winston said. 'And he came anyway. So maybe there'll be others.'

'You want to roll the dice,' Danson said. 'Do it.'

No one spoke. Cady's arms began to ache a little from holding out the gun. She briefly let go and wiped a tear from her cheek. The box still sat on the steps, not even near the gap but pushed up against the far edge. They couldn't reach it without Danson. But they had an advantage now in another way.

'Let him go, Fem,' Cady said.

His head jerked left. 'What?'

'Let him jump back over and get the box. He can open it for us and give us the key right now. Otherwise, I shoot him.'

'That's not—' Danson cut himself off. 'You have that in you, do you, Cady?'

'After what you just did? I bloody think I do, yes.'

'If she doesn't, I do,' Winston said.

'Me too,' Naz said.

'Oh, now you're a team. Avengers assemble. Well ... all that's ... sad to hear. Understandable ... but I think, once all is clear, you might come to under—'

Femi yanked him back again, harder than ever, and this time Danson did yell with pain as the small of his back bent over the fibreglass side.

'Don't you dare say we'll understand this.' Spit flew from Femi's lips. 'Don't you dare.'

Danson didn't respond. The only sound he made was his

heavy, agitated breathing. A stream of snot escaped from one nostril.

'This is what happens,' Femi said. 'I'm going to count to three and let go. You jump over and—'

'I'll need you to hold my hand,' Danson said, voice compressed but still so unerringly calm. Almost mirthful.

'Once you get over there, open the box. Don't run, or we shoot. Don't make the box destroy the key. Just sit down as soon as you get over, open it, and hand over the key. Understood?'

'Yes, but I'm going to die anyway, Femi. Why would I care?'

'I'm gambling on you still having things to do,' he said. 'Rubbish to spout at us.'

He smiled like he enjoyed being out-thought. 'You're cleverer than you come across, Fem. I always forget that.'

'Repeat it,' Femi said, 'What are you going to do?'

'I'm going to step over. Sit down. And not run. And I'm going to get the box for you.'

'Or.'

'Or Cady will shoot me.'

Femi nodded and murmured his content. But he didn't let him go. 'I don't trust him,' he said eventually.

'I thought you had it all worked out,' Danson said.

'Cady,' Femi said, 'give me your cardigan.'

She looked down to where it was tied around her waist and reached down to unknot it with one hand. 'Why?'

'Just trust me.'

She wasn't sure she did. Not entirely. If they did end up here when the sun came up, the cardigan might be the only way she could shield herself. But they needed to stick together, didn't they? And now more than ever they needed a united front. She freed her cardigan and Femi told her to put it on his lap. Then he told Danson he was going to let him go, so if he didn't want to fall, he had to clutch the side of the car.

'Keep the gun on him,' he said.

Femi let go and Danson stood to his full height pressed up against the outside of the car. Femi grabbed the sleeve of her cardigan and tied it around Danson's left wrist. Then he squeezed the knot, and Danson uttered a yelp. His foot slipped on the track and he fell.

But Femi grabbed his arm again and steadied him. The two of them exchanged a look that said they both knew they'd just gotten away with one.

'Okay, go,' Femi said, and Danson nodded once. He took a breath and stepped over, still clutching Femi's hand. The cardigan sleeve hung over the gap. When Femi let go, Danson stepped towards the box. His foot slipped on a drop of Jag's blood, and his free right arm shot out to steady himself. He looked back with wide eyes and a shocked smile. Then he edged towards the box again. Femi let the cardigan go inch by inch, its other sleeve wrapped around his right arm and wound into his clutched fist. Danson sat down beside the box, the cardigan now taut.

'Open it,' Winston said.

'Now,' Femi added.

Danson grinned and began to shake his head. 'I do have things to do still. I didn't lie. I've never lied to you. But in a way, if it ends here, so be it. There's poetry in it.'

Cady pushed the gun in her hands forward and knew instantly that she didn't want to shoot him. She really, really didn't.

But she still could. All she had to do was picture Jag.

Remember how touched and excited he'd been at the idea of possibly getting the return job to pick her up.

'I'm not going to open it for you,' Danson said. 'Shoot me if you want. Tonight, I was going to fly to the South of France. There was a camp site there my mum and I went to once and had the best time. I was going to remember her. And Eloise. And then take some pills. It'll be a shame to miss that, but so be it. In a way, it sort of proves my point about you all. You'd rather kill a man than look at yourselves in the mirror.'

His smile fell away and he stared straight at Cady.

'What do you want me to do?' Cady said to the others.

Of course, no one said a thing. Danson picked up the box and got up, moving more casually than before now he'd revealed his play. He walked right up to the edge of the gap and held out the box in his arms. The cardigan drooped towards the gap. Femi wound the cardigan around his wrist to reduce the slack, a reminder he was still in charge.

'Take it,' Danson said. Now he was staring at Femi. 'Give yourself a chance. It'll be such a waste if I drop it.'

The brief standoff ended with Femi giving Cady a last defeated glance. Then he reached out with both hands. Cady doubted Danson would drop it. But she was relieved that Femi hadn't called his bluff. That he believed in Danson's danger now. She lowered the gun.

Femi's fingers touched the box, but he couldn't grasp it. He tried to lean further over, and Danson moved towards him.

Then he slipped. Just a little, perhaps some residual blood on his sole, but he let go of the box. The box fell. Femi grabbed for it, touched it, but it bounced off him. And away, and down. Femi lunged for it as best he could, reaching over with his right arm. But that was the arm still tied to Danson.

'Femi—' Danson yelled.

But his cry was too late. Femi had yanked Danson off the side. Off the side and into the gap. The same gap through which Jag had fallen. Cady could only watch as Femi was yanked against the side of the car, caught in a tug of war between Danson and his restraint. A moment later came a tearing sound. Femi's shocked face swivelled around to look at her.

They stared at each other and listened to the gradually fading sound of Danson's terrified screams.

Femi lay against the side of the car for a few seconds. Cady held her breath.

'Oh, shit,' Winston said. 'Oh no, please tell me that didn't happen. Please, please, no.'

'He fell?' Naz asked.

When Femi finally heaved himself back into his seat, he turned to Cady again. He was breathing heavily, eyes wide and mouth open.

He wasn't holding the box.

He was still holding the cardigan, though. Or at least the torn cardigan sleeve. The rest of it was still tied to Danson.

PART THREE
STILL

Danson, Then

Went back to Mum's today for the first time since she went into hospital. Back to 'mine' now, I suppose. Found a half-finished cup of tea sat on the dining table and tidied it away, because no one else will now, will they? Just like no one else will sort the funeral or legal stuff.

Whole thing is a mess. I always thought she'd bought the flat outright with the lump sum from Dad's death, but no, she'd only been paying interest. And due to some legal issues with the leasehold, the place isn't worth the money she bought it for. If I sell it, I'll still owe the bank money unless I renounce the inheritance. But if I renounce the inheritance, any money Mum left gets swallowed up paying the mortgage debt and I won't get anything.

I've done the sums, and my best option is to work and live here until the leasehold stuff resolves eventually (which it might never do), at which point I can sell for a profit. But that basically means I can't move to London with the No Tomorrows lot after graduation. At least for now.

I got pretty angry with it all. I had that feeling I get when the injustice gets too much. The one that gets me into trouble. I paced around the flat, swarmed by memories of Mum, and of Dad. Especially of Dad. How bad he'd been to Mum. How he used to hit me at the back of the head if I said something stupid. Sort of a downward dig with his knuckles. Three times, knock, knock, knock. Hiding the bruises.

'Straw man, straw man, anything in there?'

I just used to live with the rage. Go for a run when it got really bad. Yeah, I cracked open Matty Tamplin's skull with a cricket bat when he said I stank once, but mostly I could outrun it. These days, though, I'm not as fast. Sometimes, it catches up with me.

I ended up on the floor in Mum's kitchen, looking up at the wonky cupboards all teary-eyed, thinking about that bloody cowboy builder, and about how much Dad had let her down over the years, with the drinking, with all his terrible jobs. She should have left him. We deserved better.

I balled my fists, staring at an old heirloom hanging on the wall, a framed story, calligraphy on glass. It recounts the folk tale of the lady who lived in a vinegar bottle. She isn't happy about her situation, and a passing fairy hears her complaints and magics her into a nice cottage. But eventually the lady grows unhappy with her cottage, and so the fairy puts her in a mansion. But then she complains about that, too, and so eventually the fairy, cross with her now, puts her back in the vinegar bottle.

Never liked the story. It was all about appreciating when you had enough. The lady is supposed to be bad for always wanting more. But I always thought the fairy was the real villain. Always listening in on you. Judging. Building you up and knocking you down.

What a terrible lesson. Don't strive! Know your place. Mum knew her place and look what it got her. Maybe I'd have ended up crushed like her had I not met the No Tomorrows. If I hadn't been inspired by their singular purpose and energy, and their constant belief in me. If we hadn't all committed to follow our dreams.

I feel a bit better now, but God, in that kitchen, feeling like I was going to be trapped in the West Midlands forever, miles away from the No Tomorrows and my dreams, I lost it. I took down the framed story and threw it on those badly grouted tiles where it smashed to pieces. And afterwards, while I was trying to calm down, I wondered if I might have more in common with that fairy than I'd thought.

Perhaps this was how she'd felt.

CADY

Saturday 22nd June, 12.26am
Celsius: 32°, Fahrenheit: 89.6°

Hysteria swayed, more violently than it had before, and Cady braced to grab the restraint handles on instinct. The structure groaned. The weathervane skirled. Mourning sounds.

Femi's mouth hadn't closed since Danson fell only moments before. Now, a word fell out. 'I…' He shook his head.

'What happened?' Cady said, desperate for him to confirm the box hadn't gone over the edge.

'I… I… don't know. It was too quick.'

'What happened to the box, Femi?' Naz said. 'What happened?'

'I don't know.'

'Oh, you've killed us, haven't you, you silly bastard? You've actually killed us.'

'Naz. I...'

'It was an accident,' Cady said, confident that was what she'd seen. 'Where's the box, Femi? Has it gone?' When he shook his head, she held back a swell of relief.

'No, I got my fingers to it. I wedged it against the side... I had it. But it dropped down on to the track.'

'I can see it,' Winston said. 'It's hanging over the gap right beneath you. We're cooked.'

'There has to be a way to get it,' Femi said, leaning over the side to see for himself.

'I doubt it. Unless you could lasso it somehow. If you dropped, like, something down.'

Like a cardigan? Only that had gone over the edge with Danson, hadn't it? As had all their hopes of escaping. Because Danson was dead. He couldn't have survived the fall, and any doubts they might initially have tried to entertain were unsustainable once they heard and felt him strike some hard part of Hysteria on the way down. The impact had reverberated through the car floor.

'Jesus,' Winston said, the seriousness of their new predicament hitting him.

A hopeless silence descended on the remaining members of The No Tomorrows Club. Cady manoeuvred the gun back to the floor and closed her eyes, trying to control her rapid breathing. A cocktail of fear and adrenaline charged through her body. What the hell were they going to do?

It was some time before Femi, in a small voice, said, 'I... I'm sorry, guys.' Realising the other two might not be able to hear him, he spoke up and repeated, 'I'm so sorry. I didn't mean for him...'

'I can't hold it anymore,' Naz said.

'Hold what?' Winston said, and then he understood. 'Oh.'

'I know how this might sound,' Femi said, bereft of any of his usual swagger, 'but we might want to consider trying to preserve—'

'I am not drinking my own piss, Femi,' Naz yelled.

So Winston helped her get her dress up and supported her back while she tried to shuffle down again to relieve herself over the edge of the seat. It hurt her, and it took some time. And from the sounds of her whined, 'Noooooo,' it hadn't gone well.

Cady was grateful her own urge had passed, although she doubted that was healthy. She suspected it meant she was dehydrated – her mouth certainly felt that way. Winston decided to go, too, out of solidarity, he said. And when they were done, Naz croaked a perfunctory thank you.

'Guys, I swear, it was an accident,' Femi said, looking to Cady with such wide-eyed desperation that she felt an initial stab near her heart.

'I know,' she said, although immediately she flashed with anger, remembering that it had been his deceit that started all this. That he hadn't helped keep things cool earlier when they'd needed to.

'What does it matter?' Winston said. 'You're going to hell, anyway.'

The remark sent out a shockwave as palpable as the impact Danson made striking Hysteria on the way down.

'You did exactly the—' Femi cut himself off, his anger quickly dispersing. 'Well, I won't be there alone.'

Cady assumed he meant Winston at first, or perhaps even Danson. But the looming matter of what Naz had told Eloise about her lurked close to her surface thoughts, and as much as she wanted those answers, their first priority had to be getting the box back. Focus on something practical. Get them out of this loop of blame and recrimination.

'Could you use your trousers?' Cady said. 'For a lasso.'

'I could try,' Femi said. He undid his belt and kicked off his shoes. 'Guys, I fucked up. But I'm going to do everything I can to get you out of this. I promise you.' He started to shuffle off his trousers, leaning over the restraint once they had passed beneath in order to pull at them on the other side. His voice began to gather energy. 'I know I'm to blame here. I know, if I'd never given Eloise what she wanted and just… I should have told my parents and lived with that. I knew it about five minutes after I told her. And I know our situations aren't comparable, Winston. Of course I do. But I'm still an okay guy, you know. I've lived a lot of years since university. I'm still… I'm not perfect. But I know when I mess up. And I know when I need to make it right.'

He managed to slide his trousers off the rest of the way with his feet and brought them up to his waiting hands. Cady noticed a tattoo on the inside of his thigh, one she'd never seen before despite how often Femi had cavorted around their shared houses in his boxers. It was a single word: Captious. She didn't know what it meant, but perhaps, because it was on his leg, it was connected to what happened to him on the football pitch. He had no other tattoos she could see.

Trousers in his hands, Femi held them out by the bottom of the legs, assessing the waist area.

'Just don't drop them,' Cady said. 'If we're going to make it through this, we really need as much clothing to shield us from the sun as we can.'

'I'm sorry about your cardigan,' he said. 'I'm going to give you my T-shirt, if it comes to it. To cover your head and face.'

'You can't go without a top,' she said. 'I won't let you.'

'I'll be fine. I've got more melanin than you.'

With that he leaned over the side and began to lower the trousers, testing the length and which end he might use. Winston helped guide him, and between them they decided their best chance was to hook the V of the crotch underneath the section of the box hanging over the rail. If they tried to lift it slowly, though, they would quickly lose control, and it would fall. Either into a position beyond retention, or off the coaster entirely. And there was no way to retrieve it without getting under it, which would again create a slow tilt liable to lead to disaster.

'You have to yank it quickly, up and to the side of the coaster,' Winston said, sounding somewhat despondent. 'That's the only way.'

'And if it goes wrong, we're basically dead,' Naz said with the tone of a question.

'It won't go wrong,' Femi said. 'I've got this.'

There was no way he could be as certain as he sounded. Cady couldn't see the box from her seat: it was below Femi. But from Winston's description, it sounded like they'd need a lot of luck. Yet, despite everything, she now found his confidence reassuring, as she'd often done in the past.

Naz didn't appear to feel the same way. 'Sorry, hang on,' she said, trying to control her suddenly very rapid breathing. 'Can I just... Please. Everything's going too fast. I'm going to have a heart attack.'

'I won't go without your say, Naz,' Femi said.

'I don't see other options here,' Cady said, eager to get on with it. 'Let's just pull the plaster off.'

'Make sure you pull towards you at the same time as up,' Winston said. 'You're not quite at the halfway point, so it'll tip if you don't get under it.'

'Got it. Naz, trust me, it's going to be fine. I'm going to smash this.'

'I don't fucking trust you,' Naz snapped back, her voice suddenly shrill. 'You're a cocky prick, Femi. You have a surplus of self-esteem and a complete lack of appreciation for the concept of hubris. Things are never going to be fine again, don't you get that? There are some things you do that you just can't come back from.'

'Naz,' Cady said, 'can we just—'

'I just fucking hate him so much right now. The sound of his endless bullshit.'

'I'm trying to reassure you,' Femi said, jaw clenched.

'Fem,' Winston said. 'Just don't.'

'Fine,' Femi said, suddenly dragging the trousers back inside and tossing them across the car. They struck the opposite side and almost fell out, but Cady managed to lean forward and grab them just in time.

'Femi,' Cady said, stunned by what he'd almost done.

'Look, I've done my best to apologise.' He had tears in his eyes. 'But if you guys can't find it in you to have a little bit of forgiveness or understanding, after all that's gone on between us, as if you're all so bloody perfect, then screw it. I could have got that box, no sweat. And if it went wrong, I would have sacrificed myself for you.' He jabbed his chest with his forefinger on the area above his heart. 'That was my plan. That's how much I still love you. Always have. But no. If this is how it's going to be, if there's no way for me to at least try and make it up to you, forget it. We'll just wait it out, shall we? See who lasts longest once the sun's up.'

'Oh, my God, Femi,' Naz said. 'Are you serious?'

He folded his arms. Cady noticed that his shoulders were trembling. 'Deadly. Fuck the lot of you.'

CADY

Saturday 22nd June, 12.44am
Celsius: 32°, Fahrenheit: 89.6°

'Great,' Winston said. 'Well, maybe this is no less than we all deserve.'

'Speak for yourself,' Cady said, still staring at Femi's trousers in shock.

Until someone told her something to the contrary, she wanted to actively resist being lumped in with them. What they had done to one another, and possibly to her, was terrible. There was no other word for it. She had a tiny bit of sympathy for Winston, and perhaps she might for Naz, if she knew exactly what she'd told Eloise, but she couldn't really understand the mental trade-off Femi had made in selling out Winston the way he had done. And they could have all chosen to pay Eloise. They could all have found a way to afford it somehow, surely? A loan or credit card. That's what she'd have done in the same position, wouldn't she?

Or was she being unfair? How could she really know without having been in their shoes? After all, they had no idea how long Eloise planned to keep blackmailing them. How frightening it must have seemed. Regardless, no matter how they felt about one another, and however much they felt they deserved some sort of punishment, they had to remember she was innocent in all this, no matter what Danson said.

Convincing Femi. That was what mattered now. The only problem was Cady couldn't think of way to do it. Every utterance between the others felt like the erection of another eternal wall between them. Pleading her own case wasn't likely to sway anything.

'Stop being dramatic, Femi,' Naz said, oblivious to the small opportunity Cady had created for her to reveal the secret. 'This isn't all about you.'

'No, it's fine,' he said, with the bare-legged look and whiney sound of a petulant teenager. 'I step aside.'

'Grow up, man.' She paused for a while and came back sounding more reconciliatory. 'I know you, Femi. And when I hear that ego in your voice, it just worries me. There's a lot of lives at stake, that was my point. I wanted you to be certain.'

'It's fine, Naz. My ego hears you. You hate me. And I step aside.'

'Femi, I don't know how I feel at—'

'I don't want my ego to put the three of you at any risk.'

'Four,' Naz said.

'Four of us, fine.'

'Femi, no. There's four of us to consider. And you.'

Femi took a moment and straightened in his chair. 'What do you mean?'

'I need to tell you something. Okay?' Naz took three very deep breaths. 'You said you were certain, I know, but the stakes… It's only fair you know them first. And maybe it will explain why I am struggling to feel anything but hate for you right now.'

Femi glanced at Cady but she could only mirror his surprise. 'What are you saying?'

'Are you happy for me to talk about us, Fem? You know, all of it? Is that okay?' From the way her tone had softened, her voice in a deeper register, Cady had a sense of where this might be going.

Laughing bitterly, Femi said, 'There's no secrets here now.'

'Let me start by saying you were so cold about the baby at university. Maybe you didn't realise it, maybe you were just young. But you were … so decisive. And I think your certainty swayed me into thinking I was more ready than I was. To end it. It's not that I regretted it. But I regretted not being certain that I didn't regret it. And so I partly blamed you, Femi, for that uncertainty. Maybe that sounds pathetic.'

'No,' Cady said, and Winston made a similar mutter of denial.

'But then … that thing happened in Oxford. In the hotel. And lying on the bed after Winston left, I saw your tattoo. The one on your leg. And I felt so relieved, because it meant what happened hadn't been what I thought happened. It meant that on some level it had mattered to you.'

'Of course it mattered. I told you, I was distraught.'

'You never showed it, though. Not to me. Even when I told you Eloise knew, you were just like, pay her. Like you just wanted nothing to do with it. But anyway, that's why.' She took a breath. 'So Femi and I sort of started seeing each other after

Oxford. You know, casually. Just for fun. A couple of times a year if we were crossing paths. And part of that for me was, for want of a better term, to fall in love with you again. Because I'd been holding so much anger towards you about what happened. So I wanted to … fuck it out, you know? Bond again.'

Femi turned to look out in the direction of the mountains. 'I had that tattoo done after Becky divorced me. She never said it, but it was because of kids. Maybe because I wasn't around enough played a part, but it wasn't happening for us. We had the tests and everything, they were inconclusive but she blamed me because she'd been knocked up by an ex before. I never mentioned getting you pregnant. And I really wanted kids, too. Like, so much. I wanted to show my dad it could be done, being a good father *and* having success. And it's really the best way to a legacy, right? More so than all this other stuff we do. But maybe my body knew I didn't want them with her. The whole thing got me thinking about how sad it would be if the only time I'd been able to. And I'd not even realised it. I got a bit drunk and had the tattoo done.' He touched the word on his thigh. 'Captious.'

'Captious,' Naz repeated.

'What does it mean?' Cady asked.

'It means quick to anger,' Naz said. 'We didn't mean to name it. But I'd always joked to Femi that I thought that word sounded like a girl's name. So we started calling it Captious when we were talking about what to do, which was really stupid in retrospect.'

'Yeah,' Femi said.

Naz began to cry. 'Well, Femi…' Her soft sobs began to turn into laughter. 'Here's the thing. Guess what? I'm pregnant again. So…'

Cady had already started to piece it together. Her rounder face, the big dress. 'Oh, my God,' she said.

'And you came on a roller coaster,' Femi said, 'is that even … safe, Naz?'

'I don't know,' she said, still sobbing and laughing. 'When I found out, I wasn't sure I wanted it. Because when I called you, Femi, you told me you'd started seeing some woman called Samantha. So I was so upset, because I'd stupidly thought we'd been given a sort of second chance. Which was utterly insane, I know, but I was upset and… I wanted to maybe discuss it with you, but I was also scared that it would all happen again, like before. That coldness. And … well…'

'So you decided to put the roller coaster in charge?' Femi said. 'Out of spite.'

'No,' she said. 'Not spite. No. I was confused and I just … ran out of time. And when I realised you were here tonight, I sort of got angry again that we had to act like we hadn't been seeing each other. And I sort of felt fate was obviously in charge, so I'd let things play out. Because I didn't know if I even wanted a family really, or if I wasn't just overreacting to Mum's death a few years back, and the fact I've had zero relationship with Dad or Has since *Corruption* came out. I spent most my adult life thinking kids were for suckers. So why was it any different now? But it's all so stupid, the stories we tell ourselves when our desires don't match the beliefs we have about ourselves. Because now … now I know for certain, after all this tonight, that I really want this baby. I really do. All I keep thinking about is that we have to get out of this because I can't die with it inside me, Fem. I want to meet him. Or her. I want to tell Dad he has a grandchild, even if he completely ignores me. It's enough he'd know.'

Femi closed his eyes and was still. 'So, you wanted to tell

me this now, because you wanted to know what the stakes were?'

'Yes. It's us and *our* baby.'

'Gotcha,' he said, and was still for a while. Cady watched him, and couldn't quite tell if he now wore the minutest of smiles. Very suddenly, he grabbed the trousers from Cady, leaned back over the side, and yanked his arms towards the car.

Cady cried out. So did Winston. Femi made another quick movement, reaching with his left arm. Something clattered against the car. Winston swore. Femi swore. And then everything went still.

Had it fallen? Was it over? Femi didn't move.

Then Winston spoke, his voice thick with emotion. 'Femi, you are a complete bastard. But Jesus, thank God you're our bastard.'

Femi slowly brought himself back into the car. Tight against his chest were the trousers and the mystery box. 'Told you.' His voice wavered. 'No sweat.'

All four of them began to holler in celebration. Wild and unbridled, a pack again, even if only for the moment. Had anyone been on the ground to hear them, they would have thought that The No Tomorrows Club was having the ride of their lives.

CADY

Saturday 22nd June, 12.59am
Celsius: 32°, Fahrenheit: 89.6°

Femi sat the box on his lap, a palm at either end. His chest rose and fell, and he kept opening and closing his jaw, moving it from side to side.

'You okay?' Cady asked.

'Just getting myself together,' Femi said. 'Now for the hard part, right? Let's hope I didn't cause the stuff inside to get destroyed.'

'Well, at least it hasn't exploded,' Cady said.

The mystery box looked so unremarkable up close, it was hard to imagine it might have anything sophisticated inside. She could smell the freshly sanded pine from her seat, redolent of school woodworking lessons. Cuboid in shape, and not much bigger than her jewellery box at home, a line ran around the front and sides of the box to a set of hinges at the back. On the front, the lid was sealed by four metal clasps of the sort she'd seen on Dad's briefcase, growing up. And a little like that briefcase, underneath each was a six-figure dial, with each wheel set to zero. Calligraphic letters had been scorched into the wood under each lock.

C.F.N.W

Femi raised the box above his head and read out the word scorched on the bottom. 'Liberatio.'

'Yes, please,' Naz said.

'That sounds promising,' Cady said.

Femi's face screwed up with puzzlement, and he turned his head and brought the box to his ear.

'What is it?' Cady said.

He carefully handed over the box. 'Do you hear it?'

The box was heavier than she'd anticipated. She put her ear to it and heard a quiet whirring. 'Yes, I hear it. It's just stopped, though.' She handed it back to Femi. 'There's something mechanical in there.'

'Is it destroying the key?' Winston said.

'No way of knowing until we get in,' Femi said. 'And that might take some time. Unless anything is jumping out at any of you.'

After a long silence, Naz said, 'What if we get in and it's another trap? I mean, what if it really is a bomb or something? We've got no reason to trust the bastard, do we? All that crap about honesty, after he lured us out here.'

'Again, we're not blessed with alternatives,' Cady said, wanting to keep their post-retrieval togetherness going as long as possible.

'Well, what about the gun?' Naz said.

'What about it?' Cady said.

'It's another option.'

Winston said, 'That's pretty dark, Naz.' His closed fist manically bobbed on the clamshell's arm rest.

'No, not that,' Naz said. 'I meant, you know, we could fire it to get attention. Maybe while we're working out the box stuff. Or in the morning. Someone might hear. Or what if someone comes looking for that guy?'

'Jag,' Cady said.

'Yeah, the driver.'

'You want to shoot them?' Cady said.

'We can attract them over.'

'If anyone hears that gun, they'll probably think it's just kids, or criminals they'd want to stay well away from,' Femi said, staring at the box on his lap. 'And by the time anyone comes looking for that guy, it'll be too late for us. At least, if we believe what that guy told Danson.'

'Jag,' Cady said again. 'His name was Jag.'

'Of course. Jag. But let's be blunt.' He still didn't look up from the box. 'It's about as cool as it's going to get right now. And I'm still sweating. I don't know if it's even dropped below forty yet. Come six, maybe even five, things will start warming up again quickly. We might be okay until nine or ten. But after that… Especially given your condition now, Naz. Danson wasn't lying that we might not survive the first day, and if we do…'

Naz groaned. 'Yes, fine. We know it's a bad scene. But someone *might* come. We can't know they won't.'

Femi shook his head. 'It's natural to want to wait it out. Just in case. But Danson went to a lot of trouble to get us here.'

'Jag got through,' Winston said.

'Which to me makes it more unlikely anyone else will. That was our lucky break. We've exhausted it. And be honest now, is anyone back at home going to start worrying if you don't get in touch tomorrow? Or even the day after? Enough to contact the authorities? I know I'm out of luck there. Me and Samantha broke up two weeks ago and haven't spoken since. And I'm between agents right now, so…'

Cady experienced a pang of sadness at her own situation. Because Tom would simply assume she'd forgotten him. At first, he might put her lack of contact down to her usual troubles with times and dates, especially with the time difference. But after a few days, he'd be more likely planning their break-up than planning her rescue.

'I'm pretty solitary these days, anyway,' Winston said. 'Mum won't be wondering about me for a while. She's used to me being away months. And the band won't notice for a few weeks at least.'

'I have some friends that might wonder about me not replying to messages,' Naz said. 'But I'm mid structural edit, and they know I can get distracted. It would be a few days before anyone actually worried. At least.'

Femi waited for Cady to add something. She simply shrugged and Femi understood. 'And even if someone in our empty lives gets a funny feeling tomorrow,' he said, 'and acts on it early enough to spare us, how long will it take the authorities to follow up?'

'I'm not sure I'm finding this helpful, Fem,' Naz said. 'We know this. What's your point?'

'I'm just saying, we need to be aware that, at some point, our hope is just hurting us. So, let's forget about the gun. For now.'

Cady laughed at this. Every single one of them in this car

was a hope junkie. They'd built all their lives following their ephemeral ambitions. This was the wrong crowd. Or perhaps it wasn't.

'Femi,' Winston said, 'we're not all shooting ourselves, if that's what you mean.'

'It won't come to that,' Femi said, and paused. His hand rose and began to absently scratch in the general area of his heart. 'We have the box. That's our plan until it isn't.'

Cady hadn't liked that pause. That touch. Was he thinking about his ICD again? Had he changed his mind since finding out about the baby, and was that why he didn't want them using the gun? He was planning to kill himself to bring about their rescue. There had to be a better use of it than that, though. In all the panic of the last hour, it hadn't crossed Cady's mind that they might be able to use the gun to escape. She racked her brains, trying to think of all the coasters she'd ridden over the years. All the videos she'd watched about them by other YouTubers and the experts she'd interviewed. She looked around and behind her at other cars. She couldn't shoot the harness free without endangering them, but what about the train itself?

Hysteria was a chain lift coaster. A bit of metal under the train, called a chain dog, hooked on to a motorised chain which dragged the coaster to the top. Usually, when the chain doubled back on itself just beyond the very top, the dog disengaged, handing the coaster over to gravity, which took the train down again.

So how had Danson kept their train in place? He'd cut the power. They knew that because the chain stopped and the lights went off. So, if she had to guess, perhaps Hysteria worked something like a dive coaster at the point they were at. Baron 1898 in The Netherlands, maybe. An opposite-facing chain dog caught on a separate, slower moving chain. That second chain was designed to slowly bring them over the drop and hold them there for a short time.

She twisted her body as far as she could, and then her neck. Through the seat back she could see where their car connected to the one behind. She could also see a portion of track and the chain. Was this the same chain that brought them up, or had they transferred to the second at the start of the straight section? Given the slope, she guessed the second.

The question was then, could they somehow disengage whatever was holding them to the chain? If it was a chain dog holding them, could a ripple through the chain itself possibly dislodge it, allowing gravity to take over? The whole ornamental front portion of Hysteria was over the edge now, the weight was enough to pull them down.

But it was a long shot. There might be an electrical or magnetic component needed to disengage the brake. If that were the case, the gun wouldn't make a difference.

But a gunshot might make a ripple. It wasn't much of a plan, but it was something. Better than a bomb in a box or a bullet in the head. And if the chain dog came out…

'We fall,' Femi said, when she'd finished explaining her idea.

'What use is that?' Naz said. 'Down there, up here, we're still stuck.'

'If we go over, the momentum might take us all the way back to the start,' Cady said. 'We'd be in the shade. We'd live a hell of a lot longer.'

'Longer than Danson anticipated,' Femi said. 'Maybe long enough for someone to find us.'

'Yes,' Winston said. 'Yes. Now we're talking.'

'But what's the worst-case scenario?' Femi said.

'Well, worst case scenario is what Naz said. We're stuck down there instead of up here. Maybe we land in a patch of shade. Maybe we don't. The sun set somewhere behind us, didn't it? It'll rise and be over us all day, so … we're not worse off.'

'Only up here we're more visible,' Naz said. 'Down there…'

'*Down there* is still pretty high,' Cady said. 'I didn't see a section of track that didn't tower above the ground. But you're right, we'd be below the mountains. But that potentially will give us shade considerably earlier. I think on balance we'd be better down than up.'

'Do we need to decide now?' Naz said. 'Can we'—she adjusted herself with some effort—'keep our options open? Just in case we need to use the gun to get someone's attention?'

'I don't know about you,' Winston said, 'but I'm liking the get down plan a lot. Not sure I could bear waiting to know.'

'How many bullets are there?' Femi said. 'Can you see?'

'I checked the magazine. It held six, and there are three left.'

Apparently now moved by the spirit of democracy, Femi suggested they vote. Cady, Femi and Winston all voted to shoot the chain. Naz simply abstained.

'And what happens if you shoot and we come off the rails?' Naz asked.

'Nah,' Cady said, 'the cars are attached to the rails by the wheels. The chain is separate.'

Naz murmured, unconvinced, but she didn't object any further. She knew this had all come about because of her doubts about the mystery box.

Cady instructed them all to get as low down as they could in their chairs in case of a ricochet or flying bits of shrapnel. She lined up her shot through the gap and steadied her hand.

'If we start moving, grab your arm rests,' she said, and licked her parched lips with her dry tongue.

She fired, pulling her head behind the headrest at the last moment, and almost losing her grip on the gun when it kicked back.

Nothing happened. She had a feeling the gun had jerked to the side.

'Damn it,' she shouted. 'Sorry, I think I missed.'

She lined up her shot again and asked Femi to reach over and pin her hand down. In a soft voice, meant only for her, he said, 'Maybe we should keep one bullet.'

'Why?' she said, turning to face him. She watched a bead of sweat slide down his upper lip and off. As if she didn't know.

'Just in case.'

He stared at her intently. She still smelled the faintest trace of his aftershave. She would swear his brand hadn't changed since university. It had been in her nostrils the time they'd kissed.

'Hold tight,' she said, and fired. This time she heard a high whining sound, like something from an old Western, and the car shook ever so gently.

'Everyone okay?' she said.

She got three yeses. She'd struck the chain, she was sure, but it hadn't dislodged them.

'Cady…' Femi said.

She tried to picture it. Femi, sitting beside her, pulling the trigger. While she sat there and let it happen. One of her oldest friends, who, despite all she knew, she couldn't help but love, maddening as it was.

'No,' she said, and fired again.

The bullet whined, the car shook, far more than before, and…

Nothing happened.

The bullets were gone and her plan hadn't worked. The train remained in place.

'Bugger,' she said. She turned and kicked the wall in front of her.

They all sat in silence for very long time. Ten minutes. Half-an-hour. Time had started to work strangely up here, so it was hard to tell. They all knew what lay ahead now, and Cady suspected that, like her, none of them wanted this ceasefire to break.

Eventually Femi said, 'Shall we try and open the box, then?'

She heard Naz sigh. 'Where the hell do we start? Do any of you remember being tested by him? What does it even mean?' Naz started sobbing. 'Everything fucking hurts.'

Winston's arm came across to comfort her, but it was sent straight back.

'If we do this,' Cady said, 'we have to try and stick together. Femi, Win, you both said that earlier and it's still true now. Whatever we talk about, and we have to be honest, we can't get into fighting again.'

'Easy for you to say,' Naz said. 'But yeah, I agree.'

Cady bit back her urge to ask about Eloise. 'We can sort everything else out when we get back to earth.'

'Yeah,' Winston said.

'He said he tested our love,' Femi said. 'And we failed. So maybe we all need to talk about what we found out earlier first. Coolly. With empathy. We might be able to piece it together from that. He must have made us talk about all that for a reason.'

'He wanted us to know we were terrible people,' Naz said. 'So, what terrible things have we done to him, guys? Any ideas? Just in case any of us weren't feeling miserable enough.'

'I've got an idea,' Winston said. 'It's something to start with, anyway.'

'Really?'

'Yeah.' He exhaled the word, and his deep voice rasped. 'Think so. Before that … before *Jag* turned up, Danson was about to say something. He was like, you guys all got your dreams, or something, while I—" He cut himself off just as Danson had. "This was right before he noticed the car. And we still have no real idea what we're doing here, or what his plan was, do we? But yeah, that to me sounded like half a motive. It's about success. And in all the chaos, I told myself to remember he said that. And so yeah, on that subject, I do remember something that might have been a test of his love. See what you guys think.' And with that, he began to talk.

Danson, Then

Happy twenty-seventh birthday to me! It's been ... weird.

Went to the job centre for a careers chat. Woman was baffled that I had an Oxbridge degree but had only worked temp roles. So I gave her the whole story, about my magic, and how I'd given that up as it wasn't paying, but that now I'd started singing in a punk band, like when I was a kid, so I still needed flexibility from a day job.

She said I was a real Renaissance man, with a tone. But then she said she'd played in bands when she was younger, too, and admired me following my dreams. And by the end we'd bonded – though still had no idea how to make more money without selling out.

Then, on the way through reception, it happened. I recognised a song on the radio, a jaunty, indie-pop thing, with an over-the-top mockney vocalist. It was Winston's band – I knew the song from his scruffy old demos! They were on Radio One! Got home and found out they're in the bloody charts. They're signed to a massive record company and are touring with Coldplay next year.

Not sure how I feel. It shook me a bit. Maybe I should get in touch, it's been ages. I could send him some of my band's demos maybe.

———

Drove out to the care home today. Winston on the radio – again! Eloise didn't look great. They've stopped dying her hair. It's grown since the last operation, but it still doesn't sit right where she hit her head. Her eyes were open. Mostly it was that stuffed-toy stare, but sometimes when I moved around, I felt they were following me. It was odd.

I stuck some gems to her face and caught her up on the last six months: my band's gigs, being fired from the crap call centre job. I joked that perhaps I should have cashed in my degree in the city, to try and bait her, but obviously she didn't budge. Eventually, I went and talked to Mona, one of the nurses. Apparently, her mum's not been in since my last visit and I'm one of the only regulars now. Mona said I was a good friend!

I went back and Eloise had closed her eyes. The odd vibe remained. I decided to tell her about Winston. Baiting her again with the radio-play stuff. When I mentioned I'd sent him my demo, and that we were all meeting up soon, her eyes flew open. I actually jumped. It was probably as deliberate as a knee jerking after the strike of a doctor's hammer, but God, the idea she'd been listening, and that on the inside she was still raging at her old enemies…

I stared at her for a long time. Eventually, her eyes closed and I decided to leave. Before I did, I cleaned the dust from the plastic flowers at her bedside.

———

So much for the big reunion! Everyone cancelled but Cady. We decided to go to Drayton Manor anyway, and had a bloody good time reminiscing. Found out we've been on similar paths since Chamberlain, both of us temping while trying different creative things, neither of us managing to make anything stick. Funny, she's just started singing with a band again, too!

We laughed about other people being more successful than us, and she made this depressing point that us comprehensive kids weren't really taught about networking and stuff. Later, she mentioned in passing that Femi had used some of his sister's contacts from Cambridge to start working at a big talent agency while looking for acting work (apparently, he finally told his parents he wasn't studying medicine last year, and the reaction wasn't great). And Winston's *Little Shop* contact from all those years back had been a music lawyer for many years. He'd put his demo in the hands of a number of industry folk and they'd all flocked to see his band's gigs.

It was odd hearing someone other than Eloise say something like this about the others. Suddenly I felt very unworldly and stupid.

I played her my band's new demo in the car before we left. I told her we were called Magic Circle, which she liked. When she asked if I'd sent it to Winston, I told her he'd not got back to me. She told me to nudge him, because she reckoned it was decent.

It's been four months now. I'm not angry with Winston, it's only in his email he said he'd definitely give it a listen. Maybe it's shit and Cady was just being polite. I went on a really long run tonight. Whole thing is giving me bad energy.

I mean, I've kept his bloody secret all these years. For him. Without me, if I hadn't done what I'd done for him… Well, we all know the end of that story.

As always, I have to be the bigger man.

Met the No Tomorrows at Koko in London to watch Winston's band – and we picked up right where we'd left off, vibes wise. After the show, we all got to hang out in the secret talent rooms and catch up. Cady and Fem were on good form. And Naz was aglow with the news she'd signed with a literary agent – which of course made me all the more determined to ask Winston about my demo given it's been six bloody months now!

Yet we kept bouncing off one another like bumper cars. Eventually, when I caught him sitting alone in a little curtained-off alcove that looked like a Turkish bath, he started unburdening himself about how stressful he was finding the band's success. His mum is quite unwell and frail, and he can't get any time off touring to see her. Given their identities, too, I imagine all this attention isn't easy.

Eventually, he asked how I'd been and I pounced. I told him about Magic Circle, and how we'd had a nice write-up in a local fanzine and were ready to go to the next level, hint, hint. But he only nodded and looked at the floor, so in the end I just asked him about the demo outright.

He said he loved it. Not liked. Loved. So I asked what he thought about us doing a gig together. Or maybe helping us get a manager or something. He said he'd love to, but then started twisting up his face like he was in pain, telling me everything was out of his hands now they were signed. It was like watching an eel navigate a labyrinth.

I stared at him, and for a while he stared at me, an enormous canyon growing between us. I got the rage. I would never have done it, but I imagined saying, 'I could destroy you, you know?'

But in the end I opted for levity. I got on my knees and put my hands together. Smiling, so he knew it was a joke, I asked him if he wanted me to beg. Because I would if he wanted me to. Oh please, Winston. Please, give me a shot.

He laughed eventually, so he got it – although while I was down there I did worry he thought I was serious. Anyway, he said he'd see what he could do. And then, knowingly, he winked. God bless the guy!

CADY

Saturday 22nd June, 01.35am
Celsius: 31°, Fahrenheit: 87.8°

'It was strange,' Winston said, 'it was like there was a darkness between us. I was a bit stressed anyway, the gig had sold out, and we'd just found out we were going over to the States to perform on TV. But what I remember the most from that night is being in that room with him and feeling … scared. And on reflection, like the whole thing was a sort of test.'

Curious, Cady asked, 'So did you try and help him?'

'It wasn't like I could just make things happen. I tried to think of ways I could get him on the right track, but, being honest, did you hear his demos? They weren't good enough, you know? I wrote him an email about things he could do to make the recording sound better. You know, hoping he'd get the hint. Maybe come back with something better.'

'Did he?' Cady said.

'No. He wrote to thank me and then asked if I'd sent the demo anywhere. And I couldn't lie. So I ignored it.'

'You didn't write back?'

'I don't know, I felt annoyed. Like, get your own record deal. I mean, yeah, I know my mum's friend Martin helped us get people to those first shows, but we worked our asses off getting *really* good. We got in the best shape we could and Martin… He didn't have to like us. It always felt like that with Danson, though, didn't you think? He was always sort of just … there. Waiting for someone else to do something for him. And you know, I'll be honest now, something about him always unsettled me. Acting like he knew something you didn't.'

'Well, he did,' Femi said.

Winston paused. 'Jesus. He would have known then. Fuck. I wonder if he thought about blackmailing me?'

'He didn't, though,' Cady pointed out. 'Like he said, he kept all your secrets.'

The remark was out before she had time to stop herself. She had no desire to defend Danson after tonight, but she had talked to him a little bit over this time, and the two of them had bonded over being a little on the periphery of the group. And it was interesting that he could have blackmailed the others, and yet he hadn't. Why had that been?

'Come on,' Winston said, 'I never wanted to be cruel, but screw that now, he was a leech. You must know what I mean?'

'Maybe,' Naz said. 'I always regretted him coming to live with us in Chamberlain House. I wonder if we got swept up in all the drama of that car accident. Maybe it trauma-bonded us.'

'We had to have him,' Winston said. 'We needed five and everyone else had sorted themselves. Otherwise, we'd have lost the blockhouse. And after that, it would have been hard to kick him out in the third year. But yeah, I remember thinking he'd saved our lives. I still think he did.'

'I forgot all that,' Femi said flatly. 'To me he seemed pretty harmless. And he *was* good at all the organisational things behind the scenes. He did stuff for all three of my plays. He was solid. But yeah, he never really knew his way. He seemed a bit in awe of us all, copying what we did, like he wanted something we had. Maybe that flattered us, too.'

'He was sort of a pet,' Naz said. 'He wandered around in his own world getting petted and fussed. I see it now. It's pathetic.'

Cady bridled at all of this, again, without quite knowing why. Perhaps it was because, without realising it, they could just as easily have been talking about her. She hadn't known her way at university. And she had often felt that the others were all part of some secret club she didn't know about. How often had she felt that after university, too? Especially as one by one they all became successful. And not just them. So many friends and acquaintances from Cambridge had gone on to high-flying careers. Three from their year were now in the current government. At one point, it had been almost a monthly occurrence, seeing someone familiar on the television, or reading them, or about them, in a newspaper.

'I always liked Danson,' Cady said, shaking her head. She had always found him to be so thoughtful and patient. So helpful and loyal. He was almost like the grown-up in their midst. Sage beyond his years. If she'd ever noticed anything unusual about him, it would have been nothing compared with some of the other students at Cambridge – it had been a hotbed for all sorts of weirdness.

If anyone heard her, they didn't acknowledge it. Instead,

Naz said, 'I think Winston might be on to something with this, you know? I had a similar experience when Danson was trying to write novels. What about you two? Does anything similar come to your mind?'

Femi said, 'Maybe. I... Cady, what about you?'

'No. I don't remember. I mean we talked a few times over the years. But I was always supportive of his ambitions. I tried to encourage him. Because, you know, we were often in the same boat. I was in a band when he was. I was writing stuff when he started writing. I think we even talked about acting once when he was dabbling in that. Thing is, you guys all knew what you were doing by the time we left Cambridge, but Danson and me... I don't know, I still don't know why I'm here.'

The others fell silent. Then very quietly, Naz said, 'No, you really don't, do you?'

Cady bristled and felt her head throb. 'Pardon?'

What had she meant by that, exactly? She was pleased the other three were working together now, even if that meant using Danson's memory like a punching bag. Who cared? The man had been intent on torturing them. But just like at university, Cady suddenly had the sense of being outside the club again. What was Naz hiding? And did the others know, too?

She had to ask about Eloise. Get this sorted. Now. She opened her mouth, but a sudden fear stomped on the urge. She didn't really want to know, did she? She had no idea why that was, either. But her body was vibrating, just as it had when she'd tried to wriggle under the restraint earlier.

The opportunity to ask passed by, and Femi asked if Winston could even recall the date of his encounter.

'I remember it,' Naz said. 'I had my first ever full manuscript request from an agent that week and I've often gone back to that email because it was the very start of everything that happened for me. April 2013.'

'A decade after we all first met. Should we put it into the box then?' Winston asked. 'I'm more sure than ever that this is what he's asking for. His test.'

'Maybe let's hear Naz's thing first,' Cady said.

'Yeah,' Femi said, and glanced over at Naz. 'Don't want to get this wrong.'

'Works for me,' Winston said. 'Naz, what have you got?'

Danson, Then

Last night, Dom the druggie was having an all-night gaming sesh with his mates in the flat below, so I stuck on some serial killer film to drown it out. Guess who showed up as one of the cops? Only bloody Femi. Went online and found out he's been in loads of things in the four years since I saw him at Koko! Films, telly – even a cameo in one of Winston's music videos.

How am I so out of the loop? Last time I spoke with him, he'd still been auditioning and doing admin at that talent agency. I remember it made me feel okay about my own crappy situation. I watched the movie up until Femi's character got murdered, and afterwards buzzed with that feeling I had when I heard Winston's song at the job centre that day. And when I'd read that article about Naz's book deal not long after I started writing my magician novel. A sort of elation, but also a kind of panic.

I messaged Cady, and she replied immediately. She knew already. So much for us all being in this together! She'd even gone to see him in a play alongside some A-lister recently.

I felt very alone. So, I had a few drinks, and before I knew it I found myself at about four in the morning staring at the photograph of me and Mum in the kitchen. I started thinking about that woman who lived in the vinegar bottle, and about Eloise.

———

Saw Cady today and feel a lot less untethered. We met at the Pleasure Beach in Blackpool after the others made their usual excuses. She asked about Magic Circle, so I told her about my fist-fight with the drummer, and how I'd been putting all my efforts into my novel ever since.

As usual, we were completely in sync, as she's been writing, too – a screenplay about trying to make it in the arts while paying the bills. Maybe I was reading my own feelings into it, but it sounded like she might be struggling with the success of the other No Tomorrows, too. But she suggested I hit up Naz when I finished the book, and that its similarities to *The Prestige* might make it more marketable.

But I told her I was only really writing for myself, not an audience, and we had a great deep-and-meaningful about how obsessed we'd all been at Chamberlain with getting 'out there' and 'doing something' in the world. Like we were all emotionally a bit neglected or something, and were looking for emotional sustenance and attention from that spectral 'audience' out there consuming all the other art we worshipped.

Cady said she'd been experimenting with writing on mescaline recently to try and take a purer, less success-driven approach to her writing. Still, we did agree that making a living from it like the others wouldn't be terrible!

We wound up reminiscing about the night in our first year when I got that awful mescaline ice cream from Dom the druggie. That night Cady told Naz her secret.

I came close to telling Cady I knew. That Eloise had told me. It would have been connected to what we were talking about, about how similar the two of us are. Because, for us, art isn't only about seeking the love of an audience. Our mutual drives to succeed also come from outrunning things in our past. Trying to right wrongs, or at least keep ourselves busy enough to forget them.

I said nothing, though. Because I'm not sure Cady is even fully aware of what she did. Unpicking all that might be messy.

We rode The Big One together, and afterwards she stared up at it, an imperious blue and red brontosaur.

'It's sort of beautiful, isn't it?' Cady said. 'Maybe we should design roller coasters.'

'No,' I replied. 'That would be both artistically satisfying and financially worthwhile. Why on earth would we want that?'

I did it. I went to Naz's book signing. When I got to the front, she didn't mention my novel, but agreed to go with me for a drink after. Stupidly, I got my hopes up. In a noisy wine bar, Naz constantly looking out for her editor, I asked her why agents weren't getting back to me. She told me how tough it was these days, which I already knew.

So I asked her if she'd read my book yet, because it had been a while since I sent it, and she said she'd been busy working on a screenplay for the film adaptation of her debut, and that she didn't even have time to read for pleasure these days, ha ha ha. Then she asked if I'd heard of the *Writers' and Artists' Yearbook*, and that, if I hadn't, I should get a copy.

My mouth went dry. I wanted to strangle her. But instead, I did what I'd done to Winston that time at Koko. Just to see the reaction on her prim, poised little face, I got on my knees and begged her to help me, all the nearby patrons watching on like I was proposing.

When I got home, I took out my battered copy of the *Writers' and Artists' Yearbook* and set it alight in the bath. Then I took the ashes and smeared them on my face like war paint.

———

A terrible understanding has settled inside me. Eloise was right all those years ago when she said the others were fundamentally different to us. When you're young, you don't see it. You're just all humans going about your existence; the miraculous fact you're conscious is enough glue to hold you all together.

It's the years that show you the truth. How all the little differences snowball.

We were all clever at Cambridge. Eloise was wise.

———

To celebrate my thirty-second birthday, I went to the care home. I dabbed some of my mescaline ice cream on Eloise's tongue and put on some music. My gaze on the floor, I told her about what happened with Naz, and about how I was starting to understand Eloise's point of view.

When I finished talking, I looked up and was so shocked by what I saw that I kicked out my legs, sending myself and the chair I was on backwards into the wall with a noisy scrape.

Honest to God, Eloise had turned her head. She was looking at me. Gem-framed eyes wide and alive. Many of her teeth had been lost in the fall, but I knew a grin when I saw it.

Through stiff and parched-sounding vocal cords, she rasped a single word: 'Art.'

I ran back to my car, and only on the drive back did I start to laugh, laugh, laugh.

CADY

Saturday 22nd June, 01.45am
Celsius: 31°, Fahrenheit: 87.8°

'It was *just* like you described,' Naz said. 'He was begging me. Grinning like it was all some joke he was making, but it didn't feel like a joke. I'll be honest, I was so embarrassed at the time, but after, I felt really sad for him. When I last saw him, and he was doing so well with his career, I was actually really happy for him. I only came here because I stupidly believed he was in a good place.'

'Yeah,' Winston said. 'I thought he'd really got it together.'

'Well, he played on our egos, too,' Cady said. 'Let's be honest. He made us think we'd get something out of this. Having access to Dreamland this early for me would have been a real hit on my channel. Then there was all that Ryan Coogler stuff for Femi.'

'He made it seem like Beyoncé was on the guest list,' Naz said. 'He knew I always had a soft spot for her. I'm so stupid. Now I'm playing it back and he never said any such thing directly. He made me say it. He led me. I wasn't thinking straight. I was so desperate to get away from my flat, from the routine of worrying about the baby and the endless hours I spent at my laptop with imaginary friends.'

'For me, it was Louis Cole,' Winston said. 'Again, he never said it, but he implied that he was going to play here. I love that guy, and I've never made it a secret. See, that's always been my weakness. I should have stayed at home with Mom – I'm living with her now, by the way. I should have just got on with sorting all the band stress out and making life small again. But just like when I couldn't help myself sending Martin that demo, as soon as he mentioned Louis Cole, I had to come, didn't I? I'm like a really dumb magpie. Just like Dad.'

'Smoke and mirrors,' Femi said, and Cady looked at him. 'He studied magic for years. Maybe at last it all paid off. He knew what we were like. God knows I came here looking for a bit of good PR.'

'Oh?' Cady said.

'Well,' Femi said, 'like I said, I'm between agents.'

His attention remained on the mystery box. Winston and Naz continued talking amongst themselves about what happened to them, how test-like the encounters had seemed. It sounded like they were closing on a decision, the similarities swaying them towards certainty.

The problem Cady had was that she had no such comparable memory of Danson. All the times they had met up after university had been nice. They'd fashioned their own special relationship, often out of group reunions the others had pulled out of, making a tradition of meeting up at amusement parks and…

Her hand rose to her mouth. Was that it, perhaps? Had he reached out to her for help once she'd broken through with her channel? God, that had some plausibility. Enough plausibility that she felt the smallest shiver. How could she be certain, though? If she got the incident wrong, she'd get the date wrong, and the key would be destroyed. So, when had he come to her? Or more to the point, when had he come to her with a test?

'I think I'm ready to commit,' Winston said loudly. 'It makes sense. We all succeeded doing something creative, and he didn't. He found out he was dying and thought he'd bring us down a peg or two. To show us.'

'You think it's jealousy, then?' Cady said.

'Well… yes… but specifically he asked us to help him,' Naz added. 'And we didn't. He tested our friendship and we failed. Because for him, friendship was conditional on helping him succeed. Which is so unfair. Because … what was I supposed to do?'

'I know,' Winston said. 'It isn't like you can just make something happen for other people that easily. When you get a break, it's still all so…'

'Precarious, yes. Yes. It still is, even now. I never know if my publishers will re-contract me. I still have whole books rejected. Every author is only a few failures from the slush pile again.'

'Did you ever read his book, Naz?' Cady said.

She was silent for a moment. 'I didn't have time, Cady. I had to—'

'This isn't important,' Femi said. His gaze hadn't left the box. 'Cady, did he ever ask you for anything?'

'I'm trying to think,' she said. 'I do wonder if my … sort of late bit of success tipped him over the edge, maybe?'

'Why's that?' Femi said.

She told them about their meet-ups and the role amusement parks had played in their friendship.

'So, how did he react when he found out?' Femi asked. '*How* did he find out?'

'Well,' she said, and started to think. And it didn't take long for her to remember. And at that point, her thoughts aligned like numbers on the combination lock of a mystery box.

There *had* been something that happened between them that, on reflection, might seem like a test.

'Oh,' she said. 'I just remembered something.'

'Thank God,' Winston said. 'And Fem, do you have something that fits?'

'Sadly, yes.'

Winston punched the air. 'This has to be it, then. We've cracked it. Come on, let's get this over with. Put the code in. April 2013. I'm certain I'm right.'

'Wait,' Cady said. 'Shouldn't we talk a bit more? Just to make sure. Given what's on the line. Do you want to at least hear mine and Femi's stories, because, I mean, it's a long time to have been testing us, isn't it? Like, has he really been planning this for a decade?'

After a pause, Winston said, 'He had us all talking about our salad days earlier. Seems like he's been holding grudges a long time. And we could spend hours talking about all the ways we might have let him down, which was maybe what he wanted.'

'That's a good point,' Femi said.

'And I don't think I'm going to find another—'

clack

Cady turned to Femi, and when he only had eyes for the box, she looked down. The last of the four clasps pointed towards the stars and gleamed in the white light.

'It opened,' Cady said.

'What opened?' Naz sounded shocked.

'April 2013,' Femi said.

'The box,' Cady said. 'Winston's lock opened.'

Winston threw up his hands and yelled into the night. Naz screamed, and even Cady couldn't help but smile.

'Jesus, Femi,' Winston said. 'I… What if I'd been wrong?'

'You weren't.'

'I could have killed us.'

Femi said, his voice flat and determined, 'What's your date, Naz?'

She blew out a noisy breath. Then another. 'Definitely 2018. And I'm quite certain it was August.'

'August,' Femi said, and began to roll the dials. 'Hundred per cent?'

'Yeah, I'm sure. I met him at a signing at this tiny village festival. I think I'd handed in a book that July, too, so I know when I did the festival it was—'

clack

Cady jumped. She put a hand to her chest.

'There we go,' Femi said.

'Holy hell,' Winston yelled again. 'Thank God, thank God, thank God.'

Cady felt the tension of the last six hours rising up inside her. She threw back her head, and screamed. She wished that Femi would be a little less cavalier about this, but given it was now working she kept her mouth closed.

Winston's face appeared in the gap between the chairs. 'Over to you then, guys. What are your dates?'

Cady turned to Femi and he finally looked up and met her gaze. She saw fear but, cemented beneath, defiance. A bead of sweat burst and ran down the side of his face. He swallowed.

Then, unexpectedly, he smiled. And so did Cady.

'Shall we talk about it first?' Femi said.

'Yeah.'

'You first.'

'No, you go.'

Danson, Then

Dreams of Eloise. In all of them, she sits between her turrets saying such horrible things to me. But suddenly she stops, cries, and tells me she made a mistake, that she does love me after all.

In one last night, I ask, 'What about your Italian man?'

'I made him up,' she tells me. Says she was scared, scared, scared of her love for me.

So she doesn't die. Instead, I tell her I love her, too, and I wake up, blissful until I remember.

———

I couldn't help myself. I browsed through some photos from Femi's latest movie premiere. There was one with Winston and Naz in it. Called in sick for the rest of the day and went for a run. Then I got drunk.

―――

Got my certificate for my project management qualification today. At the care home later, Mona told me about an opening coming up at the charity that runs the place. Maybe I'll apply? I asked her about Eloise, but she told told told me there was nothing to report. I almost mentioned that she'd spoken to me last time, but I know deep down she probably didn't.

Eloise's breathing sounded like a death rattle today. But her eyes were open, staring at the ceiling. I took my little dropper of mescaline and dabbed some onto her tongue and mine. She stopped the awful noise.

I told her how sorry I was that I hadn't come to see her recently, that work had been busy. 'Eloise ... did you really speak to me last time?'

I looked down at my feet. For just a moment, the laces on my shoes looked like they were pulling themselves into a knot. Then I heard it, the soft *shoooosshing* of her head turning on the pillow. I still didn't look up.

I told her about the photo of them all grinning at the premiere. All this time, I thought they loved loved loved me like I loved them. Yet we'd never been in it together, had we?

NO.

I flicked up my head at what I thought I'd heard but was disappointed. She still lay staring up at the ceiling. I dropped my head again. I finally apologised. Crying, I told her I'd acted rashly the night she fell, that I'd been young and stupid.

Was there any way I could make it right? I asked.

YES.

I didn't look up this time. Kept staring at my laces.

'How do I make it right, Eloise?'

She made me wait, but at last she spoke again, her voice rasping like the undead, the words formed with the clumsy softness of someone who hadn't used their mouth in some time.

You're the fairy, Dan. Always watching. Always listening.

I only half understood. I needed more.

After that though, all she kept saying was Robin Hood. Again and again.

Robin Hood. Robin Hood. Robin Hood.

I can't stop thinking about it. Robin Hood! What did that even mean? Did she want me to blackmail them the way she had done? It wouldn't work now. Would Naz's family even care about something from so long ago? She might have told them everything already. And Femi's family know *his* secret. And Cady's... Well, what mileage would there be in blackmailing her with that? I'd never understood what Eloise hoped to leverage with that, unless she thought containing heartbreak would be enough.

It's only really Winston's secret that might have any potency still. Could I use that to blackmail them all? Would they all want to help him out if it came down to it?

It all sounds incredibly complicated and stressful. Yet, if Eloise is really in there, and this is what she wants, I need to consider it, don't I? I do so desperately want to make it right.

But even though I am so disappointed with Naz, and Femi,

and Winston – I could never do anything to Cady. Cady never betrayed me. Cady never became successful and ignored me. The worst thing Cady has ever done to me is get my birthday wrong – which she does so routinely it's become quite charming.

Eloise used to think Cady was the worst one of all, though. Because Cady should know better, but she doesn't, and instead she is like the middle class that side with the bourgeoisie come the revolution. Worse, she is their cheerleader, fanning the flames of their self-serving agenda.

I don't know, I just just just don't see it.

———

Met Cady at Thorpe Park. We didn't even invite the others. I needed to see her because I've been unable to stop myself obsessing, poring over the PR-heavy social media feeds of the other three, Googling them multiple times a day. Growing angrier and angrier.

Cady sensed my anger, and I couldn't stop myself telling her everything I'd been feeling. Snacking in the gorgeous sun amongst the joyous screams and yells of the punters, Eloise's words flowed from my mouth. All the stuff about me being their dogsbody at uni. Doing their bloody dishes all the time. Doing the boring admin for Femi's plays. And now they'd ditched me, and I felt used.

She calmed me down, and insisted they all loved me very much. And when I asked her for specifics, rattling off all the times they'd cancelled on us last minute, and how it was always me initiating contact, she shook her head and said, 'Come on, really?'

But I could tell Cady understood. She made a comment about them being busy, but seemed to vanish into herself. Maybe this was what Eloise had meant about her. This need to defend them. When she returned to me again, she asked, 'Do you ever wonder why we do this to ourselves? Chasing these impossible dreams.'

It was funny, because now her words came out of my mouth. All that stuff she used to say about the difference between those that made it and those that didn't was willpower. That you had to make yourself continue despite rejection. Failure was an inevitable part of success, and every failure meant you were moving along the track in the right direction.

She laughed, recognising herself, and told me younger Cady had been full of it. 'Sometimes I wonder... I made myself promise not to give up or sell out because that's what I always thought my parents had done. Thing is, why am I, a thirty-three-year-old woman, who probably wants to have a family one day, trying to keep a promise to a little girl? It's not as if *I've* never let anybody down before.'

I realised what was happening. The others were affecting her. So, I put a hand on her shoulder, and I told her it wasn't us. That the world was harder for people like us. People with our background. And I also added that our motivations were always more complicated than we realised.

She gave me a strange smile, one I struggled to understand at first. At first, I felt embarrassed I'd overshared. But, on reflection, I decided it meant she agreed with me. And she soon perked up. While swinging on a pirate ship, I mentioned my project management, and she suggested I could look into entertainment project management as a potential back door into the industry.

'Or what about project-managing for a theme park?' she said, looking around us. 'That might be cool.'

It had been exactly six months since Eloise last spoke to me. But today, I told her about my meeting with Cady. Told her that I still didn't understand 'Robin Hood', nor Cady's part in it. I insisted Cady was innocent, and a victim of the others as much as us. But she was defiant. She'd said all she had to say, apparently.

An hour later, I decided to leave. I was in the doorway when I heard her say that word again.

'Art.'

I had a nightmare I was on the porter's lodge roof, the No Tomorrows Club lined up on the turrets in the moonlight. I come up behind them, and one by one I push them off. I hesitate before pushing Cady.

Then a cold hand touches the back of my neck. And I know I have to. To make things right.

'She is the worst,' the voice hisses, sounding like a nest of snakes in my head.

So I push.

CADY

Saturday 22nd June, 2.00am
Celsius: 30°, Fahrenheit: 86°

But what if this did open the box?

Through this whole night, Cady had been convinced of her innocence. If she lost that, what else might she lose? What other hurt had she caused that she simply hadn't recognised, perhaps having stuffed it into that attic in her mind because it didn't suit her?

Of course, she'd known at the time that it might upset Danson when her YouTube career had started taking off. That was why she'd made sure he didn't find out on his own. She'd sent him a birthday message, two years ago now. The year after the lockdowns had stopped. She knew that it was September, because only after the message had sent did she remember his birthday was in *October* – a mistake she'd made more than once over the years because her initial way of remembering Danson's birthday was that it was the same date as Robbie's, only a month ahead. She just kept forgetting the month ahead part.

At the end of that message, she'd added a short PS – *you'll never guess what's happened to me* – and sent a link to her channel.

She'd known there was a problem when he took a week to reply. And what he came back with spoke volumes.

That's amazing. Wow! Would I be able to talk to you about it some time?

Something about that phrasing had made her uncomfortable. And because it was so vague, she'd given the message a thumbs-up emoji and decided to deal with it later. She'd known how that talk would go, hadn't she? And like everything that Cady didn't want to contemplate, she – not deleted it from her mind exactly – but just sort of buried it. Stuck it in a shallow grave for the worms of her subconscious to deal with.

'You go first,' Femi said now, with a decisiveness that made it no longer playful to turn it back on him but downright combative.

She felt another pulse of irritation at his skill in bossing these situations. But, in the end, she told them all what happened. The reaction was muted. Winston groaned when she revealed they had always met at theme parks. Femi nodded at parts and murmured at others. Naz said nothing.

And when Femi asked for a date, she said, 'I sent the message for his birthday two years ago. So, 2022.'

Femi began to turn the numbers into the right position.

'October, then?' Naz said.

'No, hang on,' Cady paused, making sure to get it right in her head this time. 'His birthday is definitely October?'

'Yes,' Femi and Naz both said.

'Okay, good. Right, well the thing is, I messed up the—'

clack

'…months.'

'What do you mean?' Femi said after a short silence, his voice suddenly puzzled and a little bit afraid.

'Sorry, I… I sent the message in September, Femi.'

'But…' He looked at her wide-eyed. 'I already did it.'

The clasp was upright with the other two.

'No, no, no,' Cady said.

Both of them stared at the box, waiting for it to explode, or for a crushing sound from inside. God, she'd blown it. She'd blown it all because she'd been too busy trying to frame her story in a sympathetic way to concentrate. Because of her stupid brain. Her stupid broken brain.

Danson, Then

I think Eloise wants me to kill them all.

She is coming back from wherever she has been and wants them to atone for what they made me do. And if I don't make things right, she will tell everyone what I did to her.

What choice do I have?

And I do feel hatred about the way way way they've treated me. Not enough to crucify them or burn them or bury them alive the way Eloise keeps hinting at when she says 'Art' to me. Always Art. Art. Art. Art. The word has lost its meaning. But yes, I am not averse to the idea of action, per se. To help them understand. Shock them into the truth.

I'd never hurt them though. And certainly not Cady. I have told Eloise I need time to consider. I'm going to spend some more time up in North Wales on the theme park revamp I've been managing. It will give me give me give me some much-needed space.

I had another strange dream.

In this one, I travel to meet Cady in Oxford to get lunch. I'm shown to a room in the back of a Chinese restaurant, and am sat at a table with four other spaces. I'm left there thinking there's been an error until in come Femi, Naseem, Winston and Cady.

'Surprise,' they say, and I am speechless.

My beloved friends, with whom I was so angry, have arranged a surprise party in my honour. A belated birthday celebration, they say. They buy me food and drink. Tell me how much they've missed me. They all look older, but more beautiful than ever, and they are warm to me.

They ask me about my life, and they are genuinely happy for me that I have worked so hard to keep my mother's house, and that I've managed to fashion such a unique career. At a bar later, Naz tells me she actually loved the opening of my novel, and that she wished she'd had more time to read it all and help me. And Winston pulls me aside, too, and says that he really liked my band's songs back in the day, and he's sorry for not getting back to me about it at the time. Femi has a private word, too, and tells me he hates how we've drifted over the years, and that it is his fault, but that, if I ever need him, he is there for me. That I just need to call.

And of course, I thank Cady for arranging this surprise, which I know she must have done after we last met. But she says she has nothing to do with it. She tells me how much the others all wanted to see me. And in this dream I am very drunk, and very happy, and I believe her.

Thing is, dear reader, it wasn't a dream. It should have been. But it really wasn't. I have the hangover and the gaps in my memory to prove it.

They do love me. They do, do, do. I knew it all along.

How did I allow Eloise to poison me against them again? What is wrong with me?

No more! I've been seeing too much of her the last few years. And I probably need to wean myself off microdosing. I am going to tell Eloise we are done. I'm applying for a job in the Middle East, a theme park in the desert! It's the perfect excuse to escape. And if she can't deal with that, I'll live with the consequences.

So I went back today to say farewell. Mona told me the latest scans on Eloise's brain showed positive signs. Some of the staff had heard her making noises, and they wanted to know if I'd seen or heard anything. Of course, I said no. Because, have I?

I didn't stay very long. I lost my nerve. Need more time.

Finally went back today, but things went badly. I told Eloise about my new job, and that I needed a break, and at first she said nothing. So, I sat beside her. Head down. And eventually, I heard that slow rustling. Sensed her undeniable presence.

What will you do about THEM?

Did she say it? Didn't she? I didn't know. But I told her I'd changed my mind and she was wrong. That the No Tomorrows loved me, that they'd proved it in Oxford. I heard a sound not unlike a distant saw working quickly through a knot. Then I realised she was laughing.

I didn't look up. I asked her what was funny funny funny, and she told me how ridiculous I was. How little I chose to see when it suited me. Then she spun a wild story about how Cady had felt sorry for me when we met at Thorpe Park. And that she had begged the others to come to a meet-up with me because of how upset I'd seemed. She'd probably told them I looked suicidal, to really drive it home.

Eloise said I was gullible. That I smelled of desperation.

But I knew Eloise's game now. She was trying to rile me out of thinking straight. I told her she was lying out of jealousy.

You idiot. They pity you. They laugh at you behind your back. At your music and your writing and your shitty magic.

It went on like this a while. So I got up and started pacing the room, knowing it was Eloise that had hated my magic, not them. Without ever looking at her, I told Eloise that I loved her, but that it was probably best we move on from each other. But she kept going.

If you loved me, you'd listen. Cady beeeeeegged them to see you. She felt guilty, because she looks at you and sees herself. And she can't bear it. But she isn't you. She is going to become as successful as the others. And when she does, she will want nothing to do with you, DANSON.

Each word was a slash on my soul. That name in her mouth, cruel cruel cruel. I told her to shut up, and increased the speed of my pacing. I kept telling myself that I just needed to make her understand about them. But how can you reason with someone who doesn't use the same logic as you?

Don't come crawling back to me when she betrays you, STRAW MAN, DAN.

I warned her not to call me that.

Straw man, straw man. Anything in there?

Don't say that.

Yes … there's something in there, isn't there? Something growing. Your little problem problem problem.

I hated how well she preyed on my deepest worries. Even if it was all nonsense.

Yooooooou know, don't you? And it's coming for you, Danson. But not before I tell everyone what a straw man you are. Just like your dad always said.

I screamed at her. Wanting her out my mind. And somehow I found myself by the bed, staring at the dust on the plastic flowers and telling her she was the broken one. That she was the one whose parents had messed her up.

I had my hand on her face. I was so angry, and yet I wasn't squeezing hard. Just enough to keep her nose and mouth sealed.

After a while, I sat down and apologised. I had gloves on that I didn't remember putting on. I took them off and calmly listed all the reasons she was wrong. That, even if they weren't perfect, they were my friends. And perhaps, with a little guidance, they might even be good people one day.

When I left, it was dark. No one saw me arrive and no one saw me leave. I think on some level, perhaps I'd known things were going to go badly today.

CADY

Saturday 22nd June, 2.03am
Celsius: 30°, Fahrenheit: 86°

'It's open,' Cady said, not wanting to blink.

'It's open,' Femi agreed.

A moment passed. And another. Still nothing happened to the box. It just sat on Femi's lap, three-quarters unlocked.

Finally, Winston said through the seat gap, 'Well, that was lucky.'

Cady shook her head. This couldn't be right. Nothing had happened with Danson in October. It had definitely been in September. She was certain.

'You must have got his birthday right that year, after all,' Naz said.

'I didn't,' she said. 'I remember my exact thought process.

I waited for it to come around so I had a natural reason to contact him. Then I messed it up.'

Winston laughed. 'No offence, Cady, but you and dates were never—'

'No,' Cady said. 'I remember. One hundred per cent.'

'You forgot,' Naz said softly. 'It's something you do. You always used to blame the crash. It doesn't matter. It all worked out.'

Cady wanted to yell at Naz, suddenly. At her tone, and for the part she'd played in them being here tonight, and for not telling her what she'd told Eloise. Naz didn't know what she was talking about.

'*Or*,' Femi said, elongating the word for dramatic effect, 'the whole mystery box thing has been complete rubbish.'

No one said a thing for a moment.

'What do you—' Cady started.

But Femi slid across the button on the final lock.

clack.

All four clasps now pointed skyward.

A small scream escaped Cady. Her hand came up to her mouth.

'Is that it?' Winston said, his face in the gap between the chairs. 'Did we actually...'

'I'd adjust your expectations,' Femi said, his voice grave.

'Why?' Cady asked.

Femi had a tiny smile on his face. 'This whole thing ... it's been a sleight of hand. A ... a... Another magician's trick. A misdirection.'

'Explain?' Cady said. 'You can't know that.'

'He wanted us to believe we could escape. Long enough for him to get away to wherever he was going next. Long enough for us to scrabble around trying to work out what terrible things we'd done to him, listing them all, perhaps, so we didn't pick the wrong one, thereby revealing the *truth* to each other about what total shits we've continued to be. He underestimated our overconfidence, though. He never had any intention of setting us free. He wants us to die here.'

'You can't know that,' Cady said again, fear pinching her voice.

'I can. He misdirected us before to make us think one of us had killed Eloise. Only then he turns around and says *he* did it. He was torturing us. And I wanted to believe he wasn't doing the same again now, that maybe it was some elaborate sermon, but the thought never left my mind. And when we put in Cady's wrong date… I just had a feeling. Now, I'm absolutely certain.'

'Why, Femi?' Naseem said.

Femi gave a sad smile and lifted up the box to show Cady. At first, she didn't see it. Then her gaze alighted on the numbers beneath the final lock. Femi's lock.

000000

He'd not entered anything. And yet it had opened. Just like her lock had opened on a completely random date. They could have entered anything. Danson had never been testing them at all.

'Oh, my God,' Cady said.

Naz demanded to know what was happening.

But Cady was reaching out to the box, needing to see what was inside now. She gently lifted the edge of the lid a fraction. She looked at Femi, and he nodded.

She lifted the lid. Inside were no complicated mechanics, no secret compartments or drawers, and most importantly, nothing resembling a key. It was just a normal wooden chest.

'Is it there?' Naz said. 'Please just say it's there.'

'There's something,' Femi said, and reached in to grab one of three objects Cady could see. He raised it up to get a better look in the starlight. The object made a small mechanical whirring sound.

'What is it?' Cady said.

He handed it to her. 'I think it's a speaker.'

The object, disc-shaped and no bigger than the palm of her hand, had a weight suggesting complicated innards. One flat side felt rubbery, the other corrugated. Cady found a button and pressed it. A soft boom interrupted the whirring and the device fell silent.

'It's a speaker,' she said.

She didn't need to say out loud that this had been another misdirection. That it proved Femi right. Undoubtedly the falling sensation that seemed to be pulling down the corners of her mouth and her diaphragm was happening inside them, too.

Femi still had a hand inside the box. 'The locks and numbers aren't even connected. They're just … two separate bits.' It wasn't quite amusement in his voice, but certainly from the opposing side of a bitter family feud.

Femi must have seen what she could see. A shadow at the base of the box, long and slender.

He retrieved it, his fist closed around the handle. A knife, around eight inches long. He touched the blade and his finger sprung back.

'Is there a key?' Naz demanded.

'No. He left a knife and a speaker.'

'You're kidding?' Winston said.

Naz moaned, on the verge of tears. 'Does the knife fit the keyhole?'

'There's a note,' Cady said and took out a piece of paper from the box, the last thing inside.

She brought the note up to her face. It had been handwritten. She read it to the others.

YOUR WAY OUT, AS PROMISED.

Femi started to laugh. 'I knew it. I bloody knew it.'
Naz started to scream at the night in terror and frustration.
Cady turned over the note. She read this out too.

IT'S THE HOPE THAT KILLS YOU...

'No,' Naz cried. 'No.' The car began to shake as she repeatedly kicked out at the floor.

'He lied. He told us the key was in there.'

'He didn't, though.' Femi shook his head. 'He went on about a key but he never said it was in the box, did he?'

'He did,' Winston said.

'He said our way out was inside,' Cady said. 'Liberatio.'

Winston considered this before striking his clamshell restraint. 'Sick bastard.'

'It was a joke?' Naz said.

'A joke. A satire.'

'An art piece,' Cady said, noticing something on the knife. She reached out and pointed to the blade. 'I think that's a dedication.'

For Eloise.

It was a long time before anyone spoke again. A truly deathly silence was what it was, but Cady couldn't accept that.

She would never accept it. This wasn't going to be how she died. There had to be something else they hadn't considered. She turned to Femi, again and again, hoping he might have something. But he wouldn't even look back at her. And that worried Cady, too. He had gone further into himself, and sat now staring at the knife. The box, resting on his lap, tumbled off and struck the car floor with a clatter that startled her.

But Femi didn't even blink.

PART FOUR
SUNRISE

CADY

Saturday 22nd June, 5.40am
Celsius: 28°, Fahrenheit: 82.4°

They had said little to each other during the better part of the night. All their hope, their energy and their resistance, had evaporated once they had opened the box. They returned to shouting every so often, sounding quite mad with it. They stomped and wailed and shook the car, but nothing about their situation improved.

They did all report feeling dizzy, though. Movement began to take a toll.

Femi kept staring at the knife, and Cady watched him carefully. Although at times that was hard. Sometimes she found herself gazing at the healed cut on her finger from where she'd nicked it slicing cake. Back at home it was night time, too, and Tom would be asleep in their bed. At one point Cady drifted off. She'd been looking at the desert, thinking about Tom, bouncing between vivid visions of their first reunion after all of this came to a positive conclusion and his vacant face as he read her eulogy at her funeral.

That was when she'd heard a voice. A voice from the walkway. She had turned and been surprised to see Robbie standing there, smiling and waving. Wisps of smoke floated around him. He looked older than he'd done when he died, and it struck Cady how handsome he would have become. How he would have had no problems finding his red-haired wife. Was she out there now, perhaps, that wife from another world, married to someone else?

She knew she was dreaming. And that awareness eventually woke her up. But not before she had apologised to Robbie. She'd tried to live the best life she could, live like there was no tomorrow, to make some sort of sense of his death and make her survival count for something. It should have been her that died that day, she knew that. Her parents would have preferred it, even if only slightly. He would have brought so much more to the world than she ever could. But now everything she'd done had led to this pitiful place. A stupid, pointless death. And what did she have to show for her life? Shallow videos that would leave no lasting imprint on the world, and a loving partner who she'd insisted on keeping at arm's length, especially since becoming successful. And why? Why did she do that? Was she afraid of losing something if she let him get too close? Her, Cady Ellison, who was afraid of nothing?

Robbie had said to her, 'It's going to be okay, Cady Bug. Stay positive.'

Her eyes were teary when she opened them. She would stay positive, for Robbie. But it hurt so bitterly to think of Tom mourning her. Mourning her and then moving on to someone else. Not in another life, but in this one.

When the sun had first begun to make an impact on the night from beneath the horizon, Naz had asked, 'How much will it hurt us?' No one had replied.

Now, the sun's lazy predation on them had begun in earnest. Its deep orange head was visible amid blues and purples gathered at the horizon. Around them, the desert and mountains, the empty plots and tents, looked like they had been dipped in gold. Cady could see the mounds of sand again, arranged like a smiley face. That face seemed to be mocking her.

They were sitting in silence when Femi raised his arms above his head, stretched, and flopped down back onto his restraint.

The train suddenly moved.

It might have been unconnected to Femi, but the synchronicity created a powerful illusion. All of them felt it. They sat up straight, exchanging cautious looks. It had only been a little shift forward, maybe an inch or so. But it had happened.

'What was it?' Naz asked. 'Cady?'

'I don't know. It moved, though, didn't it?'

Stay positive.

They used what little energy they had to try and shake the car again, throwing their weight forward to make it move again. But they were all too tired to sustain it for very long. And eventually they settled back into their frightened silence.

Perhaps it had been just the wind, or the shifting temperature causing the tracks to expand. But Cady didn't really believe that. To her, it had felt like the chain slipping. The train couldn't technically move without the motor. But what if the gunshot had done something? Or what if the weight of the train was causing the motor to turn?

These were the kind of good thoughts Robbie wanted her to have. Positive, forward-looking thoughts kept your brain in the right place for a solution. You got nowhere once you gave in, did you? Mum and Dad had always said they didn't ever want to retire, because too many of their friends had fallen ill or died soon after. Like your body gets the message you're done and starts shutting down.

It's the hope that kills you.

No, it wasn't the hope that killed you. It was the hope that got you places. It was the hope that kept you going after years and years of trying and failing and … and then…

Kills you. You get me, Cady?

Oh, Danson had always said that Cady *got* him. And she got him now, certainly, that bloody genius. Was this how he'd felt watching them all succeed? Feeling trapped in one place, all the while telling himself there was a chance of escape when in fact he was never going to make it. Because the world just wasn't set up for him to do that.

No, the hope saved you. She could have given up after all her wealthier friends became successful. Yet she'd pushed on. She'd made something of herself eventually.

'Let's just stay positive,' she said out loud, to nobody in particular. 'Stay positive.'

'Please, Cady,' Naz said with what was left of her voice. 'Please don't.'

The tone of her voice made Cady stiffen. 'Sorry,' she said on instinct. 'I was talking to myself, really.'

A long pause followed, and it seemed the moment had passed. Then Naz said, 'If only.'

It hadn't been loud, but Cady heard it, nonetheless. She considered her response, confused as to why Naz's remark had sounded so barbed. Were they all meant to sit here in silence and die quietly? Finally, she settled on, 'I just think it's important we don't give up.'

'And the more you say that,' Naz said, 'the more it reminds me of how fucked we are. So ... please.' After a beat, she added, 'It's the hope that kills you.'

Cady considered letting lie, but instead she said, 'I don't believe that.'

'No, you don't, do you?' Naz said.

Cady's chest tightened. 'What does that mean? Why do you keep saying things like that?'

'Because I don't know if I believe in you.'

'Is this helpful, Naz?' Femi asked.

'What don't you believe?'

'That you can be so smart and engaged and seemingly self-aware, and yet ... you're so utterly clueless about other things. Is it an act? But I don't think it is.'

'What things am I clueless about?'

'That message Danson left us. It was about you.'

'Naseem,' Femi said. 'We're all upset—'

'No,' Naz said. 'If I'm going to die... Cady has been acting like she's not part of this the whole time we've been here. But she is. In fact, I'm not sure she's not the whole reason why we're here.'

Cady's hand drew instinctively up to her chest. She was appalled and overcome with a sense of injustice. Yet she wanted to know now what Naz meant. 'I'm really confused.'

Femi held up a let-me-handle-this hand to Cady. 'Naz, back off, okay? That's rubbish, none of this is Cady's fault.'

Naz let out an irritated screech, but when she spoke again, it was slow and considered. 'I'd probably have been happy as a lawyer. Okay? Or an accountant. Earned good money. Known what I was doing each day. What time I'd finish. How much holiday I'd get. *Corruption* wouldn't exist. And I'd still have a relationship with my family. But no, every time I ever *contemplated* the thought that maybe being a writer wasn't working for me, and that I might prefer to do something more ... normal, who comes into my head? Telling me that talent is ten a penny and persistence is what separates successful artists from the rest. That rejection is the signpost telling you you're on the right path. That failures are to be bounced back from. Her. Cady bloody Ellison. Ushering us all down the runway, our tyres bursting, the engine in flames, yelling stay positive stay positive, until it's too late to stop.'

'Naz,' Femi said, 'come on. None of that is on Cady.'

'After the car accident with Danson, and even more so after Eloise, she made us all promise never to give up. Repeatedly. I know you both remember that. She was always the one telling us how amazing we all were and the world needed our art, and we had to persist no matter the cost. It was like a cult, sometimes. I'd only just made the step to walk away from one religion, and I was messed up and maybe leaning hard into that to make it stick. But I never had the space to find the real me because we had to all be focused on fucking *making it*. And the pregnancy ... I was trying to drink myself into a miscarriage, and I know you say you don't remember it, but all you kept saying was you mustn't waste your life, Naz. Which was as good as saying kill it, even though I still wasn't sure. You know that awful song, the one about getting knocked down and getting up again? Sometimes you need to stay down. You need to stay down to heal.'

'I'm sorry,' Cady said, tears in her eyes as if she'd been slapped. 'I was only ever—'

'You don't need to say that,' Winston said. 'Naz is just—'

'I'm what? In agony? Losing my mind? Desperate for a drink?' Now she sounded angry. 'Yes to all those things. But Winston, I doubt you would ever have thought about doing a band professionally if Cady hadn't insisted you send your recordings to people when you started dabbling with modern stuff in London. You obviously never wanted fame. And Femi, every knock you had, every failed audition, it was Cady building you up again. Telling you that you were talented and handsome enough, and that you would only have to turn up in Hollywood and someone would cast you.'

'Naz,' Femi said. 'This is … all due respect, this is bullshit. We supported each other.'

'Yeah,' Winston said. 'Come on.'

'You both got sad, and tired, and wanted to just … not chase the dream, sometimes. I was there. But you were never allowed to. One year, I wrote something for the *Mays Anthology*. Some famous author was editing and I think I got some sort of honourable rejection. And I didn't like that. I wrote something so personal to me, and it had been deemed *unfit*. When I finally told you all, Cady was right in there with, "you can't be a real artist without rejection. Every success rests on a mountain of failure". Which is fine if you've numbed yourself somehow to it. Somehow uncoupled the link between your art and your soul. But, if you haven't, going back again and again is torture. And maybe not everyone is cut out for it.'

'I don't know what to say,' Cady said, trying to keep it together.

'You don't need to say anything. We didn't have to listen to you. And we did okay. But what about Danson? How did he feel when you kept encouraging him to come to us with his terrible projects that were bound to get rejected? Is that why he's torturing us now? Because chasing the dream was a nightmare for him. And on top of it all, you go and make a success of something right in his wheelhouse.'

'That's enough,' Femi said.

'No, it's not. I'm angry. Aren't you angry, Femi? She's in denial. We had the potential for a second chance and instead… we're going to die here with our baby. And I'm not going to *stay positive* about anything while she's there acting like she's blameless.'

'I don't think my soul's uncoupled,' Cady said, her voice quiet and unconvincing, utterly bereft and embarrassed that all this time Naz somehow resented her for the way she'd tried to help them all. And worse, was what Naz had said about Danson true? Had she enabled him?

'It's not your fault, really,' Naz said. 'I know that. You've got your issues, too. There was a reason we all stuck to each other.'

'What do you mean, issues? Are you talking about my brother?'

'Yes. But… Cady, come on. Do you *know*?'

'Do I know *what*?'

'I know you must do, but … do you know how your brother died? Like, in your conscious mind?'

'I don't know…' Why was her voice trembling that way, and her stomach clenching? Why did it suddenly feel like the brakes had given way on the coaster and everything at once was falling? 'My grandad crashed the car.'

'Yes. He did. But ... do you honestly not remember what you told me in the first year? About why he crashed?'

'He was old. He wasn't paying attention.'

'That's not what you told me.'

Cady could see smoke rising above Naz's chair, like she was on fire. Wisps of it, like in her dream. Maybe this was a dream? Maybe it wouldn't matter what Naz said next because she would wake up soon, hopefully beside Tom back in England.

But she couldn't put it off any longer, no matter how scared she felt. The restraints were locked. The train was climbing the lift hill. All she could do now was let it happen.

'What did I tell you?'

Danson, Then

Today I walked in and Mona broke the news that Eloise had stopped breathing the day after my last visit. She sweetly suggested that it was like she'd held out for one last goodbye before going. Apparently, the funeral had been last month, and Mona had tried calling me but the number I left hadn't worked. When she showed me the piece of paper I'd written it on, two of the digits were completely wrong.

———

A group of us from the company were driven out from the hotel to where construction had started on Dreamland. We had to cross miles of unpaved, bumpy desert to a plain in the bowl of a mountain. It's mostly rocks and sand and mountains and absolutely inescapable heat. I don't know if it was the drive, or the temperature, but while everyone else was hyped by the place, I just kept thinking that this was what hell might look like.

I threw up behind a mound of sand when no one was looking. A gust of wind came by and howled around the rocks. And I swear to God I thought I heard Eloise saying, *It's growing, Danson.*

I'm sorry it's taken me so long to write. It's been a challenging few months.

I had a pretty distressing message from Cady Cady Cady that's put me in a spin. She sent me a 'birthday message', a month early, as usual. That she's never been able to remember is, in retrospect, a clue to her real real real feelings about me that I should have spotted earlier. But when that woman decides something, it gets locked in an impenetrable box in her head.

Anyway, in her message was a PS, with a sneaky, cowardly link at the end. A link to her new 'project'.

She has a YouTube channel now. She's been doing it since the pandemic and has multiple thousands of followers. Comments. Fans. Collaborations with other YouTubers.

My idea! She'd stolen my idea. At Thorpe Park, we saw a couple filming themselves talking about one of the roller coasters. I SAID to HER, we should start a channel. And she said she'd always thought about doing one, but that she had NEVERHADAGOODIDEA.

Her channel is monetised. She has adverts, too.

Sneaky Cady. Sneaky, schemey, snakey Cady.

It took me a week to even reply, in which time I spent every hour I was not working on Dreamland in my accommodation watching her videos. So charming. So funny. A face so pretty in portrait.

Such a thief. Such a liar. Such a … betrayer!

I told myself that, if I just spoke with her, maybe I'd feel better. I owed her that much. So I tried instigating that conversation. But days later, all I received was a little thumbs-up emoji on my message. That was it. After all these years defending her to Eloise…

I tried to calm myself down. I really did. I twisted and contorted my brain to make it okay fine better. But I couldn't stop watching her videos. At night. First thing in the morning. At work. Watching her BE HER, but as an act for camera.

Which got me thinking: perhaps it's all an act? All this time, the whole Cady show.

There was me assuming she was like me, when in fact, she is worse than I ever thought the others were. Worse than Eloise ever thought. She had only believed Cady to be a powerful enabler. A battery.

I waited weeks and realised the thumb was all I was going to get. By that point I'd started having long revenge fantasies about somehow bringing down her YouTube channel. Sending her awful messages in the comments. Threatening her. Maybe spilling her secret to her family.

The dreams have come back. Vivid enough to taint the hours after I wake. I'm having one repeatedly where where where I am digging up Eloise. I pull her from a coffin and hold my breath to stop the smell. I hold her and tell I am sorry. Tell her that she was right after all! And I kiss what remains of her lips, which give and spread on mine like Vaseline.

THE DROP

There's something wrong with me. I've not been sleeping and I've been losing weight. I can't concentrate at work, and I keep making really stupid mistakes. I submitted a report last week that had multiple repeated words all the way through. I've gone back through my diaries and seen errors I've made going back a year or so.

I've booked a doctor's appointment here, just in case, because work have noticed, and I don't think stress and the heat are entirely cutting it now on the excuse excuse excuse front. But I think I know what the real problem is.

I need to see Femi. He said I should get in touch if I needed him, and boy do I need some of that love I felt in Oxford right now. I have plenty of leave to take. I think I'll fly back. Maybe he can help me understand what has happened with Cady. Because I need the dreams of Eloise to stop. And the strange fantasies.

Yesterday, I stood looking up at the lift hill, the track falling into thin air between two cranes. I imagined inviting Cady out here for one of her videos. Giving her an exclusive ride. Maybe leaving her up there a little while. Tell her it broke down. I shouldn't be having these thoughts. I shouldn't want to see her pale, freckly skin burn.

I know your secret, I could tell her. And now you can't run from it.

What is wrong with me?

CADY

Saturday 22nd June, 5.50am
Celsius: 29°, Fahrenheit: 84.2°

Cady had always been a good girl. And good girls didn't like smoking. That much Cady remembered.

She'd always hated cigarettes. Because Nan, wife of Grandad Sal, had died 'because she smoked'. That's what she had been told. And armed with that knowledge, ten-year-old Cady had gone on her own smoking cessation mission with the zeal only a child can enact without fear of reproach. Shaking her head at Grandad Sal whenever she smelled cigarette smoke on him. Telling strangers puffing outside supermarkets they were going to die if they didn't give up. Once, her parents had come home to find she had put a No Smoking sign on every door of the house in anticipation of Grandad coming to stay.

As puberty neared, though, she'd tried to soften her

approach, at the suggestion of the helpful adults around her. Still, even if she had to live with people's *stupid* choice to kill themselves, that didn't mean she had to put up with passive smoking – something they'd learned about at school. After all, they were trying to murder her!

She still worked on Grandad, too, every time she saw him. She could try to save his soul because he was family. She loved him. But he was *relentless*. And sometimes Cady got the feeling he could simply block out whole parts of the world as easily as closing his eyes, including her voice when she was lecturing him. She could do that too, and tried to block out the sadness she felt when she considered he might die just as Nan had done. That he might not even care if he died now Nan wasn't here.

At least he went outside to smoke. Or leaned out of a window. That was a compromise.

She supposed that was why she got so cross at him that day of the crash. It had been a difference of opinion over outside and inside.

'You said to me you were in the back of the car,' Naz said to Cady, 'but that he lit up while you were driving along so he could smoke through the window, and the smoke blew into the back. You started telling him to put it out, but he wouldn't, so your brother changed places with you while you were still driving. When you got in the front seat, you hadn't got your seatbelt on yet. That's why you went through the window. And just when he reached the intersection, his smoke changed direction. You said it drifted across to you and a wisp went up your nose. He pulled out just as you'd reached over to knock the cigarette from his mouth. When you did it, he looked at you instead of the road, and was still trying to locate where it had fallen on his lap when the crash happened.'

It sounded at once alien and yet so utterly true. Like a friend's obituary read by a stranger. Something like terrified déjà vu rippled through Cady, yet … this hadn't happened, had it?

'You were drunk, and high, and maybe even tripping,' Naz said, 'so maybe it was a fantasy or a lie or a … waking dream. But I never believed that. I saw your eyes.'

Cady knew it was all true. She reached up to touch her temple. Pain throbbed there, awoken from its slumber. No, it had never been asleep. She was the one asleep. That pain was always there, had been since the accident. She'd just grown used to it, like how your tongue gets used to the disconcerting unfamiliarity of a freshly chipped tooth. Your mind grew over and around discomfort, like plants on abandoned buildings. With enough time, a city could become a jungle.

Cady closed her eyes and more tears came. She struggled to grab the breaths required to compose herself.

There had always been smoke in her dreams of the crash, hadn't there? Always smoke in the car *before* the crash. Why should that be? And in those dreams, she was so often in the back of the car. Why was that? In her memories, too, she was sometimes in the front, sometimes in the back. She'd put it all down to her memory being affected by the accident, another quirk like her inability to keep dates straight. Or just dream logic and…

Femi's hand rubbed her shoulder, and she startled. 'Can we call time on this, please, Naz?' he said.

'I killed them,' she said before she could stop herself.

'No,' Femi and Naz said together.

'Guys,' Winston said, 'why are we doing this?'

'It's fine,' Cady said. 'I can… I think it's true, isn't it? I've always… I always knew things couldn't be how I remembered them. I was responsible. For Grandad. For Robbie.' Something between a moan and a cry burst from her throat unexpectedly. She brought her hands to her mouth to silence it.

Naz, voice suddenly filled with doubt, said, 'Cady, it was an accident. That's just it. It was a stupid, awful accident when you were only a child. But I think your guilt about it is part of why you're like you are. The pathological positivity—'

'I think that's enough, Naz.' Winston's voice was tinged with anger.

'Just ... let us talk, Winston. Cady, you've spent your life trying to make things happen, for yourself, for other people. More than any of us, you wanted that validation. And it was so obviously more than simply guilt about surviving. It was like ... success would absolve you. And how I wish I'd talked to you about it, Cady. How I wish it hadn't become part of this Eloise thing and something I really wanted to forget about. And I'm sorry I told her. Maybe on some level, my idiotic, selfish younger me thought it all needed to come out anyway and so would actually help you.'

'Jesus,' Winston said.

'It's the lowest moment of my life, Cady. But honestly, I was scared if my brother found out he might have killed me. But ... I do wish I'd tried to help you. Because I used to hide from you sometimes if I was feeling bad, particularly about my writing or something. Because you burned so bright, and I couldn't take it sometimes. I was worried one day you'd combust and take us all with you. Which is maybe what's happened now. Maybe Danson got scorched.'

'It's not Cady's fault we're here,' Femi shouted.

'Maybe it is,' Cady said, her own voice sounding like it was coming from someone else in the car. 'I did encourage him. I encouraged him all the time. Like ... like he *was* me. And I knew he was hurt about the channel. But I just ... locked it away.'

'All I'm saying,' Naz said, 'is that fate threw terrible things our way. But it was our choices after that led us here. And I think the three of us know that, we've lived with it, but Cady... She's a fucking nuclear power station—'

'Enough,' Femi yelled and kicked out at the front of the car.

At that moment, the whole train moved again. All of them cried out and grabbed the handles on their restraints.

Cady turned to look at Femi. It had moved an inch again, maybe a little bit more. But the jolt had been stronger than the last one.

'What just happened?' Femi asked her.

'I don't know. I mean...' She sniffed and wiped her eyes with the back of her hand. 'The chain might have given a little bit. The motor is under a lot of pressure. Probably for longer than it was designed for.'

He nodded. 'That's what it felt like.'

They all began to kick and yell and shake. But again, nothing happened and eventually their cries tailed off, their energy depleted. The four of them sat trying to catch their breath, still half-awaiting a drop that didn't come.

It was Femi that broke the silence. 'Listen, all of this is bullshit, okay? We don't need an inquisition. I'll tell you why we're up here, okay? One, Eloise Draclin was a psychopath. Everyone like that? Two, Danson had serious problems. Problems that had nothing to do with us. After that, I think pointing fingers is ridiculous.'

Cady didn't agree. She understood everything now, and the finger hovered over her head like the sword of Damocles. All this time, she'd believed her life had been driven by a quest for the love her parents had been unable to give her after Robbie's death. That search for The Audience. Putting herself *out there*. *Doing something*. But no: really, she'd been trying to get away from who she really was. What she'd done. She'd always thought she was the greyhound, the only question being was the rabbit stuffed or real? But, actually, she'd been chasing nothing. She'd been the stuffed rabbit, hurtling along through life unaware it was even being pursued. And that no amount of success was ever going to make her feel like a good person again. Was that why she pushed Tom away? Because really how could he, with the things he contributed to the world, be with someone like her? After what she'd done.

Femi's voice had grown distant to her, but she began to tune back in.

'But let me say this, guys. If you want to know who's next in line after those two, I'll tell you. Because what tipped Danson over the edge wasn't Winston ignoring his demo, or Naz not reading his book, or even Cady not returning his message to meet up. I'm sure none of our successes helped his state of mind over the years. And we have all done things we're not proud of. But I started all this by telling Eloise Winston's secret. And the last time I saw Danson, I probably tipped him over the edge.'

Danson, Then

Femi met me in a back-street pub in Soho, wearing a flat cap and a long coat. He'd shaved off his goatee, too, and didn't much look like his character on the telly. Still think the barman recognised him, and Femi made a show of stuffing the tip jar.

We sat in a booth at the back, and he asked straight out what was troubling me. I've always liked how perceptive Femi is to my emotional states. I'd been planning on some opening chit-chat, but instead I blurted out how betrayed I felt by Cady, and that I needed to talk it through with someone.

It was like a cloud came over our booth. He inhaled, finished his pint, and seemed to grow to twice his size. He leaned forward and said to me, 'Go get some shots, yeah? Like, a lot.'

I did, even though I'd smelled alcohol on his breath when he arrived and I wanted his advice sober. When I brought them back, he necked two straight away.

Then he said it was very sad I couldn't be happy for Cady after all she'd done for me. I asked what that meant exactly, and he shook his head. I explained I was happy for her, like I was happy for everyone in the group doing well. It was just that it was hard, too, given we'd all said we'd be in it together. And especially given Cady stole my idea. He laughed at that, asked if I'd been copying Winston when I played in a band, or copying Naz when I wrote a novel.

He seemed angry but insisted he wasn't. He downed another shot and told me Cady was always my cheerleader. That she had made them all come to Oxford for my birthday because she'd been worried. That she thought I'd seemed suicidal.

My mouth fell open. It was just as Eloise had said.

'Were you suicidal, mate?'

I told him I hadn't been, and he nodded and threw out the word *pathetic*. I was so stunned that I don't exactly remember the the the phrasing or context. He did add that he felt guilty about using that word, but that he wanted to be truthful honest truthful with me now for my own good.

All of it sounded familiar. Like I was back up on the lodge with Eloise.

He sank yet another shot. And another. I rued buying so many so much so so many drinks.

Primed now, he went for the jugular. Said that Cady, and Naz, and Winston had all worked hard to get where they had. That he'd worked hard. And it was unfair of me to expect them to just open doors just because we knew each other at university.

The others would never say all this to me, he insisted, because they wouldn't want to get blood on their hands. But it was making Femi sad watching me chasing all these dreams when they clearly upset me.

Obviously, I tried to defend myself, and I said I'd never expected anything from anyone. That I'd worked hard, too. That I'd not had parents rich enough or alive enough to pay for a flat in London, or family friends in the industry, or even the freedom financially to make mistakes in my twenties.

Or did I just say that in my head and stare at him with my jaw ajar?

And then he said it: 'I know you've worked hard too, but the thing is, you need to understand, you're just not very…'

He didn't even have the courage to finish. I demanded he say say say it, but he just shook his head. We danced around, and I told him that, if he respected me, if he was actually my friend, he should say what was on his mind. But he was no Eloise.

So, this is how you all feel? I pressed. About my music. My writing. My magic.

'You're doing okay, aren't you?' he said. 'Theme parks are brilliant. Do you really need the other stuff?' He leaned forward then, and whispered, 'Big secret: creative success isn't all it's cracked up to be.'

But he started laughing then, and I admit, I got cross and told him not to patronise me. Oh, how I wanted to tell HIM some home truths then. All about how none of them could have done what they'd done if I hadn't kept their secrets. That I could have destroyed them but chose not to.

But he said he wasn't patronising me. He was trying to save my life. He asked if I'd ever considered that he and the others were successful because they weren't good people. Because success required incredible selfishness.

'We're all very different to you, mate.'

'Rubbish,' I said. 'I know you, Femi. I lived with you for years. I know all of you. I love all of you.'

Again, he laughed, and with a sad shake of his head, he said, 'Danson... We only moved in with you second year because we wanted a bigger house.'

'You're lying,' I said. 'I know you love me, too.'

'You don't know anything, mate.'

Then, after a pause for effect, he told me they'd all slept with one another in a big foursome the night after we'd met up in Oxford.

I didn't know what to say to this. Nor what it had to do with love. It just felt cruel, like this was definitive proof of my otherness. And maybe, because of the nefarious spirit in which he'd intended the revelation, I actually did feel irrational hatred and jealousy – even though none of this had ever been about sex.

'Cady joined in?' I asked, and he nodded, using all the skills in his acting tool box box box to come across as smug.

But now I didn't believe him. I didn't believe him. I didn't believe. He was doing an Eloise. Trying to make me hate them so I'd give up.

'You'd gone home,' he said.

Was his implication that, if I'd been rich enough to afford the hotel, I could've joined in?

It took a long time for me to compose myself enough to reply. Finally, I asked, 'So were we never in all this together, Femi?'

'Mate, you deserve better than us.'

I didn't know what to think. I thanked him for enlightening me, and he told me not to thank him. I should be angry and hate him, he said. I should want to hit him. He stared at me for a long time, and after he was done he lunged toward me and shouted. He stopped only inches from my face and eventually retreated.

I decided to go. Because he was drunk. And because I'd learned enough.

While I walked to the tube, I cried. Just like he'd known I would.

There is no easy way to learn you have wasted your life.

CADY

Saturday 22nd June, 6.02am
Celsius: 29°, Fahrenheit: 84.2°

'Oh my God,' Naz said. 'Why, Femi?'

He shrugged. 'I wanted to help the guy. And it was clear he was making himself miserable.' Neither Winston nor Naz spoke. Cady was still reeling from what Naz had brought to light, and had no room to take on another revelation of this magnitude.

'It mostly came from a good place,' Femi said. 'Danson was a decent behind-the-scenes guy, but he never showed any signs of being good at anything while we were at university, other than managing spreadsheets. Do you remember his awful close-up card tricks? Or that show we did in the third year, the one where he asked for a part, and he got the lines wrong two of the three nights? We were constantly auditioning and submitting and creating stuff all the time, hurling ourselves into all the artsy nonsense we could. And what did he do? Everything he started he never finished. In fact, the most creative thing he did in three years was lie to us about Eloise.'

Cady couldn't help it, and in her smallest voice she said, 'He was finding himself.'

'He wasn't you, Cady.' He let that hang for a moment. 'He didn't shine like you. He didn't work like you. And he certainly never finished anything, at least not to any decent standard.'

After what she'd just learned about herself, Cady had no desire to hear about how much she shined. And they were clearly attempts to placate her and diffuse her irrational anger on Danson's behalf. But to hear Femi talk this way about him, like the world was divided up into the talented and the not talented, it… it… *offended* her. That was the only word for it. Offended because so much of what she believed about art and success depended on the creative world being far more shaded and interesting than that.

But what did she really know any more about such things? She didn't know herself, that much was certain.

'Fuck,' Winston said. 'I think it's safe to say you definitely helped him find his way.'

Femi gave a sour laugh. 'Even now, I don't regret it. At least he died knowing the truth. But I take responsibility. He came to me at a low ebb, and I made a call. And as much as I want to say I calculated it, looking back I was taking my own anger out on him, too. He was there drooling over our imaginary lives, whereas I was sitting there across from him wishing I had a life as simple as…'

His voice cracked, and he turned away and covered his face. He sucked in a breath through pursed lips.

'Oh, Christ. You know, after my parents found out I hadn't been studying medicine, I told my dad I thought art could save more lives than medicine. You can imagine how he reacted. He told me I didn't give a shit about saving lives. Said that was my ego telling a story. So I said to him he'd know all about that, wouldn't he? And then we didn't speak for some time. But he was probably right. Even though, when I said those things to Danson, I was trying to save his life.'

He fell silent and shortly afterwards his shoulders started to bob.

'Femi,' Cady said, surprised she had anything left to give anyone else.

But Femi was gone now.

And in the end, they all let him go.

Eventually, his cries morphed into laughter. 'You'll find this funny. I think. You know, coming here… I'm sort of in the process of being cancelled.'

Cady shifted in her seat, already dreading what he might say.

'I'd had a bad call from my agent about it that day I met Danson. So, about a year before, I'd been doing an American film and had quite a flirty relationship with one of the other supporting actors. And she comes up to me after shooting one night and says we should go out and get some drinks to unwind. She says she can't go out looking and smelling like she did, right? And she was … perfectly nicely dressed in a clean top and jeans. So I say, you look good to me. And she says, thanks, yeah, but no, I stink and I look awful. She was being really over the top about how gross she was in that sort of over-the-top self-deprecating American way, and I was trying to be all British and gentlemanly, so I say, no seriously, you look great, and she oinks like a pig and says, nah. So obviously, I say you look really good to me, and blah

blah blah. And then she starts saying how doing the character she's playing, this outdoorsy, hillbilly type, is really affecting her confidence, and making her feel pretty unfuckable. Her words.'

Winston groaned in anticipation of what was coming. Cady could sense it too. Knowing Femi like she did. How he was with women. How he liked high stakes. How he couldn't resist paying compliments.

He continued, 'So I lean in again, and sort of channelling Hugh Grant, I say, honestly, I would fuck the absolute shit out of you right here and now.'

Naz laughed.

'And that didn't go down well?' Winston said.

'It's not funny. No, it did not go down well. She seemed fine with it at the time. But apparently she put in a complaint, said I'd blocked her with an arm or something, which I don't think I did, and the next day I get called in by the director and told I can do one for making her feel unsafe on set.'

'Oh, Femi, you daft prick,' Naz said.

'I'm laughing, trying to explain it to him what happened, and that maybe it's a humour thing that's been lost in translation. But no, he's pretty adamant he doesn't have a choice. So I'm thinking, never mind, I've got plenty lined up. Only I get back to the UK, and my agent tells me that I need to lay low a while as a few American doors have closed. Which was fine because I've got the British stuff, but now I'm worried.'

He shook his head and pinched the bridge of his nose.

'Just before I met Danson, I learned they were killing me off the show. I was only going to last three episodes of season seven. And then my *agent* said his wife was pregnant, and I should probably keep an eye out for other representation as he was scaling back his client list. So, yeah, when I saw Danson, part of me wanted to save him. Genuinely. I'm a big supporter of MeToo, and I probably made a bad call that day, but ... shit. Is that worthy of a Game Over? What maniac would want a career so bloody random and insane?'

'But you were drunk and angry, too,' Winston said. 'When you met Danson.'

'Yeah. That's my point. I own that.'

'Great,' Winston said. 'So glad I'm going to burn to death knowing you own all your terrible decisions.'

'Well ... I just want to be clear. No matter what we did in the past, I was the last of us to see him before yesterday. And I put it in his head that we were all against him. Me, me, me. And I started it, too. It was my stupid decision not to tell my mum and dad about my degree, my stupid decision to make it so public, and my decision to betray Winston's secret. And yeah, while we're at it, accident or not, I lost my temper and it led to Danson falling.'

At first, no one spoke. Then Winston said, 'I don't think any of us come out of this wearing halos – although my cents are that Cady didn't do shit to anyone. And I'd be the first to pin this on you, if I could after tonight, Femi. But you were right before. Eloise and Danson put us here. Maybe, if we'd not been so self-absorbed over the years, we might have noticed the guy was losing his mind. But no, instead we all turn up here like lambs.'

'Eloise and Danson can't help us now,' Femi said, 'but I can. The fault falls down the ladder to me next, which is why it's on me to get us out of this.' He looked down at the knife on his lap.

'Uh uh,' Cady said, her voice sounding so measly. 'No. No. That's not happening.'

'It's going to have to,' Femi said, with eerie calm. 'We all know there isn't another way.'

Cady wouldn't let him. Despite everything he'd done, despite everything they'd all done, none of them deserved this. She would grab the knife when he least expected it. Throw it over the side. It wasn't pathologically positive to think help might still come. They didn't know what the day might bring. There really might be someone coming for Jag. Or even for them. They could never be sure enough for … *that*.

Her left hand rose for a moment, hovered in the air.

But the sun was above the horizon now. She could already feel it heating up the desert again.

It would incinerate them all soon. She would die blistered, and red, and parched, suffering with pain she couldn't even comprehend.

And so would Femi. If they did nothing. So would Femi.

Her hand dropped back to her lap.

CADY

Saturday 22nd June, 6.40am
Celsius: 29°, Fahrenheit: 84.2°

For a time, they listened to the desert. Femi would occasionally return to them from deep within his thoughts to sigh or adjust himself in his seat. Occasionally touching his jaw. Left. Right. Left. But from the way he held the knife, twisting it and staring at it in the early morning light, it was obvious what he continued to think about.

Eventually, after yet another sigh, Femi looked up and said, 'It's funny, isn't it? That Danson thought we'd *made it*. Yet, if he'd known what our lives were really like…' He clucked his tongue and shook his head. 'Maybe, if I'd just told him I was about to be cancelled instead of berating him that night…'

'I'm not sure we weren't all doomed the moment we turned up at Cambridge,' Winston said. 'But yeah, maybe I should have told him tonight that the music industry was dead. And that we got signed just as it was collapsing, and ever since we've been trying to work out how to make money. Every year we're making less and doing more. More touring, more merch, more mindless social media. I've got no social life. Barely any of it is about making music anymore. Online, yeah, it's easy to make it look like you're doing well, but in reality my life is like working a fourteen-hour-a-day admin job – without the security. I have other reasons for packing it in, like I told you, but I can't say I'd miss that stuff. It hasn't made me happy for a long time.' He let out a strange whistle, like a missile falling from the sky. 'Maybe he'd have let us go if I'd said that.'

'I enjoyed my first few novels,' Naz said. 'I processed a lot of stuff. Since then, it's been constant doubt. Doubt about getting another deal. Doubt about my ability and my qualifications for even being able to pass comment on the world around me. Doubt about a whole industry you romantically revered because now you've seen the spreadsheets. When I was growing up, an author only ever read a review of their work if they were lucky enough to get one in a paper. Now, you can read the thoughts of every single person that absolutely hates what you do. What other job is comparable? At least films are collaborative. And I'd love to say I'm strong enough to ignore them, but the bad ones are all I remember. And it really is lonely. I can't relate to anyone anymore. I'm not even in the real world. I went on a Tinder date and called him by the name of my character. I keep asking myself, was this my intention? Because I don't think it ever was. I wanted a house full of people I loved, like it was when I was a girl. I just didn't want the fear.'

'I never stop,' Cady said, her voice so much lower. She tried to lick her lips, but her tongue dragged on her cracked skin like a loofah. 'This is the first time I've been still in years. I think my boyfriend might break up with me because I can't stop working. He's been trying really hard to be patient, and I keep telling him I'll make time, but I don't. I just ... don't. I keep thinking that my success is a mistake. That if I don't keep putting videos out, or be mentally working on video ideas, the algorithm might realise the error it made and ditch me. Which, really, is just part of the same old problem with me, isn't it? I don't want what happened to catch up with me. Oh, and I think I might have a stalker now, which is nice. When we got stuck earlier, my first thought was that it was him. That he'd trapped me. And was coming for me. Which is ... mad. Because I didn't even realise how much fear I've been living with because I never ever stop.'

A while later, Femi looked out at the sun, squinted, and said, 'We're running out of time, aren't we? I think I'm going to have to make a call.'

'You can't,' Naz said. 'You and me ... have ... have too much to talk about. Okay? So we wait. That's my decision.' Her voice creaked with tiredness and emotion. 'I'm having this baby now, okay? I want it, Femi. I really, really do. And I'm not fucking doing it without you. You want to make amends, that's how you can do it. So ... so ... no, I refuse it. I'm not telling our baby this story about why he doesn't have a daddy.'

'Do you know it's a *he*?' Femi said.

'No ... I'm just...'

'Writing a story you think will make me change my mind? Because you think I'd prefer a son to a daughter.'

'I'm giving you an order,' she said. 'I really will never

forgive you if you do this. Truthfully, I couldn't give a fuck about the past now. We'd only known each other a few months when Eloise did this to us. We didn't know how close we'd become then. How much more of a betrayal what we did would become in time. That's not an excuse, we have something wrong with us, but … it's still true.'

'Son or daughter, I'd love them, Naz. And if I don't do this, they'll die.' He spoke with a stolid, detached tone. 'I can see your hand shaking from here. You're dehydrated. And dehydration and pregnancy… You think I'm going to let you miscarry here? With my child. I really do love you, Naz. Always have. And I wish I'd have been a bit less … distracted to notice it. That's why I need to do it. And I need to do it soon, guys. By my reckoning, we start cooking in an hour. And once my heart stops, I don't know how long it will take for the whole alert process to work. It might be hours until they locate you, so the sooner the better.'

'No,' Naz said. 'I … I … *forbid* it.' She was close to screaming.

Femi chuckled in a way that was both perverse and warm. 'Again, this isn't a democracy.'

Naz started on Cady then, telling her she needed to get the knife off him. That she had to do something, oh, please, wouldn't she *do* something?

But Cady was paralysed. That little nuclear power core inside her had finally run out. She had never needed motivation in her life. Had never not been in the world without knowing her purpose. It simply wasn't there now. Her mind, which had always been as simple to navigate as a ladder, now seemed rungless, leaving her atop two stilts wandering an abyss. How could she ever be confident in any belief, or decision, or action, again, when she was capable of hiding such things from herself?

And how could she ever explain what she'd done to her parents after all this time? How could she explain it to Tom? To have not known, yet somehow known … she would never be able to explain it. They would think she had lied to them. Lied every day, from childhood into adulthood, complicit in the original sin with every omission.

She understood what Femi was doing. And it gave her even more reason not to stop him. He was reclaiming his status as the protagonist in his story, wasn't he? She'd always believed in her own *protagonism*, too. But tonight she'd learned that she was really more like the story's villain. So who could blame Femi for trying to put right—

'Cady, snap out of it,' Naz yelled. 'I know I said some harsh things tonight. I'm sorry. I lost my temper and I didn't mean all this was on you. Obviously, it isn't. I just wanted … I just wanted … I'm just a fucking bitch, okay? And maybe I wanted to drag you down with us because you didn't betray anyone. And … and I was always jealous of how much you affected me. And the others. Because mostly it was for the good, Cady. I promise you that. I loved you, I really did. And what happened to your family was an awful accident. And so wildly, wildly unfair. But I need you to help me. Please. You need to stop him.'

Cady looked over at Femi, who held the knife in front of his face. He briefly glanced at her and shook his head sadly. 'I don't want to hurt you by accident. This thing is very sharp. And I really don't want to get this wrong.'

'Can't we cut it out?' Winston shouted.

Femi looked up. 'What?'

'Can't we … can't we just use the knife to cut your pacemaker out? How deep is it?'

'It's deep. It's attached to my heart. I don't think I could do it myself, and as much as I admire Cady's spirit of adventure,' he turned to her, 'I'm not sure you have the stomach.'

Every part of Cady's body experienced a flush of numbness. Had it really come to this? She couldn't … operate on him, could she? In this dim light. While he was conscious.

If it would save them all, though? If it offered her a small chance of redemption? No matter what Naz or any of them said, she knew now that she'd played a part in all this. She knew now why Eloise and Danson had thought her the worst of them. She would have to do it, wouldn't she? She would make herself.

'I could do it,' she said, so softly that it was surprising Femi even heard her.

But he did, and once again he shook his head. 'It might not even work. I don't understand how the alert system functions fully, but it's designed to ping if my heart stops. Disconnecting it from my heart wouldn't necessarily simulate a cardiac arrest. It might only stop the device working. And that's before we consider any damage we do to it trying to saw it out with this. That's not going to help anyone, especially not me. And then there's the damage you might do to my heart by pulling it out. That's if I haven't bled to death.'

No one said anything. The air thrummed with energy from the unspoken thoughts racing through all of their heads. Each one of them so unaccustomed to being powerless. Unpractised at relenting. There was always a solution. Always something they could do.

Femi was working himself up to do it. She could sense the rising tension in his body and between them. Would he do it on his wrists? Or would he go for the throat? Would the blood spurt or trickle? Oh, God, no, why why why were they having to contemplate these *things*?

Perhaps to stir herself, perhaps to slow him down, she reached up and touched his shoulder once more. 'Let's just wait. Please.' He shook his head. 'I know you want to make something good of this, I know you're thinking about your baby and about…'

The Audience. That's what she wanted to say.

'…how you'll be remembered. But Femi, I'd rather you were alive than a memory.'

'Yeah, me too.' His face briefly flashed with an expression that she read as, do you have a better plan?

She didn't. They had tried everything. And now it seemed as if whatever ground had held up her stilts was giving way, and she was falling.

'You know,' he said, 'the last time I spoke to Dad was at that spartan flat of his. After Mum died. It was a lot of grunting, and him asking about how my life worked. Cordial enough. And I thought it was going to be okay, because he was nodding along when I started opening up about my career and how hard it had been lying to them at Chamberlain. And you know, he said to me, "Boy, you broke my heart. So I'll talk to you. But don't look at me like you want me to be proud."'

Cady closed her eyes. 'Please don't think about that. Please.'

'No, Cady. It's fine. Because after I collapsed, and they brought me back, he said saving people was what we did in our family, didn't he? And that one day, I'd save someone else's life. And I thought I could do that with art, but he was right, that was ego. But this will be different. He would have been proud of this. And maybe our kid will.'

Her eyes welled up with tears, and she heard Naseem sob. They'd passed the point of no return, hadn't they? They'd reached the drop.

'I think you should all just sort of shut your eyes. For a bit. Okay?'

'No,' Naz wailed. 'Wait ... wait an hour. At least.'

'And please be quiet. Please. I don't want to make a mistake. You're a fucking mad bunch, but I really did love you. When I get to hell, I'll pour a few drinks.'

Winston swore and smacked his arm rest again and again.

Femi brought the knife up towards his neck. Cady turned away and shrank down into her seat. Her bum slid beneath the rest for a moment, and the tears ran down her cheeks. There had to be something. Oh, why couldn't her mind, her stupid, scrambled, broken head just—

And there it was. In the darkness. A rung.

She grabbed it.

Cady sat up straight, and yelled at Femi to stop.

CADY

Saturday 22nd June, 7.22am
Celsius: 29°, Fahrenheit: 84.2°

'Just wait,' she said to Femi. 'There's something we haven't tried.'

'What?' Femi said, irritated by the interruption. 'What *haven't* we tried at this point, Cady? *What?*'

She shut her eyes, trying to suppress the panic her body wanted to unleash as it began to catch up with her decision. When she opened them again, the world tried to spin, and she clutched at the handle of her restraint like it might steady her vision.

'I'm going to try and go under again,' she said.

'We did this,' Femi said. 'You said it was impossible.'

'Not like this, we didn't,' Cady said. 'Not with a knife to your throat.'

Because it hadn't been impossible earlier, had it? It had only seemed that way because she'd let the panic win. She'd started to picture her head squeezing through that little gap, and how it might pop the screws in her skull. So, she'd *decided* it wouldn't work. It couldn't work. That was how her mind worked, wasn't it? Her sneaky little mind. And after that, she'd started to *believe* it. And each time she tried to revisit the idea, to suggest they give it one more try, her mind simply dunked it back into the depths. So easy to do, too, after what had happened with Naz.

But what had she been training for all these years, if not some moment like this? All those roller coasters and drop towers and titanic pendulums. What was it to be a thrill-seeker, if not to face and overcome your terror?

At first, Femi glared at her, but she saw something soften when she glared back.

'I had a panic attack,' she said, 'because of the plate in my head. From the accident. But with some help from you, maybe there's a chance I could get through.'

'I was here,' Femi said, his expression curdling. 'You weren't going to make it.'

She shook her head. 'I think there's a chance. And the thing is, rationally, my skull is stronger than anyone else's, isn't it? So actually…' She tried swallowing. Failed because she had no spit. Tried again and forced it down. '…actually, I have less to worry about when the time comes time to go through. In fact – and this gives me real dread but, hey – I want you to push me through if I get stuck.'

Now the anger went completely from his face. 'Push you through?'

'Yeah. Push my head through.'

'With a previous skull fracture? I don't think so.'

'I told you, the plate makes my head stronger. But fine, cut your throat, if you don't want to at least give it a go.'

He was still shaking his head. But why was she even debating it with him? She'd made up her mind now. This wasn't a democracy.

Like she was about to dive underwater, she held her breath and slid down the seat back until the underside of the clamshell lap restraint dug into her ribs and the plastic fin at the end of the seat wedged against her perineum. She shuffled her feet forwards and her chin pushed against her chest in that awful way it had done before. Now her body understood what was happening, and claustrophobia gripped her instantly. She was outside the car again on the road with petrol fumes in her nose. She was being pulled out of a cave with the sounds of her terrified friends close by.

'I need your help,' she said to Femi.

'Put your hand under the small of her back,' Winston said from between the seats.

When he didn't respond immediately, she yelled, 'Now, Femi.'

She heard him put the knife down somewhere. A good start. He leaned over and she felt his hand on the bare skin of her back where the t-shirt had rucked up. 'Push up so I can slide further down.' He did what she asked.

Little by little, she managed to shuffle and twist her way down, every inch a fresh battle with distress and discomfort. Her back was the problem. She needed to create space for it on the seat by dragging more of herself into the car's front. But her chin felt like it might crush her sand-blasted voice box, and her ribs had to be worked under the clamshell. At times, it seemed her spine was under such pressure that it didn't seem any more give was possible. But then she popped through a point of resistance, and sank a few more inches with ease.

When Femi withdrew his arm, her shoulders rested where her backside had been for the last thirteen hours, both arms still above her. Cady's neck and head rested on the seat back in a way that no longer choked her, but brought about even more mental resistance than before. How could she get back from this position? Was her neck going to break?

Dwelling wouldn't help. From here, she pulled herself forwards by walking until her knees met the front of the car. The plastic fin scored her back the whole time. At this point she had to twist her hips and try to fold her body into the space to make room for the rest of her. Her breasts, never the largest, thank God, caught on the clamshell, and she had to hold them down with her arm to get them through. However, the clamshell tapered upwards soon after its front edge, and after ignoring a momentary sense that they might actually burst, Cady guided her breasts through. The fin dug into her upper ribs. It was agony, but she found a position where she could manage it.

Now most of her was in the front of the car. Almost out. It was at that point her chin met the flat underside of the clamshell.

She didn't suppose it mattered which side she faced. She turned her head to the left facing Femi. The world quietened now one ear was covered. Her cheek pressed up against her shoulder, her arms still above her, the only way to get them through was to drag them behind her. All she could see was the ridged plastic edge of the seat just an inch from her nose and her armpit. She could smell herself. She tried to keep control with sour breath after sour breath. Slow and deep.

The fin slipped into the gap between two upper ribs and

Cady stifled a yell. Unable to really hear the others, she called out that she was fine and steadied herself for the next part – to get her head beneath the clamshell.

She felt another squeeze of panic when the bulge of her cheek bone pressed into the hard bottom edge – the point of no return. With some force, she managed to slide under until the bulge of her head near her temple, the parietal ridge as the team at the hospital called it after the accident, blocked her from going further.

This was the moment of truth. If she could get her head through this point, she was out. She was into the car and they were free.

But she'd been right to panic earlier. Instinctively, she must have sized up the gap and just known. Her head wasn't going through. She began to tug herself with her legs, jerking her body side to side in an attempt to wriggle her head through. It hurt her cheek and her head, the plastic abrading the skin.

It wasn't working. And if she got herself stuck here now it would be horrendous.

She took a deep breath. That wouldn't happen, of course, because Femi would be able to pull her free.

But it was what her mind wanted the headline to be right now, because her right temple was throbbing. Pop, pop, pop. Her right eye watered. Did it feel a bit compressed, too? A bit warped, like a pinched grape.

'I'm not sure this…' she started to say, her voice sounding constricted. But she shut herself up. Shut it all up. Her sneaky, sneaky mind was duplicitous, and she needed every part of her will to stop it telling stories. Femi would die beside her if she didn't get through. She had to try. She couldn't live with any more death.

'Can you push?' she said to Femi.

'Cady…'

'I'm so close. Please.'

Femi's hand touched the top of her head. The other two were saying something but still she couldn't hear them. That was for the best; she didn't need the distraction. Femi began to push and she started to pull. Oh, God, it hurt. She could feel the skin on her skull tearing and the skin of her face being pinched against the bone.

The voice in her head began yammering. Her skull would pop. She would be stuck up here with a brain injury, pieces of her skull poking into her brain. Go back, go back, go back.

'Harder,' she said, tuning it out. Her head *would* go through. She was certain. Just a bit more force, as insane as that was. But this had to work. There wasn't any other way. She was going to be the hero now. Because then there would be a chance, a very small chance, that she might be able to live with what she'd done to Grandad and Robbie.

She was screaming now, it hurt so much. Her body was contorted in a way that warped her rib cage. The fin on the seat would perhaps split her open soon.

'Cady, I don't want to hurt you,' Femi said, and she felt his pressure relenting.

'Don't you dare stop.'

A pause, and he shoved again, and she was certain she felt her head shift forward a little. The pain was so intense, she didn't cry out. It was too much and simply stunned her.

The world was white. Arcs of light appeared in the corners of her eyes. And suddenly she was standing over her younger self, lying on the tarmac of a not-long-laid road. Even with hair covered in blood, she was overcome with a sense of comforting déjà vu. She remembered looking this way, this young. She'd seen this face in the mirror often. All those dreams enlivening those eyes.

How funny, to think she wanted to hold this young thing responsible for what had happened. This little girl and her earnest morals.

But the lie hadn't aged, had it? And it had been eventually handed down to a more culpable person as fresh as it had been when she'd first landed on this road.

The little girl looked up to her. 'What happened?'

How funny, to think at thirty-eight she was still trying to keep the promises this little girl would soon make to herself. About living like there was no tomorrow. About having to do something in the world.

'Why am I on the road?' little Cady said.

'There was an accident. That's all it was. An accident.'

She nodded, seeming to understand. There was so much blood. She hadn't ever realised how much…

Then the blackness returned. Followed by the agony, so much of it now, like her brief absence had formed a flimsy dam, the collapse of which meant her enduring the brunt of a reservoir. Her cries now were involuntary. Long, hoarse grunts that, with a force of will she didn't know she possessed, she managed to silence after just three.

Naz was screaming something, she could hear that much. Something else too, the same instinct or knowledge that had known her head wouldn't fit through this gap was now telling her that her head could not sustain any more pressure. That, if Femi pushed any more, bone would break.

But her head was reinforced with metal. She had to remember that. Her body didn't know what it was talking about. She was fearless. She would do this.

How much quicker would things be, though, if she could make the passage smoother somehow? If she had something with which to lubricate the way? If only they had butter, or oil, or...

'Femi, cut me,' she said.

'What?'

'Use the knife to cut my forehead. It'll help my head through.'

'No, Cady.' He was shouting.

'I'll be fine.'

'No. We're done here.'

'Femi, give me the knife, then,' she cried.

'Damn it, no,' Femi yelled back, and kicked his feet against the front of the car. The reverberation boomed in the ear pressed to her seat and sent another shock of pain through her head. Had he just deafened her?

'Femi, what—'

The car jolted. Forward and down. Cady felt a ratcheting of the pressure on her head. She heard the others shouting, and yet again her flight response was urging her to get back in her seat. She couldn't give up, though. Not now she'd got this far.

'Come out, Cady,' Femi said.

'Push me,' she said. 'I'm nearly there.'

The car moved again. The downward angle of the car increased. More cries followed. As did more intense pain for Cady. Dear God, the chain was actually going, wasn't it? Her weight all up here at the front and Femi's kick had... They were going over the drop.

Now she let her mind speak freely. Because, if they went over now and she was stuck here, the train's movements would break her neck. Hysteria had loops and inversions. She might be hanged.

Still, she stayed put. Because, if the train went no further, they were back where they were ten minutes ago. And she was so, so close now.

Femi's hands grabbed her. They pulled her head and yanked her top. She tried resisting, but he was too strong. Her head popped out from beneath the restraint on the wrong side, and her disappointment couldn't overpower the flood of release she felt at the sudden freedom.

'Get up now,' Femi said. 'I think it's happening.'

His hands were on her. Helping her bend and twist back up into her seat, easier this way than it had been going down but no less painful. Resigned, she gave in and allowed it. Her head still felt compressed, as if the bones of her skull had shifted like an infant's in the birth canal. Little white flashes interrupted her vision.

No sooner had her chin become free from the final upward push than the car jolted once more.

And whatever had held them finally gave way.

There was an exquisite moment of suspense as the train started to move again, trickling over the last section of the drop.

Then, it was all gravity.

Danson, Then

After running my various errands, and before the flight back to Dreamland, I went to Eloise's grave and told her I was sorry, and admitted that I'd messed it all up again.

'You were right. About them. Always.'

I let her know I'd driven up to Liverpool to find her Italian. Raf barely remembered her, but I took him out drinking and smashed in his head with the bottom part of a bike lock at the end of the night. I don't think he died, but he'll certainly remember Eloise now.

The plot where they'd buried her ashes was simple. The stone, her last and remaining mark on the world, simply had her name and the required two dates. It saddened me deeply. It didn't seem fitting.

But I will make it right. Like the fairy in that story about the vinegar bottle, who always used to terrify me so much.

Secondaries in my brain from my lungs. Six months to a year at best. Had anyone in my family been a smoker?

Thanks, Mom. Thanks, Dad. Thanks, Gran.

And thanks, Eloise, for the six months I smoked in her company. To impress her.

I spent the afternoon looking things up up up. There's a good chance they can extend my life a little bit with chemotherapy. But that would involve a lot of sickness, with no guarantees.

So, I don't think so. Besides, I have plans.

Funny how it's all coming together. Like a work of art. I got told to join an emergency meeting with Aston from head office this morning when I was meant to be chairing the Hysteria maintenance and snagging meeting. I've been so error prone recently, I was convinced I was going to be fired. It's all kicked off this last week because some bad version control on the documents flying between car design and track design have meant the the the restraints on Hysteria might now need replacing entirely.

But Aston wanted to tell me that the prince's team had been in touch and told him that we need to stop construction. Apparently, the 'business strategy has changed.' They wouldn't say any more than that, and hung up on Aston when he tried pressing further. All he'd managed to get out of them was that Hysteria should be in a saleable condition, as they might wish to move it on or run it as a standalone.

I asked if it was because of the restraints, but Aston's theory was the prince had got some bad press in the last year, and that the family had docked his pocket money. He swore a lot, and told me I was taking it all very well given it was three years of my life down the drain. I shrugged, and said I was sure my work would have value.

I got back to the meeting with the Entivate lot, under instruction from Aston to keep things on the down low until the firm had managed to get confirmation from the prince's team. One of their guys was talking about the maintenance schedule for Hysteria's three launch mechanisms, the little boosters that increase the speed all along the ride. He's had ongoing concerns that should one of the boosters fail, left to gravity alone Hysteria might be dangerous because it might not clear some of the elements – a big concern in light of the version control snafu.

Not my problem anymore. There's been so much of this sort of stuff along the way, because the prince's team insisted on the design being as close to the prince's hand-drawn sketch as possible, and many of the features are a little unconventional. I think it's why so many designers quit. The thing's Frankenstein's monster now.

I waited for this section of the meeting to end, but grew impatient. So, I interrupted and asked my question. 'How long can the pre-drop brake hold the coaster car at the top of Hysteria?'

They all looked at me like I was an idiot.

'How long,' I said, without falter, 'in theory? Like if the power cut.'

'I wouldn't know off the top of my head,' said one of the team finally.

'Could it hold it an hour? Three hours?'

They wanted details, the number of riders, where the coaster was on the final chain.

I didn't give away any details. I just asked them again. Calmly.

Eventually, one of them said it could stay up there weeks. Maybe longer. It was hard to say without doing the maths. It might hold up there months, depending on how cheap we'd gone with the motor.

But I didn't need maths. Weeks was good enough for me.

CADY

Saturday 22nd June, 7.37am
Celsius: 30°, Fahrenheit: 86°

The ground swallowed the train. Under the desert now, they shot through a tunnel much cooler than outside. Cady ducked instinctively. But they were fine. Of course they were fine. It was only manufactured terror now. And how the air at this speed refreshed and cleansed.

Spat out again, the train flew beneath the low sun, twisting left and right, escalating again to another obscene height before diving. Naz cried out in agony and joy.

Each jerk of the car sent a flash of pain through Cady's head. She suspected she'd done some damage now – a brain scan awaited her in the future. But at least there would be a future. The coaster was still moving so fast, and it would surely make it back to the shelter of the starting point.

That was unless Danson had lied about the track being complete. What if sections were missing? What if they flew right off now and…

There wasn't time to dwell. Up, around, down, they rocketed across the park, the empty lots and tents, to their left, to their right, to the side, below them, all a blur.

The ride turned suddenly, sharply, and faced the distant cliff wall and the enormous lift hill. The coaster began to climb again, up a very tall rise that gave the impression the coaster was slowing down. Losing momentum.

Femi turned to her just as she turned to him.

No, it was part of the experience, surely? Up they went, up and over. Down, down, down the other side, gaining delicious speed again as they charged into a double corkscrew. At one point, the first corkscrew turned them upside down for a good few seconds, giving the impression they were beneath the tracks. Was this a zero-G stall? For a moment, Cady's whole body was suspended above the drop below them by what felt like her thighs. But no, that couldn't be right, could it? The centrifugal force was the thing that was supposed to pin them inside. The physics.

That was unless they really *were* slowing down.

Objects flew from the car. The box. The gun. The knife.

Then the coaster righted. They reached the second corkscrew and the upside-down section was shorter here. But again, Cady's arms instinctively grabbed on to the arm rest and her core muscles engaged because for all the world it felt like she was going to drop from the seat.

Impossible. It had to be an illusion. Even if it stopped still, the restraint would pin them in place.

'This doesn't feel safe,' Winston cried out, the ride beginning to climb another giant slope.

'No,' Naseem replied with little conviction. 'We're fine. It's fine.'

But it wasn't, because a short way up a steep hill that must have been at least sixty metres, the car began to slow down. So much so, it became obvious they weren't going to make it to the top. Cady looked behind her, trying to establish where they were going to end up.

It wasn't going to be in the shade, that much was certain.

Back they rolled, screaming when they reached the straight of the second corkscrew. They were far too slow, and the short, upside-down section was agonising. But the car righted this time, and Femi said, 'This is bad.'

Then the car went into the first corkscrew. Into the extended straight portion which flipped them upside down. And that was it. The train stopped.

'No, no, no,' Cady said.

Her prayers went unanswered. The four of them now dangled above a ten-metre drop the wrong way around.

Naz screamed.

Cady's body hung from her thighs. Her backside was very slightly off the seat. The blood was already rushing to her head and her whole body tensed for fear of sliding out. She held on to the armrest handle to stop her hands from dangling down. Already it felt harder to breathe now. And the pressure on her eyeballs grew.

'We're fucked,' Winston said. 'We're absolutely fucked.'

A bleak silence followed.

The tension in Cady's neck grew too much, and she let it loosen while squeezing even tighter to the handle. Mercifully, she still hung there.

But suddenly she knew she didn't have to. Not if she didn't

want to. Had the others realised this, too? Did none of them want to say it?

'I think we could escape,' Cady said, her voice sounding like her nose was blocked. 'The ride isn't designed to be upside down this long. I think, if we tried, gravity might pull us free.'

'And what, fall?' Winston said.

'Head first?' Naz said. 'No.'

Cady looked up to look down. She wished she hadn't. A pathway snaked through the sand a long way away. She quickly returned her gaze to the back of the seats. Upside down, it was hard to gauge the distance. But it was a long way to fall. Not two hundred metres. Not even sixty. But it might not be survivable.

'I think it's about ten metres,' Femi said. 'Maybe a bit more. The top diving board at the swimming baths. Or the porter's lodge at Chamberlain. Maybe less?'

'Oh great,' Winston said. 'So we're going to end up like Eloise.'

'She was pushed,' Femi said. 'If I brace for the fall and land on my feet, I think it'll be okay. I might break a leg or something. But I'll live. And if I miss the path and land on the sand, that'll be even better.'

He was talking himself into it. He was already moving around trying to work out how best to do it. But the issue was clear to Cady. To escape the chair, they would have to inch themselves down using gravity to pull their straightened legs and body through the gap in the restraint, which currently held them at a right angle.

This couldn't be done while holding on to the handle above their laps, though. To sufficiently straighten, they would have to stretch out their arms and use their full weight to pull them down and through. That meant when they were finally set free, they would be diving head first.

That very idea was instinctively worse than remaining here upside down.

'I'll turn in the air,' Femi said, unphased.

'Fem, come on,' Winston said.

'We won't last a day now. I have no idea how long the human body can survive upside down but it's not going to be long after what we've already been through. All the blood draining to your head. All the extra pressure on your organs, on your heart. On *my* heart. A couple of hours? Three? Four? We'll have agonising pins and needles by then and won't be able to move at all.' He shook his head. 'And even if somehow we manage to stay conscious or alive until we're rescued, the baby, Naz… Your body will be under such pressure.'

Naz said nothing. She could only sob into the top of her head.

'Listen, guys,' Femi said, 'if I drop and something goes badly wrong, my ICD will kick in. If I survive, I can try to get back to the ride building and get our phones.'

'And if you break your back?' Cady said. 'And you're stuck down there?'

He had no immediate answer to this. 'I'll just have to … find a way to…'

'What, walk? Or kill yourself? I don't think either of those things is happening. I'll be honest…' She took a long, difficult breath. Was she really about to say this? 'I think we need to go in the following order. Me or Winston first and second. And if neither of us two make it, then Fem, I think you make a call about … how exactly you fall. That way, at least Naz and the baby make it.'

'Okay,' Winston said. He paused for a moment. 'Yeah, I guess.'

She took another long breath and closed her eyes. She'd made up her mind. It was no worse than what she'd just endured. 'I volunteer myself to go first,' Cady said. 'I went skydiving once, and when you land you have to roll okay. Try to land on your feet and just … Sonic the Hedgehog it, okay?'

'Cady,' Winston said, 'you don't have to. You know you really don't deserve any of this.' She heard him blow a long breath through tight lips. 'Let me.'

'Nah,' she said, eyes still shut, not wanting any interruptions now. She didn't know how much mental willpower she had left. 'I've got it in my head now. I still love you lot, you know. Even after everything.'

'Cady,' Naz said, 'I… I'm sorry I told Eloise.'

'After what we've just endured,' Cady said, 'I think we all deserve a bit of forgiveness. Maybe you were bastards, maybe we're all bastards, but you were my bastards. My family. And yeah, sometimes family's hurt each other. But we had the best time, and, you know…' She wouldn't cry. *She would not cry*. 'In a way, all I ever wanted as a kid, after Robbie, was for someone to notice me. And you all did. You really were my home. And I suppose I always wanted to be remembered for something good. And if this is how I'll be remembered…'

She let go of the handle and opened her eyes. The restraint held her for now. Now came the hard part.

'I love you guys, too,' Winston said. 'I know you are sick of hearing this, and I don't want forgiveness, but Naz, I'm sorry. I'm so sorry. I'm not sure any of us have control of anything really, you know? That we're all … on a track, and we do what we do, whatever. But just in case.'

He let go of his handle.

'No,' Cady said.

'Let's see which of us the universe wants to go first,' he said. 'Tell Mom I did my best, okay? And that I know she did hers. And that I love her. Maybe don't mention the coke, though.'

'Let me go first,' Cady said. 'If we go at the same time, we won't—'

'I love you all, too.' Femi said, and dropped his arms now. 'But this should be me. You know it should.'

'No, Femi, no,' Naz said. 'You need to do Cady's plan. Please. The baby. Don't all leave me.'

'Guys,' Femi said, wriggling quickly in his seat, 'I'm starting to move.'

'Please wait,' Cady said.

'Sorry,' he said, and smiled, moving his body up and down quickly. He began to drop, moving left and right, doing sit-ups over the clamshell to allow his legs the room to shake himself free. It reminded her of footage she'd seen of escapologists, dangling from cranes while tied up in straightjackets far above the ground. He was going too fast for her to keep up, his strength allowing him to bend in ways she couldn't.

Then he fell. Cady, who hadn't even started moving yet, grabbed her handles once more and stared straight ahead.

Saturday 22nd June, 7.45am
Celsius: 30°, Fahrenheit: 86°

She heard the landing. A soft *crump* and a grunt.

Naz began shouting his name. Then Winston.

Cady looked down and saw Femi's body in the pale light, still. 'What happened?' Cady said.

'Femi,' Naz yelled.

'He couldn't spin in time,' Winston said. 'He... I think he got over near the ground and landed on his side, though. Fem. Femi.'

Cady's heart raced. She grabbed short, shallow breaths.

'He's alive,' Winston said. 'I swear, I saw him move after. His arm moved. His arm definitely moved.'

'What do we do?' Naz said.

Cady hadn't seen any movement, so it would have to have

been small. But, if there was any chance he'd survived, he could be badly hurt. And his pacemaker certainly wouldn't be sending for help.

'He shouldn't have gone first,' Cady said, unable to comprehend that, after the night they'd had, with everything they'd learned, Femi had just acted on his own impulses again regardless of logic. 'My turn now.'

'No,' Winston said, but she ignored him.

'I've given away a lot of my life to hope,' Cady said. 'But I'm not letting it kill me. Just do me a favour, okay? Tell my boyfriend that I'm sorry I didn't call him. And that I love him. Tell my parents, too. About Robbie. Tell them that I'm sorry, and I love them, and hope they forgive me. See you down there.'

She let go again, wanting to do this before her exhausted nervous system exercised its veto. Her torso swayed from her thighs. She crunched her stomach muscles as if doing sit-ups, trying to get her backside lower and the armrest to slide further down her thighs. Her skin was torqued and squeezed, her bones ground and jabbed. She blocked out the pain easily this time: it was nothing compared to what she'd felt earlier. She straightened her legs, trying to make it easier for gravity to work. The car jiggled with every clench and release of her abdomen.

Gradually, she slid downwards to the point of no return. Winston was still trying to protest, but she was too far gone now. With a final squeeze and relax, she slid down far enough, and began to fall.

Unlike Femi, Cady anticipated coming free. It didn't stop both her heart and stomach lurching, nor did it prevent her hands reflexively reaching up to grab something. But it did mean that she retained a very small amount of control. She allowed the momentum to spin her into a seating position diagonally opposite to where she'd been hanging. Her body began to tip forwards at that point, but she pedalled her legs instinctively to try and stop it, throwing out her arms to slow the descent.

But it wasn't going to work, not entirely. The ground was coming up too fast and she was still tilted towards it and moving backwards.

Just before she landed, it struck Cady she had no idea about what the emergency number even was here. They probably should have discussed it before. Never mind, it probably didn't matter now.

The fall had been further than she'd anticipated. Much, much further. She really had no control of it at all, did she? So maybe it was for the best she'd blink out of existence before discovering—

She hit the ground moving backwards and tried to bend her knees. The impact crashed through her: legs, knees, hips, ribs, neck, all crushed and jarred. Her brain slammed against her skull, and when she came back around seconds later, she was pleased that, despite all the pain she was feeling, she had remembered to roll. And when she stopped rolling, her head struck a hard patch of ground again, knocking her out once more. Before she drifted off, she had enough left about her to want to smile.

Her landing had been soft. It had been very, very soft.

CADY

Saturday 22nd June, 7.47am
Celsius: 30°, Fahrenheit: 86°

Her face was covered in sand. She licked and tasted it with a parched tongue before remembering where she was and what she was doing. Quickly, *too quickly*, she pushed herself up and a screaming pain in her left wrist sent her back down on her front. She cried out and rolled onto her back, spitting sand from her mouth as she did so.

She tried sitting up using her other elbow, but now her ribs and shoulder had an opinion. A burning, liquid opinion.

Cady took a moment to compose herself before trying again. This time she found a combination of knee, ankle and foot that didn't hurt enough to stop her kneeling. Her ear felt sore now, and she reached up to it and felt hot blood and more sand.

But none of that mattered. She heard the others above her yelling at her, cautiously jubilant.

For once, their caution was misplaced. She was alive. Better than alive. She was alive, and free, and despite what were no doubt a number of broken bones, she could move. Both her legs were intact. She opened her mouth and let out a volcanic cry of relief.

Wincing, Cady made her way back towards where she'd come from. She tried to call out and her voice locked. She coughed, and yelled again, 'I'm okay. I did it.'

They were cheering with mad abandon, and she fed on the energy. She found her landing site. Incredibly, it had been a small ridge of piled sand, now marked by two deep impressions from her trainers.

Femi hadn't been so lucky. He lay just metres away, body half on sand, half on the paved path. One leg stuck out at a horrible angle. She tried not to focus on it. She knelt down beside him and saw blood around his mouth. But he was breathing. Unconscious, but alive.

Above him they were silent, braced for the worst.

'He's alive,' she shouted up. 'But he needs help.'

It took her another twenty minutes to drag her body back to the start of Hysteria. She'd followed the pathway towards the lift hill, and when she reached the end of it, she recognised where she was. It was the main footpath from the entrance. They'd walked along it in what felt like another life.

By the time she first sighted Hysteria's main building in the distance, she'd decided that her wrist and ribs were definitely broken, and that she'd torn something in her shoulder and possibly both her calves. There was something odd about how her hip felt when she bore weight on her left side, too, but while it hurt, and while she worried all her movement was making everything worse, nothing was going to stop her.

All in all, she'd been incredibly lucky. Her mind, still stunned and adrenaline-high, kept replaying the fall to her, reminding her how wrong it could have gone. She would have to forcibly remove herself from these neck-breaking, skull-smashing reveries, aware when she did that time had passed and she was much further down the path. It was quite possible that she was a little concussed.

When she reached Jag's car, she tried the door. It was locked. The alarm began to wail. She backed away, but already she felt better. If worst came to worst, the car key was likely still on one of the two dead bodies at the foot of Hysteria. She didn't want to consider how she might get it, but it was an option.

It might have been quicker to use the exit queue line to access the ride building, the way Danson had earlier. But Cady guessed correctly that it would leave her on the wrong side of the track – and she wasn't in any condition to climb across. So she zig-zagged back down the queue line, walking the entire length because it hurt too much to bend underneath the barriers. The air-conditioning and the main lights were off inside the museum, and the exhibit was now lit even more dimly by a blue security light.

There wasn't any chance that Danson survived the fall, yet she couldn't help but imagine him being there when she reached the booth. Grinning and bloody. She imagined her man in a beanie, too. Mr Yellow Fiat. He'd been behind the whole thing, after all. Here to tell her she was full of it.

But when she stepped out on the platform, it was dark and profoundly empty. Her footsteps echoed when she approached the little booth where he'd taken all their belongings.

She anticipated resistance when she pulled down the door handle. None came. She stepped into the booth. On the wall that looked out onto the tracks was a console. Here were the ride controls and multiple dead screens. To her right was a shelf, on which sat the grey tray he'd held out to them earlier. It was the same tray, because in it were all the other belongings they'd handed over.

But where were the phones? Where were the *bloody* phones?

She searched the booth, trying to ignore the hysterical voice telling her Danson had done something with them. Destroyed them, perhaps, so they couldn't be tracked. The needling little voice started to insist that there weren't any other phones on the whole site either, because why would there be? Everyone used mobiles, and they would have taken their mobiles with them when Danson stood down the staff. That would mean their only escape would be Femi's ICD again. Femi, who was still very much alive.

After an agonisingly painful search of the building for an emergency phone, her suspicion about what had happened to the mobiles was confirmed. She found a blackened pile of phone parts at the back of the building. She smelled petrol and burning plastic, and when she grabbed one of the parts, it was still warm.

She'd had to sit down then. Even though it hurt to do so, she needed to get some composure, because she was on the verge of losing it completely. Her mouth was so dry now, and, despite the stress and exertion of the last hour, she wasn't sweating at all.

She had to make a decision about what to do next. Did she search the site for another phone or form of contacting the outside world, or use what little energy she had left to walk back to civilisation? She doubted she had the capacity to do both. And Femi, and perhaps the others, didn't have the time.

She refused to entertain the other possibility. Not now. Perhaps not ever. Before any of it, though, she first had to grieve. Just a little bit. Because to get her here, she'd fantasised about phoning the emergency services, and then calling Tom. Telling him she loved him and that she was safe. And now that wasn't going to happen. In fact, how *would* she even contact him now, once they'd been rescued? She didn't even know his number off by heart. All these years together and she still relied on her phone for that.

The few sobs she allowed herself were dry. She promised herself that she would memorise his number, if she survived this. And that was just for starters. Up on Hysteria, it had been Tom she craved. Tom she wanted to live to see again. If she was going to live like there was no tomorrow, she wanted today to be spent with him. If she was going to do something in the world, it had to be with him. And while right now she still didn't feel like she deserved his love in return, had perhaps never done really, she at least knew now that she had good in her. And that the guilt she'd carried all these years might not need the love of the whole world to be assuaged.

And with that, she got to her feet. She turned her head up towards the summit of the roller coaster, a shadowy spike on the brightening sky. They had escaped from there, they could surely escape from the park now. There had to be a way. There had to be a computer somewhere, or an old phone in a—

Her gaze still on the summit, the solution hit her. She knew what she had to do. A brief smile appeared on her face, quickly wiped away by a grimace.

Danson's body lay scattered beneath Hysteria. Clothing had burst and there seemed much less of him. A large part of him lay in a patch of stained sand to the right of one of the thick support beams. Cady tried only to look when she needed to, but she still saw things she would never be able to remove from her memory. Textures and shapes that could not be, and yet *were*, human.

But it was definitely Danson. She recognised some of his clothing. Which meant the other body, about four metres away, was Jag's. She really hoped the phone and key would be here. She really didn't want to disturb Jag.

She tried to ascertain the location of Danson's trousers, but from what she could tell the impact had folded him like an accordion. If Jag's phone was in there, and it had survived the impact, she would have to…

She'd been squinting, and had a hand up shielding parts of her vision while she circled the body. So, when she came across the phone, she almost stepped on it. Her toe connected with the edge, sending it skittering towards Jag.

Cady ran to it, cringing with every sore step. She knelt down. The screen was cracked and the plastic rim was scuffed, but God damn it if Jag, that beautiful man, hadn't protected the phone with a heavy-duty phone case and a laminate screen cover. Her heart swelled with adoration for him.

She pressed the button on the side and nothing happened. She touched it again, and again, and her heart began to sink.

Then she realised she was trying to turn up the volume. She tried the button below this and again nothing happened. After a moment, though, the phone buzzed. Then, the phone logo appeared on the screen and a jingle played. She watched open-mouthed as the phone came on.

But of course, the thing was locked. At the bottom of the lock screen, though, there was a green phone image. Please, God, this had to be what she desperately hoped it would be. She pressed it, and up came a keypad.

She stood up and began muttering her thanks to the universe. On the screen was an option for Emergency Contacts. Before leaving the others, she'd shouted up to them that she'd not known the emergency services number. Winston said that he was convinced it would be either the same as the UK or America.

But she pressed the emergency contact button first, and it began to ring. After three rings, she reached the answer machine of a company called 'Desert VIP'. Jag's company. She felt a deep sadness for the man she barely knew, his closest contact having been work.

She left a message anyway. A short one, just in case the phone died now.

Emergency. Two people dead. Four injured, one seriously. Dreamland. Help.

Then she dialled 999. It started to ring. It actually started to ring.

To the lady on the other end, who could speak perfect English, she gave a longer, more emotional version of the same story. And when she finished, and started to walk back to tell the others, she couldn't remember a thing about what she'd just said, to the point that she wondered if she had imagined the whole thing.

But that wasn't what had happened. And if she needed to feel safe, she simply touched the side of the phone, and the luminous screen would remind her that it was going to be over soon. That it wouldn't be long. Maybe even less than an hour.

She hadn't known how to direct the emergency services to where the train had stopped. She wasn't even sure if it was accessible by road. So she'd told them to meet her at Hysteria's entrance. When she had reassured Naz and Winston that Femi was still okay, and that help was on the way, she left them again.

It took every ounce of her will to do it, and she almost passed out twice. At Jag's car, she grabbed a rock and tried to smash the window. Inside she could see a bottle of water in the cup-holder between the seats. She couldn't do it, though. She didn't have the strength.

When she got back to Hysteria's entrance, she sat down on the path and noticed something wedged in the twisted steel of the post holding up the ride's sign.

It was an unsealed blue envelope marked: 'For the Police'.

When she'd recovered from her walk, she opened it, and was unsurprised to find that it was from Danson.

She read it a number of times with fascinated horror. Mostly it was a lot of pompous philosophising about whether an artist's intentions mattered when judging a work of art. Because, terrifyingly, that was how he viewed what he'd done to them. As a work of art. But ultimately he claimed his own intentions were too complex to fully know, adding he'd simply been unable to stop dreaming about Hysteria. He did go on to suggest that, in part, his work was a tribute to Eloise, a 'fellow artist'. And partly an act of revenge, a shot fired across the bows of privilege. But worst of all, Danson believed all this had been a way of giving The

No Tomorrows Club what every artist secretly desires. Immortality.

> *Their names will live on forever as bywords for hubris and there-by-the-grace-of-God-go-I, their story the subject of endless books, films, documentaries, message boards, social media and grim YouTube essays.*

Halfway through re-reading that paragraph again, she considered destroying the letter. Saving the world from the poison of Danson's mind. But that was when she heard joyful cheering from far away. The others, perhaps. They'd seen help arriving. They must have.

Cady smiled, and once she'd folded the letter back in the envelope, she stared at the healed cut on her finger. When she got home, she had to remember to buy Tom a Twix. It was vital she didn't forget.

With some slow experimentation, she found a way to rest her head on her knees without her body berating her. She closed her eyes.

She could be still now. She'd earned it.

She was just dozing off when she heard sirens.

PART FIVE
ART

CADY

Now

The story had made the news before Cady's plane home landed. Before she could get a video up on her channel to stem the flood of comments and emails. Hysteria remained in the headlines for two days, and after that there was mileage for journalists in the victims of the crime all being well known in their respective fields. After two weeks, though, the story moved deeper into the internet, where it continued to sink, and it was almost two months after when Cady stumbled across a dark tourism video, where three twentysomethings high on energy drinks roamed slack-jawed around the abandoned Dreamland.

By then she had left a short video on her own channel, asking for patience while she decided on what her next move would be. And that while she was shaken, and superficially injured, she was ultimately fine.

She grew restless in the flat, in any confined space, really. She slept now above the covers, left the shower door open, and took gradually less painful walks many times a day. She noticed men looking at her more than before. Tall men sometimes, in yellow hats. Her pulse would quicken, and she would change direction. Pick up her pace. Routinely look over her shoulder.

Tom took her away on a barge because it was one of the few methods of transport without seat restraints. It was there she proposed to him that she was thinking of giving up her YouTube channel. That, as much as she didn't want Danson to steal anything else from her, she didn't see a way of continuing. But Tom made a different proposal, one Cady liked infinitely more than her own.

When enough time had passed, and Cady felt she was ready, Tom started coming to amusement parks with her. At first, he took on the role of producer. To make *Coasting with Cady* a team effort. Tom learned the ropes of production and managing the channel, which meant she could have a break when required, and he could keep an eye on the boards for toxic comments. He proved to have other uses, too.

One weekend at Drayton Manor, Nick, the fan from Birmingham Airport, had run up to her and got right in Cady's face, asking if she remembered him, and whether their last meeting had been right before the incident at Dreamland. His desperation to be part of the story was barely concealed. Tom had stepped between them, reminded Nick they were in the real world right now, and sent the bloke on his way. While having a hot bodyguard wasn't essential – Danson's diaries had revealed to the police that *he* had been the one stalking Cady that night in Sherwood Forest, apparently to scare her into giving up her channel – it was a luxury of which she was happy to take advantage.

Then Cady started bringing Tom on camera. And things went even better. The viewers loved his cameos, and demanded more 'Dr Tom'. He rode the coasters and reviewed them for Cady until, with the help of time and a good psychiatrist, she was able to get back on herself. Soon, Tom started doing his own solo videos on the channel when Cady needed a longer break. And her fans didn't mind.

None of it sent the channel into the stratosphere, but equally she never felt she was chasing clicks or likes. The channel just kept growing. Eventually, the money enabled Tom to work a bit less, which allowed them to spend even more time together.

―――

Tom had done so much to get her back on her feet. She loved him for that. And for his forgiveness and patience. And for not letting her allow Dreamland to define her. She was grateful, too, that he had come with her when she told her parents about Grandad and Robbie. That he had sat there while the three of them held one another and cried.

Dad and Mum had always wondered why she was in the front of the car that day. Grandad often smoked while driving, and one of the police officers had suggested to them they strongly suspected he'd been smoking when the crash happened. That it might have distracted him. And they'd known how Cady felt about smoking, so it wasn't like the notion hadn't crossed their minds before.

But they'd never asked her directly. Because in the end, they said it never mattered to them. At the start they'd been angry with Grandad, and with themselves for not being there. But after time had passed, the whole thing began to appear almost inevitable. Millions of tiny things could have been different that day. The drivers in the other cars might have set off a little earlier. Grandad might have set off a little later. Nan might still have been alive to help look after them. When you really thought about it, "accident" was the only word for what happened that had any meaning. The conclusion they'd reached had sounded eerily similar to how Winston had described feeling up on Hysteria, but she quickly banished that thought.

'I wish we'd talked,' Cady said.

'Maybe we should have,' Dad said, rubbing her back. 'Maybe we should.'

Something else occurred to Cady then, about how so much of her chivvying along of the other members of the No Tomorrows Club had come from a desire for them all not to regret their lives the way she'd always perceived her parents did. They had been creative like her in their youth, but ultimately they had settled down. Then it had all come apart when Robbie died, so what was the point? Selling out only led to heartache.

How unfair that interpretation now seemed, basking in the

glow of their love for her. Was that why she'd kept Tom at arm's length all that time, too? Why she didn't want what they had to become *too* important?

Later, when it became clear that her parents wouldn't be disowning her, she told them she was getting married. This time, Tom joined in the hugs.

CADY

Now

She'd known they were coming. She had sent the invitations, handled the RSVPs and organised all of the catering requirements. But none of that prepared Cady for when she first saw Naz and Winston standing at the back of the receiving line. She'd been too distracted during the ceremony to notice anyone except Tom, but now she was conscious of their approach, and grew increasingly nervous the closer they drew. In the two years since Dreamland, they'd communicated plenty online, through video calls and in text messages, but seeing them in the flesh felt different.

Naz's baby boy was over a year old, and the television adaptation of her second novel had just debuted on the BBC. In private conversations, she knew that Naz's recovery from what happened had been greatly assisted by the distraction of having a newborn. There hadn't been time for her to grieve and process more than was absolutely necessary – she had an infant depending on her.

She was still finding time to write, though, and had found motherhood unlocked places in her mind that she hadn't known existed. *I have things to say again*, she'd declared, which had surprised Cady, not least because of how much Naz had sounded like she resented her life as a writer. How angry she'd seemed at Cady for having encouraged her to persist.

'You look amazing,' Naz said when she reached the front and embraced Cady.

'You too,' Cady replied.

'We must find a moment to catch up,' Naz said, standing aside to hug Tom.

Winston stepped forward and took her in his arms. 'You're a vision, Cady.'

She wished she could truthfully say the same to him. But she knew he had taken what happened to them all hard. He'd freely admitted drinking and drugging to cope, and holding him now, his body brought to mind how skeletal Danson felt when she'd first held him at Dreamland. Winston had left his band, which Cady'd read about in the online music press first. When she'd asked him why, he said that it was because he needed to find himself. That up on the top of Hysteria, he'd had some dark thoughts, and realised some things about his character that he needed to deal with.

Not long after he quit music, he moved back to America. He'd been thinking about doing a podcast about his family. About maybe even coming clean about his real identity. Just to be done with it, he'd said.

He stepped back and grinned at her with a mouth that now

missed one of its front teeth. His skin appeared waxy and his pupils looked too small. She kissed his cheek.

'Catch up later?' he said.

'Yeah,' she said, unsure why that idea heightened her nerves. She reached across and grabbed Tom's hand. 'Of course.'

When the dinner was over, and the band was playing, Cady did the rounds. She thanked everyone she could find for coming and being part of her batshit, wonderful bloody life. She was a bit tipsy by then, and the dehydration from that, and the non-stop tears, were bringing back unwanted memories of the Middle Eastern desert.

She grabbed a bottle of water and went down to the river at the back of the hotel's grand gardens. Naz and Winston sat on a bench beneath the shade of a tree. Sitting with them in a wheelchair, was Femi.

'Oh my God,' she said, and ran to him. 'You came. You came. Thank you so much.'

She bent down and held him, smelling a mixture of hospital chemicals and moisturiser. She stepped back, and he gave her a wonky smile that trembled at the edges. He'd worn a suit. The lovely bastard had come in a suit, even though she'd told him not to. Because she'd known how exhausted he got these days, and didn't want anything to stop him making a short appearance if he felt up to it.

'Bloody hell,' he said, appraising her, 'you're a goddess.'

His powerful voice had withered with his muscles. But it was easy to focus on the changes the fall had brought about. What remained was that sparkle in his eyes, and that bottomless charisma. And he looked so, so much better than he had done when they'd first visited him in the hospital, when they hadn't even known if he would wake up.

But he had. And now, he was out in the world again. It wasn't out of the question that he might walk again one day, in time. He might even return to acting. But that wasn't his priority, he'd told Cady on the phone. For now, he was happy that he could hold his baby. Change a nappy. Feed him. He and Naz had started trying to fashion a life for themselves together. They were living in the same house now. And while they weren't exactly in a relationship, it wasn't something that was out of the question in the future. They very much loved each other, but they wanted to take their time.

Taking time was a good thing. There was no rush anymore.

She drank champagne with them. She touched their arms, their faces, their hands. They talked about anything they could that wasn't connected to Danson. Which, in the end, was hard to do. Their friendship was another work in progress, because they all knew they would have to start again. Build new bonds. New memories.

But they could do that from today. Because today was a new chapter for her, and a new chapter for all of them, having finally been reunited in person.

Right now, though, she knew she should leave them. She had to divide her time equally amongst her guests before the end of the night. And Tom. She couldn't forget Tom. She'd arranged to meet him to cut the cake at 4pm.

'I probably need to get going,' she said. 'Has anyone got the time?'

Naz started to open her handbag to retrieve her phone.

'Listen, before you do,' Femi said, 'we've been talking and

have something that we wanted to ask you about, a sort of proposition.'

'Not now,' Winston said.

'Oh,' Cady said. Naz held up her phone and it said two minutes past four.

'Bugger,' she said. 'Sorry, can I borrow that?'

She typed in Tom's number from memory and he picked up after the second ring with a laugh. 'Have I lost you?' he said.

'No, I'm just coming. Sorry, sorry, sorry.'

She hung up and handed back the phone. 'Can we come back to this? I just need to…'

'I'll be quick,' Femi said, holding up a hand with oddly angled fingers. 'I've drawn up a pitch for a documentary, and I've been approaching studios about getting some funding. I've been getting some really big interest, Cady. I mean … really big. American studios.'

'That's… cool,' Cady said. 'What's it about?'

'Dreamland.'

Cady stared at Femi, at his dazzling eyes and granite jaw. He didn't blink.

'Dreamland?'

'Yes,' Femi said. 'I've told the others and they're all on board in theory. And if I could get you involved, it will really seal the deal. To have all four of us … the studios would bend over backwards. Hollywood studios.'

She looked at Naz. And at Winston. And they stared back at her, each wearing a big smile. Hopeful. Only the very slightest hint of doubt, perhaps. If she was being charitable.

'We'd get to own the story,' Naz said. 'Stop all the conspiracies and rubbish.'

'Could be fun to all work together,' Winston said. 'Spend some time out in the States.'

Femi just kept smiling.

'So ... you want us to talk about what happened,' Cady said. 'All of it. The truth.'

'Well,' Femi said, 'we could work all that out. The main focus would be what we went through. How we survived what that bastard did to us. How we went on and ... thrived.' His mouth twitched.

'Right.'

She waited, sensing their hope and expectation and ambition reaching out for her. Squeezing her. Pushing her.

Femi cocked his head. 'Honestly, all of our profiles would benefit hugely. Be a way to stick it to Danson, too. And imagine what it would do to your subscribers.'

Cady took a last look at her friends, drank them in, then took a long, deep breath.

'No, thanks,' she said. And with that, she turned and ran back to Tom.

She bumped into her dad on the way inside. He laughed and said, 'Careful there, slow and steady wins the race, Cady Bug.'

She found Tom by their cake, a tiered affair with two Twix fingers poking from the top beside the miniature bride and groom. At the base was a small figurine of the goddess Saraswati, a gift from Jag's mother. They'd met her while filming a video at Nicco Park last year, and stopped by the family home to answer her questions.

She kissed Tom and picked up the knife.

And sliced. Carefully. Considerately.

Slowly.

ACKNOWLEDGMENTS

Thanks so much for reading *The Drop*; I hope it terrified you. If you're still here, allow me to just thank a few people, and then I'll tell you a joke. First, Helen. I love you. Boot and Noodle, I love you too – and if I was allowed to draw something here, I'd make sure it was some goal posts and a moose, just for you. In a way this book is about brothers, but I've already dedicated the whole novel to mine, so I'll skip those losers here. Except I can't, can I? Especially because of their help with YouTube stuff and general toleration of all my random text messages (*do you think a story about people stuck at the top of a roller coaster could work???*). So thanks again guys. Now seriously, enough! Mom, Dad, you're the best. Helen, Beasty, massive kisses. Lily, Robin, Katie and Sophie, you can have some, too. And kisses to the four Morans, your support is so appreciated.

Okay, I've run out of kisses. I have a huge bag of thanks though, and none are more deserving of some than my small team of roller coaster advisors, who were incredibly helpful in making this book as realistic as possible. John Wardley (designer of countless big rides, including Nemesis at Alton Towers) was extremely generous with his time and expertise, and his autobiography *Creating My Own Nemesis* is an essential (and entertaining) read. I'm also indebted to the excellent Harry Davies, who runs the incredible YouTube channel "coaster bot". Both of you put up with a lot of silly questions, and I am so grateful for your time. I want to be clear: I have taken many liberties to serve the story, and any errors, including those related to coaster mechanics and amusement park culture, are entirely mine. I'd also like to add that the amusement park industry is very safe, and what happened on Hysteria was very much the fault of you-know-who.

Thanks also to my favourite musical, *Little Shop of Horrors*, and the brilliant team of Alan Menken and Howard Ashman who created it, particularly the song "Don't Feed the Plants" (1982), which we catch our amateur production singing in one of the early university chapters. Thanks also to the brilliant artists on my playlist of rock classics, which served as the perfect soundtrack to Musicland. Finally, thanks also to Jennie and Shana, my brilliant editors on either side of the Atlantic. Thanks so much to the whole One More Chapter and Sourcebooks Landmark teams. And thanks to Joanna Swainson for continuing to believe in me.

Okay, so that joke I promised. What did the cheese say when he looked in the mirror? *Halloumi.* Sorry, it's my daughter's favourite. She's five. I thought it might take some of the edge off after being up on that roller coaster for so long. Hope it did, and you'll come back for more (novels, not jokes). Maybe see you then?

Quote on page 143, Credit: Alan Menken and Howard Ashman, "Don't Feed the Plants",
Little Shop of Horrors (1982)

'Pacy, dark and highly entertaining, with a real sense of menace'
SUNDAY TIMES BESTSELLER T.M. LOGAN

Would you sign up to a medical trial if you didn't know the possible side effects?

It seems like the opportunity of a lifetime. An all-inclusive luxury trip abroad, all you need to do is take a pill every day and keep a diary…

AVAILABLE IN EBOOK, PAPERBACK AND AUDIO

'Captivating, unsettling and filled with gasp-inducing shocks… plunges you into a fascinating and disturbing community'
SUNDAY TIMES BESTSELLER, B P WALTER

What if the kindest thing you could do meant hurting someone?

The village of Nether Appleford calls itself 'England's Kindest Village'. Overseen by the Kindness Committee, this close-knit community strives to live their lives with kindness at the heart of everything they do…

AVAILABLE IN EBOOK, PAPERBACK AND AUDIO

The author and One More Chapter would like to thank everyone who contributed to the publication of this story...

Analytics
Imogen Wolstencroft

Audio
Fionnuala Barrett
Ciara Briggs

Contracts
Laura Amos
Inigo Vyvyan

Design
Lucy Bennett
Fiona Greenway
Liane Payne
Dean Russell

Digital Sales
Laura Daley
Lydia Grainge
Hannah Lismore

eCommerce
Laura Carpenter
Madeline ODonovan
Charlotte Stevens
Christina Storey
Jo Surman
Rachel Ward

Editorial
Rosie Best
Kara Daniel
CJ Harter
Charlotte Ledger
Lydia Mason
Jennie Rothwell
Sofia Salazar Studer
Caroline Scott-Bowden
Helen Williams

Harper360
Emily Gerbner
Ariana Juarez
Jean Marie Kelly
emma sullivan
Sophia Wilhelm

International Sales
Peter Borcsok
Ruth Burrow
Bethan Moore
Colleen Simpson

Inventory
Sarah Callaghan
Kirsty Norman

Marketing & Publicity
Chloe Cummings
Grace Edwards
Katie Sadler

Operations
Melissa Okusanya
Hannah Stamp

Production
Denis Manson
Simon Moore
Francesca Tuzzeo

Rights
Ashton Mucha
Alisah Saghir
Zoe Shine
Aisling Smyth
Lucy Vanderbilt

Trade Marketing
Ben Hurd
Eleanor Slater

The HarperCollins Distribution Team

The HarperCollins Finance & Royalties Team

The HarperCollins Legal Team

The HarperCollins Technology Team

UK Sales
Isabel Coburn
Jay Cochrane
Sabina Lewis
Holly Martin
Harriet Williams
Leah Woods

And every other essential link in the chain from delivery drivers to booksellers to librarians and beyond!

One More Chapter is an
award-winning global
division of HarperCollins.

Subscribe to our newsletter to get our
latest eBook deals and stay up to date
with all our new releases!

signup.harpercollins.co.uk/join/signup-omc

Meet the team at
www.onemorechapter.com

Follow us!

@onemorechapterhc

Do you write unputdownable fiction?
We love to hear from new voices.
Find out how to submit your novel at
www.onemorechapter.com/submissions